Explore a world where...

The bite of a dead man is the least of Dr. Arus' problems.

People from the distant past send messages of ill-intent to the future.

Danny must deal with what happens when the Internet escapes.

Meet fascinating people...

Nate is all about loyalty and companionship—but aren't most werewolves?

Anna works in a factory, where her magic won't even provide for her barest needs.

Harric has only two hours to live, unless he can win the gods' favor.

Some folks have the strangest powers...

Yvina hopes to bring peace to her war-torn peoples, if only she can channel her inner bear.

Caleb's family keeps him in utter darkness—perhaps for good reason.

Keani's parasite can make her look like anyone, but who is she really?

Discover a future where...

Trading cards hold the title to entire worlds.

Liza can manufacture dinosaurs, if she can find the raw ingredients.

David must battle incendiary monsters, and risk becoming a monster himself.

The last sunset on earth is quite beautiful, but a bit sad.

L. Ron Hubbard Presents Writers and Illustrators of the Future contains these stories and more from award-winning authors, along with articles on writing and art by some of the world's foremost authorities.

What has been said about the

L. RON HUBBARD

Presents

Writers of the Future

Anthologies

"The Writers of the Future Award has also earned its place alongside the Hugo and Nebula awards in the triad of speculative fiction's most prestigious ackowledgements of literary excellence."
— *SFFaudio*

"If you want a glimpse of the future—the future of science fiction—look at these first publications of tomorrow's masters."
— Kevin J. Anderson
Writers of the Future Contest judge

"Where can an aspiring sci-fi artist go to get discovered?... Fortunately, there's one opportunity—the Illustrators of the Future Contest—that offers up-and-coming artists an honest-to-goodness shot at science fiction stardom."
— *Sci Fi* magazine

"The Illustrators of the Future Contest is one of the best opportunities a young artist will ever get. You have nothing to lose and a lot to win."
— Frank Frazetta
Illustrators of the Future Contest judge

"The Writers of the Future Contest was definitely an accelerator to my writing development. I learned so much, and it came at just the right moment for me."
— Jo Beverley
Writers of the Future Contest winner 1988

"The Contests are amazing competitions because really, you've nothing to lose and they provide good positive encouragement to anyone who wins. Judging the entries is always a lot of fun and inspiring. I wish I had something like this when I was getting started—very positive and cool."
— Bob Eggleton
Illustrators of the Future Contest judge

L. Ron Hubbard PRESENTS
Writers of the Future

VOLUME 32

L. Ron Hubbard PRESENTS

Writers of the Future

VOLUME 32

The year's thirteen best tales from the
Writers of the Future international writers' program

Illustrated by winners in the Illustrators of the Future
international illustrators' program

Three short stories from authors
L. Ron Hubbard / Sean Williams / David Farland

With essays on writing and illustration by
L. Ron Hubbard / Brandon Sanderson / Tim Powers /
Sergey Poyarkov / Bob Eggleton

Edited by David Farland

Illustrations Art Directed by Bob Eggleton

GALAXY PRESS, INC

"The Star Tree": © 2016 Jon Lasser
"Images Across a Shattered Sea": © 2016 Stewart C Baker
"Möbius": © 2016 Christoph Weber
"How to Drive a Writer Crazy": © 1997, 2012 L. Ron Hubbard Library
"The Last Admiral": © 1949, 1999 L. Ron Hubbard Library
"The Jack of Souls": © 2016 Stephen Merlino
"Swords Like Lightning, Hooves Like Thunder": © 2016 K. D. Julicher
"Where Steampunk Started": © 2016 Tim Powers
"Hellfire on the High Frontier": © 2014 Dave Wolverton. First published in *Dead Man's Hand, Tales of the Weird West*
"Squalor and Sympathy": © 2016 Matt Dovey
"Dinosaur Dreams in Infinite Measure": © 2016 Rachael K. Jones
"Cry Havoc": © 2016 Julie Frost
"A Glamour in the Black": © 2016 Sylvia Anna Hivén
"The Broad Sky Was Mine, And the Road": © 2016 Ryan Row
"The Fine Distinction Between Cooks and Chefs": © 2016 Brandon Sanderson
"The Jade Woman of the Luminous Star": © 2011 Sean Williams. First published *Ghosts by Gaslight*, eds. Jack Dann & Nick Gevers, 2011
"Freebot": © 2016 R. M. Graves
"Last Sunset for the World Weary": © 2016 H. L. Fullerton
"The Sun Falls Apart": © 2016 J. W. Alden
"Flawless Imperfection": © 2003–2004 Sergey Poyarkov
Illustration on pages 5 and 393: © 2016 Killian McKeown
Illustration on pages 21 and 395: © 2016 Paul Otteni
Illustration on pages 37 and 397: © 2016 Talia Spencer
Illustration on pages 78 and 396: © 2016 Irvin Rodriguez
Illustration on pages 95 and 401: © 2016 Maricela Ugarte Peña
Illustration on pages 139 and 402: © 2016 Eldar Zakirov
Illustration on pages 179 and 390: © 2016 Rob Hassan
Illustration on pages 191 and 392: © 2016 Adrian Massaro
Illustration on pages 220 and 399: © 2016 Preston Stone
Illustration on pages 230 and 394: © 2016 Vlada Monakhova
Illustration on pages 259 and 391: © 2016 Brandon Knight
Illustration on pages 265 and 398: © 2016 Jonas Špokas
Illustration on pages 314 and 400: © 2016 Daniel Tyka
Illustration on pages 329 and 389: © 2016 Dino Hadžiavdić
Illustration on pages 345 and 388: © 2016 Camber Arnhart
Illustration on pages 355 and 387: © 2016 Christina Alberici
Cover Artwork: *Don't Stop* © 2001 Sergey Poyarkov
Interior Design by Jerry Kelly

ISBN 978-1-61986-502-0
Library of Congress Control Number: 2016934876
Printed in the United States of America

CONTENTS

Introduction

BY DAVID FARLAND

David Farland is a New York Times *bestselling author with over fifty novel-length works to his credit.*

As an author, David has won many awards for both his short stories and his novels. He won the grand prize in Writers of the Future Volume III *for his story "On My Way to Paradise" in 1987, and quickly went on to begin publishing novels. He has since won numerous awards for his longer works, including the Philip K. Dick Memorial Special Award, the Whitney Award for Best Novel of the Year, the International Book Award for Best Young Adult Novel of the Year, and the Hollywood Book Festival Book of the Year Award—among many others.*

Along the way, David has written a number of bestsellers, designed and scripted video games, such as the international bestseller StarCraft: Brood War, *acted as a greenlighting analyst in Hollywood, and worked as a movie producer.*

*David has long been involved in helping to discover and train new writers, including a number who have gone on to become #1 international bestsellers—such as Brandon Mull (*Fablehaven*), Brandon Sanderson (*The Way of Kings*), James Dashner (*The Maze Runner*), Stephenie Meyer (*Twilight*), and many others.*

David currently lives in Utah with his wife and children, where he is busily writing his next novel, teaching workshops and judging entries for L. Ron Hubbard Presents Writers of the Future, Volume 33.

Introduction

Just over thirty years ago, I was a college student at Brigham Young University, where I soon found myself in a writing group. We were an odd bunch—science fiction and fantasy writers trying to figure out how to make a career. At the time, there were almost no writers in our area who were making a living in this field, so we were trying hard to figure out how to make a start. We organized a science fiction writing symposium, called Life, the Universe, and Everything (which is still running) and were able to bring in big-name authors like Fred Pohl and Tim Powers and Orson Scott Card. We started a little magazine called *The Leading Edge,* which is also still running, so that we could learn how publishing works and also publish some of our own stories.

Mostly, though, we wrote like mad and critiqued one another's work. In that way, we were much like hundreds of other little writing groups across the country. But everything changed one day when my friend M. Shayne Bell came to our weekly meeting with a copy of *L. Ron Hubbard Presents Writers of the Future Volume 1.*

Shayne explained, "They've got the coolest contest ever. L. Ron Hubbard was a Golden Age science fiction writer, and he set up this great contest to help discover and promote new writers!"

For a young writer aching to break into this business, it sounded almost too good to be true. Shayne and I both decided to enter, worried that, as I put it, "If we don't get in quick, these folks might go out of business."

So I wrote a science fiction story and became a finalist on my very first entry. Later, both my friend Shayne and I became first-place winners.

Looking back, it's kind of humbling. I had no idea how large this contest would become–it has grown to be the largest of its kind in the world. Certainly, we broke all of our own previous records for submissions this year. Now, at 32 years, it has also become one of the longest-running writing contests in the world.

When I first heard of it, I didn't quite understand the vision of the contest. As Algis Budrys once put it to me, "When we talked about creating this contest, we considered what our goals would be. I knew that with the contest, we wanted to offer three things. First, if someone won this contest, they would win enough money to make a difference in their writing lives." So the contest offers generous cash prizes in addition to payment for publication. "Second, we wanted to offer validation to the new writers." So the stories were to be judged by some of the biggest celebrities in the writing field. "Third, we decided to try to help the writers by training them, by teaching them the business of writing." Thus, L. Ron Hubbard and Algis Budrys began offering a writing camp and retreat each year for new writers, where they get to meet with celebrities who help teach writers the ropes.

Yet I think that there was something even more that L. Ron Hubbard hoped for from this contest. I believe that he was looking for a new generation of dreamers, of authors and artists who might be able to envision a better, brighter future for the world. He saw speculative fiction as the "herald of possibility," and said, "A culture is only as great as its dreams, and its dreams are dreamed by artists."

As a young author, I don't know that I saw how vast that vision was. As an old editor, I understand it much better. With that in mind, each year I go through thousands and thousands of stories, looking for authors with great talent, but also searching for authors with an even greater vision.

With that in mind, I welcome you to *L. Ron Hubbard Presents Writers and Illustrators of the Future, Volume 32.*

The Star Tree

written by

Jon Lasser

illustrated by

KILLIAN McKEOWN

ABOUT THE AUTHOR

Jon Lasser lives in Seattle, Washington with his wife Laura and their two children. Although he's been writing since he was six and has long been a published author of technical nonfiction, he only started focusing on speculative fiction the last several years—ever since his wife told him to "put up or shut up" and take writing seriously.

When not writing, working in technology, or taking care of his family, Jon scuba dives. He prefers the Northwest's cold-water diving, but won't turn down a free trip to Hawaii or Bonaire if offered.

This is Jon's second speculative fiction sale, following the flash story "The Saviors," which appeared in Penumbra #32 *(May 2014).*

ABOUT THE ILLUSTRATOR

Killian McKeown is the founder behind Vision Images. Killian started as a young adventurous entrepreneur, with a father deeply involved in professional photography, so it was a given that Killian would follow in the creative vision industry.

After his dad's passing, he decided to further his father's legacy and direct his vision into photography. Mentored at Empire West Studios by Arizona's top fashion photographer, Clayton Hall, Killian learned studio lighting, equipment setup, shooting, editing, printing, and the overall start-to-finish product presentation for clientele.

Killian was able to build on his talents and soon moved into graphic design, developing right into a triple threat in the world of visual imagery. Since the age of nineteen he has worked on multiple sets as film crew, videographer, photographer and Assistant Director. Killian has created pieces for Lucky Strike Bowling, Salute the Troops 5k Run, Java Magazine, *and* Industry Magazine. *He has been a press photographer for Phoenix Fashion Week, Laughlin International Film Festival, Comic-Con International, and the world-famous Harlem Globetrotters. Killian acted and was the camera production assistant for the movie* Goats. *Additionally, he has filmed, produced, and directed rap artist Heaven Sent's very first music video. He currently works with New Angle Media in advertising.*

Illustrating has become a way to bring his imagined epic space adventures in far-off lands into reality, using a mix of all his photography, drawing and Photoshop/multimedia skills. It's almost a necessity for Killian to do what he does or he'd go crazy with the epic characters and adventures stuck within his mind.

The Star Tree

I was fourteen years, not yet grown, the summer that my father, my brother, and I moved across the vast red desert from one domed city to another, a dusty two-and-a-half day trek in a pressurized train car whose glass dome looked so much like the ones over the cities we passed between, as if it were our world in miniature. The car smelled of solvents, aerosolized lubricants, and unwashed bodies.

We were the only people traveling first class on an oversubscribed train, though a number of miners squatted in our car, smudging the seats with dust from their rough, ill-fitting work clothes. The women had the same broad shoulders as the men, the same short-cropped hair and flinty gazes, the same fingertips stained with miners' grease, even under their close-bitten fingernails. Only the men's thick beards, bushy and unkempt, distinguished them from women. A shiver passed through me: I'd never seen miners up close. Some of them weren't any older than I was, perhaps even younger. One woman, a little older than me, had my mother's piercing green eyes. She saw me gazing at her, and made an obscene gesture with her pinkie.

The first evening on the train, when the lights went out and stars blossomed bright overhead, Chiq gawped at the constellations. He was half my age: seven years old by standard reckoning, two seasons by our local metric.

"See, Marq?" He pointed up with one trembling clay-red finger. "That's the star tree, Rhyonon. If miners in the Northern

Desert lose their gear, they walk to her. There's a ring of oases, and it's another day to Tonnish City from there." Chiq collected stars. I didn't doubt he could name each star in Rhyonon, and number each system's inhabitants.

"We're not miners, Chiq." I knew a "trunk" of stars pointed north, "rooted" in Tonnish City. I'd seen fanciful drawings of that tree in the sky flush with leaves and blossoms. Whenever I looked up, all I saw were stars, glittering but haphazard, without a tree in sight. The stars were of no use to me.

"We're all miners here," my father insisted. We'd never lived near the mines, always in cities, in homes suitable to his diplomatic post: private apartments with room for personal belongings.

I knew what he meant. We were obligated to treat the miners as equals. They were the source of our world's wealth and prestige. We adopted their mental habits, their pecuniary and emotional parsimony, their disdain for softness in all its forms. Had I traveled to another world, I would have claimed I'd descended from miners. My own hypocrisy sickened and aroused me.

"Papa," Chiq asked, "Can you point to Jiri?" He pointed up through the glass dome at the starry sky. "I want to see Mommy." His eyes glistened. Surely he wouldn't embarrass us all by bursting into tears?

The star Jiri wasn't visible from north of our equator. Surely Chiq knew that. Was he testing Dad? When I had been his age, my faith in our father was unbroken—though it had not yet been put to the test the way that Mom's departure had shaken Chiq. I held my breath and waited for Dad to lie to Chiq.

Dad patted him on the shoulder. "It's too far away. We can't see her from here." Which wasn't exactly true, as I'm sure Chiq knew—but might have been close enough to reassure him. I also heard the other things Dad didn't say: he wanted to see her too. She couldn't cross the gulf that separated us. Not just the distance between the stars, too expensive to bridge except when interstellar politics demanded, but the distance between her and my father as well. Ah, the look in her eye when my father told diplomats from other worlds that his was a mining family!

KILLIAN McKEOWN

She'd seen how miners lived. As I recalled how he'd "plucked" her—his word—from a dusty mining settlement, it dawned on me that she'd never forgiven him.

I looked through the bubble, across the vast and unlit desert. The atmosphere here was so thin that the stars didn't twinkle like they did under containment domes. Tens of millions of stars shone dispassionately upon us. My father mourned for a woman on a world so far away that he couldn't have pointed to it in the southern hemisphere, her star a grain of sand in the sky's infinite fractal lode.

I woke in the morning to the train's gentle shimmy and the drone of Chiq's voice. The three of us were alone in the car and he was reading his cards. His mouth twisted around names his tongue could never tell, in languages we didn't have the anatomy to speak, as he stared at each system card in turn. His collection was childish but appropriate, not so mortifying I'd have to pretend he wasn't my brother.

"Coyopa, Nintoku, Tiye," he recited. I couldn't guess what worlds the names were for, how many billions of lives my brother held in that deck of star systems.

"Will you stop that, Chiq?" Dad snapped. "You and your foolish game."

"It's not a game, Dad. It's real." Chiq believed he held legal title to the stars and planets in his deck, systems destroyed by disease or asteroid, by their own hubris, cultural fugue, or unforeseen catastrophe. Worlds rebuilt by The Unexpected Delight Company's enormous fleet of autonomous self-replicating terraformers and repopulated according to records of the genetic, epigenetic, and cultural state of the world at its peak—only to sell its title for a child's subsistence budget.

Chiq's friends in Vervi Arrill, the city we had left, kept score of how many lives they ruled, little emperors and empresses. I considered myself mature and worldly, too old for such toys. I affected amusement, not amazement, at the scale of a universe where distressed worlds were so common as to become children's playthings. What would happen should one of those little empresses set foot on a planet to which she held title? Did The Unexpected Delight Company maintain a fleet of autonomous soldiers and bodyguards for their customers' benefit?

Nor did I understand the gap between reality and the story spun by marketing feeds. It would be years before I understood the worlds had once been real, but the one-of-a-kind cards represented their only continued existence. They contained enough data to simulate worlds, or reconstruct them to their last statistically significant inhabitant, but physical reconstruction of a single world dwarfed even The Unexpected Delight Company's seemingly limitless resources.

I'd gleaned from my brother's cards that most planets vulnerable to such tragic fates were the lone inhabited worlds within their systems; in those cases, the deed was for an entire star system. I never saw any sign that Chiq and his friends cared about the scope of their possessions, outside of counting the number of sentient beings they putatively owned.

"It's not real," Dad repeated. "They're just cards—paper! Not even digital."

"Smartpaper, Papa. A cryptographic certificate of legal planet ownership. It's electronic inside the paper." Chiq parroted the promotional copy that sheathed each card. Dad was too old to understand paper. I was too old for planet cards, but Dad was so far beyond that he couldn't even see what they were.

"So, what? You could fly to one of those planets and they'd worship you as the embodiment of the local deity? Because you have a piece of paper?"

"That's religion, Papa. This is economics. Money."

"And people turn their lives over to you—for money?"

"The people didn't exist when title was granted," I explained. "No sentient being existed at the time of the title grant, prior to reconstruction."

"It's absurd." Dad rolled his eyes.

"Look: He's learning cartography, economics—does it matter if it's real?"

"It matters to me!" Chiq butted in. He looked down at his cards and resumed taking inventory.

Dad didn't answer. I was old enough to know he was remembering Mom. Remembering the arguments they used to have. I was young enough to despise him for both their arguments and his sentimentality.

I dropped my voice to a whisper. "They're important to Chiq. If you want him to forgive you, show some interest in what he likes."

Dad blinked.

"My systems!" Chiq shouted. "They're missing!"

"They're right there," Dad said. "You're holding them."

"Not these. I have a hundred planets I've lost. Seventeen billion citizens."

"Paper." Dad sniffed. "Not worth a thing: you can't search it, can't back it up."

"Paaaapa!" Chiq burst into tears. Here he went, embarrassing us in front of the whole train car.

"Are they in your bag?" I asked. "Have you checked your pockets?"

We looked through Chiq's meager belongings: the Keensa-bark coat that Mom had shaped for him, the hollowed-out Tonsu shell she'd given him for a suitcase.

"They're not there," Chiq wailed. He looked up. "I must have left them in Vervi Arrill." He'd hidden his cards in an old food canister, just inside the ventilation unit behind our shared desk. I'd pretended not to know where they were. Keeping secrets was as childish as it was embarrassing, but not so immature as prying into them.

"You're sure they're not here?" Dad said. "Can you replace them?"

"Replace them?" Chiq shrieked. "Every system's one-of-a-kind. There's only one Coyopa." He waved that card in Dad's face. "Did I have two mothers?"

That got Dad's attention. A look I didn't understand played across his face, perhaps an amalgam of guilt and resolution. He had to be everything to us now, didn't he?

"We'll find them," he said in a low voice. He sounded alert, focused in a way he hadn't for a long time. "Wherever they are, we'll find them." He took Chiq's hand. I turned away and pretended we weren't related.

"They're not here, Papa. I left them back home. I know it." Chiq hadn't yet learned that none of us had homes.

"I'll send a note. The Dwelling Council can forward them along, if they turn up." Dad didn't sound very confident, for a diplomat.

Chiq seized on that. "They won't send along my cards. They'll keep them for themselves, or incinerate them." He was right.

Dad sighed. "We do have rights to that unit for another week, so nobody'll be in there yet. If we get off the train at the next stop"— he looked up at the pulsing diagram that ran like a frieze around the bubble—"at Korga, we can catch the next train back to Vervi Arrill. We'll pick up your planets and take the next train back. We'll make it to Tonnish City before my work assignment begins."

That was true, but he wouldn't get much rest, and I wouldn't have time to taste the various delights of Tonnish City before we were all too busy.

I seethed: why would he do this, turn around for a handful of cards you could buy for the weekly pittance allotted to children? Why was Dad so weakened by Chiq's baby tears? Wasn't he always saying we were miners?

"You go," I said. "I'm staying on the train." It would be just me and the miners. I ached at the half-formed thoughts that bobbed just beneath consciousness.

Chiq looked as if I'd socked him in the jaw. We'd long ago learned that a united front held Dad hostage to our demands. We'd maintained an unspoken agreement, a tit-for-tat system. We backed each other against his resistance. I'd just broken that truce.

"Your planets are stupid," I explained. "You own them, but so what? You'll never see them, like you'll never see Mom again. Nobody on those planets will ever know who you are. It's just a

9

baby game." He'd started collecting cards when Mother received her work assignment, months before her departure. I didn't think a lot about how the two things were related for Chiq; it was enough to know that they were. "No way am I going back to that old dump, just for your stupid game."

"Fine, Marq. You stay on the train. Papa and I will go back. See you in Tonnish City." His lip quivered only a little.

"Chiq, Marq, I don't care which way we go, but we're staying together." Dad seemed old, frightened. I wanted to agree with Chiq just to make him happy, but something wouldn't let me do that. It was being an adolescent, I suppose: I despised how both Chiq and Dad behaved. Chiq, awed by our father, treated Dad's every act as deeply meaningful. He couldn't see that Dad was doing the same things again and again, that they'd lost any meaning they'd ever had, like repeating a word over and over until it sounded strange, the way he repeated Mom's name when he thought we were asleep. It struck me that he felt about Mom the way I felt about the miners we were sitting with on the train, but I buried the thought.

Nobody said anything for a long time. I heard the high harmonics of the vibrating rails and the low whoosh of the air filtration, smelled the cooking grease, felt the sun beat down through the bubble. I paid close attention, as I wanted to fix this moment in my memory.

I couldn't stand the silence any longer.

"I'm going to the dining car. I want a snack."

"I'm coming too," Chiq said.

"No you're not."

"Let me."

"Let him," Dad said.

"Fine." I pressed the airlock pressurization button without waiting for Chiq, but he stood beside me before it hissed and opened. We pulled the door of our car shut and passed quickly into the next.

"Can you keep a secret?" Chiq looked up at me, tears welling in his eyes.

"You're such a baby. Can you stop crying for even one minute?"

"I—" Chiq lost it. I hurried him into the single-occupancy restroom at this end of the car.

"What is it?" I hissed, furious.

"The cards—"

"Not this again."

"Jiri's in my lost cards," Chiq wailed.

I hugged him tight and didn't say anything. Chiq's revelation crushed whatever secret hope I'd nurtured, of my improbable emigration or Mom's inconceivable return, like a lump of ore by the refinery. It left me with nothing but slag in the pit of my stomach. I was going to be sick.

"You can't tell Dad," Chiq said. "He'd—"

"I know." I hugged Chiq as if we were both babies. I'd half-felt his desperation, but now I knew Mom, like everyone else on Jiri V, was truly gone. Dead. Dad was lost and the two of us were alone, with nothing to steer by in the infinite and bosomless universe. In the face of that, I was no more grown than Chiq.

I studied him with a sudden sense of wonder. How had he kept this secret for so long? No wonder he blubbered in fits. "Fine. I'll go with you."

"Don't tell Papa."

"I won't." I hugged him again, as though I were the child. I wasn't hungry anymore, but Dad would know something was wrong if we came back without our snack. "Let's get something to eat."

Dad didn't ask any questions. He was just happy we'd agreed on something and didn't want to know what kind of bribery was involved. I let him presume that Chiq would be giving me a chunk of his subsistence budget.

We transferred to the Vervi Arrill train at Korga, a mining depot too small for even a proper station. The air was full of dust, as though their bubble had been permeated. But of course they had no bubble.

Miners hunched over, now and then convulsed with coughs, as we waited for our train. Some ideas I'd previously considered in isolation formed new constellations: the cheapness of the miners' air filters and how infrequently they were replaced; the way the trains between Vervi Arrill and Tonnish city elided the continent between them, and with that distance the dignity of manual labor; that the economic underpinnings of this planet were hidden in plain sight, its domed metropolitan spires just froth from the subterranean churning.

I stared frankly at the miners on the platform, willing any of them to look me in the eye. Father would never stand for it, a miner in the family. That just made me want them more. Most of the miners wouldn't meet my gaze. One—a boy too young to beard, or perhaps a woman—bared his teeth and hissed at me. Blushing, I turned away and didn't look back until the train came.

We boarded the first-class car. This train was less full, and no miners camped in our car. I plotted to enter the second-class cars but lacked the nerve when my chances came. Once, a miner passed through our car, but he never looked my way. My heart shouted, but my voice remained silent.

We arrived at the Vervi Arrill station and rode a pedal cab to the housing unit. The cabbie's musculature differed from the miners' physiques. He wore his hair long and his cheeks smooth, but he'd earned the same bold workman's hands. I stared at them the whole ride. My father shook me when we arrived, so still was I that he thought me asleep.

We took the creaky lift to the third floor and walked to the end of the hall. Its curtain had been pulled open and the unit emptied. Chiq dropped to his knees and searched the ventilator, but the food canister wasn't there.

"We had another week," Dad muttered. "The council will be hearing from me about this."

I tugged his arm. "You're not a constituent anymore. They won't care. Let's go." He tugged Chiq, and I pulled them both into the passageway. A maintenance worker, her long hair knotted into an elaborate tapestry, squeezed past us.

A day ago I wouldn't have seen her, but now I tugged gently at her uniform as she passed.

"Hey!" She slapped my hands away from her as she turned toward me. "What gives?"

"This unit—"

"I can't help you if you're looking to move in. You'll need to talk to the council rep—"

"No, this was our old unit." My heart beat so loudly I could hardly hear myself. "We left—something."

"Anything you left should be in the reclamation depot, level minus two."

Chiq raced to the stairwell and launched himself down, not even waiting for an elevator.

"Thank you." I smiled at the woman. She didn't see me, the way I wouldn't have seen her before the train. I'd always counted Dad's rank a blessing. Now I felt it a cage, perhaps the way that Mom did. Had. The maintenance worker continued down the hall away from us, clucking softly and shaking her head.

Dad and I waited for the elevator. By the time we'd arrived at minus two, Chiq had located the corner with the detritus we hadn't honored as possessions, opposite the small electricity-generating incinerator where all this trash was headed. He dug through the pile, looking for his canister.

"It's not here," I said. I kicked at one midden heap, but I wasn't looking. There wasn't anything here for me any longer. I didn't want Chiq to have more to care about than I had.

Chiq found the canister. He held it aloft, like an archaic trophy. Its top popped off, and dozens, hundreds of worlds floated to the floor.

Chiq screamed. He and I dove for the floor with the same thought: we had to find Jiri before Dad could. But Dad knelt next to us.

"You don't have to do this," Chiq said. "They're my cards."

13

"No," Dad said, "I'll help." He began to pick up cards, reading them as he went, naming worlds, counting lives.

"This is a children's game?" he asked nobody. "Millions— perhaps billions—of children, collecting lives as though—" He trailed off, astonished beyond speech. "And all of these dead worlds, lives lost. We mean...."

He trailed off again, but I heard the direction of his thoughts: the infinitely capricious universe, arbitrary as the unspoken laws that interposed themselves between my body and the miner or the maintenance worker.

"We've got it, Dad," I said, but he ignored us. Chiq and I exchanged looks.

"Jiri." My father picked up the card. "Jiri?" He moaned and lay flat on his back among the middens. He sobbed. I hadn't ever seen my parents cry. Neither of them cried when Mom left. My father hadn't cried when his own mother died, not in front of me. I'd never even seen Chiq blubber like my father did now. I turned away, embarrassed, even though nobody was watching.

All of what my father had held onto, beyond any reason or possibility—all that had fled. He was alone, and neither Chiq nor I knew how to comfort a man who had lost everything. His emotions stung me.

I ripped the card from his hand as though that would stop his inappropriate display.

"Give it back!" Dad squealed. He sounded like Chiq, a soft city boy who still revered possession. I held it near his outstretched hand, then snatched it away. Dad collapsed back into the heaped discards, moaning.

It was wrong to torment Dad, but I couldn't help myself. Everything he'd told me about the world was a half-truth, a way to possess me by directing my path—a set of rails like those the train ran on, twisting this way and that around inconvenient realities.

We drained the miners: took from their bodies and their minds and their pockets. We gave them as little in return as we could manage, not even the air filters that would protect their lungs.

14

Children of privilege, me and Chiq included, were kept away from the other classes, taught to hoard our collective wealth, though we claimed to disdain ownership. ("I don't own this, citizen: it belongs to Tonnish City!" But not to Korga, no.)

Most inconvenient of all, Mom was dead. I looked at the card: it was fresh from late this season, long after Mom would have arrived. The card would document how the planet had been destroyed, but I couldn't read it through my own blurred and welling eyes.

If only she'd taken me with her. But I had this card, the billions of lives reclaimed from death by the self-replicating automatons of The Unexpected Delight Company. Assuredly, the resurrected were identical in number and statistical variety to the deceased. As assuredly, she wouldn't be among them. Nobody who preceded the catastrophe would be. I pictured her as a column of ore-dust, of ash, blown into clouds by a gentle breeze.

I held the card. My hand trembled. I could crush it, tear it, stomp the chip—throw it into the incinerator. I heard Chiq wail at me, but he seemed very far away.

I looked at Dad. I had power over him, yet I wanted more than anything for him to tell me what to do. I wanted that direction from my strong father, not this whimpering animal.

"Please," he said.

I listened to the furnace churn. I heard Dad's ragged breathing and my own pulse thrum in my eardrums. So many systems, and nobody to tell me what to do.

I took his hand, as though I was the father. "She's not there, Dad. These are reconstructed planets. Places nothing survived."

"I know that, Marq. Still, it will remind me of her."

"Why would you want to be reminded of something that makes you feel like this?" I nudged him with my foot, as though sizing him up for a good kick.

"It tells me where I am in the universe, Marq."

"But none of it means anything."

"The miners, they use the star tree to navigate across the desert. If they'd been given different stars, would the miners be lost? They'd navigate by whatever they saw above them, whatever new Rhyonon they dreamed. The constellations are arbitrary, but they're all we have to go by. One day you'll understand."

I felt warm and tingly, as though something of great import had been passed on to me. My family, like the constellations, was composed of separate bodies that sometimes seemed related only by chance. Still, despite the nearly uncrossable distances that separated us, and the powerful forces that tugged us apart, its power to guide me remained strong.

"Maybe I'm beginning to." I handed him the card.

We collected all the others we could find and bundled them safely in Chiq's coat pocket. We sat together on the long slow train to Tonnish City, the only passengers in the first-class car. Chiq nestled up against my father and slept, while I looked out the dome and dreamed of a steady star to guide me.

Images Across a Shattered Sea

written by

Stewart C Baker

illustrated by

PAUL OTTENI

ABOUT THE AUTHOR

Stewart C Baker is an academic librarian, haikuist, and writer of speculative fiction. He has been a reader since he was very young, but didn't start writing until his mid-20s. Stewart's poetry has appeared in various haiku magazines, and his fiction has appeared in places like Flash Fiction Online, Nature, *and* Galaxy's Edge, *but he has not yet found a reliable way to successfully combine the two forms.* Writers of the Future *is his third professional short story sale.*

Stewart was born near London, England, and can speak in a convincing English accent if the mood strikes him. Since leaving England at the age of eight, he has lived in South Carolina, Japan, and Los Angeles, and currently makes his home with his wife and two children in Oregon, where he spends far too much of his time cleaning up the vomit of cats. When he's not doing that, spending time with his family, working, reading, or writing, he is usually asleep.

ABOUT THE ILLUSTRATOR

Paul Otteni was born in September in 1992, in Kirkland, Washington—a lakeside city near Seattle. As a child, he found himself with an unquenchable thirst for creating, mostly in the form of drawing. Raised in a family that was big into movies, Paul was surrounded with fantastic images of distant worlds and futuristic landscapes. These images would, over time, leave a lasting effect on him. As he grew, film continued to establish itself as a great influence in his life.

During his schooling, Paul's interest in drawing faded somewhat: he never saw much of a career in it. It wasn't until he enrolled in Vancouver Film School that his passion was rekindled. Taking classes in production design opened him to the idea of drawing and painting as a means of design for film, games, and stories.

Soon after, he invested in a Wacom tablet and software to pursue his interest in digital art. After a year of classes, Paul went on to graduate from VFS with a diploma in film production.

Currently, he is spending his time back home in Kirkland, working on digital paintings, short screenplays, and finding occasional work on film sets, ranging anywhere from production assistant to visual effects artist. He hopes to continue to improve his illustrations and make a career for himself as a concept artist.

Images Across a Shattered Sea

The air on the cliffs above the Shattered Sea was hot as a furnace and twice as dry. Still, Driss couldn't suppress a shiver at the way the shimmering message-globe moved through the sky, dozens of meters above the churning, black waves.

He had seen the globes before, of course, but only after they'd been captured and put on display in the village's cozy museum. It didn't quite seem real, the way the little ball bobbed and danced on the breeze, drifting ever so slowly toward Fatima where she stood atop a heap of boulders at the edge of the cliff.

"Here it comes," she said, waving her net back and forth as she hopped from foot to foot.

Her eagerness just made the dangers of the place worse. It was as if she didn't care that one misstep would send her tumbling to her death. Driss himself would have been happy never to have seen the coast in person. It had always been a deadly, desolate place, even in the days when the message-globes blew across the sea in huge clouds which blotted out the sun. And those days were long since past: They had seen only three globes during their two week hike, and this was the first that had come anywhere near them.

"Gotcha!" Fatima leaped into the air, hooking the bubble-like ball in her net and pulling it down from the sky. "What do you think is in it?"

She clambered down from the rock, looking for all the world like a goat rushing down from an argan tree after eating the last of its fruits. Driss laughed at the absurdity of the image, the tension flowing out from him as she moved away from the cliff edge.

"A book of law?" she continued, ignoring his laughter. "Perhaps philosophy? Machine schematics? An encyclopedia?"

"A recipe for pie," Driss countered. "A picture of a cat and a joke that makes no sense. Lewd sexual acts."

For all of these, as well, had been found in the message-globes. Driss' father, who had lived through the mad rush to the coast when they first appeared, still spoke with derision of the women and men who had bragged that they would recover the priceless lore of the past, only to find themselves the owners of meaningless trivia.

Fatima *tsk*ed as she sat on a rock. "You have no romance, Driss. No soul. Even those are treasures, to have traveled so long and so far."

"Activate it, then. Let us see what 'treasure' has come to us across time's yawning chasm."

"You are as eager as I am," she replied, waving the globe in its net. "Just admit it, and I'll open it here, where you can be the first to see."

Driss crossed his arms. "Kha! Didn't I come with you on this fool's hike? Didn't I leave a steady job with my father to chase down meaningless messages from a dead civilization? Of course I am as eager as you!"

Fatima grinned and set her catch on the rock.

Up close, the globe looked much sturdier than it had when drifting through the sky. Its surface, which shimmered with the translucence of soap bubbles when viewed from afar, had taken on the sheen of polished glass, or of the mirror pieces sometimes found in the old, abandoned tunnels to the south. The structure of the thing was not what it seemed, either; far from being smooth, it was made up of hundreds of tiny hexagons, each adjoined to the other in a pattern that shifted subtly as it crossed the message-globe's surface.

As solid as it was, the globe clearly wanted to be off; it bobbed at the top of Fatima's net, held to earth grudgingly at best.

PAUL OTTENI

"It's so beautiful," she murmured. "Let's see..." She flipped the net over and took the globe in her hands, twisting the top portion around so it popped open with a click to reveal a palm-sized gray square. "There."

A small red light flashed, and then the square in the globe's center came alive, showing not information from the past, but an image of Driss and Fatima in miniature, echoing their expressions and movements in jerky fits and starts.

In the dimness of the panops room, a solitary monitor flickered to life, bathing Jen's face in a sickly, stop-motion glare. She sucked in her breath and pushed a buzzer, then passed several minutes by staring at the scene on the monitor, which showed two people who did not yet exist having a discussion about events that had not yet happened.

The door to the room opened and a man in a beige suit entered. "Whaddawe got, kid?" he asked, clicking the door softly shut behind him.

In the sanctity of her own head, Jen bristled. *I have a PhD in quantum mechanics,* she wanted to say, *and one in electrical engineering. I am not a "kid."* But these were not the sorts of things one said to the man directly responsible for funding one's research, even if he was a jumped-up bureaucrat with delusions of being a general from a World War II movie.

Besides, he'd called her "kid" so many times now it barely offended. In revenge, she referred to him as "hog" in her thoughts. Hog for his sideburns. Hog for his chauvinism. Hog for the way his eyes narrowed in concentration every time she tried to explain how the panoptic shards worked.

Hog leaned up against the next console over. The smell of his stale sweat, insufficiently masked by strong cologne, wafted toward Jen, making her wrinkle her nose. "So who are they?" he asked. "You picked somebody important, right? The descendants of one of their kings or somethin'?"

Jen sighed. "That's not how it works. The panoptic shard can only broadcast what it happens to find—we can send it to a general place and time, but we can't target it at specific hypothetical individuals."

Hog did the eye thing.

Funding, Jen thought. *Remember the funding.* "Even if we don't know who these two are," she continued, "their appearance and the way they act can tell us plenty about the state of society two hundred years from now. For example, we can assume from the fact that they were able to activate the shard that they have at least a basic understanding of technology. And we can see that the surface is livable, given that they're not wearing any kind of breathing device or other protection.

"It's very general information—certainly not the sort of thing a market analyst would want to know—but since we're only interested in generalities, it serves our purpose well. And because the images we see in the shards derive in part from the actions we take in the short term, we can use them as a sort of gauge to measure those actions' effects."

"So I map out where we're gonna bomb, and this'll show me how far back into the Stone Age we knock 'em?"

Jen winced. "That's a gross oversimplification. There are so many variables that we can't definitively say a chosen military action alone is responsible for what we see. Even our observation itself causes variation with these people's hypothetical 'control state.'"

"What?"

"Think of it like measuring the temperature in a room. If you send someone in with a digital thermometer, both the person and the thermometer are going to add a small amount of heat. And the shards are very sophisticated pieces of equipment— especially given that we've tried to disguise the ones that transmit by putting them in groups of shards which act only as information packets. The mere fact that we've sent them will have impacted the course of future events."

Hog grunted. "But planning a military action *will* have some observable effect?"

"It should, yes."

"Then I'll leave the 'hypotheticals' to you, kid," Hog said with a grim smile. He jabbed one finger at the screen. "Give me a live stream of this in the situation room. I got meetings to hold."

Then he left, clicking the door shut behind him, leaving Jen alone with the light of the monitor, which showed the silent images of two people she feared she had killed long before they ever had a chance to be born.

Brightness. Heat. The bone-deep sense that something was wrong.

Fatima staggered across a landscape her body insisted was not what she saw, a splitting pain in her head and a hard, silvery ball clutched in one white-knuckled hand.

The ball was important, that much she knew, but the how and the why of it she couldn't quite grasp. And what had driven her to leave the safety of their shelter in the caverns? She had lived there all her life and never felt the need to see the festering, ruined surface world.

A misstep sent a jolt through her brain, and her vision exploded with silver-white sparks. Somehow, she managed to hang on to consciousness, head spinning, until the pain faded and her vision cleared, and then she stumbled to a seat on the steps of a ruined hut near a hissing stream which stank of burning hair. A yellowing skull rested against some stunted lumber which had fallen into the waters, and she wondered briefly who its owner had been, whether she would meet the same fate.

The pressure of the ball against the muscles of her hand was a throbbing counterpoint to the thudding in her head. She glanced down at it, away from the skull and the stream. What was it? She had a vague idea that it was what was wrong, somehow. But all it showed was a picture of her, with her eyes scrunched up tight against the brightness of the surface sky, and with several layers of fabric around her face to stop the poisoned air from choking her.

She wondered if she'd been out too long. If the vapors were making her paranoid.

24

But no. There *was* something out of place. Something she couldn't spot, yet which was as persistent as the throbbing in her temples and palms.

Fatima lay back and closed her eyes, hiding the sun's bloated orb behind the crook of one arm. She needed to rest. She needed to remember.

Jen shivered as the woman on screen drifted into a fitful sleep.

If the local environment was any indicator of the average global condition, most of the planet was an irradiated waste. *And all this in only two hundred years,* she thought with a glance to the door. *What in the hell are they planning?*

Jen had always known, intellectually speaking, that the military wasn't exactly going to use the panoptic shards to make the world a happy place. She'd tried to tell herself that even if they used it to kill people, the technologies she could develop would serve the greater good in the longer term. That she needed the funding. That the ends justified the means.

But this was too much. She pushed her chair back from the console and pressed her fingers against her eyelids until she saw spots, then let out a long, slow breath. She thought of her generation's children, working so hard for what they believed in. They deserved better than this, and the woman and man she'd seen on screen did, too. Everybody did.

She licked her lips, gave the door another nervous glance, and—before she could change her mind—severed the shard's connection.

It was warm in the café, but the kind of warm that was tempered just enough by breezes from the nearby ocean to be pleasant instead of stifling.

Driss sat at a table with Fatima near one glittering window, breathing in fragrant steam from a cerami-steel cup of boiling hot tea.

The panoptic shard with its recording device lay nestled in the center of the table. Fatima had attached a jamming device and nanocarbon tether, then opened a virt-screen from the terminal on her wrist. As Driss looked on, she scrolled through reams and reams of data.

"It's astounding," she said, pausing to take a hasty sip of her tea. "We've known about the shards for decades now, but this is the first we've retrieved that definitively acts as a transmitter."

Driss nodded. "Makes you wonder if they've figured out we know how it works."

"Mm."

He couldn't tell if she meant it in agreement or if she'd found something interesting, but her pupils had that half-dilated look of a woman focused one hundred percent on her virt-screen, and he knew better than to interrupt Fatima when she got like that. Instead of saying anything more, he went to the counter and ordered a bowl of olives. When he returned, Fatima had moved from reading to writing, her fingers a blur across a projected keyboard.

"Sending them a message?" Driss asked.

"Not quite. Take a look." She flipped the screen his way.

Driss popped an olive in his mouth as he skimmed what she had typed—line after line of equations, algorithms, and other, more arcane code. "All I see," he had to admit after a few seconds, "is a bunch of stuff I don't understand."

Fatima rolled her eyes and unflipped the screen. "You ought to apply yourself more," she said as she resumed typing. "They offer free classes in all sorts of things at Cadi Ayyad. Even poetry, if you're not into the sciences."

Driss spat out a seed and fished another olive from the bowl. "Maybe I'll check it out sometime. But, come on, don't taunt me! What's on the screen?"

"Okay, okay. Given where the shards originate, I highly doubt the senders' intentions are good. They're probably trying to get an edge in one of those unsuccessful 21st-century genocides. There's a signature in their programming which matches what we know about recon and intel work in—"

Driss waved his hands. "Spare me the tech-speak. I won't understand it anyway."

She grinned. "Basically, they're trying to use images of us to change our reality by altering the actions they take against us. So I'm giving them an image. Just...not the kind they're expecting. And after that, well..." She made a few final keystrokes and flipped the screen his way again. "Look."

Driss glanced at what she'd done and let out a low whistle.

Jen flinched as the door slammed open and Hog stormed in, then she went back to pretending she was hard at work trying to regain the connection. In reality, she'd used the time since her act of sabotage to copy all her research onto a secured solid-state drive that now nestled in her coat pocket.

"Get it back," Hog growled. "Now."

"I'm trying, sir. So far as our system is concerned, we haven't even lost the connection. It insists we're getting images broadcast like before. I don't know what..."

She trailed off, jaw slackening, as the monitors that lined the walls flickered on, each showing images of ruined buildings and poisonous landscapes. The console was alive with data, reporting hundreds of activated shards. "All of them?" she muttered, tapping away at the keyboard. "But we only have one transmitter. Unless they somehow figured out how to—"

"Oh my dear sweet Jesus."

Jen's heart skipped at the whispered reverence in Hog's voice. Then she looked again at the images on the monitor. A satellite image of Florida, barely visible beneath a frothing Atlantic. The Eiffel Tower, half-collapsed across a ruined city barely recognizable as Paris. The Vatican afire, bodies strewn from windows and across its many steps.

"What did you do?" Hog asked.

Jen shook her head, but before she could respond—before she could repeat that she had no idea, that this shouldn't even be possible—the screens all flickered off and on again. Only this time, the screens all showed a single image: a timer, set to twenty minutes and counting down.

Hog looked her way, eyes wide. "Turn it off," he said, his voice hoarse.

Jen swallowed. The console was still streaming with data. Hands shaking, she entered the de-activation sequence—and was not much surprised when it failed to work. "I'm locked out," she whispered. "I'm sorry."

Hog didn't say a word. He just turned away and walked through the door, pale and insubstantial as a ghost.

As soon as he was gone, Jen grabbed her coat and ran. It wasn't until she got outside and halfway to the Metro station that the adrenaline poured out of her in one big rush that left her shaky and weak; she had to stagger to a bench before she fell.

She sat back, eyes closed, breathing in the crispness of the early spring day, listening to people's murmured conversations as they dined on the patio of a nearby bar, to the swish of cars and buses driving past. The city smelled of rain, with a hint of the Japanese cherries that dotted the park across the street from where she'd stopped.

In her mind, she kept playing back that final image: those numbers counting slowly, irreversibly down. She wanted to scream, to yell, to run through the city like a mad prophet, warning of the coming destruction. But what would be the point? They couldn't stop it—not now.

A muffled cheer rang out from inside, and Jen opened her eyes. She could just make out some sort of sports game on the TV above the bar. Still shaky, she let out a long, ragged breath. Maybe, she thought, there would still be time to have a drink or two before it happened.

She stood to go inside, then froze when she saw, out of the corner of her eye, a telltale glint of a panoptic shard in the sky above the park.

A shard. Not a weapon!

Had she misunderstood the message? It didn't seem likely, with the images the future people had sent. But even just the tiniest hope of it made her heart beat fast and her shakiness vanish. She dashed across the street, dodging traffic, keeping one eye on the tiny mirrored ball as it drifted below the tree line and came to rest in the fronds of a sumac bush.

She picked it out and activated it, and her mouth went dry. Pages and pages and pages of text describing fantastical technologies scrolled past, complete with diagrams and instructions on how to construct them. One was a machine that, as near as she could figure, would establish a real-time audiovisual link between the future and the present.

And there were more, some of which she couldn't even understand. She was standing there, stunned, wondering how they'd targeted her so precisely, when there was a gentle bump on the top of her head. She reached up and retrieved a second shard, which she opened with shaking hands to find an identical payload.

Heart hammering, she looked out across the city. Hundreds more of the bubble-like objects were drifting westward, some landing on empty tables in street-side cafés while others made it into open windows or the upstretched hands of pedestrians.

They hadn't targeted her. Of course they hadn't: They didn't even know she existed. Instead, they'd delivered an instant revolution to everyone around the world. Hog and his ilk wouldn't know what hit them; they'd be so busy dealing with the consequences of this that they'd never get around to wasting resources on some hypothetical future reality.

She set one of the shards on the path, where it would be easily found, and headed off for home, laughing for the sheer joy of it. Above her, the skies streamed with glimmering secrets, coming down to earth from somewhere far away.

Möbius

written by

Christoph Weber

illustrated by

TALIA SPENCER

ABOUT THE AUTHOR

In 2014, after spending years on novels too big for him, Christoph Weber wrote his first short story—a little piece titled "Möbius." The electric rush of short form had him hooked, and he penned more than a dozen stories over the next year, one of which appeared in the journal Nature.

Christoph atones for his habit of writing on dead trees by working on live ones, as a certified arborist and tree climber. Prior to that, he was a firefighter on two U.S. federal hotshot crews, and before that, a tour guide in China, while at Peking University.

He enjoys shooting (and occasionally making) traditional bows, botany, foraging, and serving on the University of Nevada Arboretum Board. Though lately all is taking a back seat to finishing The Descent of Man, *his adventure novel depicting what happens to humans in a world without bees.*

Christoph is fairly certain that he holds the distinction of being the only winner to answer his finalist notification call impersonating Arnold Schwarzenegger. In his defense, he thought the call was from a telemarketer.

ABOUT THE ILLUSTRATOR

Talia Spencer was born in 1994 and raised in Burbank, California. There she spent her childhood dedicated to the practice of making imaginary worlds real.

At the age of twelve, she lost her single mother to an undiagnosed disease which ate away her brain. Watching her mother become a vegetable was a wake-up call that catalyzed an intensified passion to create and succeed.

Her passion is inspiring love and the acceptance of pain through her art and storytelling.

She currently attends Art Center College of Design where she majors in entertainment design.

Möbius

Detective Elizabeth Arus surveyed the illegal laboratory through her nightsight monocular. *Boarded up,* she noted. *But not abandoned.*

"So what should we expect to find inside?" Musk asked. He flexed his trigger finger, as if to warm up for the coming raid. A patch reading GCTA: *Enforcement* stood stark on his black uniform. The acronym for GeneCrime Termination Authority was, by no accident, comprised of the four nucleobase letters in the human genome. The original genome. Before gene-tweakers synthesized six more letters.

"Could be cloning, genhancements, maybe even some good old-fashioned organ harvesting. Maybe we'll find someone crossing cats with spiders. I might even let that one slide," Liz lied. In her career with GeneCrime, Liz had never let off a gene-tweaker.

"You're the detective—shouldn't you know what's inside before you send my boys in?"

"We haven't seen anyone come or go, and we have no sources," Liz said. "Whoever's running it is careful."

Musk studied the derelict warehouse, its roof sagging under the weight of age. "And why doesn't that just tell you it's empty?"

"I found this place by scanning energy records. It's sucking the grid dry, and the listed owner is a company that doesn't exist. It's a black lab, all right."

Musk's radio crackled to life. "In place at the rear exit, boss. But it's boarded up. I don't think anyone's getting out this way."

"Just post up there, Wallace. Call if you see anything. We're moving in."

"Copy that."

Liz and Musk activated the vacuums on their BioPro suits; the thin protective layers molded to their bodies like second skins, allowing maximum mobility. Along with two of Musk's enforcers, they made their way to the warehouse entrance, where they pried away the old boards. A locked steel door greeted them.

"Someone's hiding something," Musk said. "Rogers, kick it."

Rogers placed an adhesive charge on the lock and directed everyone to stand aside. The charge bloomed in a hissing flower of white-hot slag. Rogers kicked the door. It mocked him with a thudding snort.

This place is better secured than the average lab, Liz thought. She glanced at the men with her. *I should have requested more.*

"You trying to let them know we're here?" Musk hissed at his man. "Blow the door down!"

Rogers placed four more charges. Light drove back the night. Liz turned around, her ears ringing, to find the steel door twisted on smoking hinges. She followed the men inside, shielding her eyes from the concentrated overhead lighting.

Two Enforcers raced ahead to clear the compound while Musk covered Liz, allowing her to begin her detective duties. He rapped his knuckles on one of the spotless steel vats lining each wall. The ring echoed down the hallway. "Blast door, good lighting, sterile equipment... this isn't our run-of-the-mill lab."

That's what makes me nervous, Liz silently agreed. Most labs, forced underground by GeneCrime's relentless enforcement, operated in the city's darkest, dirtiest holes. Some argued for regulation of gene-tweaking rather than complete termination, on the premise that there would always be gene-tweakers, whether it was legal or not. Those people insisted that forcing labs underground only made them operate in squalid conditions, unsafe for patients.

Liz was not one of those people.

Rogers' voice burst over the radio. "Next room's clear, one stiff."

Liz photographed the vats and followed Musk into the next room, which contained three steel slab tables. Atop the middle slab, a white sheet half-covered a corpse. Fat oozed like hollandaise from sores and growths over the man's torso. Another victim of gene-tweaking.

Liz began documenting the scene: she photographed the corpse, the tube leading from his arm to the bag of red fluid suspended above the table, the sores and growths—

The growths, Liz remembered with a shudder.

When Liz was five, her mother was killed after a lab mate inadvertently released a virus he'd been gene-tweaking in secret. Liz had only two vague memories of her: one of her at the helm of a tandem solarcycle, pushing her hair behind her ear as she turned to smile at Liz. The other was of her mother on her deathbed, covered in cancerous growths caused by her lab mate's illegal virus. That memory was the fuel that powered Liz on her relentless quest to hunt down every gene-tweaker in the city.

Rogers' voice came over Musk's radio, "Compound's all clear. But there's something you should see."

"Copy that." Musk turned to Liz. "You okay on your own for a bit?"

"I don't need a babysitter."

Musk snorted and paced out.

Liz opened the room's coolbox. *Bingo.* Inside was a glass cube. Inside the cube, several dozen vials of red fluid, same color as the solution the corpse had been receiving. Stamped atop the cube was a symbol: a loop of red ribbon with a half twist. Liz recognized it at once. *A Möbius strip.*

She took a Quarantainer from her bag and pulled the tough silver fabric over the cube, ensuring that the side coated with incendiary powder faced inward. On the Quarantainer's screen, she entered her thumbprint and four-letter passcode. The nanovacuum sealed, airtight and impermeable. Three attempts to open the Quarantainer without Liz's print and passcode would ignite the incendiary powdercoat, destroying the contents.

Finding nothing more of much interest, Liz walked back to the corpse for another look.

Am I losing it, or did he just breathe?

Liz put the sound-permeable earfilm of her suit to the corpse's mouth, listening for breath while feeling for pulse and watching for the subtle chest rise she thought she'd seen.

The man sank his teeth into her ear.

Liz screamed, tried to jump back, but his teeth held tight. She struck at his face, over and over, but he latched onto her ear like a gene-tweaked Doberman. Liz palmed his head with both hands and pushed, hard as she could.

A *crack* rang through her skull as the cartilage of her ear tore away. She screamed, clutched the hot ragged wetness on the side of her head, fell backward over a table. Beakers crashed down around her.

Training finally overcame shock, and Liz reached for her sidearm. Too late. The man leaped on top, straddling her, pinning her arms to the floor. A piece of her suit—along with her ear—dangled from his teeth like a dog's chew toy.

She watched helplessly as the naked, sore-ridden man reached for a beaker shard, swung it above his head, and drove it deep into her trachea.

Liz screamed, but only a bubbling gurgle came out. She bucked, tried to free her arms, to stem the flow of life spurting out of her, but her hands remained pinned, useless.

As Liz's last breath bubbled from her throat, she had one final thought. *How absurd, to be killed by a dead man.*

Liz woke, tried to sit up, failed. She could see around her, but was immobile, as though she were encased in ice. A woman, about Liz's own age, stood above her. A brief sense of familiarity flashed through Liz's mind, replaced by anger and confusion. A desire to strike out, to hurt, surged through Liz, checked only by her paralysis.

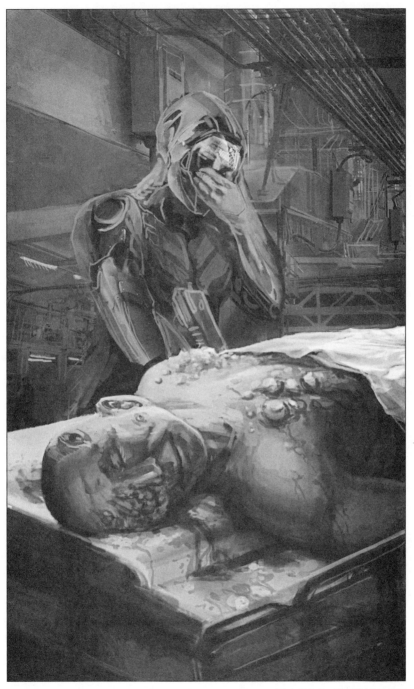

TALIA SPENCER

She screamed. A twinge of relief cooled her rage as she realized she *could* shout.

An older man hurried into the room and gestured for the woman to leave.

"Dad!"

"Shhhh. Quiet, Liz. You'll be okay."

"What's going on?"

"You're in my office at the hospital. You instructed your coworkers to put you under my care if you were ever injured. Do you remember that? You suffered a severe head injury."

Liz recalled giving those instructions. Her father was among the best doctors in the city. A specialist in emergency medicine and infectious disease, Dr. Nicolas Arus was well-versed in a dozen other fields. He often joked that he was a jack of all trades, master of none, but the medical establishment regarded him as a leading authority in several branches of medicine.

A phantom pain burned in Liz's trachea. She tried to reach for her throat. "Why can't I move!"

"I gave you a partial paralytic. Disorientation and aggression are common after the type of head injury you sustained. The drug is standard." He pushed another drug into Liz's catheter. "This will help."

When Liz was finally able to reach for her throat, she let out a long breath at finding it fully intact. "What happened to my neck?"

"What do you mean? I already scanned your c-spine—it's perfectly fine."

"I swear this...corpse...came to life and stabbed me in the throat. After..." she shuddered. "After biting my ear off."

Nicolas frowned, put his hand on his daughter's head. "I'm sorry, dear. Concussions as severe as the one you suffered can cause false memories. Sometimes terrifying ones."

"But how did I get a concussion?"

"They didn't give me a history."

"Who's they? Who brought me in?"

"The nurses brought you to me, and I assume your coworkers brought you to them, as you'd instructed in case of an accident."

Liz got up from her bed. "No one from Detective Division checked on me?"

Nicolas shook his head.

Disappointment flickered through Liz's confusion. "I need to get to GeneCrime."

Her father frowned, placed his hands on her shoulders. "Liz, you had a severe head injury. If your blood pressure spikes, you could suffer an intracranial hemorrhage. You need to stay here."

"I feel fine, Dad. Better than ever, actually. I have to go." She hugged her father and noticed the pendant he always wore on a fine chain around his neck—a serpent wound around a staff—was missing. "I don't think I've ever seen you without your Rod of Asclepius."

Nicolas smiled. "I'm glad to see the detective in you wasn't harmed. It broke off recently. But Elizabeth," his face grew stern as he took her wrists, "I *must* insist that you remain under my care."

Liz shook free and hurried to the door, pleased at the absence of stiffness she'd expected. "Don't worry about me!"

She barged through the doors of GeneCrime's Detective Division. "Really, not one of you came to visit me?"

Her answer was a room of wide eyes.

Liz glanced behind her, sure some gene-tweaked monster had barged in. "What the hell? You all look like you've seen a ghost."

Stroger, a detective Liz liked, stood up and looked her over. "Are you okay?"

"Aside from a concussion and some wonky false memories, yeah, I'm fine. What's wrong with you? Did you figure out what was in my Quarantainer?"

"Liz, we didn't know there was a Quarantainer. We didn't even know if you, well…" Stroger pointed to a poster on the wall. Liz's photo stared back at her from under a single word in bold print: MISSING.

"Is this a joke?"

Stroger shook his head. Liz looked around the room. Nobody laughed. She checked the poster's date stamp. March 11.

"What's today's date?" she asked.

"March 15."

"I've been out four days! What happened?"

"That's what everyone is hoping to ask you. All we know is what Enforcement reported: when Musk came back to the room he left you in, you were gone, along with a corpse."

"What? Then who took me to the hospital?"

"Hospital? Liz, we checked every hospital. Most of us thought you were dead."

"Why would I be dead?"

Stroger's eyes roved Liz's body, searching. "The only thing we found in the room Musk left you in was a large puddle of blood, streaked with signs of struggle. Almost four pints. We had the lab analyze it.

"Liz, it was your blood."

Liz stormed back into her father's office.

"How can I have lost four pints of blood and not have a wound? And why didn't you tell me I was out for four days?"

"I was trying to tell you when you ran out of here, against my orders! But what about blood?"

"I said, how can they have found half my blood volume at the scene, yet I don't have a scratch on me?"

Nicolas furrowed his brow. "That's not possible. You had a cerebral contusion with multiple microhemorrhages, which is why we kept you sedated for four days and why I *insist* that you stay here. But you had no external bleeding."

"Dad, our labs identify gene-tweaked chimeras with DNA the world has never seen. I think they can do a simple human blood analysis."

Nicolas shrugged. "I don't know what to tell you, Liz, other than they must have had a contaminated sample. You had no external wounds when you arrived."

"That's the other thing. How did I get here? No one from GeneCrime brought me in."

"Then who brought you to the nurses?"

Liz was already on her way out the door when she answered. "That's what I'm about to find out."

She marched up to the nurses' station. "Who was on duty the night of March 11?"

A dark-haired nurse looked Liz up and down. "I was. Can I help you?"

"Someone checked me in that night, and I need to find out who. Do you remember me?"

The nurse stared for a moment, shook her head.

"I would have been unconscious."

"I'm sorry, I really don't remember. But there were three of us on duty—one of the others may have admitted you. The log will show. What's your name?"

"Elizabeth Arus."

The nurse typed into her terminal. "Nothing under that."

"Try Liz."

The nurse tapped some keys, shook her head. "Sorry, nothing."

Impossible. Unless whoever brought me in gave a false name. "Do you keep photos of admitted patients?"

"Yes."

"Show me."

"I can't. Patient privacy."

Liz flashed her badge.

The nurse's eyes widened. "Oh. GeneCrime. Still," the nurse said uncertainly, "unless you have a warrant..."

Liz reached over the desk and turned the screen toward her. "I do."

"Ma'am, really, can I please—"

"Yes, I'll have it sent right over," Liz lied as she scanned the photos.

Her face was not among them.

Liz walked long through the warm night air. Usually, she hated the overcrowded city streets, but tonight she lost herself in the river of bodies flowing the sidewalks, hoping a change of scenery might give her some insight into what was going on.

It didn't help. Unable to make sense of anything, Liz concluded that she needed more information. She stopped, stood like a stone in a river as pedestrians streamed past, and turned back the way she'd come.

The door gave a shrill creak, as if to chide Liz for this breach of trust. She winced and squeezed through.

In the course of hunting gene-tweakers, Liz had snuck into hundreds of places without guilt. But this time was different. This time, the office was her father's.

I know he cared for me after . . . well, after whatever happened four days ago. Liz rammed her toe into a chair leg, muttered a string of curses. *But someone brought me to him, and he's not saying who.*

She flipped her light to its lowest red setting, shuffled through the consultation area, and crept into her father's personal workroom. In the crowded city, as in most of the country, space was at a premium—for a doctor to have his own consultation area, personal office, lab, and two patient rooms was testament to his standing in the medical community.

Liz powered up the photoroller on her father's desk and flicked through the projected images. Some ancient, two-dimensional photos of open, rolling landscapes. A familiar three-dimensional shot of her and Nicolas, some more of her father with colleagues, and a few of him receiving various awards. *But not a single one of Mom.* Liz had once asked her father why he never kept photos of her mother. He said he couldn't bear to be reminded.

She moved on to the lab, opened the black coolbox, and froze.

Inside, wrapped in a silver Quarantainer, was a cube the same size as the one she'd found four nights earlier.

She tried to talk down her rising heart rate. *Okay, let's not jump to conclusions. I'm sure Dad uses Quarantainers, and there are probably many med boxes this size.* She pressed her thumb to the Quarantainer's screen. It recognized her print and prompted her passcode. She swallowed, entered the letters. The Quarantainer accepted and presented two options: OPEN or INCINERATE.

A voice cut the silence behind Liz. "I couldn't crack it, even when I had your thumbprint."

Liz spun around.

"I tried your mother's name, but it informed me two more wrong entries would incinerate the contents."

"What's going on?" Liz demanded.

Her father's face was lined, weary. "I've wanted to tell you this for a long time, Liz, but I didn't think you would understand. Now, though, I need you to try. Now it is a matter of life and death."

"Enough with the dramatic generalities." Liz held up the Quarantainer, trembling in her hands. "Tell me why you have this."

"Think, Liz. You're the detective. You applied them to the wrong goal, but you've always had smarts."

Liz's head swam as she tried to put it together. The puzzle was incomplete, with too many missing pieces to see the big picture.

"Stop the games and tell me what's happening."

Nicolas sighed. "Very well. What if I told you the memory you have, the memory of the man in the lab attacking you, is not the result of a head injury, but is an accurate recollection?"

Liz shuddered, recalling the helpless terror of that moment. "I—that man was a dead. His skin was rotting."

"Yes, he was dead when you found him."

"Then how did he attack me!" Liz said, her voice rising.

"I gave him back his life."

Liz looked from one eye to the other, searching for a lie. "Impossible."

Her father keyed his mobile terminal, put it on speaker.

A man answered, groggy. "Nicolas?"

"Sorry for waking you at this hour, Arthur, but could you please come into the lab? It's important."

"Anything for you."

Moments later, the door behind Liz opened. She spun around, recoiled. The corpse from the lab, his face now free of growths, looked nervously from Liz to Nicolas.

Only when her shoulders hit the wall did Liz realize she'd been staggering backward. "How...how can he..."

Pride erased the weary lines on her father's face. "Liz, there is an ailment that has plagued mankind throughout history, a disease with one hundred percent prevalence and mortality."

"No, don't..."

"Yes, Liz. That ailment is death, and I have developed the cure."

Liz shook her head. "That's not possible."

"Isn't it? Liz, in both our lines of work, we must make conclusions based on the best evidence available. The evidence is before you. You found this man, dead, just four nights ago, and yet here he stands."

"Who are you?" Liz asked the man, the wall cold on her back.

"Arthur Teasdale. I'm a geneticist."

"A gene-tweaker," Liz corrected.

Her father *tsk*ed. "Among those you label gene-tweakers are some of the best minds in medicine. And Arthur was on the cutting edge."

Arthur nodded. "But even the best make mistakes. I accidently exposed myself to a virus I'd been manipulating. It was supposed to help people—to stop cancer cells from dividing—but it was incomplete at exposure. At that stage, it was destructive. My one hope lay with your father. We used to work together, and I knew of his research."

"And I gladly helped an old friend," Nicolas said. "Liz, you should know enough about viruses to understand the basic concept behind my cure. Death, in many cases, results from errors in genetic material. Take the case of cancer, which arises from mutations in—"

"I know how cancer works." Liz's memory of her mother on her deathbed, riddled with tumors, flashed through her mind.

"Of course you do." Nicolas frowned. "All too well. And you'll remember that your mother's cancer resulted from an experimental virus—a virus that made changes to her genome, not unlike the one that killed Arthur here. But my virus can reverse those changes. All I need is a patient's genetic code from before their cancer. I load chromosome segments into viral vectors I've bred not to reproduce, but to search for anomalies between the patient's pre-disease genome and their current, diseased DNA. When a virus finds an inconsistency, it replaces the damaged code with a healthy copy. Once the process is complete, the patient returns to a pre-disease state."

"This just sounds like advanced gene therapy," Liz said. "And what you're saying, if true, is that you've found a cure for cancer. That is not the same as a cure for death."

"True. But then I administered the virus to someone who'd died in my care, just hours before. At the time, I thought it was a long shot, but it brought them back, Liz! In retrospect it makes sense: our bodies function to support life—when the structure to fulfill that goal is returned to perfection, function follows."

Liz shook her head and pointed at Arthur. "Four days ago, his skin was rotting. There was a hole in his arm nearly to the bone. Even if your treatment repaired his DNA, it wouldn't reverse physical damage."

Nicolas smiled. "Good point. That step was difficult, but inevitable. I have been doing this longer than you want to imagine, Liz.

"Because a dose of the virus contains all of a patient's genetic information, the virus *knows,* in a manner of speaking, exactly how the patient's body should be structured. Once I pump the virus through the body, I map morphological inconsistencies and activate the genes coding for missing or diseased tissue. You are right that this is all basically gene therapy; it's just more comprehensive than anyone previously envisioned. I call it Möbius, after the Möbius strip. You remember it?"

Liz nodded.

"When viewed from above, the strip forms the basis of the recycling symbol—the symbol for recovering what has already been used. And when viewed from the side, the strip forms an infinity loop. Do you remember what curious result you get when you try to divide a Möbius strip into equal halves?"

"It remains in one piece."

"Very good. This is precisely what my viruses do: they recover used, aged DNA to provide infinite life. When the processes of disease and injury try to break down the body, to cut life short, Möbius allows us to remain whole."

Liz stared at her father, searching for any hint of a lie. *He's telling the truth.* She felt a twinge of awe; the feeling was quickly replaced by a sense of betrayal.

"You're just like every other gene-tweaker," Liz said finally, addressing both men. "Never considering the consequences of your work. You forget history. It was gene-tweakers, trying to increase food production, who tweaked the crops that killed the bees. And then it was gene-tweakers who brought back the Neanderthals the North enslaved as pollinators. And when the Civil War broke out, it was gene-tweakers who created the bioweapons we're still chasing down. Misery and war—these are the fruits of gene-tweaking. And now, in the most overpopulated era of human history, with death the only thing saving us from our own destruction, you would eliminate it?"

"Liz, I am trying to save man, not destroy him! I offer him the gift of immortality, without the decrepitude and senility of aging. People will make sacrifices for such an opportunity. If need be, we can make sterility a condition of treatment, and people will accept it as a small price to pay for eternal life."

Liz shook her head. "You overestimate people. They already know the consequences of overpopulation, yet they continue to pop out hordes of children."

Nicolas threw up his hands. "But that won't matter any longer! Overpopulation is only an issue because Earth has finite space and resources. Imagine what the greatest minds of our time will accomplish if they have five, ten, even hundreds of lifetimes to solve humanity's problems, and with no cognitive deterioration! Near-light speed space travel? Done in a few generations. We'll be colonizing not just other planets, but other solar systems, other galaxies! With the inevitable technologic developments, and with life spans suited to extrasolar travel, we'll have hundreds of exoplanets to choose from. The worries of this little rock will be a memory.

"Liz, right now you can play a role in ushering in the greatest era of human history. All you need to do is open that Quarantainer."

Liz looked down at the cube in her hands. "Möbius is in here?"

Nicolas nodded. "The rest was in my lab. Your people undoubtedly tested what they found, and just as surely failed to recognize its significance. This is all I could salvage while getting you and Arthur out."

The Quarantainer's entry screen timed out, Liz once again entered her thumbprint and passcode. Two options presented themselves: OPEN or INCINERATE.

Liz envisioned the probable consequences of each choice. With OPEN, she saw inequality and destruction—a world where only the wealthy could afford Möbius, leaving the poor to become subjects of immortal gods. She saw Earth stripped of its resources, other worlds stripped of theirs, and a mass of writhing human bodies spreading unchecked through space like a cancer. With INCINERATE, she at least saw some hope.

"I've devoted my entire life to stopping everything this represents." Her finger hovered over INCINERATE.

"Wait, Liz—there will be very real consequences if you destroy those vials."

"How's that?"

Arthur answered. "You will kill me."

"You're full of shit. *He,*" Liz said derisively, nodding at her father, "already brought you back."

"Yes, I revived Arthur and repaired the physical damage. But the virus that killed him is still in his system. Möbius does not eradicate other viruses, it simply repairs damage. And neither does Möbius replicate—if Arthur does not receive boosters, there will be nothing to repair the damage done by his virus, and he will die."

"Bullshit."

"Show her, Arthur."

Arthur lifted his shirt and turned. On the skin of his back, above his kidneys, were dark, raised blotches surrounded by red, inflamed skin.

"Symptoms of my virus," Arthur said, pulling his shirt back down. "And these are just the early signs. If I don't get that," he pointed to the box in Liz's hands, "I'm dead in a week. Eaten by a virus, inside and out, just as when you saw me the first time."

"But you're already dead!" Liz shouted. "You had your chance at life and you chose gene-tweaking! You deserve death—you're no different from the man who killed my mother."

Arthur bit his lip.

Liz looked into his welling eyes and understood. She staggered back, turned to her father. "No...you brought back the man—the monster—that killed Mom?"

"That was an *accident,* Liz. He was developing that virus to one day cure cancer, not cause it. Your mother was working on the same project."

Like frost spreading across a window, a cold desire to hurt built within Liz. She re-entered her print and passcode, and moved her finger to INCINERATE.

"Wait, Liz," her father pleaded.

"I've heard enough."

"Arthur is not the only one to die if you press that button."

"Who else, then?"

"You."

Liz probed her father's face, saw only truth.

"You're too overwhelmed to process all this, I know, but I already told you, the memory of Arthur killing you in the lab, that memory is true. An acute stress response is common when I revive a patient. I'm sure you remember your own rage and confusion when you woke this morning."

Liz remembered—a phantom of the fear and desire to strike out shuddered through her.

"It's why I gave you a paralytic, the same one I was about to give Arthur when you raided my lab. Once your team barged in, I only had time to hide under Arthur's slab—the hidden outlet to the access tunnel I built, the tunnel I used to slip you and Arthur out."

Liz looked at the Quarantainer in her hands. "But if the only remaining copies of Möbius are in here, how could you have brought me back?"

Nicolas tapped the fine chain around his neck. "I didn't wear the Rod of Asclepius for good luck, Liz. The staff and snake contained both blank versions of Möbius. I wore it as a precaution, as a way to revive someone if I ever lacked access to my lab."

"If you'd let me die," Liz said, realization washing over her, "you'd still have a copy you could rebuild from, and you wouldn't need this." She held up the Quarantainer.

Nicolas nodded. "I had a choice, and I chose family. Now you must make the same decision. Before you do, you must know that when Arthur attacked you, he gave you the virus that killed him. If you destroy that box, you destroy yourself."

Liz rocked back and forth, the Quarantainer quaking in her hands. Arthur looked at her pleadingly; her father's face was stoic. *Don't let them get to you. You don't know if they're telling the truth. And even if they are, it doesn't change what you have to do.*

"I cannot forgive what you've done. If I have to die to stop this abomination...well, I made an oath to do that the day I joined GeneCrime."

Nicolas lurched forward, his palms to his daughter. "Stop, Liz! You have conviction, I'll give you that. But before you kill Arthur and throw away your own life, I need you to see one more thing. I know you are not ready for this, but you've forced my hand." He opened the door leading to his patient exam room and gestured for Liz to follow.

On the exam table lay the woman who'd stood over Liz that morning. She was about Liz's own age, pretty even through her obvious illness, and very, very familiar. She sat up, smiled, and pushed her hair behind her ear.

Recognition struck like lightning. Liz turned, incredulous, to her father.

He spoke softly. "It was your mother's cancer that fueled me through sleepless years of development. She was the first patient

Möbius brought back. I wasn't sure if it was ready, the day she died, but at that point I had nothing to lose. My joy when it worked was quickly replaced by terror of what GeneCrime would do if they found out. They would destroy it, and probably us as well. I've had to keep your mother in hiding all these years. But she's alive, Liz, and every booster repairs her genome to the state Möbius knows—her genome at thirty-one."

"Hi, Liz," her mother said, straining to smile through pain. "There's so much I want to share with you, but I was due for my booster the day you raided your father's lab. For us to enjoy the years we should have had, I need that." She pointed to the Quarantainer. "My life, as they say, is in your hands."

A torrent of clashing emotions raged within Liz, swelling until the maelstrom grew too strong to contain, until it overflowed in twin streams down her cheeks. Liz gazed into her mother's face, now blurred through tears, then down at the box of life—or death—in her trembling hands. She pressed her thumb to the screen, her index finger to the passcode keys, G . . . C . . . T . . . A. The Quarantainer posed its question: OPEN or INCINERATE?

And Liz entered her answer.

How to Drive a Writer Crazy

BY L. RON HUBBARD

Since its inception, L. Ron Hubbard's Writers of the Future Contest has become the single most effective means for an aspiring author to break into the ranks of publishing professionals.

The Contest, of course, was created by L. Ron Hubbard, who Publishers Weekly *proclaimed as, "one of the greatest literary figures of the 20th century." He was a bestseller as a young man, with his stories gracing the covers of the hottest popular fiction magazines of the 1930s and 40s. Ron published nearly 250 works of fiction in all the popular genres of his day, including mystery, adventure, thriller, western, romance, horror, and fantasy. Ultimately, he helped to usher in Science Fiction's Golden Age with such genre-creating stories as* Final Blackout, Fear *and* To the Stars.

His broad understanding of the field, along with his proven techniques for generating tales quickly and gracefully, made him one of the most qualified people in the world to launch the Writers of the Future.

He knew the rigors of a writer's life and how the publishing industry worked. He also recognized the vital elements a tale needed to be publishable, from story ideas to research to that intangible known as suspense. He pondered the depths of story vitality, and addressed the importance of an author researching his topic deeply, so that he understands the intricacies of his tale. He also understood the importance of the relationship between the writer and his editor.

Among the more revealing notes on this business of writing and of particular significance to anyone who has faced a fickle editor is Hubbard's "How to Drive a Writer Crazy." What he describes is not just amusing, it is also the ruin of many a young literary talent.

How to Drive a Writer Crazy

1. When he starts to outline a story, immediately give him several stories just like it to read and tell him three other plots. This makes his own story and his feeling for it vanish in a cloud of disrelated facts.

2. When he outlines a character, read excerpts from stories about such characters, saying that this will clarify the writer's ideas. As this causes him to lose touch with the identity he felt in his character by robbing him of individuality, he is certain to back away from ever touching such a character.

3. Whenever the writer proposes a story, always mention that his rate, being higher than other rates of writers in the book, puts up a bar to his stories.

4. When a rumor has stated that a writer is a fast producer, invariably confront him with the fact with great disapproval, as it is, of course, unnatural for one human being to think faster than another.

5. Always correlate production and rate, saying that it is necessary for the writer to do better stories than the average for him to get any consideration whatever.

6. It is a good thing to mention any error in a story bought, especially when that error is to be editorially corrected as this makes the writer feel that he is being criticized behind his back and he wonders just how many other things are wrong.

7. Never fail to warn a writer not to be mechanical as this automatically suggests to him that his stories are mechanical and, as he considers this a crime, wonders how much of his technique shows through and instantly goes to much trouble to bury mechanics very deep—which will result in laying the mechanics bare to the eye.

8. Never fail to mention and then discuss budget problems with a writer as he is very interested.

9. By showing his vast knowledge of a field, an editor can almost always frighten a writer into mental paralysis, especially on subjects where nothing is known anyway.

10. Always tell a writer plot tricks as they are not his business.

The Last Admiral

written by

L. Ron Hubbard

illustrated by

IRVIN RODRIGUEZ

ABOUT THE STORY

In the introduction to Battlefield Earth, *L. Ron Hubbard recalls a now legendary meeting "of old scientist and science-fiction friends" he attended in 1945, in the very infancy of the Space Age. "The meeting was at the home of my dear friend, the incomparable Bob Heinlein. And do you know what was their agenda? How to get man into space fast enough so that he would be distracted from further wars on Earth."*

It was indeed a greater vision of man in space, of the stars as mankind's destination, and intrinsically, of science fiction as the imaginative catalyst for the journey, that L. Ron Hubbard under the nom de plume Rene Lafayette brought to his Conquest of Space future history series.

It was Marion Zimmer Bradley—later author of The Mists of Avalon *and other books—who, in a letter to the editor, characterized "The Last Admiral" and its suicide mission against the first pirate colony in space as "the finest story you have printed in many and many a day!"*

ABOUT THE ILLUSTRATOR

Irvin was born in the Bronx, New York in 1988. He graduated from the Fashion Institute of Technology with a BFA in Illustration in 2010. While attending FIT, he studied simultaneously at the Grand Central Academy of Art with an emphasis on academic drawing. In 2011, Irvin was the Golden Brush Award winner for the 27th L. Ron Hubbard's Illustrators of the Future Contest. He has also been featured in various publications such as Spectrum 17, Creative Quarterly, 3x3 *and* CMYK Magazine. *He currently lives and works in Brooklyn.*

The Last Admiral

Admiral Barnell sat at his desk, chin upon his threadbare chest, and read his final orders: "Complete dismantling of last surface craft and Portsmouth Naval Station. Disband all crews and personnel. When duties assigned are complete, report to Secretary General of Military Defense for final retirement."

He had been sitting where he was for two hours reading that somber message but now he straightened and put it on the desk before him. He was a fighting man, a deck officer used to all weather. Defeat, he told himself, was something a sailor had to learn to face. But it was very hard facing this.

The Navy was no more. He was the last of it: the last of a race which had started with John Paul Jones and Biddle. He was the last admiral, as David Glasgow Farragut had been the first. It was hard to take, hard to be the last man to be piped over the side of a gleaming man-o'-war, hard to know that after him the traditions of the blue and gold were dead.

He stood up and pulled his boat cloak from the rack and wrapped it around him. The offices were empty as it was late, but the sight of these desks chilled him with their bare expanses, clean of all work. These desks would be serving tailors and bonfires in another week.

He went into the yard, walking slowly over the wet and grimy cobblestones, holding his boat cloak up against the steady rain which drummed on Portsmouth. He should have gone home but he did not and wandered instead down toward the fingers of light which reached to him across the water from the town.

The docks were deserted. Half a dozen men-o'-war, all but one of them decommissioned and all of them scheduled for scrap, lay in their berthings, silent, gloomy in the downpour.

These were the last ships: a cruiser, three submarines, a tanker, and an old destroyer, unseaworthy and eaten up with rust, foul with barnacles and salt rime. Soon they would be ships no more but twisted metal plates at so much the pound.

"An indulgence of a sentimental and conservative society," General of the Air Gonfallon had called this ghost of a Navy, and Admiral Barnell, sitting in the dark and rain, stirred uneasily as he remembered those words. They had somehow included himself, yet he was only fifty-four.

The scene of the final hearings rose before him out of the mists. The politicians, the generals, and only himself from the Navy. The lofty, grating patronage of them had eaten into him deeply. They humored him. They laughed "understandingly" about his "hobby," and they cut the Navy off from all appropriation of any kind whatever.

He had faced them then like a badgered old sea lion. "You tell me," he had said, "that the day of navies is done, that man has transferred all his fighting techniques to the air! I want to remind you, gentlemen, that there is yet another arena of battle about which you have no thought. The Army has placed satellites spinning around Earth to guard her from illegal atomic manufacture. Airplanes can land in any weather and carry any troops to any scene of action in a matter of hours. But, gentlemen, there is this one thing on which you have not thought: space."

They had looked at him with pleasant smiles. They could understand the reluctance of a "battleship admiral" to see his service vanish forever from the eyes of men. A few words from him could do no harm; he was entitled to say them, of course.

"Two hundred years ago," he continued, "the Navy attempted to carry out a project of a voyage to the Moon. Private researches and Army jealousies forestalled that effort; but it was naval research data which actually made space flight possible. You are entered now upon a period of space conquest. Every few weeks explorational expeditions return from the stars to tell us of even wider horizons for man. Daily, exploitational vessels put out from our major spaceports. And five major colonies have been planted on as many planets. The significance of these things should not be lost upon you.

"Far colonies mean commerce. Commerce will come to mean piracy. The day is already over when the mere fact of being a space voyager makes one a noble hero. There are lawless elements already adrift among the far planets and there will come a time when these constitute a real menace to our expansion into the stars."

They heard him out. After all, the old gentleman had a right to say his say. After all, he was losing a good job.

"I wonder if any one of you have given any thought," continued Barnell, "to the problems incident to warfare in space. And yet those problems are complex and in need of solution. An airplane, even a stratosphere airplane, is one thing. A space vessel is quite another. A service which has the somewhat hit-or-miss experience of piloting aircraft of various small sizes is entirely and completely incapable of appreciating the problems of manning, handling, and controlling spacecraft.

"Gentlemen, a space man-o'-war is essentially no different from a large submarine. It is not and will not be a gigantic aircraft, up for a few hours or days and then back to solid ground again. Sloppy discipline, lack of routine, and bad morale are relatively unimportant to aircraft. But in a space man-o'-war we will have to return to the days of Nelson to discover the means of keeping crews in close confinement, in strict and alert obedience for possible years at a time.

"Have you ever thought of planetary blockade? I think not. Have you ever conceived the mathematics necessary to space gunnery where one ship's speed combined with its opponent's may amount to hundreds of light-speeds? I think not.

"A man-o'-war is essentially a gun platform. She is devoted to seeking and destroying enemies, to blockading and to punishing whole communities. She is a vibrant life force in herself and is not only a complicated mechanism of machinery but also a complicated and intricate problem in humanity.

"If you, gentlemen, with your aircraft, your infantry and your space transports, can solve these problems, then I willingly abandon this fight for my service. But you have not solved them, gentlemen. And there will come a time when the very existence of Earth itself will depend upon the learning and tradition which has now its last repository in a service you are disbanding—the United States Navy."

They smiled and the chairman thanked him. And they cut off the last appropriation. And sitting here in the dark and rain with the final orders like an ache in his mind, old Admiral Barnell knew how much he had failed. But he was failing not only himself. He was failing the few hundred bright young officers and technicians and the few thousand men who remained. He was failing John Paul and Farragut. And he was failing Earth.

He was stiff and cold when he rose. Tomorrow he would have to brace into the last task. He had better go home and get some rest. He had dismissed his aide earlier with his car and he went down to the gate to find a cab. The two Marines in the box, apprehensive and sensing the doom which was overtaking their proud service in common with the Navy, hurriedly stood to attention while the corporal of the guard ducked across the street to the cab stand.

The old admiral stood, unseeing, beside the guardroom table, steadying himself with one hand. He felt strangely ill. The evening paper was under his fingers where the corporal had hastily dropped it. To distract himself from the way the room had sought to tip, he looked fixedly at the headlines.

COLONY BLOWN UP
JOHNSONVILLE ON TWAIN
DESTROYED
EXPEDITION REPORTS
DISASTER

Barnell shook his head sadly and was about to put the paper away from him when the text caught his eye:

"According to the expedition commander, the attack must have come from outer space. The 116th Cavalry post and the 96th Antiaircraft Battery were evidently unwarned and the majority of the soldiers were found in the ruins of their buildings. The entire area was still radioactive and Expeditionary Engineer Martin Thomas expressed the opinion that a crude order of atomic fission had been used, such as plutonium. The planes of the Twain continental patrol were still in their hangars.

"Discounting all possibility of alien invaders, pointing out that foodstuffs and equipment which would be known and useful only to men had been looted and that the wealth of Johnsonville radium had been the evident goal of the raiders, Extraterrestrial Secretary Sime warned against panic. 'Earth,' he said, 'is amply and adequately protected against such raids and has been for the past century. There has been no relaxation of the atomic defense organizations nor will there be. This is obviously the work of some antisocial group of men who have possessed themselves of the means for one raid. We do not expect any repetition. I have asked the Army to send relief transports and further garrison to these invaluable possessions. . . .'"

Barnell had been holding the paper closer and closer to his face as he read. Now he thrust it from him with an anger which tore it. At that moment the corporal of the guard, startled by the expression on the admiral's face and the sound of the paper, stood stiffly to attention.

"Your cab, sir."

"Confound the cab! No, keep it there. Where's your phone? Where's your phone?" He snatched it off the desk and called the civil airfield.

The Navy had no planes now, having long since lost them to the Air Command of the Department of Military Defense. But his quarterdeck voice brought the admiral a civilian plane on charter in less than a minute. He rang again and futilely fumed into the mouthpiece at aides who disappeared when they were needed. Leaving orders for Lieutenant Mandville to follow him as soon as possible, he got into the cab, headed for the airport. Ten minutes later he was roaring upward through the rain toward the nation's capital.

Washington received him coolly. It had no time at the moment for admirals. Officialdom was trying to press into service transport by which to send to outflung colonies the means of defending themselves against raids, and was discovering that whereas spaceships could carry men and animals and baggage with ease, the number of ships available which could transport a 10,000-ton psi-screen dynamo was exactly none.

Old Admiral Barnell spent what he considered three precious hours trying to catch Extraterrestrial Sime. Cooling his heels in that gentleman's office put Barnell in no mood for further attempts. He took himself on an even more complicated search, the discovery of Defense Secretary Montgrove.

It was three o'clock in the afternoon before Admiral Barnell could finally lay a few salvos across the desk at this florid politician. Montgrove had been distractedly cordial at first greeting but that had cooled quickly when the admiral's proposal was only half stated.

"My dear sir," interrupted Montgrove, "you fail to realize that you have not, in all your organization, one man competent to pilot and navigate a space vessel. Further, there is no existing appropriation—"

Barnell exploded. "Confound the appropriations! Are you not aware, sir, that out there somewhere is a condemned, cowardly crew—a pirate, sir, a condemned pirate! And since when, in all the annals of time, can you find where the Army has run down pirates? You can't, sir. I defy you to, sir. And all the antiattack forces in the world, mounted around the colonies, will not do more than protect the immediate confines of some town. Sir, you don't understand the situation. It is beyond you, sir. And *I* am going beyond you, sir. I am going to the president by right of national security. Forbid me to see him, sir. I defy you to forbid me!"

Montgrove had been raised a ward heeler for all his bluster. He folded fast before the noble rage of old Barnell and was heard to utter a relieved "Whew!" when that officer had gone his angry way.

But the president, like all presidents, had "entrusted these matters to competent authority and reliable men" and "disliked to interfere with the duties of his departments."

"You have no department with that duty, Mr. President," said old Barnell. "I respectfully ask you to call any or all of your departments to discover whether or not there is a single effort afoot to patrol planets in outer space or even to perform that most vital function, the seeking out and shooting into splinters, sir, shooting into splinters of that condemned pirate!"

"There has never been an occasion," said the president, "to delegate such a duty, but I am sure the Department of Air has some thought for this."

"Call them!" demanded Barnell.

The call was made and then several calls. And at last, with a puzzled look on his face, the president stared at the old admiral.

"They hadn't," he said slowly, "thought of it. Not until just now. I—" His phone rang and he picked it up, talked for a moment and looked relieved. "Well," he said, brightening, "I was wrong. The Army is going to man a transport and send it out looking."

"A what?" cried Barnell.

"Why, a transport. One of their troopcraft. I imagine—"

"Mr. President," said the admiral, "since time immemorial the Army has had troop transports. And since the first day they got them the Navy has been pulling them off rocks and convoying them through danger."

"But you have no crews. You have no competent navigators—"

And now Admiral Barnell could smile craggily. "Mr. President, in the past hundred and some years we have had very little work for our officers. We were called the idle service and the burden on the public purse. So we have been happy to loan officers to private enterprises." He leaned forward in triumph. "Thirty percent of the membership roll of the Explorers Club is composed of naval officers or ex-naval officers. Navigation, sir, is the Navy's strong forte! I have the men!"

This was a stopper to objection. But only for a moment. "My dear admiral, even if, as you say, naval officers have been commanding private expeditions for a very long time into space, there is still the matter of a ship. I am sure your sea vessels cannot cope with space, and I am equally sure that funds could not be made available in so short a time to purchase such a ship—"

"Mr. President, what are those things which whir past Washington every day hundreds of miles out? Sir, they are satellites."

"But satellites! Good heavens! They've been abandoned for these many years. Just the other day the Army engineers were debating whether or not it was worthwhile to salvage them. They decided that until they were proved a serious menace to navigation they should remain—"

"I want those satellites!" said Barnell. "The Army put them out there a couple of hundred years ago. There is no corrosion in space. They have never served any purpose whatever. Now I want them."

"But what could you possibly do with them?"

"A naval vessel is a gun platform. I've got the guns. I've got guns that will shoot charge enough to destroy a town five hundred miles away. But they need a platform—"

"This is going to take money," said the president, getting confused.

"I have several old naval bases, two Navy yards and a few ships to sell for scrap. I can raise a hundred and ninety million dollars in twenty-four hours and use it, if you will direct that all naval property be struck off as expended."

"Isn't that a war measure?"

"This is war," said old Barnell. And he so thoroughly looked it that by six he was in the one remaining office the Navy had left in the Defense Building, burning phone wires, authority gripped in a big, seamanlike hand.

And outside the window a newsboy was hawking his wares with "Mines on Ballerdice Raided! Five Hundred Dead in New Disaster! Army dispatching forces to stop space raider. Read all about it!"

Barnell didn't care to read. From the files he had records of thirteen officers, engineers, ordnance men, former expedition men and electronics experts. And by long distance they were replying to his barked commands, "Aye, aye, sir. Right away, sir."

Mandville, the aide, a harassed young man, entered, already briefed by the old chief yeoman in the outer office, somewhat stunned by all this activity in a place which had slept for generations.

"Any orders, sir?" said Mandville.

"Yes!" barked Barnell. "Get the chief of supplies and accounts and start him unloading naval property and have him grab up, commandeer if necessary, every scrap of space equipment on the continent not already in Army hands. Get recruiting to grab, press-gang if necessary, every space mechanic they can find. Tell hydrographic to collect all the space charts they can locate. And have ordnance down at Portsmouth start getting ready to receive Commander Stapleton tomorrow when he goes down to break out guns!"

"Will that be all, sir?"

"Oh, yes. Have somebody bring me in some dinner. On the double."

"Aye, aye, sir!"

The United States Navy had begun to move into space.

During the ensuing days, while the newspapers unknowingly played up Army relief attempts and civilian experts offered sage opinions on how to make a colony safe, Admiral Barnell and a frantic staff scooped together the ingredients of the first space battleship. It would be cumbersome and uncomfortable and it would never be able to land anywhere. But it could carry guns— missile atom guns and lots of them.

In their files they had found the design, drawn by a naval architect long since dead, of an "ideal" space dreadnought. It had features which they could not even approximate, not for lack of technology but for lack of time. Appended to that drawing were a series of comments which had followed its publication in a magazine after the Navy had smiled on it. Chief among those comments was one which hurt.

"Who would be so stupid as to drain the public treasuries for the construction of such a useless monstrosity? It cannot carry freight. Its two-hundred-and-fifty-man crew would be useless in any construction project. Its bases would place undesirable populations in the vicinity of our colonies...."

They could not build that battleship. They could not even attempt it. But it had several features which they used. Its principles were sound. A space man-o'-war would have to be able to depart from any course and assume new courses hurriedly. This meant "side-wheeler" drives which were mounted in turrets like guns and which could be swung in any direction, imparting, without upsetting the ship itself, new courses. Four such drives were instantly begun—exterior engine rooms to be fitted in a girdle around a hull.

The next principle was conservation of air in event of hits, which meant intricate compartmentation. The satellites had this but they planned to double it.

The next principle was steady gravity. An electronically inclined commander, by a simple device, tuned the ordinary gravity circuits to the engine throttles so that all acceleration would be attended by proper resetting of gravity, a thing which would keep men comfortable and, more important, would make for steadiness at the guns.

Another principle was the ordnance recoil adjuster which operated to adjust automatically the turret engines each time hits upset the speed and direction of the vessel.

A detector arrangement was developed and built in two hectic days which, using fifth-order magnetism, instantly located anything within four light-years and trained the guns upon it. They stripped twenty cargo vessels, hurriedly commandeered, of their drives to fit up the four turrets. They gutted them of gear.

They compounded their meteor force screens into a kind of force armor. Then, in a mad scramble, they loaded all they had in the twelve freighters they had chartered and roared out in a ragged flotilla to intercept the first satellite. Out of the eight satellites available, Commander Simpson had chosen this one in an initial scout. But even so, its long-disused condition made the Navy men heavy of heart when they grappled to its sides and boarded.

These satellites had been built by dumping materiel in orbit and then assembling it in space at the speed of twenty-five thousand miles an hour. It had been quite a feat at the time— two hundred years before. The engineer and spotting crews, alert for atomic work below, had idly rebuilt the interiors now and then so that little of the original was as it had been planned.

Nevertheless, despite the ragged and insecure bulkheads, the ancient metal, the fouled oxygen machinery and a hundred other drawbacks, Admiral Barnell tackled the work with a fury before which anything would have surrendered.

Bluejackets in spacesuits swarmed over the old satellite, burning and welding, fitting and throwing away. For some thousand years or more before that ancient time, sailors had carried well the repute of getting things done. And their ingenuity was displayed now in a hundred ways.

For two weeks, living aboard the grappled freighters which remained while the balance ferried up new materials, officers and men hammered away at the satellite. And then, out there in the absolute zero of space, unattended by throngs or bands, old Admiral Barnell and his bluejackets cracked a bottle of champagne across her hitherto unchristened bows and blazoned upon her nose in red lead the scrawled name "USS *Constitution*."

A brief pause of pride and a few shy grins to hide emotion and that weary, grimy lot heaved aboard her supplies, pulled her throttles and broke her out of the orbit which she had followed for two centuries as a hulk.

Old Ironsides did not at first lend herself to man-o'-war routine. She was crude, cold and uncomfortable. Her "Officers' Country" was a ledge of bunks with no springs just abaft her bridge. Crew's berthing was anywhere a man could find to put his blankets down and not get stepped on. The galley for the first week consisted of burning torches aimed precariously at coffee pots. Her battle stations were wherever a man thought he should be when action came.

But there was Navy about her. Not just in the dungarees and the lace on the officers' dirty caps. Boatswains' pipes peepled and shrilled through her and commands were received with a cheery aye, aye. Where she was going now, heading out well over ten light-speeds and building up, up, up with every hour under the able hands of her conning officers, was known only to her captain and Admiral Barnell.

Her captain, "Ten-Ike Mike" McGranger, had received his orders in a brisk, brief quarterdeck snap and he was obeying them. He was a full captain and the veteran of five space expeditions on loan to the Explorers Club, and he had ten officers who had tasted space before.

"Sir," said Admiral Barnell, "you will head in the general direction of Twain with all speed and there rendezvous with supply vessels. You will not, under any circumstances, contemplate the landing of this ship anywhere, since I conceive that battleships, to be effective, must be big enough to fight and that's too big to handle alongside a planet. You will keep all detectors alert and report any other craft. And you will hold the usual drill and general quarters to fit the men for their duties. The ship is yours. I shall not interfere. Carry on."

And the days narrowed their distance to destination. Old Admiral Barnell stayed cooped up in his cabin with mounds of space charts. All they saw of him was his aide, his yeoman, and his steward.

They came to quarters twice each day. They held battle practice. And worked out their various bills for fire and damage control. But no one even tried to figure out how one would go about abandoning ship. That would be something to think about when the time came.

They held target practice with their batteries and coordinated their fire so that by the time they had held five drills, they could pick off a meteor or bit of dust at six thousand miles with a considerable air of confidence. With all formulae relating to gravity not counting, with their missile projectors unimpeded by air, they were finding that their sea weapons had surprising potentialities. The proximity fuses they managed to stretch so that a mile miss was a clear hit. And well before the rendezvous was reached they had screens so rigged that a fifteen-thousand-mile salvo could be fired with an accuracy of three hits out of ten shots.

They reached Twain and had to wait two days for their supply vessels which, however tardily, finally came up. The assorted cargoes were insufficient in many instances and failed to fill up the lists which department officers had anxiously and hopefully made of things they could use. One set of drives had soured and they gutted a freighter to get another.

Admiral Barnell, in a fast gig he had made en route, went down to Johnsonville to see what they faced.

He came back grim and tired. They piped him in through the air lock and he stiffly returned the salutes of the side boys. To Captain Ten-Ike Mike he said:

"All officers in wardroom country, sir."

When they were there he sat at the head of the green-covered board, head sunk on his chest, looking tired and old.

They waited quietly until he told them to sit down and then Ten-Ike said, "Things pretty tough down there, sir?"

Old Admiral Barnell raised hot eyes to the *Constitution*'s captain. "Sir, you are not old enough to recall the last atom war. I myself was a boy. But Johnsonville is old Chicago again. Dead."

The officers waited. Barnell brushed the ugly scene from his eyes. "They were attacked without warning from outer space. The missiles were probably fired from six or eight hundred miles. Eighteen thousand men, women, and children are down there—cooked."

Faces grew hard around the board and the younger officers fidgeted, anxious to slash out to a new destination and come to grips with an enemy.

Barnell looked at them. "I understand your feelings, gentlemen.

Atomic war was theoretically banished forever from Earth. It was 'banished forever' five times. And now it's out here in the stars. It means that every small community, every mine, and trading post among the planets is open to attack. Gold doesn't burn. Radium and uranium aren't affected. And while there is greed among men, these things will continue to happen—unless we are successful in this initial quest. I do not need to remind you, gentlemen, that the life term of our service is short. This will be the end of the road unless we succeed. Naval tradition has been fully ten thousand years in building. If we vanish as a service, there will be none to undertake this task of guarding space. There is more at stake here than Johnsonville, gentlemen, although heaven knows, that's enough.

"Have any of you looked at space charts? Some of you are old hands in absolute zero. Most of you are not. But all of you realize, I think, the immensity of space. There are literally millions of stars within a few hundred light-years of this point and thousands upon thousands of habitable planets. We do not have much time for several reasons. Have any of you any suggestions as to how we should locate and destroy the perpetrators of this crime?"

They had several suggestions. And after listening to them a few minutes, the old admiral nodded.

"You are all too right in that we work under enormous difficulties," he said. "We have invented insufficient technologies; we have a battleship that doesn't dare touch ground anywhere, lacking chemical jets and proper stress analysis. We have no intelligence force in operation and we have no escorts. But we have some advantages, gentlemen. We are on the scene and we have good guns and brave men.

"Commander Thorpe, I am assigning you to the command of the freighter *Gaston*. Mount one of our spare missile racks in her bows and take her crew and twenty men from this vessel. I am commissioning the *Gaston* as a cruiser. You will proceed to Radioville on Canova Bear. On arrival you will ground and search all space vessels for any of the goods which might have come from here and for all suspicious characters. Act with a high hand even if the Army tries to stop you: there is no defined authority in space.

"Lieutenant Carter, I appoint you..."

He spoke for twenty minutes and at the end of that time the only experienced space officer he had left was Captain Ten-Ike. The others had been given the freighters, newly created "cruisers," and various destinations in space.

"Gentlemen," he told them as they stood up to leave, "you are a scout force. You are poorly manned, under gunned and may well be in dangerous situations. The merchant ships which you are using are badly fitted for their tasks. But those tasks are important. You must procure intelligence as to the whereabouts of a raider base and protect at all costs the planets and colonies to which you have been assigned. You are empowered to act with complete discretion to achieve these ends. And you are reminded that upon you and your judgment rests not only the future of our service but the safety of all commerce throughout space. That will be all."

The designated ten officers took their caps and filed out. And then Barnell looked at Ten-Ike.

"Now whip the rest of these people into top deck watch officers, Captain. By trial of arms and the taking of prizes they may be commanding vessels of their own before this year is out."

It was ambitious. But that it was nearly hopeless old Admiral Barnell dared not think. What he had seen on Johnsonville had told him that the enemy was powerful. Very powerful. Johnsonville had been heavily protected by a major action force screen, a thing he had not known, by six batteries of excellent area defense weapons and by adequate warning systems. Yet, even though she had been commanded by an Army colonel whom Barnell knew by repute to be astute and alert, Johnsonville had fallen like a card house before a hurricane.

The enemy they faced was ruthless, well informed and greedy. *And he had bigger and better guns.*

During the next watches the old admiral paced the bridge, pausing from time to time to watch units of his newly

71

commissioned flotilla, weirdly silver in the bright blaze of Mizar and backed by the absolute black of space, depart upon their missions. He had left one freighter and one passenger craft, the first to service him and the other to carry the marine expeditionary force of two companies which had tardily arrived. He didn't like to think how undermanned was the *Constitution* now or how she would fare with inexperienced deck officers. Instead he indulged himself in hope that one of his scouts would bring him intelligence and that he could soon close for action.

With only his two remaining vessels beside his flag, he turned to his orderly.

"My compliments to the commanding officer and he will get underway immediately for Rangerton of Beta Centauri."

There, he thought to himself, in that welter of outcast humanity and amid the pooled riches of six planets he could most likely find (1) vital information and (2) men to replenish his crews. And he would be in the hub of the wheel he was scouting, ready to strike in any direction.

The big craft began to shudder under the impetus of drives. They were getting underway.

But Admiral Barnell need not have been quite so impatient for news. Less than one week later the battle circuit opened up with a message from Lieutenant Carter commanding the *Miami*.

INTERCEPTED BY HOSTILE CRAFT AND FIRED UPON. AM REPLYING. EVIDENTLY OUTRANGED . . . ATTEMPTING TO CLOSE . . . SEEM TO BE . . .

That was the end of the message. No further word of any kind ever came from the *Miami*.

Captain Alonzo Schmidt sprawled on a rug in the shade of a large rock and watched his ship fitters patch up the gap in the keel of the *Guerra*. To hand was a gallon of lemonade liberally spiked and served up by a girl scantily clothed.

"*Ach,* Emanuel! What nonsense, Emanuel," said Schmidt.

"Some expedition with naval men loaned. You haf heard of such. *Ach,* such worryings. No wonder you are anemic!"

Emanuel, a dandified little Argentinian, a full Spaniard, unlike Schmidt whose people had come to the country only a couple centuries before, dabbed daintily at his forehead. He found more than the rays of Aldebaran hot this day. He was a very brave man. But he was cautious.

"But they have never carried guns before," he protested.

"*Ach,* popguns. Shooting corks! So they haf heard of trouble in space and they mount popguns. Darling, more lemonade."

"They fired remarkably well," said Emanuel. "And I myself saw the bodies in the debris. They were naval officers and men. United States."

"What would they be doing in space, now? *Eh?* What? Just some private expedition that wanted to fight."

"I didn't see a single piece of expedition equipment," said Emanuel.

"*Ach,* worrying. Always it gives worryings. Besides, we outranged him at least ten thousand miles. My little darlings. My own poppets. They shoot so sweet, *ja?*"

"Admitted your people have a flair for invention," said Emanuel. "You've practically taken over our whole country with them. But..."

"*Ja,*" said Schmidt, suddenly dark, "and they kick the best of us out because we are too smart. But never mind, Emanuel. Someday we go home. We make a big colony, a big Navy, and we go home. And we take what we want, *ja?*"

"I think we ought to quit for a while," said Emanuel. "Besides, we require people for our project and all I have seen so far is murder for baubles. We should stay right here and build up our ships with what we have already. It is risky. Our guns are good. Our technicians good. We will soon be able to return and do what we wish with Earth. But that ship last month, it worries me. Naval officers, naval crew. And no equipment."

"Bah, my chicken-livered friend," said Schmidt, "you get goose bumps in any zephyr, *ja?* Didn't we shoot him to pieces?

Was there enough left to bury? Could we even salvage that old tub? No. Well—"

"She had '*Miami*' painted in red lead on her bow. I saw it. The United States Navy used to name ships after towns and *Miami* is a town."

"Bah. She's dead. They're all dead. Forget it. Two, three days we get word from Don Alvaro about Rangerton and back to work we go again. I hear it is heavy with gold shipments. Nice, yellow gold." And he chuckled in sheer good nature and reached toward the girl.

Admiral Barnell sat on a packing box in an office the Marines had tossed together for him on the outskirts of Rangerton. His five-star flag hung limply in the blazing breath of Beta Centauri. The khaki of the sentries outside was black with sweat.

The man between the two intelligence JGs was also sweating but it was not from heat. Water dripped from his palms and ran from his brow into his eyes. He had a frantic air about him and he kept twitching his head as though to get it out of a vise.

"Now let's be calm about it," said Barnell. "We do not intend to torture you—"

"I've had no food or water!" whimpered Don Alvaro Mendoza. "I'm dying of uncertainty. That's torture enough!"

"Pirates," said the old admiral, "I think we hang in chains to dry. That's right, isn't it, Colbright?"

Colbright, a clever young officer, nodded brightly. It was he who had spread the report of rich shipments while pretending drunkenness and had brought Don Alvaro prying down upon him.

"Of course we try them first," he added. "*Unless* they tell what they know *when* it is some use to us."

"But the Army post never bothered me! What are you doing here? This is a nightmare!" cried Don Alvaro. "What is the Navy doing here?"

"Protecting commerce, guaranteeing the freedom of space, and just now," said Barnell, "questioning a renegade and a thief.

You are an Argentinian. You admit you are descended from the Germans who migrated there. You admit you were thrown out of the country about ten years ago for plotting its overthrow. Now tell us where your friends keep their ships."

Don Alvaro went white. He could see Schmidt smiling while he flogged a man to death. He could see Schmidt shooting a traitor, wounding him here and there. He could see Schmidt sticking a seaman's hand out of the air lock into space and then bringing him in to knock the frozen member off like a piece of glass. He began to sweat harder.

"The difference is," said Barnell acutely, "that you are in our hands. How far away is your leader?"

"Sir, I don't think he'll talk," said Colbright. "I have his code. I'll just send a message to space at large that he has told all. That will save a lot of trouble."

With a thin scream Don Alvaro leaped back. "No!" he said, chattering with fear. "No! I'll tell you. This is the next place of raid. They'll be here in five days. *Capitan* Schmidt is the leader. We intended to build up a fleet and attack the Argentine, using Schmidt's developments. Now the base..."

The *Guerra* sailed down toward Rangerton. It was a bright afternoon there, rewarding his calculations. It would make gunnery simple. Good Don Alvaro. Schmidt trusted his friend had wit enough to stay clear of the firing area. Rangerton would make a good haul in metal and perhaps there would be two or three ships at the spaceport.

The planet looked pretty, he thought, as his detectors sought the concentration of metal which would train him dead on the town. This was his fifth attack on such places and he felt very sure of himself. The Army had nothing which could worry him and these persistent rumors about naval vessels were so much beer froth. Nobody had guns which could touch him. Nobody. Hadn't his own people shown him how to make guns? And did anyone else know? They'd brought all that from Germany a long time ago at the end of some lost and forgotten war. There. He was just about dead center. Now—

"*Capitan!*" said Emanuel. "There's a ship!"

"Ah, more for the pot. Let him land and we'll—"

"No, no," said Emanuel, excitedly, staring into the screen. "It is coming toward us, about thirty thousand miles, closing fast. A small ship. A freighter. Very fast. Twenty-one thousand—nineteen thousand—sixteen thousand—"

The *Guerra* bucked under an impact and Schmidt reeled at his station. In a sudden fury he trained his guns and pressed all firing trips. The *Guerra* rolled as her course shifted and the planet was lost for an instant. Then there was a bright blaze in the sky off to port, a blaze which had bursts in it.

"Hit him!" said Emanuel. "He's done for. But I don't like it. He almost did for us. Our steering jets are ruined!"

"*Ja,* got him," said Schmidt, all cheers again. "What a pretty lot of fire. Emanuel, I am a gunner. Now we change course with the main drives and get back to business."

Admiral Barnell's face was grim and hard as he stood, hands jammed angrily in his pockets, on his bridge, glaring at the sputtering fire which was all that remained of Commander Thorpe's *Gaston*. But it had served. It had clearly served. And swooping up from the protection of a low moon, drives all out, the *Constitution* was cutting down the range. "Eighteen thousand miles, sir," said the rangefinder.

"Captain," said old Admiral Barnell, "you may fire when on target."

A moment later the *Constitution* was shaken by a blast. A damage control circuit clanged shut, isolating the hit. A minute and a half later the *Constitution* shrilled with the whistle of launching missiles.

There was a sharp crash abaft the bridge and the emptiness around the ship blazed furiously. She bucked again under a second salvo. Damage control circuits began to close swiftly. A strained voice somewhere said, "Number Four Engine Room gone."

The shrill of a third salvo screamed through the ship. The starboard side dissolved in sparks and melting metal.

"Put on your space helmet, sir," said Mandville. "Pressure's dropping in here. We're bad hit starboard."

Barnell did not need a detector now to see the *Guerra*. The range was closed to forty miles. All drives were furiously backing and the quartermasters were trying to swing the *Guerra* alongside.

Point-blank the *Constitution* let go a salvo from her remaining guns. And then Barnell saw what was wrong. A force screen of an advanced design blocked most of the impact of their proximity shells.

"Stand by to ram!" he barked.

The quartermasters hesitated for a brief second, automatically waiting for their captain to relay. But Ten-Ike was dead on the cold steel deck and the after bulkhead was in flames.

The helm jets strained, turning into the *Guerra*'s force screen. The drives shuddered in their turrets. They were inside the *Guerra*'s shooting range, and now at three miles any salvo hitting them would also destroy the *Guerra*.

The quartermasters looked white-faced at the looming side of the *Guerra*. They were coming fast, too fast. The turrets bucked harder in an effort to hold down the impact.

Mandville snatched tight the old admiral's helmet strap and then fell himself, choking with fumes of metal turning into gas.

They crashed. There was a fiery fanfare of sparks as metal sawed through metal. Plates buckled. The bridge glass curved, almost stood the strain, and then flicked into splinters.

Air whistled out of the *Guerra* in a dying gasp. Shattered bow into rent side, they were tangled in death.

An ensign and two sailors burst through the melted compartment wall, glanced hurriedly over the bodies on the bridge and snatched Barnell from the wreckage. They stepped out into space, out of the inferno which was licking through both vessels, and fought free.

The ships did four circuits of the planet before they crashed.

IRVIN RODRIGUEZ

It was long enough for the *Memphis* to take off thirty wounded from the *Constitution* and two sailors from the *Guerra*. They found old Admiral Barnell and the three who had rescued him. Admiral Barnell was dying. His chest had been crushed.

But the old man's dying injunction was messaged back to Earth and has come down to us in our distant time in the form of Article Ten, Naval Regulations, governing the conduct of officers:

> There will be times, as there have been, when political or economic concerns seek to handicap the initiative and performance of duty of officers. It must at all times be remembered that lawless and self-seeking elements among men must be curbed by strong and effective action, often extraordinary in scope, and that whosoever threatens duty or the means to perform it threatens also the security and therefore the existence of mankind. No measure taken, no matter how far beyond the call of duty, which tends to secure to mankind the advantages of safe commerce, should be censured in any officer or man.
>
> To the Army belong the planets. To the air departments belong their atmospheres. But only to a Navy and its officers can belong the outer marches of absolute zero, the depth, the length and breadth, in all their infinity, of space.

Provided with guns from the *Guerra's* base, equipped with new knowledge and technologies, supported by generous appropriations from an appreciative nation and heralded everywhere by popular demonstrations, the United States Navy, within two years, was competently discharging its duties in space. And after it, and securely founded upon its practices, came the United Continents Navy, the Earth Navy, the Confederated Planets Navy, and through a host of others to our own time when the Intergalactic Department of the Navies regulates for us our own commerce and keeps for us peace among the hundred million worlds.

Old Admiral Barnell, sleeping in his tomb at Annapolis in the Earth National Monument of Mankind, must sleep very peacefully and content.

The Jack of Souls

written by

Stephen Merlino

illustrated by

MARICELA UGARTE PEÑA

ABOUT THE AUTHOR

Stephen Merlino lives in Seattle, Washington where he writes, plays, and teaches high school English. He lives with the world's most desirable woman, two fabulous kids, and three attack chickens.

"The Jack of Souls" is a story taken from his novel of the same name.

Stephen's path to writing began at the age of eleven, when he discovered Tolkien and dreamed of writing epic tales of his own.

In college, when a tenth reading of The Lord of the Rings *no longer delivered, he discovered Chaucer and Shakespeare and fell in love with England and its literature. Sadly, the closest he got to England back then was Seattle's Unicorn Pub (and that was run by a Scot named Angus); it wasn't until years later that he'd attend grad school in Berkshire to study Shakespeare.*

One day, a professor said of Stephen's stories, "You should get these published!" and the old dream stirred. Stephen pursued it, and though those stories remain unsold, the journey showed him the world of agents, craft, critique groups, and the value of what Jay Lake called, "psychotic persistence."

"The Jack of Souls" and its parent novel are the result of that happy psychosis.

ABOUT THE ILLUSTRATOR

Maricela Ugarte Peña was born in 1986 in Monterrey, Mexico. Maricela, or "Mari" to her friends and family, had an abiding interest in creative pursuits.

Mari felt deeply inspired by her oldest cousin, Luly, who spent hours drawing chalk unicorns that Mari would collect. Mari went on to copy horse figures and developed a strong interest in creating as she grew.

Mari's grandmother, an artist herself, nurtured Mari's interests. Eventually, she began to develop her work in conjunction with an online community, where she developed many close friends.

Now, Mari is creating diverse illustrations for games; she is working hard and polishing her art and stories, so that she can develop her original graphic novels.

The Jack of Souls

In two hours, Harric would host his own wake.

By sunrise, he'd be dead.

The knowledge hung on him like a skin of lead. There would be no shrugging it off or bearing it patiently. There would be wine, and there would be cards. Plenty of both. And with luck, there would be no tears.

Standing against the sun-warmed side of the inn, he sipped his wine and scanned the courtyard for a mark to follow into the gentleman's card hall. Free men crowded the courtyard tables, a throng of road-sore bodies under a square of bright blue sky. These were drovers and wagoneers, all drinking or calling for cider. It was their masters Harric watched for: wealthy lords looking for drink and cards in the company of their peers.

A gentlemanly hustle would keep his mind off things. It would also buy the wine for his wake.

The wake.

Thought of it made his stomach twist. *They'll expect a speech of me. Something brave, gods leave me.* He gave a small snort. "We gather tonight to celebrate my nineteenth birthday, which is also my death day...."

He swallowed a mouthful of wine, and rubbed the Jack of Souls where the card lay in his sleeve. "Send me a fat mark, Jack," he murmured. "I'm thinking too much."

The scent of rose-cider announced the arrival of a reveler at his side, and he turned to find a plague-gaunt free man peering at him from a face like a skull.

Harric jerked away.

"Didn't mean to spook ye," said the man, in a voice like a wheeze.

On second glance Harric saw it wasn't plague that consumed the fellow. He bore no telltale sores, but his flesh had wasted from his bones to the point it seemed a wonder he could stand. His nose had also been removed at some distant time, the mark of a cruel master on a slave. Open nostrils reached halfway up his face, in the shape of elongated pumpkin seeds.

"You're the gentleman bastard supposed to die tonight, ain't ye?" The man gestured with a jug at Harric's bastard belt and nodded in answer to his own question. "Some kind of witch-curse, ain't it?"

Harric looked hard at the man, certain he was being mocked, but the man's open expression was not that of a joker. The stranger simply must have known that the witch in question had also been Harric's mother. He gave a curt nod and tugged his shirt over the bastard belt, but the man missed or ignored the hint. Instead, he remained uncomfortably close, grinning like a corpse and tipping his ferryman's cap to Harric. The cap marked the man as a mate or pilot on the river, but Harric didn't recognize him as one of the regular crewmen. He'd have remembered such a scarecrow among them.

"Heard you was buying the free folk drinks tonight," said the man. "I been free ten year."

Ah. He only wants an invitation. "Feel free to join us in the inn after sunset. That's when we'll raise our cups in hope that my doom proves swift and painless."

The man coughed a thin laugh. Black eyes glinted from sunken sockets. "I thankee. And for that, I'll tell ye this. *Maybe ye don't have to die.*" He leaned close, the stink of cider thick on his breath. *"Not if ye can get the attention of a god."*

There it was. The glib prescription of every sage and know-all in the north. Now he knew he was being mocked; one of the local wags must have sent this walking skeleton to stoke his fears in exchange for a jug of cider. Harric turned on the man, hands tightening to fists . . . but the man's pitiful condition stole all urge to violence. Fate had dealt the ferryman a harsh lot, too. Worse, in some ways, than Harric's. On what should such a wretch think if not death and gods?

"Leave me with my thoughts, neighbor," said Harric.

"Looka there." The man gestured to the opposite side of the courtyard.

Harric turned to see a lord and his guards leading a slave girl to the gentleman's card hall. The girl wore showy saffron yellow from top to toe, marking her the property of the lord, whose saffron silks bespoke his lofty yellow blood rank. Her face and hair shone with matching slave paint, and the dress wrapped her so tight that it too might have been painted on. Though the makeup made it hard to guess her age, the dress revealed her as nothing but willow limbs and ribs, no more than fourteen.

Harric glimpsed a bastard belt around her waist, and his breath hitched as if from a blow. Only luck made him a free bastard, her a slave; had he been born on the West Isle, he too would wear the paint.

"That one hasn't been a slave more than a month," said the ferryman. "See how she makes him drag her?"

He was right. Born slaves obeyed habitually; this girl radiated a despondent resistance.

Anger burned behind Harric's breastbone. "She was a free bastard. One of our own, kidnapped and made a slave on the West Isle. Gods take these West Isle dogs. They mock our freedoms."

The lord glided past him on the way to the card hall. Shrewd eyes glinted from a smooth face framed in golden curls. Seething inside, Harric maintained an expression of bland indifference. The lord assessed Harric's gray silks and gentleman's long hair, and accorded him a polite nod, which Harric returned.

Before the lord entered the hall, two of his guard preceded him, announcing, "Lord Iras of Silbrey, West Isle!"

Iras swept in after them, dragging the girl, and his rear guards followed.

Harric let out a long breath. The girl's hopelessness weighed on his heart. "No call for that much slave paint, unless you're hiding bruises."

"Aye," said the ferryman. "She's proud. She'll be broke or dead in a week."

Harric's fingers dug into the palms of his hands. A red haze obscured his vision for a moment. When it passed, his mind came into strange focus. He seemed outside himself, above the chessboard, somehow, with a view of the patterns of fate. Clear as dawn he saw he could do nothing to alter his own fate. But hers... hers he might affect, if the pieces lined up right.

He smiled. *Black hells, maybe a god would notice that.*

Draining his cup, he stepped away from the inn, and adjusted the cards in the bands inside his sleeves. The ferryman said something, but Harric barely noticed.

"You'll pardon me," Harric said, and followed the lord into the card hall.

Harric plunged into the overheated haze of the hall and immediately began to perspire. Smoke from a hundred candles and burning ragleaf stained the air, adding to the reek of a hundred unwashed and perfumed men and women. Lords and knights from every island of the kingdom thronged the hall, each as unfamiliar with the next as they were with Harric. Harric was the only local with enough coin and breeding to brave the place, so no one there knew him but the hall girls he shared his takings with.

Jostling his way between tables, Harric scanned for Lord Iras among the many games of dice-wheel and tarot poker. Candelabra on the tables made islands of illumination in the gloom. From the dark at the back, orange embers of ragleaf smokers pulsed like the eyes of watching demons.

He caught sight of Iras taking a seat at a middle table of knights wearing red and umber blood colors. Iras' saffron blood outranked everyone at the table, and indeed it outranked most everyone who'd passed through the outpost that summer.

From across the room, Harric could see his air of superiority as the slave girl sat on a stool beside him. His guards took places behind, at the edge of the candlelight.

The men at the table grew still as Iras laid out a stake of silver and a deck of tarot. The knight nearest him leaned over and spat on the sawdust floor. "We don't play for West Isle coin."

Iras cut his deck and shuffled. "Pity. It spends as well as any," he said, in a West Isle drawl. "And it has the advantage of bearing a king's head, not a Queen's."

Glaring, the men left the table, leaving Iras alone.

Harric claimed the seat across from him, and sat in such a way as to keep his belt concealed beneath his shirt. He laid silver on the table to show he was in.

Iras looked up. Laughing eyes, piercing glance. A fox in man's flesh.

Beside Harric, a silk purse thumped on the table, followed by a gust of ragleaf smoke. A gentlewoman in riding dress and boots slid into the seat beside him. Lean, and well past middle-age, she had a shrewdness in her glance. Amber highlights announced blood higher than saffron. Her split riding skirt marked her a lady of the Queen's court, which meant she'd be titled, educated, and accustomed to independence.

The sight of her sent an ache of remembrance through Harric. She was a living image of his mother, when she'd lived—sharp, independent, a Queen's Lady, too—before madness banished his mother to the frontier.

"Ardensi ot billum sincu pras," said the lady to Iras. *Bright is the silver I take from a foe.*

Harric kept his expression blank, feigning ignorance of the words.

Judging from Iras' frozen sneer, the lord truly knew no Iberg. "An educated woman," he said. "How droll."

"Does it frighten you?"

Iras shuffled his cards. "No more than a speaking parrot. Shall we play?" Without awaiting answer, he dealt.

Harric suppressed a smile. If Westies despised anything more than free bastards, it was the Queen and her ladies. There could be no better lightning rod for Iras' attention during the game, which would make Harric's game much easier. He filled the silence by introducing himself. Iras followed suit.

"I am the Lady Bettis," said the woman.

Bettis won the first hand.

As Iras dealt the next hand, Harric glanced at the slave girl. She'd slumped beside her master as if shamed by the presence of one of the Queen's famously independent ladies. When she noticed Harric's glance, she met it with a stare so bleak he felt his soul rising to meet it. Unfairly cursed—doomed, as it were, to a living death—her eyes mirrored his own despair.

This near, he also noticed a swelling above one of her cheeks: a blacked eye under the paint. And when she turned her head, a lump shone through the hair above one ear.

A week to live, the ferryman gave her? More like a day.

Helpless anger burned behind his breastbone. *Notice, gods, and blush at your inaction.*

Harric picked up his cards, and studied them. Without looking up, he said, "Lord Iras, I wish to buy your girl."

A cloud of ragleaf coughed from Lady Bettis. From the corner of his sight, Harric saw her studying him. He kept his eyes down so nothing in them could betray his intent.

"You mean rent her?" said Iras. "I'll rent her, if you like."

Harric let his eyes wander over the girl. She sat rigid on the stool, eyes desperate.

"Go see to the gentleman," Iras told her. "Sit on his lap."

When the girl only glared at the floor, Iras slapped her so hard he unbalanced her from the stool. The sound brought a hush to the nearest tables. Heads turned. The hush spread as the painted girl crawled to her feet.

A dandy bounded from an adjacent table, hand on the hilt of his sword, but when Iras' guards stepped forward to meet him, he balked, sputtering.

"Sit down, you drunk ape," said Bettis. "We don't have to like it, but the Queen gave Westies their rights. Law's on his side, and only a fool doesn't know it."

Iras' bodyguards watched him, hands on the pommels of short brawler swords.

The dandy flopped back in his chair.

Jeers sailed in from the spectators, but many directed dark looks at Iras, and the tone of the place went from rough merriment to an angry grumble.

Iras stood. He opened his arms to the crowd and spread an amused smile around the room. "We mean no disrespect to the house." He laid a hand on his breast. "You in the East have forgotten the Old Ways, so they surprise you. Your Queen even freed your bastards. But I ask you, in what way are such lordless vagrants free? Free to starve and freeze in the open air? To rob for their bread?" He placed a fatherly hand on the girl's shoulder. "Consider instead how I care for Sweetness. How I clothe her and give her labor and purpose. Without me, would she not beg and die with the rest? So do not judge me, good gentles of the East. Raise a glass with me! The West offers counsel if you'll have it."

Harric lifted his cup and drank.

Iras hadn't merely needled his Eastern brethren; he'd preached, relying on rank to protect him. And though most in the hall muttered and cast hard glances, it chilled Harric to see how many joined the toast with, "The only good bastard's a slave bastard!"

The crowd returned to its games, but Harric felt the burn of angry eyes on his table. A bloody undertone had crept between those who toasted and those who had not.

Iras sat, and pushed the girl toward Harric. "Go to him."

"My apologies," said Harric. "But I only wish to buy."

"I'll pay double," said Bettis.

Iras chuckled. "So eager to be a master? No. You would free her." He fingered a lock of hair from the girl's face, revealing a clenched jaw and frozen stare. "Tell you what I'll do, I'll add a taste of Sweetness to the pot, gratis." He tossed a token to the midst of the table. "That stands for a night in the chamber. Go to him," he said to the girl. "Earn your supper."

As the girl maneuvered toward Harric's chair, the lady clapped a hand to the girl's wrist and diverted her into the chair on the opposite side of her from Harric. "Sit here."

Iras chuckled. "As the lady wishes."

Harric shrugged.

Iras dealt again, and Harric played that hand to lose. Iras won it, so neither Harric nor Bettis won the girl's service, and though the token never reappeared, the girl remained at Bettis' side.

Iras proceeded to lose a string of small pots, but when one pot grew very large, Harric perceived a shift in Iras' focus. The lord's eyes traveled to his girl with a new regularity. When Harric saw her force a mirthless and unnatural smile in return, he recognized what was happening: Iras was using her to signal cards.

The realization took Harric by surprise. Few would suspect a lord of Iras' blood rank to hustle cards, but he was as much a trickster as Harric.

Watching the pair work, Harric recognized their system. It was one Harric's mother had taught him, a combination of smiles, long blinks, and timed counts. Part of him wanted to believe the girl was a willing accomplice and brilliant actress, but the swelling under her eye suggested she was forced, as did the falseness of her smile, which had tipped Harric off in the first place.

She could easily sabotage Iras' games. She could cause him to lose by passing bad signals, or expose him as a cheat and get him lynched. The fact that she didn't told Harric there was more at work than met the eye. Many slave lords threatened harm to a slave's family if they didn't cooperate. He guessed Iras had told her that if she caused trouble, loved ones would suffer.

The pot grew to staggering heights, and Harric dropped out. Players at other tables stopped their games to watch as Iras and Bettis kept drawing and raising the bet. Several bulky knights pushed up behind Bettis, amber arm bands marking them as her retainers. Harric counted six. Arms crossed, they stared coolly across the game at Iras' four guards.

When the lady's purse went dry, she called the game and triumphantly displayed her cards on the table. "Tens and a seven."

Iras nodded. He laid out his hand. "Princes and a nine."

Bettis blinked. Groans and laughter from the crowd.

Iras' bull-necked guards shifted on their feet, hands on hilts, eyes on Bettis' men.

The lady's gaze traveled between the two sets of cards, and back again. To her credit, her mouth hung open for only a moment. Then her jaw snapped shut, her eyes hardened, and her lips pressed in a thin, tight line. Slowly, she rose and left the table.

"No Iberg motto for us, lady?" Iras swept the pot to his side.

Bettis stiffened. Over her shoulder she said, *"Sola verto infudis qato ban"—only law protects you from my blade.* Her acid tone left no doubt she meant it.

Before the lord's good humor could wane, Harric acted. "Lord Iras, I propose you play me for your slave girl."

From the corner of his eye, Harric saw Bettis turn.

Iras glanced up from sorting coins. "I do not wish to lose her."

"Double or nothing, then. If I win, she's mine. If I lose, I join her as your slave."

A murmur of surprise rippled through the nearest onlookers.

Curiosity and suspicion flickered in Iras' eyes. "Why would I want you as a slave?"

"Surely I must be good for something." Harric feigned the bleary look of the slightly drunk.

Iras leaned back, clearly amused, but perplexed. He examined Harric as he chewed on a roll of unlit ragleaf and jingled a handful of coins. His gaze shifted to the spectators' faces, and back to Harric. A fox sniffing a trap.

Abruptly, he chuckled, and returned to stacking coins. There was greed in those eyes, but caution proved stronger. "I cannot accept. I sense fine breeding in you, and high blood mustn't stoop."

Harric groaned inwardly. He couldn't buy her, and Iras wouldn't play for her. He had only one other gambit. Harric slid his chair back and stood, tugging his gray shirt against his belly to expose his bastard belt. His mother's rank of emerald green—a higher rank than any yellow rank—flashed in a band below a band of bastard black. "Would this change your thinking?"

Whispers rippled outward through the card hall as lords and retainers craned to see.

For the second time that day, Iras' smile froze in place.

His guards turned livid. "Whoreson bastard!" spat the largest. "Toss him out!"

"A bastard's free in these parts!" someone retorted.

The hall stirred, anticipating violence.

Iras raised a hand, and his guard fell back. "What foolishness is this?"

"No foolishness," said Harric.

"Your freedom is blood heresy."

Harric gave an apologetic shrug. "Not here. Here, I am outside the game of blood rank and purity. The only way you can put me in my proper place is if you win me as your slave."

The big guard lunged for Harric across the table, scattering cups and nearly toppling the candelabrum. "I'll take his whoreson tongue!"

Harric retreated. Chairs throughout the hall scraped across the floor as men stood from their tables. To Harric's relief, Bettis' retainers stepped up beside him. "This is the East Isle," one told Iras, "and if you don't like our free bastards, you can go back where you came from."

A chorus of agreement followed.

Iras raised his hands in sign of peace. "No need for that." His genteel smile returned, but his eyes remained flint. He scooped up his cards and rose as if to leave, but one of his guards stooped to whisper in his ear. Iras' eyes flashed to Harric, and as the man spoke, new amusement flickered in his gaze.

"I see," said Iras, as the guard resumed his place. "You're the bastard they say is cursed to die on the morrow." He laughed. "How clever you must think yourself to stake your freedom in a game, when you have only a day left in your miserable life! Had you hoped to cheat me in this way, so that even if you lost, I would lose more?"

Harric bowed. "I am discovered."

Iras leaned across the table, eyes burning. "You miscalculate, bastard. I can buy another girl. But you could not buy your freedom once I owned you. And do you think because you have only a day that I couldn't make it seem an eternity?"

Harric clasped his hands to steady them. "I intend to win. If all you have are words, be gone or be silent. Otherwise, sit and prove them with cards."

Iras froze, eyes locked with Harric's. After a moment of stillness, he straightened, and smiled. The tension drained from his shoulders. "Then let us play!" He laughed. "I accept the bastard's proposal! Bring parchment so we may draw up the deed to his life."

Excited confusion rippled through the crowd.

"Don't do it." Bettis laid a strong hand on Harric's arm. "I do not believe you can win."

"I am resolved," Harric said. "I'll write the deed myself."

Someone laid out parchment and quill, and Harric wrote. It amused him that he could ink such a vile document without the smallest pulse of dread. On the contrary, he felt detached and calm. If anything could win the gods' attention, surely this would do it.

Word of the wager spread. More and more people squeezed into the card hall, and by the time he finished the deed, the space was stuffed with perspiring bodies. Stable boys swarmed the rafters. House girls stood on tables.

Two of Iras' guards loomed behind Harric and stationed themselves behind his chair to make sure he didn't cheat. Bettis and her guards stationed themselves behind Iras. As if in response to the guards' scrutiny, one of the cards in Harric's sleeve slipped out of its band—the Jack of Souls, he realized, by its location among the high cards. It must have been knocked loose in his retreat from the lunging guard.

Cursing inwardly, Harric dropped his wrist against the edge of the table and pinned the card there before it emerged.

He held it there as four witnesses signed the deed, and he kept it there as he laid the deed alongside the girl's in the middle of the table.

Iras picked up a deck and gazed across to Harric. The hall fell silent.

"Tarot poker," Harric said. "Two-draw minimum before call."

The lord shuffled and dealt. At Iras' side, the girl sat motionless, a figure of saffron marble. Her eyes locked on Harric. Was it dread he saw there? Fear of a new master? Her expression seemed to ask, *Why?* And he had no easy answer. Because he hated Iras and his kind? Because he hated his mother for cursing him? Because he saw a chance to pluck meaning from the void and maybe seize the attention of a god?

All of it, surely.

Bettis and her knights hovered behind Iras.

Harric kept his wrist immobile against the table until Iras finished dealing, then feigned to scratch his wrist so he could nudge the card back in place.

Both Iras' guards leaned in at once. "What's wrong with your arm?" said one.

Harric looked up. "Can't a man scratch?"

"You're a bastard, not a man. Keep your hands apart."

Harric shrugged and picked up his cards with his free hand. He could pin the Jack of Souls against the table until he needed it. But his palms perspired at the thought of removing it or any card under such fierce scrutiny. To have any access to it, he'd need to create a distraction.

His initial hand was terrible, but since the two-draw minimum insured he'd have at least two draws, he discarded the entire hand and drew again. Iras smiled and without dropping his gaze from Harric, followed suit, discarding his entire hand to draw again.

When Harric peeked at his cards, his breath caught in his throat. He'd drawn all four queens.

His insides froze.

Iras had won.

He scanned his hand again and verified that he had the Queen of Souls, the Queen of Cups, the Queen of Fires, and the Queen of Blades.

MARICELA UGARTE PEÑA

Iras had somehow swapped in a stacked deck, and not even Bettis and her companions had seen it. There was no other explanation. The sheer improbability of four queens in the first draw made it evident. At the same time, Harric knew exactly what Iras' hand must be: all four kings, the only natural hand to beat the queens. Since no one could prove the trick, it was an act of supreme contempt for the house, and a political snub to the rule of a woman.

"Are you well, Bastard?" A tiny smile curved Iras' lips.

Sweat slid down the back of Harric's neck. The only card he could slip from his sleeve to beat four kings would be the Jack of Souls—the only wild card—to make five queens. But if Iras had the Jack as well—and why wouldn't he, if he went as far as all four kings?—then the appearance of a duplicate Jack in Harric's hand would expose one of them as a cheat, and it wouldn't take much to show that it was Harric who held the false Jack. He didn't dare try it.

The pressure of the Jack against his wrist mocked him, dared him.

Harric discarded his fifth card—a six—and drew the Prince of Fires. Of course. The highest remaining card after kings and queens, so he now held the second-highest possible hand. If there had been any doubt Iras was playing him, it died now.

A roar began in Harric's ears.

He had to breathe. To think. He'd been out-cheated before and still won. The trick to winning in such cases was always to think *around* the game—to find the game outside the game, and win that.

When the Jack slipped and nearly peeked from his cuff, he knew what he must do.

He laid his cards face down on the table and called the game.

Iras' eyebrows rose. "So soon? We've had only two draws."

"Show your cards." Harric sat back. Since his cards were now on the table and beyond tampering, Iras' guards made no protest when he dropped his hands beneath the table.

All eyes went to Iras.

The girl watched, her face a mask of intensity.

Iras spread his cards. All four kings and the Jack of Souls.

Harric stared as if shocked. Out of view, his hands dipped in and out of his sleeves.

Iras turned Harric's cards over to reveal the queens and prince.

A general groan from the spectators.

Iras laid a hand on the deeds, and locked eyes with Harric. "Queens," he said, softly. "That shall be your slave name."

Harric lunged over the table and clapped a hand on the back of Iras'. "Wait."

Iras did not struggle. "Cold feet, Queens? There are witnesses here. I am now your master."

"You cheated. The game is forfeit."

A snarl formed on Iras' lips. "For such a grave accusation you'd better have proof. The mere coincidence of the two highest hands is not proof."

Harric's other hand flipped Iras' discard pile, revealing a duplicate King of Fires and a second Jack of Souls.

Iras stared in shock. The girl's jaw dropped. Anger rippled through the spectators.

"Last I heard," said Harric, "there are only four kings in a fair deck, and only one Jack of Souls. How is it you had more?"

Iras closed his mouth, then opened it, but nothing came out. Eyes wild, he dove for his discard pile, but Harric slammed his hand upon the cards.

"Don't let him take the evidence!" someone shouted.

"Those aren't my cards!" Iras said. "Check them!"

From behind Iras, Bettis reached around and pressed a wickedly delicate blade to Iras' throat. The lord froze. His eyes flicked to the sides for bodyguards who did not come. Bettis' retainers were wrestling one to the floor; the others had similar knives to their necks.

The girl slid from her stool, a rabbit poised for flight.

"I suggest you lift your hand from the table," said Bettis, in Iras' ear.

"This is preposterous," said Iras. "The Queen grants us protection. You cannot harm us."

"Now you cling to our Queen's skirts? Curious." Bettis drew her knife a hair to the left, and Iras stiffened. A tiny bead of blood showed at his throat. When he finally lifted his hands from the table, Bettis eased the lord back in his seat.

"She didn't promise protection to cheats," said Harric. He lifted his hand from Iras' discard pile to reveal the offending cards again. This time murmurs boiled into shouts.

"He had all the best cards extra!"

"How many others did he cheat that way?"

At a nod from Bettis, the biggest of her knights seized Iras' lacey collar and dragged him over the back of his chair.

"House rules," said Harric. "You cheat, you lose."

The slave girl dove under the table.

Iras' eyes bugged and he choked against his collar. "Those aren't my cards! Flip them—"

Bettis clapped him on the side of the head with the butt of her knife, cutting his words short.

No one but Harric seemed to catch what Iras tried to say, or if they did, hatred made them deaf to his plea. If they'd examined the cards in better light, they'd note that the backs of the offending cards did not match the rest of the deck. And if anyone deduced that Harric had deposited the mismatched cards with the same hand that flipped the discard pile, no one felt moved to say it.

"I imagine you cheated me that way, too," Bettis said, as one of her men hauled the dazed Iras to his feet.

"Time for Liar's Leap!" cried a local.

"Liars Leap!" others chanted. "Liars Leap!"

In the growing commotion, a barmaid leaned in and swept the cards onto her tray along with the ash bowl, and disappeared in the crowd.

A dozen hands hoisted Iras from the floor to the shoulders of the crowd. The room roared in triumph as the mob swept him to a side door that opened onto the stable yard, and the cliff.

From under the table, the slave girl emerged beside Harric, eyes aflame with vengeful passion. She snatched both deeds from the table and clutched them to her, poised to flee.

Of course. She doesn't know my intentions. Harric nudged the candelabrum toward her and nodded to the flames. Her eyes widened. Warily, she dragged the candelabrum to her, and held her deed to a candle. Yellow flames fattened on the crackling parchment. When it became clear no one would stop her, a sound escaped her lips. Harric could not tell if it was a laugh or a sob. She dropped Harric's deed to cover her mouth with one hand. Tears flooded her eyes.

A weight seemed to lift from Harric's heart. He set fire to his own deed and held it before him, the flames dancing in his vision.

At the door, a shoving match broke out as a few of Iras' sympathizers tried to prevent the crowd from carrying him out. The mob overpowered them. As Iras passed beneath the lintel, he screamed to his guards, "Avenge me!" and when his wild gaze locked with Harric's, "I curse you! I curse you!"

Harric returned his gaze to the deeds. "How original."

The hall cleared, leaving Harric and the girl with Bettis and her retainers. Bettis' men held Iras' guards as one of Bettis' knights paced before them, sucking knuckles he'd bloodied in the scrum.

"We like our Queen," the knight said. "We like our bastards. And we don't like West Isle trash pissing on 'em, neither. Isn't that right, bastard?"

Harric smiled. "I thank you."

"You'll pay for this!" Iras' biggest guard spat. "The Old Ways live!" He and his comrades sputtered curses, but Harric barely heard them. To him it seemed they weren't men, they were pawns, minor pieces in a game of blood rank and status from which he'd always been excluded. Like their master, their faith in rank had proved their downfall. Harric had moved in the only way he ever knew, outside the game, and won.

"Ride home," said the pacing knight, as Iras' men were hauled from the hall. "Tell your friends on the West Isle the New Ways live, too, and if they come here they shall go the way of your lord!"

Lady Bettis gave the knight a nod. The knight followed the

captives out into the night, leaving her alone with Harric and the girl.

Outside, the mob cheered.

The girl stirred beside Harric. She placed something small and shiny on the table. A tiny blade, like a good purse knife. Saffron paint ran in lines down her cheeks. "That was for Iras," she said, in a small voice. "Or for me." She spoke in a decidedly East Isle accent, like Harric's.

He studied her, trying to see the person beneath the paint.

She looked down at her ridiculous dress, and in that act shrank back to a barely budding girl of fourteen. "What should I do?" she whispered.

"You may return home, if you wish it," said Bettis, stepping forward. "Or you may come with me. I have need of a maid."

The girl bowed her head. "My lady...I thank you."

"What is your name, girl?"

"Mara, my lady."

Bettis turned to follow the mob. "Come, Mara. You should see this."

Mara began to shake. Her face screwed into a mask of fear. "But...my sister. They said they'd steal her if there was trouble, and now they'll blame me and—"

Bettis held up a hand for silence. "Then we shall send for her as well. I will keep you both as long as you wish. I will teach you to live as a woman ought. In return, you can teach me Iras' tricks."

Mara's eyes widened, and she giggled. "Yes, my lady!" With a quick squeeze of Harric's hand, she hurried to the lady and bowed. The lady lifted her to her feet and embraced her with both arms.

As she held the girl, Bettis regarded Harric. "You seemed familiar tonight, but it wasn't until you revealed your blood rank that I understood why. Your mother was the Lady Chasia. Yes. By your look I see it is so. I knew her in court. Everyone knew her. Did you know that she was a great sorceress for the Queen, before..."

"Before she lost her mind and cursed the things she loved?" He gave a wry smile. "I know."

A shadow passed behind her eyes. "Just so."

Mara stepped away from her new patroness to gaze at Harric. She murmured something.

"Speak up," said Bettis.

"Thank you," said Mara.

Harric smiled. "It was truly my pleasure. Live fully for me."

Mara nodded, eyes wet and earnest.

"Farewell, son of Chasia," said Bettis, as she led the girl through the door. "May the gods take note of your deed this night."

Harric made no reply, for fear of cracking his voice.

Alone in the smoky hall, he took a deep breath and let it out. The ferryman's words echoed through his mind: *Not if ye can get the attention of a god....* "Well," he muttered. "Did I?" He saw no omen. No portent in the hall. Surely there would be a sign? His chest ached with loss and emptiness.

Just a bottle dream. Fate doesn't work that way.

He shoved the table from him, and stood. Grabbing enough coin to pay for the wine at his wake, he stumbled from the hall into the deepening night.

Across the yard at the cliff's edge, the mob still floated Iras on upstretched arms. They'd been toying with him, passing him back and forth along the edge of the cliff, until he raged with impotent defiance.

Harric crossed to the inn and steadied himself against a door. He found himself panting, unable to get enough air in his lungs.

The mob roared in triumph, and a falling cry pierced the night.

Lord Iras was flying.

When the mob dispersed, Harric lingered in the dark beside the inn, waiting for breathing and heart to settle.

Someone stirred in the darkness. A moment later, the funeral stink of roses tickled Harric's nostrils, and he sensed the presence of the noseless ferryman.

"Off to your wake!" said he, slurring, and swaying over his

feet. A grin shone pale in the night. "Why you suppose they call it a wake, anyhow? 'Cause it wakes ye? 'Cause it wakes the gods?" He planted a hard finger in Harric's chest. "You don't need a wake."

"Tell that to everyone waiting inside." Harric jerked open the door to the inn, spilling yellow lamplight into the yard. He gestured for the man to precede him inside. "Time for the drink I promised."

The ferryman regarded him from the gloom. In the half-light from the doorway, he seemed more skeleton than ever. He doffed his cap, baring a bald pate as pale as ivory. "Not today, thankee. I have my fare, tonight. Another soul waits at the river."

Hairs pricked on the back of Harric's neck.

The ferryman returned the cap to his head, and the shade of its brim made his sunken eyes like the pits of a skull. "Ye won my attention, bastard, and ye won another day. Tomorrow we drink. Look for me at sunset."

The ferryman bowed deep and retreated into the darkness, where he vanished.

Harric stared after. Weakness unstrung his knees, and he clung to the inn door.

A day.

One day.

Deep in his belly he felt the light rising like laughter. He laughed until tears streaked his face and strength returned to his knees. Still chuckling, he entered the bar to roars of applause, and paid for all the wine in the house.

Swords Like Lightning, Hooves Like Thunder

written by

K. D. Julicher

illustrated by

ELDAR ZAKIROV

ABOUT THE AUTHOR

K. D. Julicher has wanted to write fantasy novels since she read The Hobbit *as an eight year old. Having acquired a master's degree in computer science, she found it took her years to kick the habit of ending every sentence with a semicolon.*

In 2010 K. D. decided to take her childhood dream and lifelong hobby to the next level and pursue a professional writing career. She switched from scribbling only during NaNoWriMo to year-round writing, plotting, and editing. The story she wrote that year ended up being the inspiration for an entire fantasy world which includes this story along with the Baen Fantasy Adventure Award winner in 2014.

Her husband got passionate about editing her work when he discovered how to apply the skills for writing engineering specifications to crafting story structure. Now they collaborate on novels while raising their daughter. After living in six widely scattered states in the last twelve years, K. D. is now hoping to put down some roots in the sublime desolation of Nevada and write more stories about bears.

ABOUT THE ILLUSTRATOR

At sixteen, Eldar felt electrified after seeing a collection of American and British science fiction and fantasy drawings in his homeland of Uzbekistan. Suddenly, drawing, painting and art history all combined into a new passion for speculative fiction illustration.

Eldar credits the rich art throughout history as his inspiration—from Renaissance, Eighteenth and Nineteenth Century surrealists to the contemporary fantasy illustrations of today.

Eldar won the Grand Prize Golden Brush Award of the Illustrators of the Future Contest in 2006, and his art was featured in Writers of the Future Volume 22.

He has since expanded his technical skills and client base. He's working for prestigious magazines, museums and game design firms in Australia, Russia and the United States, including National Geographic. *He's been written up in international media, including a feature article in the* New York Times.

Swords Like Lightning, Hooves Like Thunder

When her horse stumbled near the edge of the bluff, Yvina leaned against its neck and prayed that the animal had merely missed its footing. The roan took another two steps and then faltered. Yvina glanced over her shoulder. Her pursuers rode along the treeless top of the last ridge, maybe two miles back. Too far below her, the river glinted in the early morning sun. She was exhausted from riding all night. She hadn't eaten in a day, and her tongue was thick with thirst. Acrid fear and horse-sweat clogged her nostrils. She'd never make it but had to try. She urged the horse on. *It's no use,* her bear whispered inside her mind. *He's spent.*

Can you give more of your strength to him? she asked. She'd already shared the bear's power with the horse once. It was a trick reserved for dire straits, where the risk of death was stronger than the risk of having your soul come unraveled.

His tendon is strained, the bear said. *I don't have enough strength for that.*

Then share mine, she urged.

If I drained us both, it might work, but then we'll be helpless, the bear warned.

Then she'd save her strength and the bear's for when her pursuers caught up. She slid off the horse onto the rocky ground, avoiding a clump of spiky grass. At least she had the short sword she'd taken off one of the Methlan warriors earlier. She wasn't going to let them take her alive. And she wasn't going to die easily. The horse took three steps before collapsing. Yvina spared a thought for the beast but there was nothing she could do for it.

She scrambled down the steep slope, her shift catching on the prickly bushes, heading toward the river. Even if she reached it and crossed, she wouldn't be safe. Her brother's army lay miles away. This was such a stupid way to die, after everything she and Aradon had been through. If only Aradon had listened to her warnings. Her brother was a fool. Now he was a fool in chains, surrounded by enough Methlan warriors to defeat even him. Was Aradon even still alive?

Worry about us first, her bear said.

I wish you had teeth and claws to help me fight, Yvina said. Now she was halfway down the steep slope. The scent of water made her parched mouth tingle. Her feet kept up a steady trot. Her eyes scanned the rocky hillside for safe footing. She could try going straight down the slope, while the riders would have to pick a path their horses could manage.

I'll give you everything I can, the bear promised. It was a comforting presence in her head. *We'll make them pay.*

Now that she was over the edge of the bluff, she couldn't see her pursuers, but they were back there. They wouldn't give up now, with their quarry so close. With luck, and help from the bear spirit, she might be able to kill most of them. If only she wore her armor. It lay safely back at the war camp, useless to her now. She wore a torn shift and boots much too large for her feet; she'd taken them off the same dead man as the sword. Her matted hair clung to her face and shoulders the way the seaweed had clung to her the night her father drowned, twenty years ago and three hundred leagues from here. She hadn't thought about that in years. Why now? Because she was going to join him soon?

We're not going to die, her bear said. *Look, we're almost to the river.*

Scrawny trees dotted the bank. The river was shallow here. It boiled and raged past teeth of rocks. Mountain-fed, it would be icy cold, even now at the height of summer. Her dry mouth longed for a cool drink. If she could reach the water, at least she wouldn't die thirsty.

She heard a distant thump. The bear sharpened her ears. Hoofbeats. She scrambled down the slope. When she heard the hoofbeats pause, she turned.

A band of Methlan warriors sat on their horses at the top of the bluff. They wore sturdy boots and leather pants, but their chests, tanned nearly as dark as their horses, were bare. Several stood in their stirrups to see her better. One pointed, and they rode straight for her, nearly at a gallop, down the steep slope she'd have sworn no horse could manage. She stood mesmerized for a half-dozen heartbeats as the horses surged over rocks and clattered down. She'd heard of Methlan riding skill, but this was beyond simple boasts. Their bare chests gleamed, covered in whirls of dark paint. Their blond hair streamed out behind them like ribbons. Their high-walled saddles were as gaudy as the bright sashes at their waists. Silver hoops pierced the rim of their ears, each man wearing at least three rings, and one with so many his ear looked mail-clad.

Run, her bear shouted. Yvina sprinted across the rocky strand and splashed into the river. She gasped as the water instantly numbed her toes. It tugged at her ankles. She scooped water to her lips. One handful barely wetted her mouth. Her shift quickly dampened from the splashing. She picked her way across, taking another drink when she could. The smooth stones of the riverbed shifted with every step. One foot placed wrong and she'd be swept away.

She slipped, and caught herself, arms flailing wildly. One knee dipped into the water. Her soaked shift clung to her, making her shiver despite the hot sun. Behind her, she heard the first rider splash into the water.

She stood in the middle of the river now. There was almost an island here, though it didn't quite hump out of the water. On the far shore, the land rose up gently, easy ground for her pursuers' horses. She had nowhere to run. They'd catch her almost as soon as she left the river. She changed her sword to her good hand and turned.

The riders had spread out. Four of them started across the river. Two others sat on their horses at the water's edge, and a couple had turned to greet a straggler coming down the slope. The closest riders had drawn swords from the scabbards on their saddles, leaving their bows untouched. They were grinning. "Come back with us," the closest rider said in heavily-accented Aradori. War paint covered his chest with bold designs. "We won't hurt you."

"Well, not much," his companion said in Methlan. They both laughed.

"I thought the Methlan were *noble* warriors," she mocked. They gaped at her. Probably they hadn't expected her to speak their language. "Yet now I find you are dogs, not fit to be called men."

"Dogs?" the leader spat. "Watch your mouth, bitch. You can come with us or you can die here."

"I prefer to die," she retorted, and set herself. The four riders spread out to surround her. *Now, my heart!* she said, and the bear leaped inside her.

She sprang forward. Her feet found their places as surely as a mountain goat's. The first rider's mouth barely opened, to speak or merely in shock she didn't know, before she reached him. He started to bring his longer sword down, far too slowly. She slashed, cutting his saddle-straps. The horse reared and he slid sideways toward the water. Yvina ducked under the flailing hooves. She could have reached up and touched them without danger. That was the bear in her, speeding her movements far beyond what an ordinary human could match.

Before the rider hit the water, she plunged her sword into his chest between the whorls of paint, then snatched one of his blades as it fell and spun off to the next rider.

This one had no more time to react. She swung her new sword hard with both hands. It bit deep into his thigh and sliced across his horse's neck. Horse and rider fell in a spray of blood. For a moment, they were a pile of thrashing limbs, all tangled together, and then the water caught them and swept them away.

Two down, but she could smell the rest closing on her. Yvina turned. The other two riders came together. They eyed her nervously. One opened his mouth. Not giving him time to speak, Yvina scooped a rock from the water. She wasn't cold anymore. The heat in her blood was a roaring fire. Yvina hurled the rock at one man's face. It smashed his nose in with a sickening crack. He cried out, raising his hands to his face. She sprang toward him before he could react. A thrust upward with her sword, and he toppled into the water.

The smell of blood grew overwhelming. Every heartbeat flooded her veins with rage. A distant part of her mind warned dispassionately that this was how bear warriors lost themselves in fights.

Yvina ignored the warning. She had to focus on winning. But oh, it felt so good to be alive. Her sword felt like an extension of her arm. Her feet danced in the too-large shoes.

One enemy remained in reach, staring at her in horror. His horse shied back. He started to turn. Yvina, snarling, grabbed at his leg. He tried to bring his sword into play, but she simply yanked him from his saddle.

Yvina screamed, all the rage and fear and frustration of the last day coming in a wordless roar, and the man landed on his back in the river. His horse whinnied and danced away.

Yvina swung. Blood and water arced up, spattering her, and her enemy went still.

We're not done, the bear warned. Her rage ebbed away, leaving her panting, aware once more of the water freezing her feet and calves. Her shift hung off one shoulder. She bent and picked up the short sword from the warrior she'd just killed. Now she held a pair of Methlan blades, one short, one long, just like their warriors used. She turned to face her enemies.

They weren't paying her much mind. Yvina frowned. They

milled around in a knot, surrounding one man. As she watched, they suddenly broke off from the lone rider and rode away along the river. In the wrong direction, too; they headed south, not north after the rest of the horde. What was going on?

The horses she hadn't killed were picking their way out of the river, unfortunately on the same shore as the last Methlan. He sat astride his horse, studying her. He wore an amused smile, and his swords still rested in their saddle-scabbards.

Yvina stood watching until she began to shiver. He was only one man. She could take him. But something about his manner unsettled her.

"Come out of the river before you die of cold," he called.

Yvina shook her head. "The water's lovely," she said. "Why not join me?"

The man laughed. Unlike the earlier men, there was no cruelty in it. He held up his empty hands. "I wish to parley with you, Lady Yvina."

"A kind offer, but I think I'll be going," she shouted.

"That's the wrong direction," the man said. "Your brother is the other way."

"His army is this way," she said. Why let him nettle her? She needed to get away. Yvina started across the river.

She heard the splash as he entered the river. She glanced back. The fool had dismounted and was slogging across on foot! What sort of idiot abandoned an advantage? He'd just watched her kill four of his friends. Well, so be it. She was growing tired, and the bear was nearly spent.

I am not, the bear said. *And be wary. I do not know what this one is up to, but he is different from the others.*

Different how?

How should I know? the bear asked. *He is different. Dangerous.*

Yvina watched her feet. One tricky place to get past and then she'd cross the shallows. Her pursuer was gaining on her. She cleared the last knot of rocks and splashed up the bank.

She longed to collapse to the grass and catch her breath.

Instead she turned. The man stood at the edge of the water, swords in hand. The bottom half of his pants were soaked. There were dark lines of soot-black paint on his bare chest. Methlan war-markings. All the warriors put them on when going into battle. They gave the warriors strength and speed, like the bear did. Though far inferior to the bear, or she wouldn't have been able to kill the four so easily.

"Why did you send the others away?" she asked. "You want the glory yourself? You'll take my head back to Khan Sihkun and he'll reward you for it?"

"I wouldn't bring Khan Sihkun a waterskin full of mare's piss," the man said, coming further inland. He was a little older and six inches taller than she was, and carried himself with a cat's assurance. Unlike the men before, his ears were unpierced, and he wore simple clothes without colorful sashes. "I wanted to meet you, and those fools were in my way. I told them to leave or I'd kill them."

"You?" Yvina raised an eyebrow. "By yourself?"

"You killed four," he said.

"I am an Aradori warrior," she said proudly. "Daughter of kings, sister of bears."

"I know," the man said. "Or at least, I know what you call yourself. What you truly are . . . now that I'd like to see."

"Who are you?" she demanded. "What do you want?"

The man gave her half a bow, his stomach muscles tightening, an insolent smile playing on his lips. His brown eyes echoed the same amusement. "I am Mahkah," he said. "And I want you, lady."

She raised her swords. How dare he speak to her like that? "Never." She should have been afraid, not annoyed. But his tone seemed playful, and her bear felt amused.

He shrugged. "Then I must prove myself to you? Very well." He raised his swords. Yvina set herself.

Mahkah took two steps toward her. He was shorter than most Aradori men, and not as broad-shouldered, but his arms were cords of muscle and his abdomen tight. He held the short sword high in his left hand. The long sword he kept low near his hips.

She'd seen Methlan men fighting duels a few times when she'd managed to convince her brother and whatever clan was nearby to talk instead of just fight. But she'd never fought with two swords before. She wondered if she should just drop the short blade and use two hands on the longer sword.

Mahkah cocked his head. "What is it?"

She let the short sword slip from her fingers. "If you have any honor at all, you'll match me," she said. "Or will you make me use a style I don't know?"

"I said I would prove myself." Mahkah put down his short sword. "Now, lady who rides with the storm, we will dance." He raised his sword in salute, then closed on her.

Yvina's blade caught his. She pushed, but his arms were longer, and he had weight on her. Mahkah broke away.

She'd have to beat him with speed. *We must win this quickly, brother bear,* she said. There would be no wearing this foe down. She would win fast or not at all.

Yvina whirled in, trying to strike under his guard, but Mahkah was there. He parried her blow and pushed her back.

Her foot slid in the too-large shoe and nearly tripped her. Cursing, Yvina leaped back, getting a few feet away.

Mahkah watched her. She ripped the shoes off her feet and cast them aside.

"Ready?" Mahkah asked.

Yvina swore at him in three different languages. He stood impassive. She called her bear, and strength flooded her again. Suddenly she wasn't angry anymore. He wasn't taunting her; he was honoring a worthy foe.

Damnation, here was a half-naked Methlan barbarian showing her more respect than her brother ever had.

Yvina screamed and hurled herself forward. Mahkah came to meet her. At the last second she twisted sideways.

Mahkah reacted quickly, but his blade missed hers. Her sword-tip grazed his bare shoulder. A thin line of blood oozed from his skin, red on golden-brown. She grinned. First blood, and from the way he'd moved, he wasn't used to fighting with one sword. If he'd had the short blade in his left hand, he'd have blocked that attack.

They drew apart, and together, and apart again. Once Mahkah's blade caught Yvina's shift low down and ripped through it. She ignored it. She'd fight naked if she must.

Her feet ached. She held her own, but couldn't much longer. Worse, he was playing with her. She could see it in the tiny smile on his lips, the ironic way he raised his eyebrows after a good pass. He could have finished this three times already, and yet here they were. Why?

Let him play. She'd wipe that arrogant smirk off his face. Yvina shifted her weight. She wrapped her sweaty hands tighter around her sword. *Give me everything,* she told the bear. *Everything we have left.*

I hope you know what you're doing, the bear said. It shuddered. Yvina wrapped the bear's strength around herself like armor, filling her arms and legs. The world sharpened. She could see every blade of grass, hear birds quarreling a half mile away. She pulled everything in, and threw herself forward.

Mahkah's eyes had time to widen before she reached him. Her blow drove him back two steps. They struggled, nearly at the river's edge. Mahkah's foot slid on a rock, and he went to one knee. One hand slipped from his sword. She had him.

He reached up, faster than she could respond, and grabbed her wrist. He pulled, hard, and her sword flew out of her hands as she fell against him. Mahkah caught her before she hit the ground. His hands steadied and pushed her up. She rocked back on her feet. Mahkah let go and rose.

Her sword lay five feet away, glinting at her from the river. Mahkah's sword dangled from his hand. They stared at each other. Yvina's chest heaved as she struggled to catch her breath.

Brother bear? she called. No response came. It might be hours before the bear could return. Too late for her.

Mahkah set his sword aside. He spread his arms and bowed. "Lady Yvina," he said, "you have shown me wonders."

Yvina stared. Her shift was still damp from her earlier river-crossing. Its torn cloth clung to her chest and rode up on her mud-splattered legs. Her feet stung with a dozen tiny abrasions. She lacked a weapon, and the bear was gone.

Maybe she could get the knife from Mahkah's belt. Not likely. She looked away, shoulders slumping in defeat. "My brother's army is coming," she said. "None of you will escape. Kill me, kill Aradon, and they will hunt you down and wipe you out." She shook her head, trying to hold back tears of anger and frustration. None of this should have happened. Three days ago they'd been on the verge of an alliance, one she'd worked so hard to craft. Now this.

"I have no intention of letting my kinsmen kill your brother," Mahkah said. "How far back is your army?"

She looked up sharply. This wasn't what she'd expected. "I don't know. If they learned of our capture quickly, they might be only a few miles from here."

"Oh?" Mahkah asked.

"We were negotiating with Sihkun when he sprang his trap. I escaped; so did two others. They may have reached my brother's army, or they may be dead. Either way, by now the army will know something is amiss and be on the move. Aradon left orders."

"They will not come in time," Mahkah said. "Sihkun's band will reach the conclave at Kharakor in three days. The clans are assembled there already, waiting for him. He will speak with the grandmothers; he will kill your brother and proclaim himself khan-of-khans — unless we arrive in time."

"Why do you care?" Yvina asked. All her frustration boiled up at once, and poured sizzling onto the ashes of her anger. "What do you want? Who *are* you?"

"Let's catch one of the loose horses for you," Mahkah suggested after the tiniest pause, "while we talk."

That made sense. Mahkah went to the river and retrieved her sword. He approached her, holding it out hilt-first. She accepted it and wiped the blade. Having it in her hand made her feel a little better.

She kept a wary eye on him as they picked their way back across the river. Mahkah offered her a hand across the roughest stretch. She ignored it. Her shift had just begun to dry; now it was soaked again. She shivered as they climbed the shore. It was a warm day but the cold linen pressed against her.

Mahkah half smiled as he watched her. "That garment you wear is worse than useless," he said. "You'd be more comfortable with nothing. But as I expect you will take offense at that suggestion, let me see if I can help you." He went to his horse, which had grazed a short distance along the riverbank, and rifled through one of the bags behind his saddle. "Here," he said, returning to her with two cloth garments in his hands.

They turned out to be a loose blouse, bright red with golden threads working designs throughout, and a pair of woven wool pants, both clearly made for a woman. Yvina eyed them suspiciously. "What are these?" They did not appear to have been previously worn.

He shrugged. "A wise man is always prepared," he said.

Yvina thought about refusing, but that was stupid. "Turn away," she ordered, and Mahkah did. Interesting, but she wouldn't let her guard down. She shimmied into the trousers, then ripped off the ruins of her shift. Yvina balled the shift up to throw aside in disgust, then hesitated, unwound it, and used the fabric to bind her chest. She held back a hiss of breath as the cold cloth chilled her skin, but she'd feel more comfortable riding this way. Then she pulled the Methlan blouse over. The neckline plunged down farther than she liked, making her double glad she had wrapped her breasts. "All right," she said, and Mahkah turned around.

She heard his sudden intake of breath. "Those suit you, lady," he said. His tone was mild, so why did Yvina's heart suddenly race?

"Now what?" she asked.

"We catch you a horse," Mahkah said. "And then you ride where you will. Back to your brother's army, if you wish."

"Where else would I want to go?" Yvina asked.

"I ride for Kharakor, and I want you to ride with me," Mahkah said. Yvina started to protest but he kept talking.

"I intend to stop Sihkun from killing your brother. Not because I have any love for Aradon Stormborn, but because I will not see Sihkun become khan-of-khans. One way or the other that will not happen. You wanted an alliance between our people, did you not?"

Yvina blinked. "How do you know?" She'd spent hours arguing that point with her brother and his generals. Aradon had insisted that the Methlan had nothing to offer, that all the Aradori needed was to negotiate safe passage across the steppes. Yvina felt certain there could be cooperation with the Methlan. When Sihkun offered to negotiate, she had hoped it would lead to more.

"I met your envoy," Mahkah said.

"Ikkayana?" A rush of excitement filled Yvina. "She got through?"

Mahkah's lips quirked. He took a coil of rope from his saddle and nodded. "Come."

Yvina followed Mahkah along the riverbank toward the stray horses. One was still saddled and bridled. It looked up as they approached, whinnied, and moved off. "Is Ikkayana all right?" Yvina asked.

"How did you come to have a Methlan servant girl?" Mahkah asked.

"I bought her freedom from a slaver four years ago," Yvina said. It had become obvious that the Methlan were key to crossing the great steppes, or being stopped at the edge. "I wanted to learn your language and customs."

"She said you treated her well. No beatings, and you kept her free from unkind attentions."

"Aradori do not keep slaves," Yvina said as they strolled closer to the stray horse. "And I will not see anyone in my care mistreated. She became my dear friend."

"She spoke well of you," Mahkah said. He uncoiled the rope, made a loop at the end.

Had Ikkayana's message reached its target? Even if Mahkah might know the answer, Yvina didn't want to ask him. Mahkah held the rope in both hands, playing it out. He raised it high, whirling it until she could barely see the motion, and then tossed. The loop sailed through the air and landed on the horse's neck. The horse started, and Mahkah twitched the rope. The loop closed tight around the horse. Mahkah approached slowly, making soothing noises. He took hold of the bridle and stroked the horse's nose, speaking softly to it. After a moment he removed the lasso and led the horse to Yvina. "He will serve you now," Mahkah said gravely. "I told him that you defeated his master in fair combat."

Yvina took the reins. She hesitated. "Can we really stop Khan Sihkun?" she asked.

He shrugged. "It seems worth the attempt."

Yvina sheathed her sword in the saddle's scabbard. The saddle held a bow, too, and full saddlebags. She put her foot into the stirrup and swung up onto the horse. With a horse between her legs and weapons at hand, even if there was more pursuit, she would be able to make it back to the army.

She peered north along the river. One of the stray horses grazed along the bank, picking its way through the rocks and scrubby bushes. No sign of the Methlan, of course. They'd be a full day's ride ahead by now. "Damn Sihkun," she said. "I've spent twenty years protecting my little brother and I'm not going to give up now. I'll ride with you."

They turned away from the river a little after noon. The grasslands spread out around them, tan and brown in every direction. Cloudless blue sky stretched like a taut canvas. Yvina had thought of the steppes as empty. Now she saw the rabbits and ground squirrels poking out of burrows to watch their passing. Overhead, hawks soared. The land rose and fell gently. Knots of scrubby trees indicated waterholes. A whole line of deeper green marked a stream, or at least a place where there would be water after a rain, or so Mahkah said. They crossed a wide swath of land where a herd had grazed recently, eating the most succulent shoots from the tough clumps of grasses and moving on under the care of their Methlan tenders. Her bear occasionally sharpened her nose for her, letting her smell all the life around them. *This is a good place,* the bear said. *A strange place but a good one. Not hemmed in like the coasts. I like the feel of sky above us.*

Mahkah rode close to her, like a guide, not a captor. He occasionally pointed out features, but for the most part allowed her to appreciate the steppes herself. Near dusk, she spotted smoke rising near a clump of trees a few miles off, and round yurts dotting the plain. "Is that them?"

Mahkah shook his head. "Stragglers heading for Kharakor. Our quarry passed through hours ago. We would see more signs of my people ordinarily. Right now, most of us are at the bluffs waiting for Sihkun."

"I don't understand what he's trying to do," Yvina said. "I thought...you have not had a khan-of-khans for some time, but Ikkayana told me the last khan-of-khans had a son. Prince Kharil. That's who I sent her to speak with. I thought we could come to an agreement with him. I offered him...an alliance."

"An alliance?" Mahkah raised an eyebrow. "I thought your brother wasn't interested."

"Aradon would have had no choice." She blushed. "I offered Kharil a personal alliance. Marriage."

Mahkah grinned. "I see. Is it common for women of your people to initiate a courtship?"

"No," Yvina said, "but I am not a woman. I am a kingsdaughter."

"You look very much like a woman to me," Mahkah said.

Should we take offense? her bear asked.

Yvina's stomach fluttered. *No,* she told the bear. *But he's ...very direct, isn't he?* She forced herself to laugh. "I mean I am not just an ordinary woman," she said. "Kingsdaughter means that I must marry a man who is worthy to be king. If my brother fell without an heir, or proved himself unfit, then my husband would rule our people. If he were Aradori, that is."

"I see." Mahkah looked her over. She flushed. He wasn't just staring at her. He saw into her, deeper than she quite liked. "Among my people, a man goes to another clan when he is ready to court. He looks for a woman who would make him a fine bride. He brings her gifts: clothing, and knives, and horses. And if she is willing, she rides back to his clan as his wife." He shifted his seat and let up on the reins a bit. His horse's pace quickened, and Yvina followed. "Has this Prince Kharil come courting you?"

"No," she said. "I didn't even know if Ikkayana reached her clan safely. I'm glad she did. Anyway, if Sihkun kills my brother, it'll be too late for anything else."

They rode in silence for a while. Even her bear kept still. The sun sank near the horizon. Yvina wondered if she should suggest stopping, but Mahkah seemed to know what he was doing. "I do not think you understand all our customs," he said at last.

"I'm certain I do not," Yvina said.

"Among our clans, a son does not always follow his father as khan. He earns his place by right. Our last khan-of-khans had a son, true, but the boy was no prince. Just another warrior. He may not even wish to be khan. It has been a dozen years since his father died, and he has done nothing to prove himself to us."

"Oh," Yvina said. Her heart sank. So much for her clever plans. *Mahkah must think me a fool.*

Mahkah smiled. "Do not worry. I am sure you will find another Methlan husband, if that is what you want."

"I just want to save my brother," she muttered.

Mahkah cocked his head. "Tell me of your brother," he said. "Every Methlan has heard of Aradon Stormborn. He and all your people swept onto our lands like a storm made flesh. But what sort of man is he?"

Take care what you say, the bear warned. *He is our ally for now, but the day may come when his people have their teeth in our throats.*

She considered. "Men will follow him anywhere," she said at last. "He's my younger brother. I raised him after our parents' death. He can be such a hard-headed fool that you want to strangle him." She found herself clutching at her reins, laughed, and let them slacken. "But sometimes he speaks and even I am swept along. He has this vision for our people. We have no homeland, you see. We fled across the seas in my father's day. We have a few keeps along the coast, scattered farms and fishing villages to support our people. No wealth. Swords and armor we buy from our neighbors at too high a price. But Aradon has this vision of us as strong and united. He's going to build us a new homeland, something that no one can take from us. He will make the name Aradori live a thousand years."

"He named your people for himself?" Mahkah asked.

Yvina shook her head. "My mother named him for our people," she said. "My mother was a seer. She had the winds in her blood. She said, the day he was born, that here was one who would make the earth shake. *Swords like lightning, and hooves like thunder.* That's what she said. She named him, she set him in my arms, and she died."

Mahkah didn't reply right away. "What about you?"

"What about me?"

"Did your mother give you a birth-gift like that?"

"I don't know." He'd hit on one of her secret griefs. Her bear nudged at her, wordless but present, a comfort in her mind.

They rode into the night. The half-moon shed silver light on the dark steppes, setting the sun-burned grass aglow. The grass rippled before them like little white-capped waves rolling toward a dark shore. A cool breeze brought rich, earthy scents that tingled in her throat. Above, the sky glittered with a sea of stars so bright they almost drowned the moon.

They gave the horses their heads and walked slowly, until the moon dipped low and the horses could barely set one hoof before another. They stopped and Mahkah built a tiny fire in the hollow between two hills. Yvina sat close and warmed her hands.

"It gets cold here at night," Mahkah warned. "There are blankets for us both, but if it's too cold just before dawn, wake me and I'll build the fire back up."

Yvina nodded, too tired to speak. Mahkah gave her jerked meat and hard, flat bread from one of his saddlebags. She chewed as much as she could, drank from the waterskin, and laid down under a pile of blankets.

"Forgive me for the accommodations, princess," Mahkah said quietly from the darkness.

She yawned. "I told you, I'm a kingsdaughter. Not a princess. I've slept out of doors before. While being hunted by slavers. This is much better." She rolled over and stared up at the sky. "I've never seen this many stars," she said. "Down in the coastlands, the sky is almost always cloudy at night." Now that the moon had set, she could see the dense band of stars overhead, gleaming like a path in the sky.

"The ten thousand eyes," Mahkah said.

"What?"

So he told her a legend of the first Methlan, who fled into the empty lands seeking freedom. Their old oppressors hunted them, capturing them in ones and twos and dragging them back to bondage, until the first wise woman went to the first khan. "Give me your eye," she said, and he took it from its socket and gave it to her. She burned it on a fire of plains-grass and horse-hair, and then took the ashes and threw them up into the sky, where they caught and twinkled. "Now you have ten thousand eyes to see our foes," she said, and from that time no enemy could catch the Methlan unawares on their steppes.

"That's a beautiful story," Yvina said.

"My mother used to say that wise woman was her mother's mother's mother, fifteen generations back," Mahkah said.

"Is your mother dead, too?" Yvina asked.

"And my father," Mahkah said. "I have spent a long time away from my clan, seeking answers."

"To what questions?"

Mahkah didn't answer. Yvina knew she should sleep, but she ached from the day's hard riding. She twisted around again, curling on her side, pulling the blankets tighter around her shoulders. Mahkah rested only a few feet away, but now that the fire had died she couldn't even see her own fingers. "Why did you fight me?" she asked. "If you wanted me to come help you save Aradon, then there was no need."

"I had reasons," Mahkah said. She could hear the smile in his voice. It made her heart beat quicker. Here she lay, alone under the stars with a man who had bested her in combat and then showed her utmost deference. Yet she'd heard his breath catch when he saw her dressed in Methlan clothes. A half-dozen times she'd caught him glancing at her body. Oddly, it made her skin tingle rather than crawl with revulsion. Plenty of men found her attractive, even if she was in her late twenties now, but none of them had ever made her feel so alive.

"What reasons?" she asked, trying to get her mind off this trail.

"To fight you? Three, and I do not think I will tell you."

Now he was just being annoying. "You wanted to get my attention," she said. "If you'd just said *you're free to go, but come help me,* I'd have left you behind in a heartbeat. Coming out with you was foolish."

"It might be the cleverest thing you've done, lady," Mahkah said. "I just want to stop Sihkun. You're the one who wants Aradon back alive."

"If Aradon dies, we will have war between your people and mine," Yvina said.

"Yes," Mahkah said softly. "But that might be a war my

people can win, if Sihkun and Aradon are both dead. Who will inherit your brother's throne? You?"

Now it was her turn not to answer, not to give away anything to a man who was, after all, only a temporary ally. He asked a good question, and one that had kept Yvina awake at night before. Several of the generals would try to seize power. Most likely the Aradori would shatter into half a dozen factions. Mahkah was right: they couldn't win a war that way. The only way to keep the Aradori united would be for her to marry one of the rivals and bring legitimacy to his claim. She shivered.

"What's wrong?" Mahkah asked. "Too cold?"

"No," she said, though she shivered beneath the blankets. "Just thinking about what it would cost me to unite my people if my brother dies."

"Ahh." He stretched the sound out. It caressed her ears. *He understands what you mean,* her bear whispered. *He listens, not just to your words but to your heart. Be careful. I do not want to see you wounded.*

I am on guard, dear heart, Yvina said. But it was nice to have someone who actually listened. She closed her eyes and listened to the little sounds of rabbits hopping not far off, the soft whisper of the breeze. Soon Mahkah's breathing changed, and not long after, sleep came at last.

She woke abruptly, chilled to the bone. The pale gray sky overhead promised sunrise soon. She sat up and pulled the blankets tight around her shoulders, rubbing her hands.

Mahkah lay three feet away. He opened his eyes, looked at her for a moment, then got up. He draped his blankets over her and knelt beside the fire. Yvina shivered. A little thrill ran through her as she soaked in the warmth from Mahkah's blankets. They smelled of him. Like saddle-leather and sweat and horse and a hint of something else she couldn't name. The scent excited her. *Careful,* her bear warned. *This man is dangerous.*

I don't think he wants to hurt me, she said.

That makes him more dangerous than anyone you've met, the bear warned.

Mahkah coaxed a tiny flame. He fed in a bit of kindling, then set a small pot of water near the fire. He dug out a cup and a small pouch, then sifted powder from the pouch into the cup. When the water was steaming, he drew it back and poured. He handed her the cup. Yvina sipped, looking up in surprise as the rush of flavors hit her tongue. She savored blackberry, and dried rosehips, and something with a hint of spice. "Good?" Mahkah asked.

She nodded. "I've never tasted anything like it."

"It'll warm you quickly," he said. He watched her drink.

"Don't you want any?" she asked, after taking another sip.

"I have only the one cup," he answered.

She took another sip, then handed him the cup. He raised an eyebrow but drank. They handed the drink back and forth, filling it again when the water ran low. Then Mahkah threw the dregs over the fire and kicked dirt on it. "We should get started."

Yvina helped pack the horses, rolling up the blankets and stowing them as pink streaks lit the sky. It didn't take long. They mounted.

"Look," Mahkah said, taking her reins and turning their horses to face east.

Yvina started to ask what, and then the first rays of the sun peeked above the horizon, flooding the plains with pale light. A flock of birds soared up from the brush nearby, flying upward and filling the air with their song. Nearby, a brook whispered. The sun rose higher, its disc heaving up over the horizon. "Oh," she said, and couldn't find other words.

Mahkah was watching her. "It's worth rising early just for this."

"Oh, yes," she breathed. "I've never...I've seen thousands of sunrises, but not like this."

"It is good that you like the steppes," Mahkah said gravely. He swung his horse around. Yvina followed.

"Why's that?"

"You said before that you have offered an alliance to Prince Kharil."

"Oh. Yes." She'd almost forgotten that, forgotten everything as she enjoyed the early morning with this strange man. "I suppose I never thought about it," she said. "I would have to come out and live here."

"Could you?" he asked.

"It's so lonely," she said. "For a day or three, I don't mind, but for longer?"

He laughed. "You forget. A khan will have a whole clan with him. It's hard to find privacy, not company."

"Tell me about that life," she said. "Tell me what it's like to be Methlan."

Mahkah twitched his reins and she matched his canter. After a while, they slowed to a walk again. "I am perhaps not the right Methlan to ask," he said. "I have spent many years as a wanderer, going from clan to clan or just finding my own path."

"Why?" she asked.

"When my father died, there were those who had certain expectations for me," he said. "Ones I was not sure I could embrace. We say that any man may become khan, if he proves himself. But it seems that khans' sons have less to prove. Sons often follow their fathers. I was young. Many doubted me. Still, I beat three rivals."

"And then?"

Mahkah shook his head. "The fourth was the man my sister desired for her husband."

"So?" Yvina said.

"If I defeated him, then for my sister to marry him would have brought us shame. So I left. I took my horse and my saddle and I went to wander. That was ten years ago."

"I see," she said, though she didn't. "Is this man a good khan?"

"No," Mahkah said. "I knew he would not be, but I chose my sister's happiness over my clan's wellbeing. I thought they would see through him and choose again. But he has clung to power through intimidation. And now he will make himself khan-of-khans."

"Sihkun," Yvina said, the light dawning. "So that's why you're returning now. To fight him as you should have done before."

"No," Mahkah said, shaking his head. "I cannot challenge him. He is my brother now, and for brother to fight brother is forbidden."

"Then what are you planning to do?" Yvina asked. Something nagged at her, an unformed sensation that didn't even rise to a suspicion, yet. Mahkah was more than he seemed.

"Wait and see," Mahkah said. His light tone annoyed her. More than annoyed; she was tired of being treated like a fool, by Mahkah or anyone else.

Yvina pressed her horse's flanks. The bay mare took a few quicker steps, bringing Yvina level with Mahkah's horse and only a foot away. She glared up at him. *Set him on fire with your eyes,* the bear suggested helpfully. "You are making me a pawn in your schemes," Yvina said. "I want to know what they are. No. I demand you tell me what you are going to do."

"Or?" Mahkah asked. "Surely you are used to men keeping their councils from you."

"Oh, I'm used to that," Yvina spat. "I am used to my brother and his generals shutting me out because I'm only a woman and what could I know, as they sit discussing the information my spy networks have brought them. I know very well the way men try to hide their plans from women. That's why all my informants are women. Sisters and daughters of lords too proud to watch them. Servant girls and whores who tell me what they say in their sleep. I have given my brother a dozen victories based on the secrets that men have thought they kept from women. I just wanted to think you had more sense than that. But perhaps men are the same, no matter what people they call their own." She looked away and bit her lip. Tears welled in her eyes. There was no reason for her to tear up about this. This man meant nothing to her. She shouldn't have let him get under her skin. "I will not be used," she insisted.

"Did you not offer yourself as part of a scheme?" Mahkah asked softly.

"That's different. I looked at all my options, everything I knew, and chose to make that offer."

"To offer yourself to a man you have not met, who your informant had not seen in years? To join a people you know nothing of?"

"That has nothing to do with this," Yvina insisted. Her horse's gait began to cramp her thigh. It only stoked her anger more. "You want my help, you can tell me your plan!"

Mahkah studied her, face unreadable. At last he nodded. Pulling back on his reins, he slowed his horse to a walk. Yvina matched his stride. "I am going to challenge your brother," he said. "I am going to fight Aradon in the presence of all our people, and when I am done no one will think of letting Sihkun lead."

Yvina's stomach twisted into knots. "You want me to help you kill my own brother?" She reached for the sword in the saddle-scabbard. Mahkah's hand darted out and seized hers.

"No," he said, eyes blazing. She nudged her horse away from his and he let her hand go, following closely. "Yvina. I am not going to kill your brother. I don't need to. All I need to do is impress my people. Then you and your brother may go free."

"You expect me to believe that?"

"I swear it on my own soul, on my sword, and on the dreams I dream," Mahkah said.

As Yvina struggled for an answer, a flash of motion on the horizon caught her eye. She turned to look. Mahkah put his hand to his brow. *Help me see, brother bear,* she said, and she focused like a hawk.

Ten Methlan warriors rode toward them. They were all armed. "You said Sihkun is your brother now and you cannot fight him," Yvina said. "I don't think they agree with you."

Mahkah fumbled with the pouch on his waist. "Are they wearing skin-wards?"

"Skin-wards? You mean the warpaint?" Yvina squinted. "Yes. All of them. Covered in it, like tattoos on a sailor."

Mahkah held a jar in his hand. He dipped his finger and began to draw dark lines on his own chest. "How many of them?"

"Ten I can see. Their saddles have the same markings as mine." She hadn't noticed before that Mahkah's horse wore a plain saddle, without the fancy colors and designs she'd seen on other Methlan.

"Sihkun's men for sure, then."

She pulled her bow free of its scabbard and felt for the arrows. The short bow was different than she was used to, but she knew how to nock an arrow. "We can sting them," she said.

"Good. They'll be trying to shoot us too, of course, but if we can unseat a few of them before they get here, we'll find it easier." Mahkah set aside the paint, found his own bow, and stared at the enemy. "I know three of their faces," he said. "Do not hesitate. They will show no mercy. If they overwhelm us, slice your throat before they can take you."

She nodded, unable to speak. *Are you ready?* she asked the bear.

Always, came the reply. *If today we die, we will die well.*

"Yvina," Mahkah said. She started. It was the first time he hadn't called her *lady*. "If today I die, I will die in good company."

She laughed. "That's what my bear said." She set an arrow to the string. The riders were three hundred yards away and closing fast. She drew the string back to her ear and let fly. The string twanged, stinging her fingers. She didn't waste time watching the arrow. Nocking another, she fired again. Beside her, Mahkah sent a stream of arrows so close together it sounded like a hive of bees.

Some of their arrows found marks. Three enemies toppled from their saddles, and a horse reared up, screaming in pain. An arrow whipped past Yvina's head, taking a strand of hair with it. She swallowed hard, fired off one last arrow, then dropped her bow into its scabbard and drew her sword.

The enemy was on them. A man galloped right at her, his sword high. Yvina ducked his swing, leaned forward, and put her sword in his ribs. He gaped at her even as his horse carried him past. She hung onto her hilt grimly and the blade ripped free, trailing blood. She turned in her saddle.

Mahkah held a sword in each hand. He guided his horse with his knees and Yvina wished she could watch him, because the flashes she saw were brilliant. He was music in muscle. He cut and swung, every blow perfect and purposeful. *Pay attention to the men you want to kill, not the one you want to ride,* her bear snarled, and she turned back.

They were down to four enemies. Three surrounded Mahkah, riding in circles around him, while the fourth hung back. He was pulling a bow out of his saddle-scabbard, Yvina realized. She kicked her horse and galloped forward, shouting. The man looked up in surprise just as she swung. His head flew off his shoulders and bounced three times before rolling to rest in a scraggly bush. She turned back.

Mahkah had dispatched two of the others while she was busy. The last man eyed him warily. "A duel?" the stranger said.

"Very well," Mahkah agreed. He dismounted. As he came clear of the horse, the enemy prodded his own horse and galloped forward. Mahkah's horse started and leaped away. Mahkah went down on his back. Yvina gasped. She was too far away to help. Mahkah would be trampled underfoot.

Watch! her bear shouted, and things seemed to slow. She saw the horse striding toward Mahkah. Saw him tense as he lay on his back. His abdomen tightened, and he sprang up just as the horse was on him. His fingers grabbed at the bridle, and he swung himself upward. One hand punched his enemy square in the jaw. The other yanked on the horse's reins.

The horse stumbled. Mahkah sprang free. His enemy and the horse fell. The horse got up and scrambled off. The man lay groaning in the dirt.

Yvina slid off her horse and approached. Mahkah stood over the fallen man. A trickle of blood ran down the man's lips. He writhed, but only the top half of his body moved. "My legs," he moaned. "I can't feel my legs."

Mahkah knelt. He touched the man, who stiffened and screamed. "You have broken your back," Mahkah said. "What did Sihkun tell you?"

"To kill." The man stared up at the sky, his eyes wide with pain. "He said. The woman and the wanderer, both."

"You will die in a day whether I aid you or not," Mahkah said. "It will be agonizing. I cannot spare the time to make you comfortable. I offer you the mercy of my blade."

"Mercy," the man said. "And death to Sihkun. He knew what he was doing, sending us after you."

"Sihkun is my worry now, not yours," Mahkah said. He drew his knife. Yvina watched, without hate or disgust, as he slid the blade up between two ribs. The man gasped, then his face slackened. Mahkah straightened up. His eyes met Yvina's. She gave him a tiny nod. Mahkah cleaned his knife and put it away.

"Come," he said, walking away from the dead man. "We've lost time. Sihkun will reach the bluffs tomorrow morning. We must be close behind."

The smoke from Sihkun's band smudged the horizon as they made camp and settled in. Yvina ate the same meal of dried meat and bread they'd shared for the past two days. It tasted better tonight than it had before. *Life is sweeter after a brush with death,* her bear said.

They sat and watched the fire die down without much talk. Mahkah took a flask from his bag, drank, and offered it to Yvina. She tried a sip. The liquid tasted like strawberries and honey but burned going down. "What is it?" she asked.

He shrugged. "I got it off a trader."

She took another sip and handed it back. "By tomorrow night, my brother will be free or we'll be dead."

"Yes." Mahkah drank. "When we free your brother, what will you do?"

She frowned. "The army will be here. I know they're not far behind. We saw the dust they kicked up, earlier today."

"This is not the time and place for a fight," Mahkah said. "All my people are assembled at Kharakor. There are enough of us to destroy you, but we would not soon shake off our own wounds."

Yvina said, "That's what I've feared from the first time our peoples crossed paths. I spent months laying the groundwork for an alliance, and now Sihkun's destroyed everything."

Mahkah rubbed his chin with his hand. She felt strangely fascinated seeing a grown man with no beard, no hair anywhere on his torso. The glimpses she'd caught of his legs, when his pants rode up, showed some hair there at least. She wondered what it would feel like to run her hands across his chest. "We should be more than just strangers content to ignore each other," he said.

Yvina laughed. "I've heard how our men speak about your people. They'll do anything for a chance to test our strength against yours. We cannot ignore each other. But we could be brothers."

Mahkah raised an eyebrow. "You understand warriors," he said.

"Sometimes I doubt it," Yvina said. She sighed. "Even if I persuaded Aradon to talk, who speaks for your people? You have no khan-of-khans."

"No," Mahkah agreed.

"It seemed so easy, back when I sent Ikkayana to find Kharil," she said.

"Why did you care so much about this alliance?" Mahkah asked gently.

"Maybe I didn't," Yvina said, not looking up at him. "Maybe I was just tired of my brother's generals discussing which of them would have me. As though I should be grateful for any of them to deign to claim me. I'm twenty-six, not dead."

"You've been a woman for a long time," Mahkah said.

"Yes." Yvina pulled her legs up to her chest. Mahkah was a wanderer. Maybe he understood what it meant to be lonely. "A woman who could not give herself to any man. Not until my brother secures his throne. Even now, if I choose wrong, my husband will use me to make himself king in my brother's place. That's why I thought perhaps Kharil...He's not Aradori, my people would never follow him. Instead of being a threat, he could bring my brother new allies. But I've never met him. For all I know, he's dead, or married, or he'll think I'm too old." She left a question in her voice, wondering what Mahkah would reply.

"Well," Mahkah said, a teasing note in his voice, "a Methlan khan may take as many wives as he wishes. Or as many as his wives permit. Though going beyond three is a bit gaudy."

"If you think I'd share my husband," she began, looking up. Her words and annoyance died as she met Mahkah's eyes.

He set a hand on her knee, and she shivered as the warmth seeped through the thin cloth. He offered her the flask and she drank deeply before handing it back. "Yvina," he said, and his voice was a caress. "Yvina."

"Yes," she whispered. His eyes held hers. In the fire, a stick popped. She felt warm all over, lightheaded.

"The steppes are my home. You've seen my world these last few days. Could you come out here, abandoning everything you know? Could you ride a horse day after day, birth your sons in a yurt, have only the things you can carry?"

Yvina stared into his face, searching, seeing only openness and intensity. An appealing combination, so different than any man she'd known.

A streak of light caught her eye. She looked up as a star fell flaming across the skies. She sighed. "The sky itself fell in flames, the day my father brought my mother out of the wreck of our old country," she said. "Mountains fell into the seas. The world shook and shattered. The ocean was blood and fire. But they came out of that, with me clinging to my mother's skirts, and they found a new land, among strange peoples. I asked my mother once if she was afraid, and she said no, because my father was there."

Mahkah's hand slid across to enfold her own. Her fingers rested on his wrist. She could feel his heartbeat pulsing against her fingertips. Her own heart raced like a runaway horse. "Then..." he prompted. He shifted closer to her.

"If it were with a man I loved," she said, tasting her words wonderingly. A man she loved. She'd never even dreamed of that. To marry for duty would be enough. "I could go anywhere. Do anything."

Mahkah's other hand stroked her face. She shuddered with pleasure at the light touch. "For ten years I wandered," he said. "I searched, I did not know for what. Then I found an answer, but not an answer I liked, so I said I would keep looking."

"What answer?" she asked.

"That is a story for tomorrow," he said. "But then I found a woman standing in a river, wearing her shift like the golden robes of a queen, leaving her foes dead around her. And I knew that my future stood in front of me."

"Ahh," Yvina sighed, and closed her eyes. Mahkah's fingers traced the line of her jaw, trailed down her neck, touched her shoulder. His touch made her shiver. She wished they could stay like this, hesitated to speak the words that would end this moment. "I'm a kingsdaughter of the Aradori," she said at last, gazing up into his serious face. "I cannot just go where I please. My marriage should be an offering for my people."

"You have given your people one king already," Mahkah said. "Is it not time for your own pleasure? Ride with me, Yvina, daughter of the storm. Be the wise counsel of my ears, fire of my life, mother of my sons. I will give you my sword for your defense, my cloak for your warmth, my devotion for all your years."

Yvina leaned against Mahkah's shoulder. His arm went around her waist, pulling her close. She wanted to stay there, forever. And perhaps...perhaps she could. "When my brother is free, I will be free," she said.

They sat like that for a long time, as the ashes of the fire ceased their glowing. When they lay down to sleep, they lay beside each other, fully clothed but sharing blankets and warmth, and when Yvina started awake at a wolf's howl, Mahkah's hand on her shoulder soothed her fears and let her find sleep once more.

The bluffs behind Kharakor stuck up out of the land like red and gray teeth chewing at the sky. At their foot clustered thousands of round yurts, surrounding banners bearing various devices. Mahkah told her what some of them meant as they rode.

"How many Methlan are there?" Yvina asked.

"All the clans have gathered," Mahkah said. "The messengers went out weeks ago."

They rode past herds of sheep and goats, waving to the boys out guarding the flocks. Most of the boys appeared annoyed to be there. "They know they are missing history today," Mahkah said. "Sihkun will have had his men stirring the people up. Today the future of my people will be decided."

Yvina glanced over her shoulder. The Aradori army crawled along behind, too far back. "They need to hurry," she said. "Sihkun will have my brother's head on a post by the time they get here." Even if Mahkah could stop Sihkun, she feared the army would fall on the Methlan camp. They'd spent days chasing after Aradon, they'd be howling for blood by now. She'd never get them to stand and listen.

"We will stop him, my heart," Mahkah said.

Yvina's own heart skipped a beat. "I hope you're right," she said. Her mind worked furiously. Mahkah was going to fight Aradon, to impress his people, he'd said. Her heart told her that if any man could go head-to-head with her brother, it was Mahkah.

Here was the answer to the scoffing bear warriors who asked what the Methlan could offer the Aradori. Let them see Mahkah, let them respect the Methlan skill at arms. Not just as a worthy challenge to be defeated, but as a foe that they could not easily best. Then, maybe, they'd be willing to talk.

Especially if Mahkah beat a little sense into Aradon. Just as long as he didn't kill him.

"You are quiet," Mahkah said.

"My heart is full," Yvina said.

The sun stood overhead by the time they rode near enough the Methlan encampment for riders to approach. "They won't attack us," Mahkah assured her. He pointed to the banners that studded the land near the outskirts of the camp, the same as the ones in the riders' hands. "The wise women rule here. Sihkun can try his tricks but he will not best our grandmothers."

The riders surrounded them. Mahkah raised a hand in greeting. "Has Sihkun spoken yet? Does his prisoner live?" he asked.

The men exchanged looks with each other. "The grandmothers said wait until sunset," one said at last. "The omens were strange. Greatmother Khassila said that today is a day of many changes. She could not read the winds at sunrise."

"She is right," Mahkah said.

"Then there's still time," Yvina said. She looked back over her shoulder, where the Aradori army crept over the horizon. They were a dark cloud against the land. They'd reach Kharakor well before sunset.

Somewhere ahead, a horn sounded, two long blasts. Yvina turned to Mahkah, whose face was grim. The horn sounded again, different this time.

"Sihkun calls the warriors," the rider said. "He told us last night to be ready, that the bear-clan would come for their prince and that we would fight."

Mahkah scowled. "Sihkun is not khan-of-khans yet."

Yvina set her hand on Mahkah's arm. "Can you stop him before he attacks?" she said.

Mahkah's eyes narrowed. "If your people are willing to parley."

Yvina seized a banner from the nearest rider, silencing the man's protests with a glare. "Bring my brother out," she said.

"I'll bring the Aradori. Your people aren't the only ones who need to see this fight. If we are to be more than a pair of wary dogs circling the same corpse, if we are to ride and fight together, then my people must see how strong, how honorable the Methlan are."

Mahkah smiled. "Make them see," he urged. "Tell them to let this fight decide whether our peoples are to be brothers or enemies, from now until the end of time."

Mahkah seemed so confident, so certain, but without Aradon's cocksure swagger. For the first time she realized Mahkah had sworn not to kill Aradon, but Aradon would be under no such constraints. Did Mahkah know what he was getting into?

Then it hit her. She grinned. "The second reason you fought me," she said. "You wanted to learn what a bear can do, so you can beat my brother."

Mahkah looked a bit abashed. It was a strange expression on his handsome face, and she found it uncomfortable. "Yes," he said.

"Well, my brother's ten times the warrior I am," she said. "And I was tired. And I didn't show you everything. So don't underestimate him."

"I will not," Mahkah said. "After all, if I lose to your brother, I can hardly expect you to ride with me."

She showed her teeth. "Then you'd better not lose," she said, and turned her horse's head around.

Yvina galloped across the land. Her horse's stride ate up the distance between her and the Aradori army. Miles fell away behind her. Her heart pounded with the horse's hooves. Would Mahkah be able to make his people listen? What if Sihkun killed Aradon anyway?

Three thousand mounted men, armed to the teeth, rolled like a wave over the land. Their heavy armor and dark hair looked out of place here, after the last days spent with Mahkah. The Aradori had left behind the baggage train. That meant they'd be eager for a fight, and quick to return home. Whatever happened would be resolved today.

Her bear sharpened her eyes and she scanned the banners. The scouts raced to intercept her, then fell away as they recognized her. Yvina rode up to the generals.

"Lady Yvina!" General Jorum exclaimed. "You escaped!" The whole army ground to a halt, pressing around the knot of high-ranked warriors.

She addressed the generals. "We have an ally. He will bring Aradon out from the Methlan camp. They will fight a duel in front of both our peoples. No one is to attack unless there is treachery. We ride in under a banner of truce." She shook the standard at them.

"Lady Yvina?" Jorum said, sounding uncertain. "What madness is this? After they betrayed you under the last banner?"

"A duel?" General Byorn said. He leaned in closer. "Who's this ally of yours, kingsdaughter? Is he any good?"

"I haven't seen Aradon in a serious duel in six months," a captain farther back from Yvina remarked. "I'd pay good money to see him fight a half-decent Methlan warrior."

The murmurs rippled out from Yvina. The Aradori clustered in closer, asking questions, arguing loudly with each other about Aradon's chances. She let them talk, enjoying the speculation. The only thing Aradori warriors liked more than fighting was watching a good duel. This would work.

"Are you seriously calling off the attack?" Jorum asked Byorn.

"By the hells, yes," Byorn said. "Look, if this Methlan fellow is any good at all, then when Aradon defeats him the rest of them will understand what it means to oppose the Aradori. They'll crumble without a fight."

"Is he?" Jorum asked Yvina. "Any good? Whoever this fellow is?"

Yvina wheeled her horse around. "Why ask me when you can see for yourself?" she said. "Keep your swords in their sheaths, and come see a fight you'll be telling your grandchildren about."

The assembled Aradori and Methlan stared at each other across fifty yards of empty grassland, broken by bits of rock and small, round bushes. A hawk screamed overhead. A horse whinnied. Yvina dismounted and crossed into the open space. Her brother stood bound in the midst of the Methlan. He seemed confused, with a patch of dried blood on his forehead, but otherwise unharmed.

Mahkah strode out toward her, a trio of ancient Methlan women with him. He'd redone his skin-wards, black lines sharp against his bronze skin, and his swords were in his hands. She tore her attention away from his chest to meet his eyes. His face gave away nothing. The Aradori generals hurried after her.

"Is this the fellow?" General Jorum said. "He doesn't look like much, does he?"

Mahkah held up a hand. "Will you speak my words for me, my lady?" he asked. "Word for word, whatever I say?"

"You swear you told me the truth last night?" she said.

He hesitated. "The truth," he agreed, "but not all of it."

Her earlier suspicions resurfaced. Or were they hopes? "I will translate," she agreed.

"What are you saying?" General Byorn demanded. "What is he saying?"

"I'll translate," she told them.

"Who's this fellow, anyway?" another general asked.

"Yvina," Aradon said. "They told me you were dead. I knew they lied. Do you have plans to get me out of here?"

"Mahkah does," she said, "but not necessarily in one piece. Don't worry, I think you'll enjoy this." She smiled coldly. "I know I will."

"Who's Mahkah?" Aradon asked. She ignored him.

"I'm ready," she told Mahkah. He turned to face the Methlan. She stood back to back with him, facing her people, conscious that Mahkah was only a foot away.

He raised his swords, and the crowd hushed. "People of the steppes! People of the storm!" Yvina translated as he spoke. "Some of you know me. Some of you know this man.

ELDAR ZAKIROV

But what we do here will echo through the ages, and so I will tell you what is happening today." He paused and waited for her to catch up. "Remember this, so that you can tell your grandchildren. We will decide the fate of two peoples today." The Aradori murmured as she relayed Mahkah's words, fingering their weapons and eyeing the Methlan.

Mahkah continued. "My father was khan-of-khans."

Yvina's head snapped around, but his back was to her. Her bear said, *I knew there was more to him than met the eye.*

"My father led us to drive back the farmers who invaded our western grazing lands," Mahkah said. Yvina stumbled, but translated. "He ended two tribal feuds and led us well. When he died, the women wept. I was but a boy. I knew I could not be khan-of-khans, but I thought perhaps I would lead my own clan. I met three challenges and fled from the fourth."

"Because you are a coward!" a man wearing golden rings on every finger and a dozen more in his ears shouted, pushing other men aside to reach the front of the crowd. She knew that face; Khan Sihkun, who had captured her and her brother. The men around him held him back, muttering.

"I fled rather than fight the man my sister wanted for her husband," Mahkah said. "I was wrong. I should have beaten his face in and told my sister to find a new man." The crowd laughed, Aradori and Methlan both, and Yvina grinned. Their peoples had so much in common, if they could only see it. "No matter; I wandered, alone, for years. A cloud hung over my head, the knowledge that I should have done more."

The Methlan leaned in as Mahkah dropped his voice. It was almost a whisper now, yet it traveled. "So I went to the holiest place. I climbed the mountain whose peak is white all year round. I found the sacred place of our fathers and spoke with the spirit of the wind."

The Methlan gasped as Mahkah continued. "The spirit of the wind spoke to me. She told me about the storm coming. Not a storm of air and rain, but of people. Men who were storm made flesh. She told me my destiny was to find a way for our people to weather the storm. We might be blown away, or worn down. Or we could join with the storm and ride on the winds to greatness.

"Some of you know the name my mother gave me. I was Kharil, heart of the people. The wind-spirit renamed me. She named me Mahkah, heart of the storm. She told me to seek my fate."

Yvina translated, her heart in her mouth. Why hadn't Mahkah told her the truth last night? *You already knew,* her bear whispered. *You knew from the moment he told you he'd come seeking you. Who else would have even known your name?*

Mahkah spoke on. "And so I wandered once more, until I came to a river. On the banks of that river I found my fate. I found a woman of the Aradori standing over a pile of her fallen foes. She looked at me, and I knew that with this woman at my side I could face down any storm. And so I came to the wise women of our people with one request. I must match steel with her brother— with this man!" Mahkah jabbed his longer sword toward Aradon, who grinned like a fool.

A few of the Aradori shouted approval, jostling each other. Mahkah said, and Yvina wished she could see his face, "Stand witness, people of the steppes! We will see what the Aradori are made of. Are they to be our brothers? Or shall we go to war, as Khan Sihkun has said? Let our steel give you the answer. Let us decide the future of two peoples here and now, with the sun and sky for witness. What say you?"

The Methlan gave a huge cheer, and to Yvina's delight, so did the Aradori.

"Stop this nonsense," Khan Sihkun shouted. "This is my prisoner, not his!" But nobody paid him any mind.

"Where's my sword?" Aradon demanded. "Someone give me a sword. Yvina, what's all that nonsense you said about this man taking you as his wife? Do I need to kill him?"

Yvina glared at him. "If I decide he's the man I want, that's

my choice," she said. "If you disagree, feel free to try and win."
Even though Mahkah had sworn he wouldn't kill Aradon, this
was serious combat. One of them could be maimed in a careless
instant. She wanted to tell Aradon not to hurt Mahkah, but
Mahkah waited only a few yards away, watching. She would
not show him that disrespect.

"Fine," Aradon said. "Get me a sword, someone!"

Someone cut Aradon's bonds and gave him a sword. The
crowd closed around him and Mahkah. Yvina joined the Aradori.

Mahkah had a sword in each hand. He and Aradon circled
each other. Yvina felt the surge of power in him as Aradon's
bear woke. Mahkah held himself easily. Skin-wards covered
most of his chest. *Can he match Aradon's bear?* Yvina asked her
own companion.

He beat us, her bear replied. It wasn't much of an answer.

The generals clustered around Yvina as Mahkah crouched.
Aradon stood tall, grinning wildly. He raised his sword and
charged. Yvina's heart pounded.

Mahkah rose to greet him, catching Aradon's sword with
his longer blade and coming in under his guard with the
short sword. Aradon slammed his left fist down and knocked
Mahkah's blade aside. He shoved Mahkah back, pulled his
sword free, and smashed down at Mahkah.

Mahkah caught Aradon's sword with both blades this time.
They struggled with each other, then Mahkah sprang back.

"The Methlan fellow's quick, but Aradon's got four inches
and thirty pounds of muscle on him," General Byorn said. "And
a bear, of course."

"What happens when Aradon guts him?" another of the
Aradori asked.

"My men are ready to attack," General Jorum said. "We're
just waiting for the right moment. Probably right after Aradon
puts his sword through the other fellow."

"Just shut up," Yvina said through gritted teeth, "and watch
the fight." She clenched her fists together until the nails bit into
her palms. Mahkah would win, he had to win. He matched for

Aradon in every way. But it would only take a single mistake to see him in the dirt with his life bleeding out.

Mahkah attacked this time, coming in like a lightning bolt. His longer blade caught Aradon's shirt and ripped through, but missed Aradon's body. Aradon still grinned. "You're not bad," he said in badly accented Methlan. Her bear brought every word to Yvina's ears. She hadn't realized his speech was that good. Maybe he'd listened to her after all. "If you hadn't insulted my sister, I might let you live."

Mahkah laughed. "What insult, oh Stormborn? I have made my offer, and she may decide as she likes."

"Even if you are a prince, I can't have my sister marrying just anyone," Aradon said. He shut up as Mahkah's flashing blades forced him back. Yvina felt torn between annoyance and pleasure.

Again and again they clashed and fell apart. The sun slid down toward the horizon. Most of the assembled crowd sat down on the grass. Yvina accepted some trail rations from one of the generals. "How long can this go on?" General Jorum asked. "Aradon should have had him an hour ago."

"Shut up," General Byorn said. "This is the best fight I've seen in years, and you want it to be over?"

The two combatants were her whole world. Mahkah fought beautifully. Every move was graceful and fluid, like a dance. Aradon's responses spoke of power and endurance. Two very different styles. Both masters of their bodies and swords.

This is the alliance we need, she told her bear. *Our raw strength, with their quickness. Methlan cavalry force an opening with a lightning charge while our army stands ready to smash through that opening. We'd be unstoppable together. We must have this alliance.*

Her bear felt amused. *He's won you, at least,* it said. *No matter the result?*

I don't need this swordfight to show me Mahkah's heart, she said.

So tell him that, when he's done, the bear said. *If Aradon doesn't kill him.*

He won't, Yvina said, clasping her fingers together. *He won't.*

143

The sun slipped low on the horizon, sliding behind the bluffs. The shadows dimmed everything. On the other side, an ancient Methlan woman stood up. She raised her arms and called something. Yvina couldn't catch the words but Mahkah did. He fell back and opened his arms wide. "A pause," he said.

Aradon stepped back. He came over to the Aradori lines as the Methlan brought out torches, lit them, and placed them around the field. Aradon wiped sweat from his face and accepted water. "What a fight," he said. "And what an audience. This will be one for a song!"

"Our songs and theirs both," Yvina agreed.

Aradon turned to the generals. "Good work following so fast. This fight is impressing the Methlan. After I finish this fellow, I'm going to call out Sihkun and kill him. Once he's dead, they'll listen to reason. I think you were right, sister. We can use these people."

Yvina clenched her fists. "You don't understand them at all," she said. "You never have. They won't follow you, Aradon. But they might follow him." She gazed across the field to where Mahkah stood. A trio of beautiful Methlan girls had brought him water. They giggled and smiled up into his face. "Excuse me," Yvina said, and ignoring her brother's calls, she marched across the field to Mahkah.

The girls fell away as she approached. She glared at them until they hurried back to the Methlan crowd.

Mahkah smiled at her. Her anger loosened a bit. Who was she angry with, anyway? Aradon for being stupid, or Mahkah for lying? "Why didn't you tell me?" she asked.

His smile vanished. "You sent an offer to Kharil, sight unseen. You are a woman of your word and would have honored that offer," he said. "I wanted to be sure that you were willing to come with me. That you understood what that meant. Besides, I told you. I am not Kharil anymore. That boy was foolish and put his own happiness ahead of his people's."

"And now?"

"Now," he said, "I think I can have both."

"You're not just fighting him for me," she said. "Or to stop a battle, or even to make Sihkun look stupid."

He bowed. "When I am done, they will follow me to the ends of the earth. Yvina, I am not asking you to be wife of a wanderer. I am asking you to stand beside the khan-of-khans of the Methlan and help me shape our future. The world is changing. Your people bring the storm. My people must change, or fall before it. You can help me. You know the Aradori. I know the Methlan. The sons we share will have the best of both peoples."

"The third reason," she whispered. "The third reason you asked me to fight you at the riverbank."

"Just as I am showing my soul to our peoples tonight, I wanted to see your soul and to show you mine," Mahkah said. "I did not have time for a long courtship. Not with my people's future at stake. They say we see truth in swords." And then he smiled and raised one eyebrow and all Yvina's tension dissolved like snow in spring. "Besides, a khan-of-khans has enemies and I wanted to be sure I could count on my wife's sword in a pinch."

She laughed. "I think they're ready for you to finish this," she said. The last of the torches had been placed and the crowd seemed impatient.

"I'm ready," Mahkah said. "And you?"

Yvina set one hand on Mahkah's arm. She reached up with her other hand and pulled Mahkah to her. Their lips met. She kissed him with all the passion that had been building in her like a summer storm. Mahkah's lips were warm against hers. His hand slipped around her waist and he pulled her tight.

Now that is going to make an impression on the crowd, her bear whispered, but she ignored it.

After a moment she pulled away. "Oh, no, did I smudge your skin-wards?" She looked down. One or two of the lines seemed mussed.

Mahkah laughed. "I know how to fix them," he said. "Now go watch. This will be over soon."

She marched back to the Aradori side, head high. Aradon stared at her. "What the hells are you doing?" he asked.

Yvina smiled. "Forging alliances," she said. "Go seal the bargain for me, brother."

"What does that mean?" he asked, looking puzzled.

"Just finish the fight," Yvina said, rejoining the generals. Aradon shook his head, then ran out to join Mahkah.

"Kingsdaughter?" General Byorn said. "Does this mean... I don't know what it means."

"You will soon," Yvina said.

Aradon and Mahkah raised their swords, just as one last ray of sunlight broke past the bluffs. It lit their blades, bright white in the gloom. Yvina raised a hand to her lips. "Oh," she said, the words of her mother's prophecy coming to her again. "Swords like lightning. Hooves like thunder." Then it had been a promise for her, too.

Mahkah darted forward, quicker than thought. Aradon barely got his sword up. Mahkah danced around him, Aradon turning to face him. Their swords clashed over and over. Yvina's bones shivered along with their steel. This was the turning point, when the future of two peoples would be resolved.

If Aradon won, Mahkah would be disgraced. Aradon would get his treaty with the Methlan, but they'd be uneasy, lesser partners. The alliance would last only until the first test, and then dissolve. But if Mahkah won, would the Aradori talk or attack?

"Something's changed," General Byorn said. "Look how they're moving. That Methlan fellow is desperate."

"His name is Mahkah," Yvina said. "He's not desperate; he's determined. This ends soon."

Aradon's smile disappeared. He beat back Mahkah's attacks through sheer willpower. She could feel his bear from here, keeping his arms and legs moving with the speed to match Mahkah. Mahkah's magic felt different. She wanted to know more about the skin-wards. Would learn more, if Mahkah won. They weren't alive the way the bear was, clearly, but they gave him what he needed. Twice Aradon's sword had grazed Mahkah's arm without drawing blood.

The fighters crashed together, and a sword flew glinting past the torches and into the Methlan crowd. Yvina held her breath. Whose sword?

Aradon stepped back, hands empty, face still determined.

Mahkah buried his sword-points in the grass and sprang at Aradon.

Aradon's face twisted in surprise for an instant before he went down under Mahkah's onslaught.

Yvina's heart was in her throat. She couldn't breathe. The two grappled, rolling over. Now Aradon knelt over Mahkah. He punched down hard, and the sound of fists on flesh made Yvina wince.

Mahkah wriggled out and suddenly he was on top, wrestling with Aradon. Aradon tried to throw Mahkah, but this time Mahkah kept his place. He got his arm around Aradon's neck and locked it in behind his other elbow, putting Aradon in a chokehold. Aradon flailed. Then his hands dropped to the ground. His fingers twitched.

Mahkah rose. His chest heaved. Yvina wanted to run to him, but Aradon lay on the ground nearby. Was he dead, despite Mahkah's promises?

Then Aradon groaned and sat up. His nose and chin ran red with blood. His eye was already swelling shut. But he grinned. Mahkah stooped and offered a hand.

Aradon stared at it, then took it and stood.

The roar that went up from both armies echoed to the skies.

Yvina found herself halfway across the field before she realized she'd moved. Her bear leaped inside her. She caught herself just before she reached the two men, and stared from one to the other. Mahkah wore a bruise on his face and a split lip, but looked considerably better than Aradon.

The crowd swelled up around them, Aradori and Methlan mixing together and shouting. The generals stood close by, as did Khan Sihkun and the very old woman Yvina had seen before. Mahkah held up his hands and called for silence. The noise died slowly. He looked at Yvina. "Be my voice to your people?"

"Always," she promised, and he smiled.

"Tell us what just happened," General Jorum demanded.

"I got thrashed," Aradon said. A grin split his face from side to side. "And I think I found us some new allies."

"Mahkah wants to speak," Yvina said.

"My people," Mahkah said, "you have seen a fight tonight. Was it to your liking?" The crowd's roar was answer enough. "It was to mine," he shouted. "Today I have won a wife, I have found a brother, and I have come home!"

Aradon told Yvina, "You speak their language better than I do. Tell them that my word is binding. The Aradori and the Methlan will be brothers. Khan-of-Khans Mahkah is my brother now." He grinned. "That bit's right, isn't it, Yvina?"

"Fortunately for you," Yvina said.

The Methlan crowd cheered again. "Absolutely not!" Khan Sihkun shouted. "The Methlan will never follow a herdless wanderer, a coward who ran when offered a proper—"

Aradon strode over to Sihkun. His fist moved faster than Yvina could follow, and Sihkun lay motionless on the grass. "No one speaks to my brother that way," he said in badly-accented Methlan. The crowd cheered, Methlan and Aradori both. Apparently some things didn't need translation.

Yvina went to Mahkah, who was still surrounded by well-wishers. They melted away, leaving Mahkah and Yvina with a little space.

Mahkah took her hands. "Are you pleased?" he asked.

She smiled up at him. "When can we be married? Tonight? Tomorrow?"

He frowned. "I fought your brother in front of both our peoples," he said. "What more does it take?"

"Then we're..." The shock hit Yvina. "I suppose," she said, searching for the right words.

You should shut up, her bear said as Mahkah bent and kissed her. She responded eagerly. That was a better answer, anyway.

Where Steampunk Started

BY TIM POWERS

Tim Powers is the author of fourteen novels, including The Anubis Gates, Declare, Hide Me Among the Graves, *and* On Stranger Tides, *which was adapted for the fourth* Pirates of the Caribbean *movie of the same title. His books have twice won the Philip K. Dick Memorial Award, three times won the World Fantasy Award, and three times won the Locus Poll Award.*

Powers has taught fiction writing classes at the University of Redlands, Chapman University, and the Orange County School of the Arts, and has been an instructor at the Writers of the Future program and the Clarion Science Fiction Workshop at Michigan State University.

Powers lives with his wife, Serena, in San Bernardino, California.

Where Steampunk Started

Back in 1976, a British publisher thought it might be a good idea to do a series of ten books about King Arthur being reincarnated throughout history: one novel about Arthur sinking the Spanish Armada in 1588, for instance, another with Arthur chopping open Nazi tanks with Excalibur—that kind of thing.

I'm getting to steampunk, I promise.

K. W. Jeter, Ray Nelson and I agreed to write the books, and we divvied up historical periods among ourselves, and set to work; and we had each written several novels when the British editor decided he didn't like the idea after all, and certainly didn't want any books that we might already have written in the series. (Just as well—in retrospect it seems likely that the publisher would have issued all ten novels under one house pseudonym.) I don't remember what segments of history Nelson had laid claim to, but I had drawn the early 19th century, and—portentously— Jeter had got the Victorian era, and had written *Morlock Night*.

But our peculiar King Arthur books were now without a publisher—orphaned!

Jeter and James Blaylock and I were in the habit in those days of going to a local bar in Orange, California called O'Hara's, to plot stories and complain about rejection slips over many pitchers of beer, and Jeter told us about a terrific couple of research books he'd used for his now-homeless *Morlock Night*—*Mayhew's London* and *London's Underworld,* both by the eccentric 19th century social researcher Henry Mayhew. These two big books—even though they were inexpensive modern selections from Mayhew's original vast three volume edition of 1851—were an absolute gold mine for details about day-to-day life among the brewers and costermongers and thieves and prostitutes of Victorian London.

All three of us had of course read the works of the Bronte sisters and Stevenson and Doyle and Dickens, and Jeter had even read a lot of more obscure Victorians like George Gissing and William Harrison Ainsworth—but the Mayhew books galvanized us to write books of our own set in that era; and since we all thought in terms of science fiction and fantasy, that's the sort of plots we came up with. Blaylock wrote *Homunculus,* about the misadventures attendant upon an extraterrestrial's visit to London, Jeter's *Morlock Night* had H. G. Wells' morlocks traveling back in time to Victorian London, and I wrote *The Anubis Gates,* which had to do with Egyptian sorcerers bent on killing King George III.

These didn't all get published with their first submissions; I believe *Morlock Night* was rejected at least once before it was picked up by DAW Books, and my *Anubis Gates* was turned down by at least half a dozen publishers before it landed at Ace Books. But they did all appear within just a few years of each other, which gave them the appearance of being part of a trend.

And then we went on to write other sorts of things. Blaylock wrote contemporary fantasies set in California, Jeter wrote horror and science fiction novels, and I wrote books set in other places and historical periods; but in 1987 Jeter returned to the Victorian London setting with his novel *Infernal Devices,* involving a number of outlandish plot elements including a clockwork man—and he wrote a letter to *Locus* magazine in which he said, "Personally, I think Victorian fantasies are going to be the next big thing, as long as we can come up with a fitting collective for Powers, Blaylock and myself. Something based on the appropriate technology of that era; like 'steampunks,' perhaps...."

Of course our books were by no means the first to set science-fictional adventures in Victorian England—Michael Moorcock's

Warlord of the Air (1971), and Harry Harrison's *A Transatlantic Tunnel, Hurrah!* (1973), for example, very clearly belong in the category Jeter was describing. But by coining a term for it, Jeter had, at one stroke, made it a defined sub-genre.

Our steampunk novels were not alternate histories—they took place in the actual history of this world, albeit with a lot of spectacular events that never found their way into the history books. But that was to change.

Soon William Gibson and Bruce Sterling collaborated on *The Difference Engine,* in which Charles Babbage succeeded in inventing a mechanical computer, with the result that information technology revolutionized 19th century England. Cherie Priest has followed with her *Boneshaker,* which serves up an alternate America in which Seattle has been destroyed by a mining machine and zombies prowl the ruins. And Jeter himself, in his recent novel *Fiendish Schemes,* posits an alternate 19th century England in which dealing with sentient oceans requires the use of walking lighthouses. More things in Heaven and Earth!

There's Wild West steampunk now. Imaginary world steampunk. The peculiar retrospective glamour of the idea has expanded a lot since the days when Jeter and Blaylock and I drank beer in O'Hara's and scribbled story ideas on napkins. In fact it has moved right out of printed fiction altogether, into the realms of costume, architecture, and even music. Paul Di Filippo (author of *The Steampunk Trilogy*) has written, "the medium where it all began—literature, stories, books—is now the least important aspect of the juggernaut."

But that original setting is still potent. Stories of mysterious doings in Victorian London have been entertaining readers ever since there *was* a Victorian London—streetlamps and carriages at midnight, boats pursuing secret errands on the moonlit Thames, and why not a stray steam-powered airship ducking in and out of the clouds?—and they're not likely to lose their allure. From a writer's point of view, sources like Mayhew's books have by no means been exhausted or superseded.

Back at that booth at O'Hara's on so many long afternoons in 1976, Blaylock had the advantage of actually having been to London; Jeter and I had nothing but the facts and impressions and occasional misunderstandings we'd picked up from books. But steampunk owes as much to freewheeling invention as it does to real geography and historical fact, and we had stumbled on a *milieu,* a *motif*—an evocative sort of world, to stick to English— that has evolved and gone on to capture a wider audience than was dreamed of in our philosophies.

Hellfire on the High Frontier

written by

David Farland

illustrated by

ROB HASSAN

Steampunk stories often explore such issues as "What would the world be like if this technology had been invented earlier?" or "What if history had changed in this way?"

While many of these tales are set in the Victorian Era in the mid-1800s, I've seen some fine ones that go back into the early Renaissance. For example, in one story last year, a young William Shakespeare lived in a steampunk universe where he ran afoul of an Egyptian goddess. So we have the whole breadth of history and the span of the world as our canvas.

"Hellfire on the High Frontier" began as a kitchen-sink story. I have an ancestor named Hellfire Morgan, and I always wanted to use him in a story. But I had other things that have intrigued me— feral angels, cities in the clouds, and so on. So for fun, I wrapped them all into this story. Enjoy!

ABOUT THE ILLUSTRATOR

Rob Hassan is a freelance artist based in the Chicago area. He is a former quarterly winner of the Illustrators of the Future award. His artwork was published in L. Ron Hubbard Presents Writers of the Future Volume 14.

His studio offers an eclectic mix of art styles. In tribute to his myriad graphic skills, he likes to use the handle "GraphixRob."

For all practical purposes, Rob is a self-taught artist. He has attended several traditional drawing and painting courses over the years, with the pinnacle being at the School of Visual Arts (NYC). Rob has found that "independent study" is by far the most beneficial for him. He feels keeping on top of the latest art, artists and techniques via the internet is the best way to stay creative and fresh. Most recently he has focused on his computer graphics art education and has incorporated several 2D and 3D software programs into his traditional workflow.

Rob's artistic experience includes but, is not limited to, character design, storyboards, virtual product prototype design, concept artwork, portrait art and comic book cover art.

Rob draws inspiration from many sources, including a wide variety of traditional and CG artists, modern fantasy painters, science fiction books and movies, classic (Universal) monsters, contemporary art, comic art and graphic novels.

Many of Rob's original science fiction, comic art and fantasy creations are held in personal collections both domestically and internationally.

His artwork has also been presented in an exclusive line of etched glass art and reproduced in a limited run poster collection. Rob's artwork has been used in website design, featured on book covers, in comics and magazines, and has been seen on music and movie DVD covers.

His artwork has been displayed in several Chicago area art galleries and has received art awards and honors in Chicago, IL; Hollywood, CA; London, England; Brisbane, Australia; and Trieste, Italy.

Hellfire on the High Frontier

Wyoming Territory, Circa 1876

Morgan Gray sat alone, peering into his crackling campfire, eyes unfocused, thinking of girls he'd known. In particular, there was a dancehall girl he'd once met in Cheyenne. What was her name—Lacy? She'd had red hair and the prettiest smile—so fine he almost hadn't noticed that she'd worn nothing more than a camisole, bloomers, and a green silk corset while she lay atop the piano and sang.

Out here on the range, there was little more to do than cook his beans over the campfire and remember. For weeks now, he'd been trailing a skinwalker, a renegade Arapaho named Coyote Shadow, but the skinwalker had taken to bear form and lost Morgan in the high rocks of the Wind River Range.

A schoolmarm murdered, her child eaten. Morgan hadn't been able to avenge them.

Sometimes you lose a trail, he knew. *Sometimes you lose the fight. You have to figure out how to keep fighting.*

He downed some coffee, as bitter and cold as the trail.

Out in the rocky hills, a wolf howled. It sounded wrong, a little too high. Could've been a Sioux warrior, hoping to count coup. Morgan would have to watch his horse tonight, sleep with one eye open.

The burning ponderosa pine in his campfire smelled sweet, like butterscotch boiling over in a pan. Some pitch in the heartwood popped. A log shifted, and embers spiraled up from the fire. They rose in balls of red, and seemed to expand, dancing around one another as they sped toward heaven.

Morgan watched them drift higher, wondering when they'd wink out, until time stretched unnaturally, as if the embers planned to rise and take their place among the stars.

Suddenly, The Stranger took form across the campfire, a shadow solidifying into something almost human, sitting on a rock.

Morgan had met him only once, seven years back: a man in a black frock, like a traveling preacher. He wore his Stetson low over his eyes and had a wisp of dark beard. The spurs on his boots were made of silver, with glowing pinwheels of lightning. The cigar clenched between his teeth smelled of sulfur.

Could've been an angel. Could've been the Devil. Morgan's gut told him that The Stranger was something different altogether.

"Long way from Texas," The Stranger said in a deep voice, lips hardly moving.

Morgan had no authority outside of Texas. So he kept his ranger's badge in his vest pocket. "Justice shouldn't be bound by borders," he said. "The whole world's gone crazy."

The Stranger smiled. "Got a job for you."

Morgan should never have asked this stranger for help seven years back. Might have been better to just let his horse, Handy, drown in the quicksand. With folks like The Stranger, there is always a price.

But, hell, Morgan had loved that gelding.

"A job?" Morgan asked. "I catch 'em. Don't necessarily kill 'em." He'd seen too much bloodshed in the war. After more than ten years, the scars were just beginning to heal.

Morgan wasn't afraid of a fight. Once you've stared death in the face a few times, nothing riles you. Yet...

"He's good with a gun," The Stranger said. "Few men would stand a chance against him. He's a clockwork gambler, goes by the name of Hellfire. Shooting one of them...it's not the same as killing flesh and blood humans...."

It should be more like stomping a pocket watch, Morgan realized. Clockworks were all springs and gears inside. But Morgan had known a clockwork once, a soldier by the name of Rowdy.

Morgan swore that the thing was as alive as any man of flesh and blood. Rowdy had once joked, "Us clockworks, we got souls same as the rest of y'all. Ours are just wind-ups."

"What did this gambler do?" Morgan asked.

"Fought alongside Jackson at Chancellorsville," The Stranger said, as if to ease Morgan's mind. "Is that enough?"

Morgan had always hated slavers. "The war's over."

"But this old soldier still kills," The Stranger said. "Not sure why. Some say he took a knock from a cannonball in the war. When the gears turn in his mind, he cannot help himself. The last victim was a boy, sixteen years old. Hellfire called him out. Before that, he shot a Chinaman, and before that, a snake-oil salesman. Each killing is four months apart—to the minute."

The Stranger spat into the fire. His spittle burst into flame, like kerosene, and emitted a rich scent that reminded Morgan of blackberries, growing thick on the vine beside a creek.

Morgan suspected that The Stranger was right. This gambler needed to be stopped. But killing a clockwork wouldn't be easy. Their inner parts were shielded by nickel and tin, and you never knew where their vital gears hid. Thirteen Comancheros had had a bout with one down on the border a couple years back. Rumor said it had taken twenty-three bullets to bring him down. Eleven Comancheros died.

Clockworks were quick on the draw, deadly in their aim. The Stranger called this one a "gambler," but clockworks had been created to be soldiers and guards and gunslingers.

"What brand is he?" Morgan asked.

"Sharps."

Morgan ground his teeth. He'd hoped that it might be some cheap Russian model, built during the Crimean War. The Sharps clockworks had a reputation. Going up against one was almost suicide.

Yet Morgan had taken a handout from a *stranger,* and he'd known that there would be a day of reckoning. "Where do I find him?"

"Heading toward Fort Laramie..." The Stranger said. "The gambler is like a bomb, with a fuse lit. In four days, six hours, and seven minutes, he will kill again."

The Stranger turned into an oily shadow and wafted away.

Morgan hardly slept that night. Gold had been discovered in the Black Hills, and prospectors were crawling all over the wilderness north of Fort Laramie, the biggest supply depot in the West. Tens of thousands were riding in on the new rail lines.

The Indians didn't like it. After getting pushed around for years, Sioux holy men like Crazy Horse and Sitting Bull were on the warpath, trying to drive off the miners, much as they'd tried to hold off the homesteaders and buffalo hunters.

Only this time, the way Morgan figured it, there was going to be a bloodbath. You can only steal so much from a man before he has to push back. Morgan didn't fancy blundering into such a mess. Some Sioux had big magic.

At dawn he rode east toward Frenchman's Ferry, climbing over the hills. A day later, he found a single skinwalker's track between two boulders, in a land covered by worn sandstone rocks and sparse grasses. The creature had been leaping from boulder to boulder, hiding its trail. But it had come to a place where the rocks were too far apart.

Like many skinwalkers, Coyote Shadow had turned himself into a beast once too often, and now he'd lost himself. His print was something halfway between a human foot and a bear's paw. Coyote Shadow had become only half a man.

Much like me, Morgan thought. He'd carried a torch for Sherman, had forced womenfolk from their houses and set entire cities aflame. Sometimes folks had refused to leave their homes, and he'd heard the women screaming in the fires.

He forced down the memories.

Morgan slid from his saddle and studied the print. The dusty ground here had given easily, yielding a deep track with crisp ridges. The track looked fresh—hours old.

Morgan searched the bleak landscape: sandstone thrusting up from broken ground, dry grass and sage, and little else.

During the heat of the day, any sane Indian would have stopped in the shade, though there wasn't much of it here to take solace in.

Morgan's mare nickered and shied back a step, as if she'd caught a dangerous scent.

Morgan sniffed. Between the iron odor of rocks and dry grass, he smelled an undertone—like garlic rubbed in fur.

A skinwalker.

He'd been hunting the creature for months, and now he resented finding it. He was on his way to kill the clockwork gambler.

But justice demanded that he finish this monster.

He searched uphill. A pile of sandstone boulders stood at its crown, with a single rock jutting up from it in a small pinnacle. Yucca plants and a few junipers grew tall in the pinnacle's shadow.

The skinwalker is up there, Morgan realized. *He could be watching me.*

Morgan studied the shadows. Nothing stirred. Perhaps the skinwalker was sleeping.

Morgan tied his pony to a mesquite bush, pulled his Winchester from the saddle holster, and began picking his way uphill, weaving behind rocks and bushes in case the skinwalker tried to take a long shot.

Fifteen minutes later, Morgan reached the rocks, and in the shade of a juniper found some crushed grass where the skinwalker had bedded. He'd left only moments ago.

Biting his lip, Morgan leaped to the far side of the rock and scanned the landscape. He saw the skinwalker, rushing uphill toward the next ridge, a lumbering mound of shaggy fur. His long arms swung with every stride, and he ran low to the ground, like an ape, but Coyote Shadow still wore the scrap of a loin cloth. He moved fast, faster than a horse could run.

The creature was more than two hundred yards out, and as he neared the ridge, he turned and glanced back.

Morgan had time for one shot before the sorcerer escaped. He

163

crouched behind a rock and steadied his aim. The skinwalker saw him, whirled, and doubled his speed.

Morgan's hands shook. Mouth went dry. Heart pounded. He gasped.

Buck fever.

He didn't want it to end this way—shooting the skinwalker in the back. Morgan had imagined catching Coyote Shadow, taking him to some town where a judge would see that he was hanged proper.

Morgan forced himself to stop breathing, lined the skinwalker up in his sites, and squeezed gently.

The rifle cracked and jumped in his hands. The skinwalker didn't jerk or stumble. Instead, his stride seemed clean, uninterrupted, as he disappeared over the hill.

Still, that didn't mean that Morgan hadn't wounded the beast. Morgan once had seen a rebel lieutenant die in combat—he charged into battle, swinging a sword in one hand and shooting a revolver from the other while bullet holes blossomed on his chest like roses. "Charging Dead," Morgan called it.

So he took note of the place where the skinwalker had stood as Morgan fired, near a large rock with a yucca plant, then hurried to the spot.

He found the monster's tracks and studied the ground for blood, a clump of hair, hoping for any sign that the skinwalker was wounded.

Morgan tracked the monster over one ridge, then another.

As the sun began to wallow on the horizon in a leaden sky, and bats wove through the air, he admitted defeat. Not a drop of blood could be found. He'd missed.

That night, the moon hid beneath bands of clouds, and a south wind from the Gulf of Mexico smelled of rain. Morgan camped without a fire, not wanting to risk setting the prairie alight.

He couldn't sleep. He'd ruined Coyote Shadow's rest, and he worried that the skinwalker might come creeping into his camp, hoping for vengeance. So for long hours, Morgan lay quietly listening for the crunch of a foot in the prairie soil with his pistol in hand, just beneath his blanket.

As the hours stretched, he dozed sporadically, but would wake again with a start. A screech owl hunted nearby, flying low, shrieking every few minutes as it tried to startle mice from their hiding places.

Long after midnight, Morgan decided to relax and put his hat over his eyes. Suddenly it was knocked away, and he rose up and fired blindly, just as the owl winged off.

His hat lay on the ground next to him. The bird had swooped low and struck it. Apparently the bit of rabbit fur on the brim looked too much like a varmint to the owl.

Morgan turned over, indignant, and after many minutes he slid into an uneasy slumber.

He dreamed that he was in a shop, where a tinkerman with a big, white handlebar moustache and penetrating blue eyes worked at piecing together clockwork soldiers.

One soldier lay like a patient on a surgeon's table. The tinkerman had its chest cavity open and was grasping something inside: it was a huge golden coil spring, nearly lost amid gears and pistons. Part pocket watch, part steam engine, the insides of the clockwork soldier were somehow more greasy and filthy than Morgan had imagined they could be.

The tinkerman nodded toward a crate and said in a deep Georgia drawl, "Son, would you be so kind as to fish a heart outta that box?"

The shop had bits and pieces of clockwork everywhere—a shelf of expressionless faces, waiting to come to life; arms and legs hanging from the rafters like dry sausages in a Mexican cantina; tubes and gizmos lying in heaps on counters and on the floor.

Morgan looked into the box. He found dozens of hearts in it, barely beating, covered in grease and oil, black and ugly.

Morgan picked up the largest, strongest-looking one. It throbbed in his grip, almost slipping away. He handed it to the tinkerman.

"Much obliged," the tinkerman said.

He thrust the heart into the contraption, piercing it through with the gold coil, and the clockwork soldier jolted to life—hands flexing, a strangled cry rising from its throat. Its mouth opened, and it whined stupidly, like an animal in pain.

The tinkerman smiled in satisfaction. "Perfect."

Somehow, that pronouncement scared Morgan. Would the clockwork gambler that he was hunting be "perfect?" It sounded presumptuous.

Morgan wondered at that. He said, "When God made man, he only allowed that his creation was 'good.'"

The tinkerman glanced up, lips tight in anger, eyes twinkling. "God, sir, was not a perfectionist. He failed as an organism. We superseded him."

"Superseded?"

The tinkerman smiled cruelly. "He drove Adam from the Garden of Idunn. In some tales, afterward, Adam made a spear and sneaked up on God while he was sleeping. . . ."

Morgan woke, wondering. He'd heard in the war that God was dead. He never heard any legends, though, about how it happened. He lay awake in the cooling night, peered up at he cold stars shimmering above. A fox barked in the distance, but otherwise the night remained soundless. He tried to force his uneasy mind to go back to sleep. . . .

Morgan woke with a start, afraid that someone was sneaking up on him. He lay still for several minutes, listening for the crackle of a footfall. Thin clouds filled the sky, which was beginning to lighten on the horizon. Morning would not be far off.

Small birds flitted about in a nearby sage. Here in the desert, most birds were silent, unwilling to call attention to themselves.

Morgan felt that something was wrong.

Suddenly, he realized that he hadn't heard anything amiss. It was what he *didn't* hear that bothered him—his horse. He lurched to his feet, swung his pistol around, and peered into the shadows.

His horse was nowhere to be seen.

166

Coyote Shadow had circled Morgan while he slept. After a brief search, Morgan discovered that the renegade had stolen his food, his hat, his rifle, and his horse.

Morgan must have worn himself out, trying to keep watch. The skinwalker could have killed him in his sleep, but this Indian was more interested in counting coup, humiliating Morgan, than taking his scalp.

"Hope you're getting a good chuckle out of this!" Morgan shouted to the horizon.

He turned away from the skinwalker's path and set off for Frenchman's Ferry.

Morgan wasn't the kind of man to chew on regret. In life, he believed that you have to do the best you can. Sometimes you succeeded, sometimes you failed.

He'd lost Coyote Shadow, and by now the renegade was probably heading to join up with Crazy Horse's men; either that or he'd gone up into the aspen forests in the high country. Morgan figured he'd never see Coyote Shadow again.

Yet he began to regret missing his shot at the skinwalker. He wondered about his buck fever—the shaking hands, the dry mouth.

Too many men, when they get in a gunfight, will draw and fire wild, hitting only empty air. That's what gets them killed. A more experienced man will take a moment to aim—half a second, if need be—and thus shoot his opponent.

Morgan was fast on the draw and had a steady aim, but he'd gotten buck fever.

His failure seemed a portent.

The clockwork gambler wouldn't suffer from human debilities. He wouldn't get excited and drop his gun. He wouldn't get a case of tremors. He wouldn't pause because he was having an attack of conscience.

He would just kill.

In some ways, Morgan realized, *he's better than me.*

Morgan survived the next two days off strips of sliced prickly pear cactus, which tasted like green beans, and yucca fruit, which were more like potatoes. The odd jack rabbit added protein to the fare.

167

Four days after meeting The Stranger, Morgan was hobbling along on sore feet, thirty miles from Fort Laramie. If The Stranger was right, someone would get killed today. Morgan wouldn't be there to stop it.

When he reached Frenchman's Ferry, down on the North Platte, he spotted a miserable little log shack. Bear traps, snowshoes, and other durable goods hung outside. A pair of dogs—half mastiff and half wolf—guarded the door. Its smokestack was roiling, even in the heat of the day, producing black clouds of smoke.

A bevy of greenhorns had just left the post, heading north into the wilderness.

Morgan hurried inside.

At the counter, an aging squaw sat with a basket of big turkey eggs. She hunched over a lightbox—a box with a mirror on one wall, and an oil lamp in the middle. By holding an egg up to the contraption, a person could check it for cracks or the blobs of half-formed fetuses.

The squaw's blouse was white with red polka dots—a Cheyenne design. But she wore buckskin pants like a trapper, and her perfume smelled imported. She didn't spare him a glance.

"Look around," she offered in that Indian way that was more "careful" than "slow." The shop was filled with merchandise—tins of crackers; barrels of pickles, beans, rice and wheat. On the wall behind the counter were hunting knives, a pair of shotguns—and above them hung Morgan's Winchester.

So the skinwalker had been here.

The gun didn't interest him right now. The skinwalker had stolen it fair and square. He'd counted coup and sold the gun. No sense arguing with the squaw about who owned it. Morgan would just embarrass himself by admitting that it had once been his.

Of everything in the shop, the things that most interested him were those eggs. Hunger gnawed at him. When Morgan was a child, his ma had often sold eggs to folks in town. She'd taught him young how to candle one, to check it for damage.

"Is Black Pierre around?" Morgan ventured.

"Gone for supplies," the squaw said. "Back in three, four days."

The squaw was turning an egg experimentally, studying it. She didn't look up. Morgan could see how judging such an egg might be difficult. Most chicken eggs were a uniform tan in color. Finding blood spots inside was easy. But these eggs were white, with big specks on them—some sand-colored, others more like liverworts. The shells were thicker than a chicken egg.

"I'd be right happy to buy some turkey eggs off of you," Morgan offered.

"Not turkey eggs," the squaw said, "thunderbird! Traders brought them in this morning. Found them in an old geyser vent over in Sulfur Springs."

Morgan had never seen a thunderbird egg before. Back East, they were called "snakebirds" but had been extinct for at least a hundred years. Down in Mexico, the Spaniards had called them quetzals, and some of the tribes still prayed to the critters.

"Want to see?" the squaw asked.

She held an egg to the hole in the lightbox, and Morgan peered in. Sure enough, the light shining though the egg was bright enough to reveal the embryo inside—a birdlike head with a snake's body. Many of its bones were still gelatinous, but he could see its guts forming, a tiny heart beating. Its scales were still almost translucent, just beginning to turn purple.

"Well, I'll be!" Morgan whispered. "Didn't know as there were any snakebirds left. They're fading faster than the buffalo."

"Mmm..." the squaw mused. "The world must get rid of the old wonders, so that it can make way for the new."

Morgan thought on that. He'd seen some of the last real buffalo herds as a child, darkening the plains of Kansas. Now the railroads were coming, and the railroad men were killing the buffalo off. The big herds were a danger to trains.

He imagined the clockwork gambler. Would such things someday replace men?

"Those eggs for sale?" Morgan asked.

"Not to you. They're for the Sioux—big medicine."

"How much you reckon to get?"

"My scalp," she said. "The Sioux slaughtered General Custer last week at the Little Bighorn. I'm going to need some gifts, to make peace."

Morgan didn't have a lot of money. He was able to buy back his pony and his hat at the trading post, but couldn't afford his rifle.

He set off down the Platte toward Fort Laramie, riding overland, well south of the river, far away from the pioneer trails where the Sioux would concentrate their patrols.

When he reached Fort Laramie, the post was full.

People of every kind had taken refuge just outside the fortress walls in tents and teepees—gold miners, fur trappers, homesteaders on the Oregon and California trails, Mormon converts from England and Denmark on their way to Utah, railroad workers of the Chinese, Irish, Dutch, and Negro persuasions, Omaha Indians and a few Comanches, Bible thumpers. Morgan had rarely seen such liveliness on the frontier.

He heard a rumor that there was a plague merchant in town— with bottles of black death and boxes of locust larvae.

Hell, there was even a freak show in town with a three-headed woman, an elephant, and a genuine Egyptian mummy.

The town hadn't seen rain in weeks, and so as Morgan entered the fortress, he found a rainmaker at the front gates—pounding a huge drum that sounded for the world like the crashing of thunder.

"Come, wind!" the rainmaker shouted. "Arise ye tempest, I say! Let your water soak the gnarly ground. Let cactus flowers bloom, while toads claw up from the mud!"

Morgan sat on his horse and studied the slim man—a tall beardless fellow in a fine top hat and tails, who roared as he drummed and stared off toward a few clouds on the horizon like a lunatic, with manic eyes and a grim smile.

The clouds were drawing near, blackening from moment to moment.

Morgan tossed a penny into the man's cup. "Keep your eyes on them clouds, Preach," Morgan said. "Don't let 'em sneak off."

"Thank you, good sir," the rainmaker said, pausing to wipe sweat from his brow with a handkerchief. "There will be rain soon. Mark my word."

Morgan didn't want the clockwork gambler to know that he was hunting for him. But the rainmaker seemed like a trustworthy fellow. He hazarded, "I'm looking for a clockwork gambler. Seen him?"

"You a friend of his?" the preacher asked. His tone became a bit formal, suspicious, and he backed away an inch.

In answer, Morgan pulled the badge from his pocket, a star made of nickel.

"You're too late," the preacher said. "He went on a rampage yesterday. He was sitting quiet at a card table, and suddenly pulled out his gun and shot a showgirl. There was a big row. Some cavalrymen drew steel, and seven men died in the firefight. The gambler escaped."

"See which way he went?"

The rainmaker nodded toward the clouds. In just the few moments since they'd begun speaking, Morgan realized that they'd shrunk and had begun to drift away. "He headed off into the High Frontier, where no one can give chase. There won't be no posse. Major Wiggins has got more trouble than he can handle, with them Sioux."

Morgan had heard tales of the High Frontier, but he'd never been there. Few men had. There had always been stories of castles in the clouds, but truth is far stranger than fiction.

"How'd he fly?" Morgan asked.

"Private yacht. He won it in a poker game."

Morgan wondered. The clockwork gambler was far away by now, more inaccessible than Mexico, almost as remote as the moon.

The rainmaker said hopefully, "Wells Fargo has a new line that goes to the High Frontier. Got to stay ahead of them railroads. Schooner lands next Monday."

"What day is today?" Morgan could guess at the month, but not the day.

"Today's a Wednesday."

Five days to get a grub stake together. Morgan bit his lower lip. He'd seen an airship once, a big copper-colored bulb glowing in the sunset as it sailed through ruddy clouds. Pretty and untouchable, like a trout swimming in deep, clear water.

"The dancehall girl," Morgan said. "She have any friends?"

The preacher squinted, giving an appraising look, and nodded sagely. "You thinking 'bout going after him?"

It seemed audacious. Hunting a clockwork alone was foolhardy, and few men had the kind of money needed for airfare.

Morgan nodded. "Justice shouldn't be confined by borders."

The rainmaker nodded agreement, then thrust a hand into his pocket, pulled out some bills and change, handed them over. "Here's a donation for your cause, Lawman. Lacy didn't have a lot of friends, but she had a lot of men who longed for her from afar. Check the saloon."

Morgan's heart broke at the mention of Lacy's name. He remembered the red-haired girl, her innocent smile. He'd seen her before. But what was she doing in Laramie?

She'd come here for safety, he figured, like everyone else. Scared of the renegades. They were like sheep, huddled in a pen.

He'd felt so in awe of Lacy, he couldn't have dared even speak to her, much less ask to hold her hand. In some ways, she was little more than a dream, a thing of ephemeral beauty.

The preacher smiled and began pounding his drum with extra vigor. "Come, horrid bursts of thunder!" he commanded. "Come sheets of fire! Groan ye winds and roar ye rain!"

On the horizon, the clouds darkened and again began lumbering toward Laramie.

A week later, Morgan found himself in the gondola of a dirigible.

It turned out that Lacy had had a lot of friends in Laramie. Though none was rich enough to afford passage to the High Frontier on their own, and none was mad enough to shoot it out with a clockwork, Morgan was able to scrape together enough money for his passage.

The balloon above the gondola was shaped like a fancy glass Christmas tree ornament, all covered in gold silk. A steam engine powered the dirigible, providing a steady *thump, thump, thump* as pistons pounded and blades spun.

The gondola swung beneath the huge balloon, connected by skywires. Its decks were all hewn from new cedar and sandalwood; their scent complimented the smell of sky and sun and wind.

City slickers and foreigners sat in the parlor cabin, toasting their good fortune and dancing while bands played.

Morgan could hear their music, smell their roast beef, sometimes even glimpse them dancing. But he wasn't a railroad tycoon or a mining magnate or a politician.

He'd taken passage in the lower deck, in the "Belly of the Beast," as they called it, and had one small porthole in his cabin to peer through.

Still, the sight was glorious.

The dirigible reached the High Frontier at sunset, just as the sun dipped below the sea, leaving the clouds below to be a half-lit mass of swirling wine and fuchsia.

One could only find the High Frontier at that time of day— when the sun had set and the full moon was poised to rise on the far side of the Earth. It was a magical place, nestled in the clouds.

Down below the skyship, a silver city rose—elegant spires like fairy castles, with windows lit up like gemstones. The colored glass in those windows made it look as if sapphires, rubies, and diamonds were scattered over the city.

The skyship landed amid glorious swirling clouds, and the rich folk marched down the promenade, arm in arm, laughing and joking and celebrating their good fortune. On the deck, the band came out and played soft chamber music.

Women *oohed* and *aahed* at the spectacle, while men stood open-mouthed. Morgan imagined that saints might make such sounds as they entered heaven.

The High Frontier had only been discovered four years back. Who had built the silver castles, no one knew. How the cities of stone floated in the clouds was also a mystery.

Angels lived there—scrawny girls with wings, ethereal in their beauty. But they were feral creatures, barbaric, and it was said that when the first explorers had entered the silver city, the angels were roosting over the arches—little more than filthy pigeons.

Some thought that it had once been an outpost, that perhaps angels had once been wiser, more civilized, and that they rested here while carrying messages back and forth between Heaven and Earth.

One guess was as good as another. But a new territory was opening up, and folks were eager to be the first to see it. Morgan couldn't figure how a man might make a living here. The sky was always twilit, so you couldn't grow crops. The clouds were somehow thick enough to walk on, but there was nothing to mine.

Just a pretty place to visit, Morgan thought.

When the rich folk were mostly gone, Morgan made his way down the gangplank. A fancy dude in a bowler hat stood at the top of the gangway, smoking a fine cigar that perfumed the air.

He glanced at Morgan, smiled, and said, *"Das ist schön, nicht wahr?"*

Morgan grinned back. "Sorry," he apologized. "I don't reckon we speak the same language."

Morgan walked down the gangplank, his spurs jangling with every step, and trundled through the city. He imagined that madmen had fashioned the soaring arches above the city gate, now planted with vines and lianas that streamed in living curtains.

Maybe a fellar could grow crops up here after all, he mused, *though the light is low.* Butterflies and hummingbirds danced among the flowers.

As he entered the silver city, spires rose up on either side. There was something both strange and yet oddly organic about the tall buildings, as if some alien intelligence had sought to build a city for humans. Perhaps dove-men had designed it, or termites. He wasn't sure.

People filed off in a number of directions. It was rumored that many a tycoon had bought houses here—Cornelius Vanderbilt, Russell Sage, along with royals out of Europe and Russia. Even Queen Victoria had a new "Summerhouse" here.

All the high-falutin' folks sauntered off to their destinations, and Morgan felt lost.

One fairy castle looked much like another. He searched for an hour, and as he rounded a corner, he found what he was looking for: the wing doors of a Western saloon. He could hear loud piano music inside, and smell spilled beer on its oak floors.

He walked into the saloon and found a madhouse.

On either side of the door were golden cages up over his head, and angels were housed there—small girls, perhaps eight or nine, with fabulous wings larger than any swan's. Their hair was as white as spun silver, their faces translucent.

But their dark eyes were lined with a thick band of kohl, as if they were raccoons. They drew back from Morgan and hissed.

Unbidden, a dark thought entered his mind. When he was a child, Morgan's mother had always told him that when a man dies, the angels come to take his soul to Heaven.

He could be walking to his death.

A verse from Psalms came to mind, one of his ma's favorites: "Lord, what is man, that thou art mindful of him? Or the son of man, that thou visitest him? Thou madest him a little lower than the angels..."

As if divining his thoughts, one of the angels hissed at him and bared her teeth. She scooped a turd up from her cage and hurled it. Then grabbed a corn cob and tossed that, too.

Morgan dodged and hurried past.

Inside, the place was alive. Dancehall girls strutted on stage to clanking pianos and catcalls. Men hunched at tables, drinking and telling jokes. It was much like a saloon, but it suffered from the same miserable clientele as he'd seen on the dirigible—European barons in bright silk vests and overcoats. Eastern dudes. Moguls and robber barons.

The beer wasn't sold in glass jugs, but in decorous tankards, inlaid with silver and precious stones.

The place smelled more of gold than of liquor. Pipe smoke perfumed the air.

But the clockwork gambler was surprisingly easy to spot.

In fact, Morgan gasped and stepped back in surprise when he saw him.

The clockwork was obviously not human. His face had been sculpted from porcelain, like the head of a doll, and painted in natural colors, but there were brass hinges on his jaws. When he blinked, copper eyelids flashed over glass eyes.

He wore all black, from his hat to his boots, and sat at a card table with a stack of poker chips in front of him. He had a little gambling kit off to one side. Morgan was familiar with such kits. They held decks of cards for various games, dice made of bone and ivory, and always they held weapons—a pistol and a throwing knife.

The clockwork gambler sat with three wealthy men. By the piles of solid-gold coins in front of him, he was winning.

Morgan steeled his nerves, walked up to the table, and said, "You gentlemen might want to back away."

The patrons scattered aside as Morgan pulled back his coat to reveal the star on his chest.

Some men cried out as they fled, and others ducked as if dodging imaginary bullets. The clockwork gambler just leaned back casually in his chair, as calm as a summer's morning. His mouth seemed to have little porcelain shingles around it that moved to his will, so that when he smiled, it created a crude approximation of a grin. The creature's teeth were as white as shards of ice.

"Here to try your luck?" the clockwork asked.

"Your name Hellfire?" Morgan replied.

The gambler nodded, barely tipping his hat.

Morgan felt his hands shaking, and his mouth suddenly dried. He'd never seen a man face death with equanimity the way that this clockwork did. It was unnatural. Almost unholy.

I'm betrayed by my humanity, Morgan thought. *Flesh and blood, gristle and bone—they undo me.*

In that instant, he knew that he was no match for the clockwork gambler.

"Tell you what, stranger," the clockwork said. "Let's draw

cards for your life. You get the high card, you get the first shot at me."

Morgan shook his head.

"Come on," the gambler said reasonably. "It's the best chance you've got. Your flesh was created by God, and thus has its all-too human limitations. I was made to draw faster than you, to shoot straighter."

"You might be a better killer than me, but that don't make you a better man."

"When killing is all that matters, maybe it does," the clockwork said.

The silence drew out. Morgan wasn't sure if he should let the clockwork draw first. He didn't know where to aim. The creature's chest provided the biggest target, but it was the best protected by layers of metal. The joints where its neck met its head might be better. But what was a head to this machine? Did thoughts originate there, or elsewhere? The head looked no more serviceable than that of a poppet.

The gambler smiled. "Your human sense of honor bothering you? Is that it?"

"I want justice," Morgan said. "I demand justice."

"On the High Frontier?" the gambler mocked. "There is no justice here—just a pretty tomb, the ruins of a grander civilization. This is Rome! This is Egypt!"

He waved his hands wide, displaying the ornate walls carved with silver, the golden cages with captive angels. "This is what is left of your dead god. But I am the future."

Morgan had heard a lot of talk about God being dead over the years, from the beginning of the Civil War. But the discovery of these ruins proved it to the minds of many.

"Tell you what," the gambler said. "Your legs are shaking. I won't shoot you now. Let's try the cards. I'll draw for you."

The gambler placed a fresh deck on the table, pulled a card off the top, and laid it upright. It was a Jack of Hearts. He smiled, as if in relief.

"I didn't come to gamble," Morgan said. "I came for justice."

"Seeking justice is always a gamble," Hellfire answered reasonably. "Justice doesn't exist in nature. It's just the use of force, backed up by self-righteous judgment."

The gambler cut the deck, pulled off the top card, flipped it: the Ace of Spades.

"You win!" the gambler grinned.

Morgan was all nerves and jitters but pulled his piece anyway, took a full quarter second to get his bearings, and fired. The bullet ripped into the gambler's bowtie, and there was a metallic *zing* as it ricocheted into the crowd.

Someone cried out, *"Mein Gott!"* and a woman yelled, "He's been shot!"

Morgan's face fell. He hadn't meant to wing a bystander. He glanced to his right, saw a fat bloke clutching his chest, blood blossoming on a white shirt.

Morgan ducked low and tried to aim at the clockwork, but faster than the eye could move the gambler drew, aimed, and fired. The bullet took Morgan straight in the chest and threw him backward as if he'd been kicked by a horse.

Morgan fell and wheezed, trying to suck air, but he heard blood gurgling from the hole in his ribs. His lungs burned as if someone had stuck a hot poker through them.

He looked right and left, hoping someone would help him, but all that he saw were frightened faces. He had heard that there was no law on the High Frontier, only money.

No one would stop the killing. No one would avenge him.

As he lay on his back and felt blood pooling on the floor, he fought to stay conscious. The clockwork gambler strode toward him, smiling down, his porcelain face a mockery of flesh.

Morgan realized that he'd been charging dead, from the moment he'd started this hunt. When he'd missed the skinwalker, he should have seen it as a sign.

"Your human tinkermen have made me well, have they not?" Hellfire asked. "You humans, in such a hurry to create. It was inevitable that you would fashion your replacements."

ROB HASSAN

Over the clockwork's shoulder, Morgan saw his angels—leering from their cages. One was grabbing at the lock on its golden door, trying to break free, as if to come for him.

But Morgan was on his way out, like the buffalo, and the Indians, and thunderbirds, and all the other great things in the wide world.

The gambler aimed at Morgan's head. There was no shaking in his hands, no hesitation. He pulled the trigger.

Thus, a new wonder in the world supplanted an old.

Squalor and Sympathy

written by

Matt Dovey

illustrated by

ADRIAN MASSARO

ABOUT THE AUTHOR

Matt Dovey lives in a quiet market town in rural England with his wife and three children. Despite professing to be a writer, he still hasn't found the right words to properly express the delight and joy he finds in this wonderful arrangement. His surname rhymes with "Dopey"; any other similarities to said dwarf are purely coincidental.

He does boring stuff with computers for a living. Thanks to the tireless and loving efforts of his wife, he has time not only to write but also to brew wine, photograph everything, and run around a field with a pretend sword and a silly accent in the name of live roleplay. He is very English and often has arguments over when one should add the milk to a cup of tea. For the record, this is before *the boiling water, not after, despite George Orwell's claims to the contrary.*

He has presently completed thirty-one consecutive orbits of the Sun (a personal best) and hopes to extend this record so that he will have time enough to get through his Ideas That Need Writing *list. He looks forward to the day when AI snapshots can be spun-off, set loose, and later reintegrated back into one's core personality as a method for actually getting around to everything that needs doing. It's his last hope.*

This is his first publication, though others are already following.

ABOUT THE ILLUSTRATOR

Adrian Massaro was born in 1989 in the small tourist city of Bariloche, situated in the foothills of the Patagonian Andes in Argentina.

He has drawn ever since his hands could hold anything that could leave a mark, and his mind could picture what a tree or dinosaur looked like. His older brother, a very talented artist, was always his inspiration.

Adrian went on to study Visual Communication Design at the National University of La Plata in Buenos Aires.

After spending most of his life drawing with graphite pencils and lead holders, he started his journey with digital painting using a small Wacom Bamboo. The online community, through numerous forums, magazines, articles, and blogs provided the help and tuition he was looking for to push his craft and imagination to the next level.

Adrian continues his independent studies and works doing freelance jobs for private clients. He is currently living in Neuquén, Argentina and is always in search of new experiences and roads to travel.

Squalor and Sympathy

Anna concentrated on the cold, on the freezing water around her feet and the bruising sensation in her toes. *So cold. So cold. So cold,* she thought. A prickling warmth like pins and needles crackled inside her feet. It coursed through her body to her clenched hands and into the lead alloy handles of the cotton loom. Each thought of *cold!* kindled a fresh surge of heat inside and pushed the shuttle across the weave in a new burst of power. Anna's unfocused eyes rested on the woven cotton feeding out of the back of the machine. *It looks so warm.*

The constant clacking of looms that filled the factory changed tempo, quieted slightly. Anna glanced to her right, where Sally White worked.

Sally was standing, her feet still in her water bucket, and talking to herself. "Sodding thing, gone and jammed on me again. No wonder I can't meet numbers." She was peering into the loom at where her shuttle must have caught.

"Here, let me help." Anna took her bare feet out of the bucket and stepped over. Her own shuttle slowed and stopped as she released the handles.

"You can't, Anna. If Shuttleworth sees you've stopped work, there'll be hell to pay. I'll get it sorted. Don't you worry about me, you look after yourself." Sally's fingers were deftly picking at threads of cotton, darting in and out like a chicken pecking for seed. She had good reason to be so delicate: when the jam cleared, the tension in the threads would launch the shuttle across the loom, even without power, and any fingers in the way would be ruined.

"Don't be daft," said Anna. "It'll take no time with two of us." She tucked her dark hair behind her ears then reached in and held the shuttle, letting Sally unpick the knots and tangles more easily.

"Oh you've a good heart, you have, Anna. I do like you. Ain't many folk like you around no more. The world's a selfish place these days, and always looking out for itself. I'm glad you're in it to look out for others still."

Anna stared up at Sally. Her hair and skin were so pale as to be almost white, especially in the weak sunlight of the factory. She was only twenty-two, Anna knew, only five years older than Anna herself, but she looked worn through, like milk watered down too thin. "Why don't you say something about this shuttle?" asked Anna. "It's near worn out!"

"I can't say owt about it. If I say I need a new shuttle, it'll get docked from my pay, and I can't afford that. I'm already having to work double shifts since my George shipped off to India with the Company. A new shuttle'd cost me a week's pay, and I can't have my Charlotte going hungry all that time, little angel." Sally unpicked the last knot and pulled her fingers back quick like. Anna released the shuttle and it flew across the weave, sliding to a rest.

"She not old enough to earn something herself, yet?" asked Anna.

"My Charlotte? Oh no, not yet. Well, I mean, she's five now, and I hear they're using kids that young down the lead mines 'cos they scare easier at that age. They send them down to get all frit up by the dark, and then they sit them in a bucket with a load of mined lead, and them kids look up and see a bit of light at the top of the shaft and they start lifting the bucket with their Squalor 'cos of how they're so frantic to get out."

"No!" Anna covered her mouth in shock. "That's awful, the poor buggers!" The image of her brothers down a pit, terrified and sobbing, flashed into her mind, and Anna gave a shudder that had nowt to do with the factory's winter chill.

"I know, terrible how people'll take advantage of them that need the pay. If they tried to take my little Charlotte away from me and scare her like that, I'd tell them what for. They'd be jumping down that mineshaft themselves to hide from me, I tell you. The things they do to us desperate folk are awful. I'm not surprised them Luddites are making progress like they are." Sally sat down again, feet in the water bucket and hands on the handles, and started her loom up.

Anna peered around, making sure no one was close enough to overhear, then leaned in closer to Sally. "I keep hearing about these Luddites, since I started, but who are they?"

Sally checked around herself before answering, her voice barely audible over the sound of her loom. Her shuttle never slowed: she had the knack of focusing her Squalor without thinking about it. "I hear they started off wrecking machines, right? Supposed to be this one woman called Nelly Ludd who didn't agree with engines, said they were instruments of cruelty and shackles round the poor. No one's ever seen her, but there's this whole following now, and they aren't just wrecking the odd machine anymore. I hear they're threatening to shut factories down, if Shuttleworth won't listen to their demands."

"What they asking for?"

"Saying they're the voice of the people, right? That everyone's getting worked too hard and paid too little, and it ain't fair to take advantage of people's suffering to drive machinery. Squalor's a gift from God to help them what need it most, and twisting it like this is the Devil's work."

"Sir John ain't that bad as they go, though, is he? He don't hurt no one to coax their Squalor, not like some I've heard of."

"Anna Williams," boomed a voice. Anna startled in shock, and saw Sir John Shuttleworth on his balcony. He stood with a speaking trumpet, reading a sheet of paper—probably a list of names against looms so he could pick her out from the floor. She glanced back at her shuttle, stationary on the weave.

Sir John lifted the trumpet to his mouth again. "Come up to my office please, Anna Williams."

185

Anna picked her way across the factory floor, rough stone hard on her bare feet. The clattering and clacking of the shuttles beat against her ears as her heart beat against her chest. She passed row upon row of grim-faced women, all with their feet in water buckets, all gripping lead handles tight. The cold made 'em needy for the warm cotton coming out the looms, wishing they could wrap themselves in it. That need drove their Squalor, and their Squalor drove the machines.

Sir John Shuttleworth stood at the top of the iron stairs, awaiting her. His swept-back silver hair was stark against the black cloak he wore; his back was straight and his hands were clasped behind him. He stared down his hawkish nose at Anna as she climbed, and indicated his open door.

She hadn't been in the office before. It was rich and warm, all mahogany and gilt, but the smell was what stood out. Where the factory floor was the single sharp note of sweet cotton, the office was earthy and musky and full of subtle scents, as complex as a summer forest at dusk.

She was about to step onto the plush rug before the desk, eager to feel its softness between her toes, when the noise of the factory cut out and Sir John's voice said, quiet and dismissive, "Please remain on the floorboards. The water from your feet would damage the carpet."

Anna set her foot down again and lowered her eyes as Sir John brushed past.

He seated himself and studied her over steepled fingers. "Miss Williams, pray tell: do I employ you to stand around conversing?"

"No, Sir John." *Be a meek little mouse, that's what he wants.*

"Are you singularly possessed of the unique ability to drive your loom without actually being sat at it?"

"No, Sir John."

"Then kindly explain why you waste my time and factory space on conversations with your neighbor!"

"I was helping her unstick her shuttle," Anna said, lifting her face to look at Sir John. "It's getting awful worn, and it ain't fair to make her pay for—"

"Is your shuttle in full working order, Miss Williams?"

"Well yes, but—"

"Then no one else's shuttle is any of your concern."

"But if you'd just—"

"Enough!" Sir John slammed his palm on the desk, cutting Anna off. "This insubordination will be noted on your file."

She lowered her eyes again. *So much for meek little mouse. Can't help but get involved, can you?*

Sir John shuffled through papers till he arrived at her file. "Your address is Mrs. Hobble's orphanage in town?" His voice was no longer angry, but curious. Anna didn't trust the change.

"Yes, Sir John. I been raised there these last six years, and Mrs. Hobble lets me rent a room still."

"And, in your opinion, are the boys there healthy, well-fed and strong?"

Anna stumbled for a moment. Boys? It was all women on the factory floor. Sally said men didn't have the common sense to make a loom work, they were stupid brutes that could only use fear and anger for their Squalor. *What could he want boys for? Children? There's no work for kids except—oh no, the mines! What if he sends my brothers down a pit? Daniel'd choke down there, he hates being cooped up. Even Charlie'd struggle, and Jacob's so young—*

"You seem to be having some trouble, Miss Williams."

Anna said nothing.

"Perhaps it is that you do not trust me. No, do not trouble to deny it—I fully expect you have heard mutterings on the floor...especially of late." His face darkened for a moment; he dispelled it with a soft shake. "The truth is, I do not expect you to understand. I work for the betterment of the Empire and to the glory of Queen Victoria, a goal too lofty for your concerns. Thanks to Parkes' new lead alloy, Britain alone possesses the secret to channeling Squalor for industrial purposes. The Prussians may think to challenge us, fueled as they are by the coal reserves we so sorely lack, but we are lifted anew by a fresh spirit of invention built on the Squalor of the working class. The prize we compete for is the world itself, and all Britain would prosper from its riches; and if the price seems heavy now, the reward will be worth it. You may not trust me, but I assure you that, ultimately, I work with your best interests at heart. So I ask again: are the boys at the orphanage healthy and robust?"

Anna searched for something, anything to say, but what could she do? Sir John donated to the orphanage, and if he thought Mrs. Hobble wasn't running the place right... "Yes, Sir John. Proper fed and raised well."

"Good. Do tell Mrs. Hobble that I shall be enquiring with her forthwith, and she is to ensure that the boys are ready for presentation at all times. That will be all, thank you." Sir John indicated the door behind Anna and turned to his papers, his earlier tirade apparently forgotten.

Pale faces followed her back to her loom, but Anna paid them no mind. *What have I done? If he takes my boys ... but what else could I have said? Oh, if only I'd not stood around nattering.*

She stopped, her path blocked. Maud Farlin, gruff, broad, and imposing, stood in her way.

"You all right, girl?" asked Maud.

"Yes, thank you." It hadn't taken Anna long to clock Maud. She was the mother of the factory floor, but not soft and caring. No, she was a mother fox, watching over everyone and fighting for 'em tooth and claw. Properly speaking, she was just another worker, but all the women looked to her.

"Shuttleworth didn't give you no grief now, did he?"

"No."

Maud stared intently, but Anna kept quiet. She'd let her mouth run away with her too much already today.

Maud grunted. "All right then. But you let me know if ever he does, right?"

Anna nodded and went back to her loom. In a few moments her feet were back in the water bucket, her hands were clasped around the lead grips, and the shuttle was running back and forth across the weave and filling Anna's ears and mind with noise.

The winter winds chilled Anna something terrible as she walked the two miles back through Burnley, and she was grateful for the kitchen fire when she stepped in through the side door of the orphanage.

"Anna! Oh love, you look frozen." Mrs. Hobble looked up from the tall kitchen table where she stood slicing bread. Her clothes were faded, layered on her round frame, but there was still enough color in them to clash. "Come in, quick, and shut that door. Here, have yourself a slice. You need something in you to ward off a chill."

Anna sat on a kitchen stool and unwound her scarf as Mrs. Hobble spread a thin layer of watery butter on a slice of bread. Anna took it without argument and began to eat.

"I've brought my rent," she said between slow mouthfuls, putting a mixed handful of shillings and pennies on the table.

"Oh, you daft sod. I keep telling you, we don't need your charity. You can stay here for nowt for as long as there's room."

"The house is riddled with holes, there ain't never enough to go around, and you're always taking more orphans in, so don't tell me you don't need charity."

"We need charity, love, but we don't need yours. You've got yourself to look after."

"You looked after me for long enough, so if I can help in any way, I will."

"Oh love, you don't half say some daft things. Seeing you all grown up and standing on your own two feet is repayment enough, especially seeing you grown to care for others. You're not that feral girl looking out for her own that I first met. So don't you worry. You owe us nothing."

"Even so, I ain't taking it back. It's yours."

Mrs. Hobble put the bread knife down with a sigh. She'd sliced off a dozen or more slices of bread in the time they'd been talking, but the loaf hadn't gotten any smaller.

Anna frowned. "Are you going hungry again so as you can stretch the food for the kids?"

"Needs must, love. Using my Squalor's the only way I can get enough food to get them through this winter."

"And what good is it to them if you can't get through the winter? Take the money to buy some more and have yourself something to eat now. There soup left in that pot?" Anna nodded toward the kitchen fire.

"Aye, love, some chicken broth. It's been on for three days though, so it's getting a bit thin. I don't know as it's worth stretching out any longer."

"You've gone hungry for three days? I'm not having that! Get that money put away in your desk and I'll sort us both some bread and broth. Three days, you daft bint!"

Mrs. Hobble smiled, an exhausted smile between cheeks cracked red by winter, but Anna thought she could see some pride there, too. "All right then, I'll be back in a jiffy." She went back into the house, skirts rustling as she left the warmth of the kitchen.

Anna sliced the last of the bread up, taking care with the knife against the tough, stale crust, and then took two bowls over to the pot and ladled some chicken broth out. *Three days! I can't hardly remember hunger like that. It must be bruising her insides to be so empty.* Anna's stomach clenched in sympathy, an oddly warm sensation. She filled both bowls: it hadn't looked like there was much left, but somehow it stretched. It was surprising how much these old iron pots could hold.

The door burst open and her three younger brothers rushed in, tumbling into Anna's legs with shouts of excitement.

Anna laughed, put the bowls down, and crouched to hug them each in turn. "And what are you little buggers doing up still, eh? I expect Mrs. Hobble here put you to bed an hour or more ago, yet here you are!"

Jacob, the youngest at seven, pulled Anna down into another hug and whispered in her ear, "We love you."

A tide of love and gratitude swept through Anna while Jacob's small hands tangled in her dark hair. "I love you too," she said through a choked throat.

ADRIAN MASSARO

"We miss you when you're not here," said Charlie, the oldest of the three boys. He was taller now at twelve than Anna at seventeen, and just as serious as her too. He'd been old enough when they'd arrived at the orphanage six years before to know what was going on, and he'd needed to grow up near as fast as Anna; Daniel had been only two at the time, Jacob not even walking yet.

Anna would do anything for them to keep their innocence.

"Well I'll still be here in the morning," she said, smiling, "so you can get yourselves to bed now, aye? Go on with you, up the wooden hill you go!"

They filed out the door past Mrs. Hobble. Jacob and Daniel chattered as they went, and even Charlie was smiling. Mrs. Hobble saw them up the stairs before she came back and sat at the counter for her broth and bread.

"Eat up then," said Mrs. Hobble, dipping a slice.

"You'll look out for them, won't you?" asked Anna in a quiet voice.

"Of course I will! I always have, haven't I?"

Anna smiled weakly, but she couldn't shake the image of the boys down a mineshaft, frightened and alone in the closed-in dark.

"What's on your mind, love? Not like you to ask those sorts of questions."

"Sir John had me in his office today. Asked if there were many strong boys here."

"What's he asking you that for?"

"I wish I knew. He pulled me up for talking instead of working, but when he saw I lived here, he started asking about the boys. He'd never have known to ask if I'd not been idling for him to catch me. He said he'd be by any time to inspect them, and for you to have 'em ready at a moment's notice." Anna wiped round her bowl with the last of her bread, round and round, round and round. "Mrs. Hobble?"

"Yes, love?"

"Don't let him take my boys, will you? When he comes, don't let him take them. Please."

Anna's eyes welled up, and Mrs. Hobble reached across the counter to squeeze her hands.

"I just—" stumbled Anna. "I know it's selfish of me, 'cos he'll take other boys instead, but I want them to have their childhood as long as they can."

"You're allowed a little selfishness, love. Everyone is. You think I run this place out of goodness? I'm as selfish as anyone. I only do this so as I don't have to work in them mills. Everyone has to look out for themselves these days, 'cos no one else'll do it for you anymore."

"I just don't want anyone to take advantage of 'em. I want them to know how to stand up for themselves."

"Now that's one lesson I don't think they'll have any trouble learning, not with you around to teach them."

Anna smiled again, but more genuinely this time. Still, it was tempered by sadness, like cold rain on warm skin. "I just hope they don't have to learn it as hard as I did."

Anna clenched her jaw to stop her teeth from chattering. They ached from hours of cold. Her bare feet were almost blue in the water bucket, though it was difficult to tell in the gloom. Another gust of winter wind blew through the factory, raw and biting.

Shuttleworth had declared the doors remain open at the start of the shift, "to encourage motivation and boost production." Everyone knew why: another of his factories outside of town was still burning this morning, a great plume of black smoke dropping ash all through Burnley. *Nelly Ludd and her Luddites* had been the awed rumor at first, *Nelly Ludd and her Luddites* the bitter recrimination after Shuttleworth's announcement, *Nelly Ludd and her Luddites* a whisper lurking beneath the rattle of the looms, *Luddites CHUDUNDUN Luddites CHUDUNDUN Luddites CHUDUNDUN.*

The whispering had died now, though. Only the looms clattered, lulling Anna into a chilled torpor. Even Sally, who chattered through every shift, had fallen silent.

Which made her sudden scream all the more jarring.

Anna's heart dropped past her guts as she leaped up. A scream like that meant only one thing in a cotton mill. Sally was sobbing on her stool, cradling her hand, face paler than Anna had ever seen it. Inside the loom the shuttle was tangled in yarn and glistening bright red with blood.

Sally's good hand was half to frozen solid when Anna reached for it, muttering reassurances and gesturing for her to show her wounds. *Bloody hell, ain't no surprise her fingers got clumsy if they're that cold.*

Anna's breath caught when she saw the ruin of Sally's fingers. They were splintered and twisted, bone and tendon showing white through the red ribbon of muscle. A shiver ran through Anna and her hands clenched involuntarily, itching with imagined agony.

"Oh, Sally . . ." Tears blurred her vision as she wrapped a gentle hand around those broken, ragged fingers. All her sympathy welled up inside, near to choking her, building to a heat in her chest like coals glowing under breath. Sally couldn't work the loom no more, and little Charlotte'd be crying with hunger every night. Charlotte! Sally wouldn't ever stroke her angel's face again, not tickle nor tease her.

The heat from Anna's chest started to run down her arm and—she felt sure of it—into Sally's fingers.

For a moment she stood there, confusion and astonishment locking her in place. The heat died, and her arm loosened, and she lifted her hand away.

Sally's fingers were pink and raw, like new skin after a burn, but they were straight and whole again. In a week they'd show no sign of the injury.

Maud Farlin stomped up with some of her women and looked to Sally, her gruff face set grim. "What happened?"

Sally was vacant and numb, pale with shock.

Maud looked to Anna instead. "Did you see it?"

"No, but her shuttle's stuck and there's blood all over the weave. Reckon it caught her as she untangled the threads. Cold fingers ain't fast fingers."

Maud grimaced. "Aye, girl, that's the Lord's truth. Well let's have a look, Sally. See how bad it is."

Maud reached thick fingers down and lifted Sally's hand into a feeble beam of sunlight.

"Teeth o' Jesus," said one of Maud's women, "don't know as I'd still be sharp enough after a full shift to focus my Squalor and fix myself that good."

Anna kept quiet. *What had happened? What . . . what was that?*

"This is on Shuttleworth," said Maud. "I'm amazed we ain't had more of this today. Near as amazed as I am that you fixed yourself up, Sally. Ain't many could do that." She looked at Anna as she said it, looked at her closely, before turning to her women. More had gathered as they talked, and Maud raised her voice to them all. "I ain't standing for this. No one should have to risk themselves with these long shifts and cold draughts for his profit. C'mon Sally." Maud put her hands on Sally's shoulders and gently, but firmly, stood her up and led her out of the bucket of water and up to the front of the factory floor, beneath Shuttleworth's balcony.

Anna got caught up in the group of women and hustled along with them.

"Shuttleworth!" shouted Maud. The factory slowed as all the women turned, uncertain what was happening.

No answer came from the office.

"Shuttleworth!"

Maud's voice echoed in the silence. All the looms had stilled. Thin cloth whispered as women stood and joined the crowd.

"Shuttleworth!"

The door opened at last and Sir John stepped out, expression distracted and annoyed. He seemed surprised to find the mass of workers staring at him and his factory halted. The anger in the air broke through his arrogance for the briefest second before he regained his composure and set his hawkish face in a mask of disdain.

"Pay will be docked for this stoppage. Further punishment will be meted out to the ringleaders in due course, but I have more pressing appointments in town."

In town? Oh Christ, not the orphanage! I've got to get to the boys! Anna tried to wriggle her way out of the crowd but she was held in, pinned at the front of it all.

"I will return at two hours past dusk, and I expect you all still to be working," continued Shuttleworth. "If production does not meet my expectations, then I have a number of...newly redundant workers in need of fresh employment." He turned to leave, black cloak flaring out as he spun.

Maud said, "We'll not stand for this anymore, Shuttleworth."

If the floor had seemed silent before, it almost ached with the absence of sound now.

Anna could feel the wrath in Sir John from here. The way he moved back to face Maud Farlin was too controlled, too *tight*, with none of his usual flamboyance.

"I do not care what you will stand for," he said, knuckles white as they gripped the railing, "because it does not matter to me. You think your petty concerns are important when set against the empire? Against progress?"

"You think us less important because we have to worry about food on the table each night?" Maud's voice was just as quiet, just as angry.

"I think you less important because you *are* less important, woman! Learn your place and keep to it, else I will find someone else to fill it. All of you!" He stormed down the iron steps and out the factory, rage in every step.

"You hear that?" yelled Maud, face still upturned as if Shuttleworth remained on his balcony. "You hear what he thinks of us?" The crowd grumbled. "He thinks us inferior! He thinks us contemptible! He thinks us desperate!"

We are desperate. Anna tried to worm her way out of the crowd, her terror growing lockstep with the mob's fury.

"Are you going to let him talk to you like that?" Maud faced her audience now, gesturing roughly. "Put you down like that? He

196

ain't no better than us. He's no God-fearing man like he pretends. He's sent by Satan himself! Building his dark mills on our fair moors! He's a canker on our land and a canker on our souls. Why should we let him drag us down with him? Why should we suffer at his tainted hands? No more of his abuse or his scorn or his evil! No more!" Maud turned and stomped out, the looms seeming to quake as she passed, all the women behind her.

Anna followed out the door and then fled up the road, leaving the mob to their riot.

Anna ran for the orphanage, ran with abandon and fear, ran as fast as ever she could.

When Shuttleworth's black and gold coach passed her, going back the other way, she ran even faster still.

She burst in through the front door and raced through the old house, searching for Mrs. Hobble, searching for the boys.

"Hello, love." Mrs. Hobble's voice was soft.

"Where are the boys? Where are the boys?"

"I'm sorry, love, I tried to keep them back... he had me gather all the boys in the front room, and I made sure your lads were tucked away, near hiding behind the sofa, but he went straight to 'em... walked past all the boys standing proud and confident, like he wanted the frightened ones. I'm so sorry, love, I really am." She twisted her colored skirts between her hands.

Anna swallowed back the tears and the screams and the panic. Her throat hurt when she spoke. "It's not your fault. Thank you for trying." She gripped Mrs. Hobble's arms in as reassuring a manner as she could muster, and then turned and fled before she could break down.

He wants the frightened ones. Boys that'll scare easy down a mine. Where's these mines he's taking 'em to, though? He said he'd be back at the factory past dusk, he must be taking them there first.

Anna ran. The exhaustion of a full day's shift and the bitter Lancashire winter dulled her thoughts till she became focused on the run, the run to the factory, the run to the boys, eyes glazed and feet pounding and lungs burning like they were on—

197

Fire.

Fire, filling the horizon, blazing orange against the night.

Fire filling the factory and eating it up and casting the dark iron beams as shadows, huge black ribs bending inwards like a consumptive wreck on his deathbed.

"No..."

The heat of it washed against her face from all these hundreds of feet away, and the sharp smell of burning cotton stabbed at her nose. The fire flared in a gust of wind, and part of the roof collapsed.

"No!" she shouted, lurching forward into a sprint. Maybe there was a corner that hadn't caught yet, maybe they'd gotten out and were standing the other side, maybe she could find them and help them and—

Strong arms wrapped themselves around her and lifted her off the ground.

"Careful now, girl, easy now. Easy!"

Anna kicked her heels and struggled against the grip, but she was held tight, and she was exhausted. She went limp, and let herself be lowered to the ground. A half-choked sob burst from her throat.

"Easy now, girl. You don't want to be running down there."

Anna looked up through tearful eyes. "Maud? Maud Farlin?"

"What you doing back here, girl?"

"I—my brothers—I—" and Anna collapsed again, a broken doll with strings cut by grief.

Maud waited. Anna wept out her tears, and mumbled, "They were in the factory."

"Say what, girl?"

"My brothers. They were in the factory."

"Can't have been. We made sure no one were about. What would they have been doing in there?"

"Shuttleworth took them from the orphanage earlier. He picked them out special and took 'em in his carriage, so now they've burned with him in that factory." She broke down in tears again.

"Nelly!" shouted a new voice, rising up the hill—one of

Maud's women, thunder on her face. "We best get going. We've dallied too long."

Maud—Nelly?—turned to the new woman. "Aye, in a moment. You lot need to vanish. Go on, all of you."

"You can't hang about. If they catch themselves Nelly Ludd, they'll go hard on you."

"I'll be all right. I can look after myself, can't I? Now get on with you."

The woman clenched her jaw, but walked away without further argument.

Anna picked through what she'd heard. "Nelly...Ludd? *You're* Nelly Ludd? What's been attacking all the factories hereabouts? But you work in ours!"

"Aye, girl. So as I could keep an eye on that toad Shuttleworth. So as I'd know when he wasn't about and we could burn his factory without burning him. I ain't becoming a murderer on his account."

It took a moment for Nelly's words to sink in. "Sir John... wasn't there?"

"No, girl. Nor was your boys. We knew Shuttleworth was coming back, so we waited till he left again."

Relief washed through Anna. *They're ok, they're ok, they're not dead, they're ok.*

"Where are they, then?" she asked, looking up from the damp grass. "Has he taken them to his mines?"

"Shuttleworth ain't got no mines, girl. Where'd you hear that?"

"But—why else take them? Where could they be?"

"Damned if I know. But they ain't here."

"You've got to help me find them!"

Nelly barked a single laugh. "I've got to get away from here is all I've got to do. I've got my own worries, girl."

Anna stood. "No. No, you will help me. 'Cos I know it was you now, what's been burning the factories."

Nelly's face darkened. "You threatening me, girl?"

"What you gonna do? You wouldn't burn Sir John for all he's

done, but you'd hurt me? Kill me? No, I don't reckon that's your way. I reckon you'll help me. Because whatever he's got planned with my brothers, stopping it would hurt his cause, and you'll do it for that, if not for my boys."

Nelly stared for a long moment, and then her broad face cracked a wicked grin. "I like you, girl. You got fight. Come on, then."

"Where we going?"

"To Gawthorpe Hall. To Shuttleworth's home."

Habergham Drive was a tunnel through trees made bare by winter. The full moon slipped through the naked branches and littered the path with fractured shapes.

Anna and Nelly had walked in silence since turning away from the burning factory.

Nelly said, "Girl, say what's bothering you."

"Why did you burn the factory?"

"To stop Shuttleworth. To show him he can't have it all his own way."

"Like what?"

"Like chilling the factory floor so we work faster. Like us suffering the poisoning from Parkes' bloody lead alloy. Like paying us in pennies and promises of an empire we've got no interest in."

"Like you, then."

"Careful how you speak, girl. I ain't like him."

"No? Burning that factory down to get back at Sir John? There's people on that floor need those wages to eat, for their kids to eat, but you've made the decision for 'em. You've dragged them into your fight whether they wanted it or not."

"I'm being brave for them. They'd never stand up otherwise."

"I expect Sir John'd say the same about his empire, if you asked him. He's being strong for 'em, showing them how to stand up tall so as they can build something magnificent."

"Tell me, girl, how does your Squalor work? Yours, mine, everyone's?"

200

Anna's indignation stumbled at the swerve in the conversation. "Well...necessity. Deprivation, I suppose. Squalor gives you just enough of what you need most, and you've got to really need it."

"Exactly. Anyone could use Squalor, even all the toffs. But you ain't got that necessity if you're comfortable. So you think Shuttleworth and his kind'll ever let us share in their wealth? No. They need us poor to build this empire. Their machines'd stop dead if we ever had it good enough. The rich'll get richer and the poor'll stay poor and they'll keep us in our place so as they can keep exploiting us."

"And you don't exploit people? You use them as tools to try and change the world in a way you reckon is best, thinking you know better. There's ways of changing the world without ruining lives like you have tonight."

"I ain't the one who's stolen your brothers," said Nelly, quiet with rage.

"No, I suppose you ain't at that. You're the one helping me get 'em back. But even then, you're doing that to get at Sir John, not out of charity. You and everyone else in this world, you're all so selfish now."

Nelly didn't seem angry at that. If anything, she looked sorrowful. "Aye, girl, the world's a selfish place now. Time was people cared for others. We didn't only have Squalor to save us then. We had Sympathy too." Nelly looked askance at Anna, an odd expression in her eyes, but she put a finger to her lips before Anna could ask more. She stepped behind an ash tree at the edge of the wood and motioned for Anna to join her. "We're there."

Gawthorpe Hall was imposing in the night, a looming black shadow detailed in silver moonlight. The gravel drive was flanked by open lawns and ornamental gardens. Two coaches stood by the stables, one large and ornate, the other simpler but detailed in gold. Shuttleworth's coach.

Men in red jackets and towering bearskin hats stood at the entrance, watching the approach.

"What are they doing here?" muttered Nelly.

"Who? Those soldiers?"

"Soldiers? Girl, they're the Queen's Guard."

"Shouldn't they be with the Queen, then?"

"Aye, girl, they should. But the Mourning Queen hasn't left London for four years now. Not since Prince Albert died."

"How we going to get past them?"

"We ain't. Let's try round the back." Nelly moved off through the trees, keeping an eye on the Queen's Guard and warning Anna into stillness whenever a mounted patrol moved round the garden.

A handful of Douglas firs lined the side of the River Calder behind Gawthorpe Hall, enough of them to hide Anna and Nelly as they crept round. A painted wooden door stood at one corner of the hall, a warm light spilling from the kitchen window next to it.

"You're faster than I am, girl. See if you can work that door open."

Anna hunched low and ran across the lawn, a tingling fear at the base of her neck as she crossed the open space, praying against any guards rounding the corner. She grabbed at the black iron handle but it held firm and wouldn't turn—locked. She tried again, heaving her shoulder against the door, but it remained stubbornly solid. The crawling fear was growing stronger, pressing in, and with a curse Anna turned and ran back to the safety of the treeline.

"No good," she said, panting clouds of breath in the cold air. "There's got to be another way in."

"Hold this," said Nelly, taking off her winter coat and passing it over.

"What you doing?" asked Anna.

"This hall's been here more than two hundred and fifty years. Penny to a shilling there's still a privy that drains into the river. If I can find the grate and work it loose, you might be small enough to make your way in." Nelly finished taking her boots off and dropped into the river before Anna could question it further.

Anna was near frozen after a few minutes standing there. A frost was already settling under the clear, starry sky, and the wind bit through to her skin. *I don't know how Nelly's managing in that water. I can bare feel my toes just stood here.* The exhaustion was catching up. She'd worked a full shift that day, and Squalor came at a price, drained something out of you. Two guards passed by on horseback, and Anna ducked down behind the trees. Crouched there, tucked away from the wind, Anna's eyes and limbs grew heavy.

The sudden splash of Nelly heaving herself onto the riverbank shocked Anna back awake. "Help me out, girl," said Nelly, teeth chattering.

Anna grabbed Nelly's outstretched hand and hauled her up onto the grass. Anna put the winter coat around her, but it didn't seem to help stave off the chill.

"Found...the grate," said Nelly, coughing and shaking, "but...couldn't open it...lead, not iron, so...not rusted." Nelly pulled the coat tighter around her, but she still convulsed with shivers. "Stayed in...too long. Had to try though..."

"Nelly, you're gonna freeze to death! You need to warm yourself!"

"Too cold to...focus...my Squalor." Her coughs were already weaker, rasping in her throat.

Oh Christ, she's going to die on my account, that wind's cutting through me and I ain't soaked through with river water. I can't imagine how cold she must be, in her guts and in her bones. Anna wrapped her arms around Nelly and tried to warm her, tried to give over some of the heat that was churning in her own chest, but the wind and rain stole away what little she had to give. She looked around, desperate, and her eyes caught on the kitchen window and the door next to it.

Anna heaved Nelly up, an arm around her waist and Nelly's arm over her shoulders, and all but dragged the big woman to the door. She pulled hard at the handle but it was as firm as before, even with Nelly lending what strength she could.

Oh Lord, that's it then! The chill'll get in her bones and she'll die out here, stuck the wrong side of a door from the stove that'd save her. She only needs to get through this door and get in! And as Anna felt the cold that she knew Nelly was feeling, felt it inside her, a new warmth flared out of her bones and through her fingers and the door gave way—

—and they stumbled into the kitchen, trying to catch their balance. Heat washed over them as Nelly slumped against the stove and Anna shut the door against the bitter winter.

"How…how did you do that…girl?"

Anna's mouth opened and closed, but she had no answer.

"Doesn't…matter. Find your brothers." Nelly's voice was settling, the shivering lessening. "Go!"

Anna nodded and went to the kitchen door, cracking it open so she could peer through to the hallway beyond.

Tall canvases lined one side of the hall. Dark figures looked down from centuries past, repainted as ghosts by moonlight through the full-height windows. Warm light leaked from a door at the other end of the long gallery, but the hallway itself was empty. It seemed all the guards were outside.

Anna scurried down the hall, but as she passed through the bright shafts of moonlight, two Queen's Guard on horseback turned the corner outside the house, clearly visible through the leaded windows.

She ducked inside the door at the end, heart pounding, eyes closed, throat clenched. As the seconds passed with no sound of alarum, she slid to the floor and breathed again.

The rushing in her ears subsided, and she opened her eyes.

Sir John was in the room, crouching over something in the flickering candlelight.

Panic and bile rose up her throat, and Anna cast about for somewhere, anywhere to hide. A plush sofa sat in the corner nearest her, and she scrambled toward it.

As soon as she crouched behind the sofa she peered back round it. A few candles struggled against the darkness, barely illuminating the rich hangings and thick carpets. An enormous chandelier glinted in the half-light above where Sir John crouched with his back to her, busying himself with a wide metal bowl. It must have been five foot across, and made of lead alloy to judge by its dull reflection. A bundle of cables trailed off behind an ornate modesty screen.

The door opened wide, and Anna pulled herself back into the corner.

"Ah," came Sir John's voice, "Your Majesty."

Queen Victoria stepped into the room, yards from where Anna hid. She crossed the drawing room and sat in a large high-backed chair before the bowl, projecting authority, expectation, and not a little impatience.

"Well then, Sir John, let us be on with it."

"Of course, Your Majesty, a moment's more preparation," said Sir John with a bow. He moved smoothly from the bowl to the modesty screen, careful not to show his back to the Queen.

Anna moved to the other end of the sofa and tried to see where he went, but it was too dark behind the screen to see what he was up to.

She heard a whimper from behind it, though. A whimper she knew.

Boys!

A deep thrumming sound swelled up from the large lead bowl, and a cold light cast new shadows across the drawing room, stealing the darkness Anna had been about to move through. *If he's hurt them behind there...*

The shining figure of a gentleman stood over the lead bowl, floating inches above it, as if on a step. He wavered, like a mirror underwater, and there was a leaden sheen to him. He was staring at Anna with a stern, unblinking expression.

The Mourning Queen stood and reached out one gloved hand to him.

Sir John stepped back into the room from behind the screen. "Prince Albert returned to you, Your Majesty. As promised."

He's calling the dead back! How in the Devil's name is he doing that? Oh, this ain't no good thing. It can't be. I've got to get the boys out of here!

Anna watched Prince Albert, waiting for him to look away, but he remained completely still.

Completely.

Queen Victoria stared at Prince Albert, and Sir John at Queen Victoria.

Cautiously, Anna slipped out from behind the sofa and along the wall. The shining image of Prince Albert pivoted to follow her, unmoving and static, but always facing her. *He ain't real!*

Sneaking with absolute care, Anna passed inches behind Sir John's back, in full view of the Queen and saved only by Her Majesty's fixation on the shining apparition. Anna kept her eyes on Sir John, ready to run at the first sign of him turning, until she was behind the screen and stepping over the bundled cables.

Charlie. Daniel. Jacob.

Her brothers were sat on plain wooden chairs, wide-eyed and terrified. All three held a pair of lead handles, like the ones on Anna's loom, cable trailing from the bottom and into the room.

Anna rushed to Jacob, youngest of the three and nearest her, and hugged his face to her neck. He felt cold—not winter cold, but deathly cold.

"Oh Jacob, what's going on?" she whispered beneath the resonant thrum of the machine.

Jacob pulled his head away and stared over her shoulder, face taut with fear. Anna followed his gaze to a canvas of Prince Albert that hung on the screen. The image was the spit of the apparition in the bowl.

Charlie, the eldest, sat in the center, and met Anna's gaze as she turned back.

"Charlie! What is this?" she hissed.

"Anna, get out of here!" he whispered in reply. "You can't risk getting caught!"

"I'm not going anywhere till I know what's going on."

"We have to bring Prince Albert back! Sir John told us of the Prussians and their invasion, how we need Prince Albert to stop them rampaging about with their filthy coal machines!"

"Rampaging Prussians? What nonsense is this? Look, there ain't no way of bringing the dead back. That ain't Prince Albert out there, it's only an image!"

206

"Please, Anna, we have to do this!"

Anna looked at Charlie—really looked—and across at Daniel and Jacob. They were terrified. Desperate for salvation—salvation they needed from Prince Albert. That desperation was driving their Squalor and creating the image.

She had to get them out of here. But how could she do it without Shuttleworth knowing? If the image of Albert disappeared, he'd know something was up and catch them before they got away.

I'd take their place if I could, but I ain't frightened enough for Shuttleworth's machine. Oh, if only I could be as scared as them! Think, Anna, think. You've got to feel their terror like you felt Nelly's cold, like you felt Sally's pain, like—

—oh good Lord, that's it. That's how I've been doing it. It ain't just what I need. It's what anyone *needs, if I feel it strong enough.*

Not just Squalor. Sympathy.

"Give me these," she said, taking the lead handles from Charlie's hands. "Get your brothers and get out. Go to the kitchen. There's a woman there called Nelly, she'll help."

"What are you going to do?" whispered Charlie.

"I'll bring Albert back, don't you worry. Now go!"

As Charlie went to his brothers, Anna gripped the handles tight. *They're so young. They're so scared. Terrified of the Prussians, and only Albert can help. Albert. Albert.* Her stomach lurched with a hot fear. The lead handles were cold in her hands, a cold that spiked up her forearms like ice needles in her veins. Charlie was talking to Daniel and Jacob, and the cold surged as they released each handle. Her arms were numb now, and the ice was stabbing at her chest, roiling against the heat in her stomach. The light in the room began to dim.

The boys had all stopped to watch her. She turned to them with gritted teeth. "Go!"

The cold ebbed as her concentration broke. *Stupid! Think of their fear, think of their fear, think of their—*

"What is going on?" hissed a new voice.

Sir John stood on the other side of Anna, his eyes filled with anger.

All the fear and terror and uncertainty in Anna, hers and the boys' both, coalesced into a white-hot rage.

"You tell me, Shuttleworth. Scaring young boys like this? Terrifying them? No. You'll not do it to them. I'll do it for 'em."

Shuttleworth's face was dark and clenched, quivering with anger. "Fine. Do it, and drain yourself. Divided among three, they would have had the strength to survive, but you will lose your life in this, *fool*. And see if I care."

Another voice broke in. "One is alarmed at the mention of the loss of life."

Shuttleworth almost jumped out of his skin as Queen Victoria spoke from behind him. Anna's brothers stepped back into the modesty screen, knocking it over.

"Your Majesty," said Shuttleworth, "my most abject apologies. Merely technical difficulties and nothing to be concerned with." Sir John all but scraped the floor in his obsequiousness.

"On the contrary, the welfare of my subjects is of the utmost concern to me. What precisely is the arrangement here?"

"Ah...well, the lead alloy handles are a conduit for the emotions and energies of the—"

"One presumes you are about to lecture on Squalor. I assure you, Sir, I am aware of how my country prospers. My confusion pertains to the presence of these children and the apparent threat to their lives."

"My apologies, Your Majesty. The apparatus concentrates a desire for the Prince Consort, in this instance produced through fear, hence the requirement for such young...volunteers. The girl, however, is an intrusion shortly to be removed."

"Fear? Why would anyone be afraid of my Albert?"

"The children were told of a threatened Prussian invasion, Your Majesty, that only Prince Albert could stop."

"What utter nonsense!" Queen Victoria looked at the boys, at Anna holding the lead handles, and finally at Shuttleworth with imperious disdain. "No, this will not do. I will not stand by while one of my subjects sacrifices herself to save others. It is a Queen's duty to protect her citizens, and it is my place to make the sacrifice. I thank you, young lady, for reminding me of it. If you would be so kind?"

The Mourning Queen gestured. It took Anna a moment to realize she wanted the lead handles; she passed them over in a stunned silence, cables trailing.

The Queen spoke as she took hold of them. "A desire for the Prince Consort, you say? Who could have a stronger desire for Albert than I?"

"Your Majesty," Shuttleworth panicked, "please, no!"

But his voice was lost beneath a sudden swell of noise from the bowl, an enormous hum that Anna felt in her ribcage, and the image of Prince Albert bloomed anew above the bowl: a thousand times more brilliant than before, and moving now, turning to face the Queen and look upon her, and despite the piercing blue light of that figure, Anna could see, quite clearly, the smile upon his face.

The Queen returned the smile, eyes shining with delight, and then collapsed to the floor, dead.

Dawn's light stained Gawthorpe Hall with shades of pink and peach, and the frosted lawn twinkled copper and silver beneath Anna's feet.

"You realize what you are then, girl?" asked Nelly.

"I figured it out in there. What you said earlier about Sympathy. Squalor's a selfish thing, but Sympathy, caring for other people ...why me, though? Why now?"

"You care about other folk, girl. You're selfless in a way most have forgotten. And you're of an age now where you're not just thinking of yourself. Children are all wrapped up in themselves, but you've grown up. You think of them around you. I wondered if it was you as fixed Sally White's fingers yesterday. Reckon it was."

The Queen's Guard marched Shuttleworth out of his own front door in shackles and threw him into a coach. Queen Victoria was borne behind him on the shoulders of her guardsmen, held high on a stretcher, lead handles still gripped in her hands.

"What'll happen to him?" asked Anna. Daniel and Jacob

hugged her from each side, and Charlie stood close by her shoulder.

"For regicide? They'll strip him of his title and hang him."

"I didn't want him to die. In his own way he was trying to do the best for people."

"If he thought he was what was best for folk, we're better off without him."

They fell silent as the carriages rolled past, gravel crunching in the crisp winter air.

"Come on then, girl," said Nelly once the carriages had passed into the freezing mist that clung to Habergham Drive. "We can use you in the movement. A Sympathy witch looks good for us."

"No."

"No? Don't you want to help?"

"Aye, I do. But I want to do it my way, Nelly Ludd. You ain't what's best for folk neither. You can follow me if you want, and Lord knows you'd make a powerful difference, but I'm changing the world my way. We can make the world a better place without having to make it worse first."

Anna squeezed her brothers close in the chill morning air. "Come on then, boys, best get you home. Mrs. Hobble'll have fretted herself half to death by now, worrying about us all."

Daniel looked up from her side. "Haven't you got to change the world, though?"

She smiled. "I have, aye. But I reckon I've got to get you lot to bed first. Now go on with you!"

She walked down the drive with her brothers beside her.

A moment later, Nelly Ludd followed.

Dinosaur Dreams in Infinite Measure

written by

Rachael K. Jones

illustrated by

PRESTON STONE

ABOUT THE AUTHOR

Rachael K. Jones grew up in various cities across Europe and North America, where she picked up (and mostly forgot) six languages along with and an addiction to running. Now she lives in Athens, Georgia with her husband. She is a writer, an editor, a podcaster, and a secret android.

Rachael has been a voracious consumer of the written word since elementary school, when after she'd read all the books in the classroom library, a teacher gave her the dictionary to keep her occupied. She went on to get a degree in English, but didn't do much with it until National Novel Writing Month got her back into creative writing years later.

These days she is pursuing a master's degree in Speech-Language Pathology at the University of Georgia, which combines her love of linguistics, science, literacy, and communication. In her free time, she writes stories about her favorite things: dinosaurs, friendship, feminism, and upwardly mobile brains in jars.

ABOUT THE ILLUSTRATOR

Preston Stone was born and raised in Loveland, Colorado. In preschool he began making images of superheroes and monsters with markers. From there, he expanded the subject matter to include studies of various wildlife, eventually developing a fondness for drawing insects. There was even a time when it seemed he might pursue entomology as a career. Instead, he stayed on the art path, realizing that he simply had an aesthetic appreciation for what most people viewed as ugly or creepy.

High school brought with it the discovery of new art and entertainment. Anime and tabletop fantasy role-playing games occupied much of his time, and he began to emulate the themes and styles found in their art.

He continued his education at Aims Community College where he earned certificates in game design and animation. In 2013, he earned a Bachelor of Art and Design, with an art emphasis and drawing concentration from the University of Northern Colorado.

He's currently working as a freelance artist in fantasy and science fiction, and he hopes to one day have his illustration work on the covers of books and his creature and character concept work used in video games and movies.

He credits any success to the support he received from his parents, who provided the tools, the studio, the artistic foundation, and an attitude of complete acceptance toward his decision to choose a career as an artist.

Dinosaur Dreams in Infinite Measure

Mom had hands like dinosaur bones: fragile at a glance, but old and strong, hardened by time and pressure. Fossils endure. My mother had endured 80 years already, through disease and bereavement, through a long career ended in humiliation and disgrace, and now this final insult: her own daughter demanding she leave it all behind, the house and farm and everything in it.

"I've worked hard for this house. I worked for everything I ever had." Her voice was a tight, tense warble. Fossil-hard fingers bent around a mug painted with a cowgirl on a lavender T-rex, lasso roping round the handle.

It wasn't just the house, not really. Primrose Farms Poultry had forced her from her life's work as an industrial engineer, and thanks to an intellectual property clause, Mom hadn't even kept the rights to her own inventions.

"No one's trying to take away your stuff," I told her gently. "We're just worried about you, alone out here and with the animals, and the house like this." The farm was expensive, too. The upkeep outstripped its worth.

"I can take care of it myself. I'll clean it up. I just need time."

The kitchen looked shabbier than usual. A stack of textbooks took up most of the table: engineering, animal anatomy, evolutionary biology, paleontology. The top one read *Principles of Gene Manipulation*. The house had accumulated snowdrifts of clutter over the years. A baby gate held back a tidal wave of dirty clothes from the laundry room. Usually a pink stuffed bunny sat crammed against the bars. Uncle Louis called it *The Convict,* but it had gone missing today. I plucked a folded sheet of heavy orange construction paper from the table, the creases grayed with age. One of my childhood paintings, a long, skinny purple splotch labeled BRONTOSAURUS in neat adult block letters.

"See, stuff like this is the problem. You need to let go of this sentimental crap."

She swiped the drawing from me and tucked it into the genetics book's cover. "That's not yours anymore." Her tone was bitter, like pith.

"Brontosaurus isn't even a real dinosaur, you know," I said. I meant it as a joke, but her mouth sagged into a frown, creases wrought by years of disappointment standing out like canyons.

"You have no idea what I know and don't know, Liza," she snapped. "Truth is, you never did."

It stung. In my childhood, Mom had wanted me to follow her footsteps into science. She'd been bitterly disappointed when I became a music teacher instead. I don't think she ever forgave my rejection of something so important to her. But even still.

"That may well be true. But the real estate agent's coming next week."

I finished my drink and showed myself to the door, letting the screen bang shut behind me. My head felt hot and heavy, like superheated tar. I decided to take a stroll, clear my thoughts before heading home. Best to see what shape the property was in, anyway.

In the chicken yard, some hideous demon-birds about the size of a golden retriever clustered around a dead rooster, tearing wet strips from the bones with sharp little teeth. Wicked black talons tipped their stubby, arm-like wings. My stomach lurched. One demon-bird snapped its head up and peered at me sideways, its pupil a vertical slit, like a rattlesnake's. Those black, fingerlike claws unsettled me. Something wasn't right.

I followed the gravel path toward the barn where Mom kept a few horses. A wheelbarrow sat beside the door, piled with an odd tangle of papers, pickle jars, a bucket of bright plastic dinosaur toys, and the large pink bunny that used to live squished against the baby gate. I leafed through the papers. Blue

214

pencil sketches on grid paper—machinery of some sort, stamped with the Primrose Farms logo.

A cow lowed in the field outside the barn, and something answered it in a rising tone, like a question. Beneath a pecan tree, an animal reared on its hind legs to grab and shake the lowest branch, eleven feet up.

It had a long, iguana-like body and thick, heavy legs like an elephant's. A double row of spade-shaped plates ran from head to mid-back, where they changed into giant spikes all the way down its long tail. Another spike jutted backward from each shoulder. On all fours, it was about my height, close in size to a cow, but much longer. It snapped a branch off the pecan tree and ground it to a pulp in its powerful jaws.

An electric thrill shot down my spine. Every hair on my body stood on end, as if I'd plunged into ice water. I flung open the barn doors. Inside was chaos. Leathery lizard heads and spiked tails and horns and wicked claws stomped around inside the stalls. Next to the door, something like the demon-bird, but taller than me, was roped by the neck to a brass ring. It hissed and strained forward. I stumbled into the warm dimness and fumbled for the light switch.

In the room's center stood a machine, something like a huge metal cube, taller than a refrigerator. A cone-shaped flange big enough for a car to drive through faced me, a holding tank with a chute attached to one side.

"Close the door, or you'll let the raptors out," said my mom from behind me.

"The...*what*? Mom, what *is* all of this?"

Mom rolled the wheelbarrow up to the machine. "It's a dinosaur engine," she said.

"A what?" I followed her, because the raptor by the door kept trying to nip my shirt.

"It makes dinosaurs. I invented it." She opened the hatch covering the big chute and tossed in the giant pink bunny.

It didn't make any sense. "This is crazy."

"Grab that stool over there. You can remove the staples." She

215

jerked her chin toward the wall. A three-legged wooden stool hung among the riding gear and grooming brushes. I lifted it down and settled by the wheelbarrow. Mom passed me a little staple remover. It looked like a T-rex mouth. Chomp, chomp.

"So," Mom said, "I'm not supposed to talk about any of this because of my non-disclosure agreement, but screw it. They ousted me, so they get what they get. Everyone's going to find out soon enough, so my daughter might as well hear it first. You want to know the secret behind Primrose cornering the organic chicken market?" She tapped the metal cube, and it rang. "This baby. Or at least, they have the prototype. This is the real deal. I tooled theirs to extrude chickens. When you feed in the right ingredients and calibrate it right, it'll generate chickens until you turn it off or it runs out of material. They extrude chickens right onto the production line and slaughter them the moment they pop out. They keep a small flock of dummy chickens out in a sunny field somewhere for the inspectors, while this thing cranks out all the meat you need. Poof. Organic meat at a fraction of the cost."

I wouldn't have believed her, if not for all the dinosaurs in the barn. "So those, um, chickens in the yard...they're not chickens," I said.

Mom shook her head. She unscrewed a pickle jar and tossed in the whole thing, minus the lid. "They're called Mahakalas. Small raptors, basically. One of my first successes. After all, what's a chicken, if not a newfangled dinosaur?" She chuckled under her breath. "Primrose doesn't know crap about my invention. That's what they get for giving me the boot. But the dinosaurs are mine. My life's work."

As I removed the staples and passed Mom the papers, she chucked them into the chute. "Just how long has this been going on?"

"A while." Mom paused, considered it. "A *long* while. Decades. It's taken me some time to figure the prototypes out, to reconstruct them from the clues I could find. I had to guess for some of them. They're not perfect, but they're here. And I'm working up to bigger ones. That's why I need the space, Liza. Don't you see? I can't move yet. I need more time."

In the dim, sepia glow of dangling light bulbs, her face took on a lean, hungry look I hadn't seen since my youth. It scared me. I'd never seen her *want* something so much. There was pain in that look. Maybe, for some people, the worst thing that could happen might be something that never happened at all.

"Mom. *Mom.*" My voice broke. She paused her frenetic activity and really considered me. "Mom, where is all this going? You make a lot of dinosaurs, and then what?"

She held my gaze with eyes that were also mine. "That's it. There is nothing else. It's enough to have brought them into existence. As many as I can, before they make me stop." I gaped at her. I had no response for that. But she cracked a gentle grin, and added, "Do you want to see how it works?"

The responsible part of me—the part that held down a job, and called on Mother's Day, and paid the Internet bill once a month—told me to call Uncle Louis immediately. And the police. And maybe Mom's doctor. But the part of me that really had liked that Brontosaurus drawing and her tacky dinosaur mug, and wondered what it would be like to ride the Tyrant Lizard into the sunset—that part had to know. "Okay. Show me."

Mom pushed a power button that booted up an LCD in the dinosaur engine's control panel. "Load the rest of that stuff into the chute. Try to sort out the metal, though. It mucks up the Raccoon."

"What raccoon?"

"The decompositer. I call it 'the Raccoon' because it eats garbage."

I tossed the junk from the wheelbarrow into the chute. It reeked of pickle juice. The plastic dinosaurs bounced and slid through the brine into the chamber below. Mom pressed a button, and the tank roared to life, churning like a garbage disposal, grinding everything to a pulp.

"It's separating the compounds now," Mom yelled over the roar. "What should we make?" She turned the screen toward me. It displayed a list of dinosaur names, most of them unfamiliar.

217

"Where's the Stegosaurus?" I asked. "I saw one out in the yard."

Mom shook her head. "Kentrosaurus. Same family, different animal. Like dogs and dingoes. I haven't tried a Stegosaurus yet. Here, we'll do another Mahakala. They're easy." She tapped out something and hit enter. Now the whole engine roared to life, and together with the Raccoon, it was deafening. Mom lifted down a pole with a loop attached to one end and crouched near the great black flange that faced the barn door. She motioned for me to stand clear.

The dinosaur engine kicked into a frenzy, and then suddenly cut off. Something chickenish catapulted from the dark hole with a loud lizardy shriek, flapping its arm-like wings before it hit the floor. Mom quickly lassoed the Mahakala's neck and tightened the noose so she now controlled it at pole's length. She offered me the stick. "Take it out to the chicken coop, will you?"

I obeyed, trotting down the road with a tiny raptor scurrying ahead of me, screaming its panic until I released it into the yard with the others. Back outside the barn, the Stegosaurus— *Kentrosaurus,* I corrected myself—lazed in the sun with two unconcerned cows.

"So, that's how it works," Mom said when I returned. She leaned against her invention, a woman in her element. "Any questions?"

It was so impossible. It was marvelous. Something long-dormant inside me re-awoke, the part that believed in infinite wonder. "Can we do another?" I asked, a little shyly. "Do you have a T-rex in there?"

Mom scrolled through the list. A black and white T-rex skeleton loaded on screen. "The only trouble is feeding in enough material for the decompositer. I'm limited by what the tank can hold. This guy is big, though." She rubbed her chin. "Maybe, *maybe* we could pull it off, if we keep feeding the engine while it's extruding. It'll take hours, anyway. You'll help?"

"What do you want me to do?"

Mom toed the wheelbarrow. "Fill this up with whatever you can find. Remember, not too much metal. Then load it in. I'll get the program going."

Once the dinosaur engine roared on, Mom and I hurried back to the house. She threw open the sliding glass doors on the porch so we could roll the wheelbarrow right into the living room, then we raided the clutter. Mom grabbed anything she could reach: old plastic high school trophies, Halloween costumes, brand-new bed sheets in their packaging, dog toys, potpourri sachets, mittens. I followed her lead. When we had a full load, we rolled it back to the barn and loaded the chute. The tank had already drained 10% according to the gauge, so we went back for more.

I felt astonished when Mom threw it all in without comment or complaint. All the irretrievable memories, fed into the dinosaur engine in hope of extruding something terrible, something beautiful.

Something *awesome*.

On our fifth trip back from the house, the dinosaur began to emerge snout-first, those wicked teeth slicked with saliva. Mosaic scales covered its snout, giving way to feathers behind the brows. Those deep black eyes, bestial, alive, flickered around the room as it struggled and tossed for a body still materializing in the engine's bowels.

"We'd better get a rope in its jaw while we still have the chance," my mom said after we made another trip. She wiped sweat and dust from her cheeks and squatted down for a breather. "I think we'll put it in the south pasture. Plenty of space, electric fencing, cows to eat."

"Mom!"

"Well, it's true." She fixed me with a glare almost as reproachful as the T-rex's. "It needs to eat something. If we let it go hungry, it'll be dangerous."

I realized at that point I should have called Uncle Louis and the police hours ago, but it was too late now. I wanted to see the T-rex roam free. "Where do you keep the rope?"

It turned out that anything that big and wild isn't so easy for two people to wrangle. Fortunately, the T-rex was a little dazed when it flopped, newborn and trembling, upon the floor.

PRESTON STONE

I brought my pickup around and attached the leads to the trailer hitch. In the meantime, the King of Lizards helped herself to a couple of Mom's larger raptors in the barn, but we didn't mind. They were easy enough to extrude. Using the truck, we led the beast by her jaw up to the south pasture and let her free.

I don't know how to describe the feeling, watching her stand and run on those huge, thick legs that shook the earth, her banded black-and-tan feathers like sunlight flooding through cage bars. I knew, though, that I couldn't betray Mom now. I would have to see this through to the end.

Like most kids, at one point in my childhood, I wanted to be a paleontologist. I was over the moon when, for my eleventh birthday, my family made the nine-hour drive to Washington, D.C. to visit the Smithsonian Museum of Natural History.

"Dinosaurs! That way!" Mom grabbed my hand and hauled me forward, but stopped short. I rammed into her legs. "Oh, no." A temporary carpet-board wall blocked off the exhibit's central room: *Under Renovation: Coming in the Fall.*

"You mean we can't see any dinosaurs at all?" I worried at my lower lip with sharp incisors.

She paged through the brochure. "Well, they've got some paleontologists doing restoration work on a Tyrannosaurus skull a little further down. How about we take a look?"

"Okay. I guess. If we have to."

Down the hallway, the fake wall opened into a grating like malls use when they're closing for the night. Behind it, four people in jeans tapped at computers and completely ignored us. On the closest workbench lay the Tyrannosaurus skull. I'd never seen a skull so big. I held my arm against the grate and compared it to those teeth. I tried to picture what the skull would look like with skin on, how the teeth would gleam when slicked with saliva. I ran my tongue over my canines and bit down just until my tongue hurt. Those fangs must have eaten things when the dinosaur was alive. It had gotten so big. How long did it take a T-rex to grow up? I wondered.

"What do you think, Liza? Do you want to work there someday?" My mom flicked on the camera.

Around me, other kids and their parents piled in, watching the scientists raptly. I didn't get it. They weren't doing anything particularly interesting. They weren't tinking at bones with chisels. They weren't wearing lab coats, or even khakis like a paleontologist should. It wasn't what I'd pictured when I said I wanted to study dinosaurs. There, in the presence of the Tyrannosaurus skull, while everyone gaped at the scientists as if they were bears in a zoo, I felt that dream fade away, leaving a little numb spot. Mom snapped the shutter, and the flash flared. One scientist shot her a dirty look.

I shrugged and studied my shoelaces. "I dunno. It's okay, I guess. Let's go see the mummies now."

I started down the hall, but Mom didn't follow. She lingered, fingers interlaced in the grating, gazing at the scientists, her face contorted in a hungry, spare expression as if she were seeing something ephemeral, something she'd never set eyes on again.

"Mo-om!" I yelled. "Come *on*."

She turned, and for a second it was as if she didn't see me. "Oh," she said. "I'm going to pop into the restroom. I'll meet you at the mummies."

Later, when she found me, Mom pressed a gift shop bag into my hand. "So you can remember seeing a dinosaur the first time," she said. I unwrapped the heavy thing inside. It was a mug with a cowgirl riding a lavender T-rex.

I called Uncle Louis and made excuses to delay the real estate agent. "I don't know how we're going to sell the place, with all her garbage in there," he said, but I told him not to worry.

Mom was spinning garbage into gold.

Together we made a list. Mom worked tirelessly on her computer with the genetics books fanned around her in concentric circles, while I hauled material from the house to feed the Raccoon. In went Mom's porcelain place setting for twelve, the one patterned in blue cornflowers. Out came a dun-colored Allosaurus and two Triceratops. In went my high school yearbooks. Out came a Dimetrodon and a peacock-tailed Archaeopteryx. My baby clothes got us Pachycephalosaurus. Her wedding portrait in its heavy oak frame gave us a flock of quick-footed Compsognathus specimens. By the end of the week, the floor was cleared in every room of the house. When it got too dark to work in the barn, I vacuumed and dusted the empty spaces until exhaustion took me.

The farm was utter chaos. We couldn't find three of the cows anywhere. Putting the Giganotosaurus and T-rex in the same pasture turned out to be a big mistake, even after tethering them to separate trees. Once they caught wind of each other, the ropes gave out, and they got territorial. I could hear their battle-roars from the shower. I toweled off in a hurry, dressed, and chased the T-rex around with my truck until Mom could rope her and lead her to a different field. It all struck me as terribly irresponsible, but there was so little time.

"What's next on the list?" Mom would say. "What's next?" That fierce determination never left her for an instant. For years, I'd considered her a fragile old lady, but now I saw that I'd misjudged her. Here was a woman at the height of her power. Her mind brimmed with dinosaurs until they spilled out into reality, and the world would never be the same because of it.

We made long-winged Pterodactyls. We made an ill-tempered, sluggish Ankylosaurus which took down a paddock with one strike of its tail. Dinosaur dung lay everywhere. Some hunted each other. Some mated. The Mahakalas ushered little reptilian hatchlings around the chicken yard. Mom made enormous omelets with runny whites and yolks the size of my palm, and served them with a side of Iguanodon bacon.

"What's next?" she asked while the engine rested from a round of Protoceratops extrusion.

"I don't think the dinosaur engine is big enough for a sauropod," I said. "It might break the machine. I think we might be done."

Mom grabbed the notebook and trailed a finger down the list, each name checkmarked and dated. The house was nearly clean now. All the furniture vacuumed, all the closets tidied. "No, we're not done yet. We haven't made you a Brontosaurus."

I snorted, but she looked dead serious. "You know that's not a real thing. They never existed, Mom. They were a mistake. It was just an Apatosaurus with the wrong skull."

She smiled a secret smile, a wicked one, the grin of a woman who won't hear *no*, because she could make her own *yes*. "They'll exist now."

But sauropods were big. *Big*. They made the other dinosaurs look like a child's action figures. "The Raccoon's going to need a lot of stuff."

"Well, you'd better get moving, then," she said, pulling up schema on her computer.

"No, Mom," I said, trying again. "You don't understand. It's going to take *everything*. We'd have to empty your whole place— furniture, mattresses, fridge, clothes—*everything*. Heck, we'll probably need curtains and carpet, and everything in the tool shed for that matter."

She tossed the notebook into the chute. "Pack me a suitcase."

I finally understood. She'd known. She'd known about the finances—why wouldn't she? Mom was brilliant, competent— I'd underestimated her. She hadn't needed me or Uncle Louis policing her decisions, telling her what she'd already known years ago. She'd planned this so that she could leave on her own terms.

I'd always loved my mom for the unwavering faith she put in me. In that moment, I realized I liked her, too.

We moved the dinosaur engine to the driveway. The Brontosaurus needed room to stand as it extruded. The stars were radiant in the 4:00 AM dark. We drank coffee in silence. I'd gotten the cowgirl mug this time. She sipped from a handmade clay mug, a gift for my grandmother in her own girlhood. We tossed our cups down the chute when we finished, then we got to work, hauling and breaking furniture to feed to the Raccoon.

The Brontosaurus head emerged around sunrise. It towered

over me when it wobbled out on a shaky neck, blinking in the new sun. It opened its mouth—such huge, flat teeth!—and lowed. I stroked the ridge above its eye, and that seemed to calm it. It pressed its nose into my middle and snuffled, its hot, moist breath sucking and pulling at my clothes.

"We're going to need a lot more stuff," Mom said from the porch. With each trip to the machine, the neck got longer and thicker until the whole body was straining at the flange. The Brontosaurus lowed its distress, this time louder. The dinosaur engine shook and bounced and rattled on its wheels, and the power dimmed and flickered. It was like watching a live birth.

By noon, the Brontosaurus stood on tree-trunk front legs, and its neck extended past the chicken yard, where it chewed up the blueberry bushes with muscular jaws. By 3:00 PM, the hind legs cleared the flange. Mom hobbled the legs with rope to keep it from moving before the tail was done.

The last foot of tail finally snapped free after 7:00 PM. By then, we'd emptied the house into the Raccoon, even the bedroom doors and the carpet. One of the last things to go in was Mom's framed PhD.

"It only mattered because of the memories," Mom said when we added it to the Brontosaurus slurry. "Now we'll make new ones."

And then it was over. The dinosaur engine shuddered and switched off, and we cut the hobbling ropes. Mom and I sat arm in arm on my truck's hood and watched our creation shamble away into the field. With each slow, ponderous step, it fought gravity and won.

How did anything ever get to be so big? How can anything so big ever die?

"This is something entirely new," said Mom, her weary voice triumphant. "No one has ever seen this before, because it never existed until right this moment. There has never before been a Brontosaurus. Now there is." Wood snapped and cracked distantly as it took down all the walls and fences in its path. No holding back the dinosaurs anymore. It was out of our hands now.

My mother had done this. All these years, and I'd thought I

had her figured out. What hubris, that I'd ever called myself her daughter, having come from her body. But the dinosaurs had come from her mind.

"It's enough," I said. "It's enough to have brought them into existence. Whatever happens next."

She smiled and ruffled my hair, and she was just my mom again. "Whatever happens, kiddo."

ORDER FORM

ORDERS SHIPPED WITHIN 24 HRS. OF RECEIPT

WRITERS OF THE FUTURE

L. RON HUBBARD PRESENTS WRITERS OF THE FUTURE volumes: (paperbacks)
- ❑ Vol 22 $7.99 ❑ Vol 23 $7.99 ❑ Vol 24 $7.99 ❑ Vol 25 $7.99
- ❑ Vol 26 $7.99 ❑ Vol 27 $7.99 ❑ Vol 28 $7.99 ❑ Vol 29 $7.99
- Trade paperbacks: ❑ Vol 30 $15.95 ❑ Vol 31 $15.95 ❑ Vol 32 $15.95

L. RON HUBBARD PRESENTS WRITERS OF THE FUTURE: THE FIRST 25 YEARS
(hardcover) $44.95   _____

L. RON HUBBARD PRESENTS THE BEST OF WRITERS OF THE FUTURE
(trade paperback) $14.95   _____

OTHER SCIENCE FICTION/FANTASY BOOKS BY L. RON HUBBARD

- ❑ BATTLEFIELD EARTH trade paperback — $19.95
- ❑ BATTLEFIELD EARTH unabridged audiobook CD — $59.95
- ❑ FEAR paperback — $ 7.99
- ❑ FEAR abridged audiobook CD — $14.95
- ❑ FINAL BLACKOUT trade paperback — $11.95
- ❑ FINAL BLACKOUT abridged audiobook CD — $14.95
- MISSION EARTH trade paperback — $22.95 each
  - VOLUME: ❑ 1 ❑ 2 ❑ 3 ❑ 4 ❑ 5 ❑ 6 ❑ 7 ❑ 8 ❑ 9 ❑ 10
- MISSION EARTH abridged audiobook CD — $14.95 each
  - VOLUME: ❑ 1 ❑ 2 ❑ 3 ❑ 4 ❑ 5 ❑ 6 ❑ 7 ❑ 8 ❑ 9 ❑ 10
- ❑ TO THE STARS hardcover — $24.95
- ❑ TO THE STARS unabridged audiobook CD — $25.00

❑ **Check here for a complete catalog of L. Ron Hubbard's fiction books.**

SHIPPING RATES US: $3.00 for one book. Add an additional $1.00 per book when ordering more than one.
SHIPPING RATES CANADA: $3.00 for one book. Add an additional $2.00 per book when ordering more than one.
*Add applicable sales tax.

Tax*:   _____
Shipping: _____
TOTAL: _____

CHECK AS APPLICABLE:
- ❑ Check/Money Order enclosed. (Make payable to Galaxy Press.)
- ❑ American Express ❑ Visa ❑ MasterCard ❑ Discover

Card #:_____

Exp. Date:_____ Signature:_____

Credit Card Billing Address ZIP Code:_____

Name:_____

Address:_____

City:_____ State:_____ ZIP:_____

Phone #:_____ E-mail:_____

You can also place your order by calling toll-free: 1-877-842-5299
or order online at www.GalaxyPress.com

Select titles are also available as e-books and audio downloads at Amazon.com and other online retailers.

BUSINESS REPLY MAIL

FIRST-CLASS MAIL   PERMIT NO. 75738   LOS ANGELES CA

POSTAGE WILL BE PAID BY ADDRESSEE

GALAXY PRESS
7051 HOLLYWOOD BLVD
LOS ANGELES CA   90028-9771

**Fold at dotted line and tape shut with
payment information facing in and
Business Reply Mail facing out.**

WOTF 32

Cry Havoc

written by

Julie Frost

illustrated by

VLADA MONAKHOVA

ABOUT THE AUTHOR

Julie Frost was raised as an Army brat by parents who taught her to love reading by the age of four. She started writing in high school, but didn't pick up her keyboard seriously until she was in her 40s. Since then, she's written an eclectic mixture of short science fiction and fantasy, which has appeared in Cosmos, Unlikely Story, Plasma Frequency, Stupefying Stories, *and many other venues, and has been a finalist at the Hidden Prize for Prose. Her first novel,* Pack Dynamics, *was published by WordFire Press in 2015.*

She lives in Utah with her family, which consists of more pets than people, along with a collection of anteater figurines and Oaxacan carvings, some of which intersect. When not writing, she enjoys traveling to zoos, wildlife refuges, and National Parks to take pictures. When not traveling, she cuddles with her husband, cats, and guinea pigs and watches bad werewolf movies and good TV.

This fine story was her 29th entry to Writers of the Future, which she hopes teaches everyone the value of psychotic persistence. "Never give up, never surrender."

ABOUT THE ILLUSTRATOR

Vlada Monakhova is a freelance illustrator working in the genres of fantasy and speculative fiction. She has studied fine art at MacEwan University with a specialty in drawing and painting. She has done work for Strange Horizons, Lightspeed, *and the special issue of* Fantasy Magazine: Queers Destroy Fantasy!

Her personal aesthetic is heavily influenced by Slavic mythology and Eastern European folk art. She aims to combine decorative and elegant treatment with dramatic and often unsettling subjects, favoring powerful women and expressive characters. She is interested in costume, set, and character design.

She lives in Edmonton, Alberta, and survives through the harsh winters by reading long books.

Cry Havoc

I wanted to feel something, anything, as I gazed down at the body of my packmate on the medical examiner's table. All I could muster was a kind of numb stoicism. Katrina was the eighth, and last. A single silver bullet to the back of her head had burned her brain to a crisp and left her beautiful face a ruin. She hadn't even had the chance to see it coming.

But as a werewolf, and, moreover, her alpha, I didn't rely on facial recognition. Not only could I smell who she was, even over the stink of death, chemicals, and stainless steel in the morgue, but I knew her, down in my marrow. I'd felt her die, a lightning-stab through every nerve ending and a scorching blaze in my skull that jerked me awake screaming in the wee hours of the morning. She'd gone in for some kind of crisis at the all-night restaurant she managed—and been ambushed.

Brushing a strand of her dark-brown hair behind her ear, I swallowed and closed my eyes, nodding. "Yeah, Lou." After four meetings very like this—the last time, I'd had to identify five of my pack all at once—the medical examiner and I were on a first-name basis. "It's her."

He knew better than to touch me; the first time he'd laid a hand on my shoulder in solace, I nearly snapped it off at the elbow. Back then, immediate rage had been the overwhelming emotion.

"I'm sorry, Nate," he said.

A stray wolf had come through a couple months previous, pulling a serial killer shtick that precipitated this particular hunt.

VLADA MONAKHOVA

A local hunter had bagged the stray before I could, and then everyone else decided my pack was next. It was an excuse for them to be more bloodthirsty than they thought we were—with no season and certainly no limit. The law turned a blind eye, regarding our status as a gray area somewhere between human and not, and leaving us and the hunters to duke it out without interference. No one would face justice for her death, at least not in court.

I heaved a heavy, hopeless sigh. "Well. This'll be the last time you see me." Unless I ended up on his slab myself. But no one was left to claim my body.

On autopilot, I made my way to the Snake in My Boot, the little tavern I'd chosen for my go-to brooding nest, even during the week. A country song about lost love twanged on the jukebox, a stock car race played on the small-screen TV above the bar, and a pair of couples two-stepped on the parquet dance floor. It was a working-class place filled with working-class people, and the odors of stale beer and cheap whiskey predominated.

I ordered a double Jack Daniels, straight up, and the cocktail waitress took one look at my expression and left the bottle. I didn't know if I was drinking to remember, or forget. Either way, it wasn't working.

A hunter and several of his friends walked in, chattering and laughing. The miasma of silver wafted after him, reaching my corner table, and he stood at the bar with his elaborately stitched cowboy boot on the brass footrest. When his beer arrived, he lifted it in a toast. "The only good werewolf is a dead werewolf."

I'd heard that too many times to count, but hearing it again after IDing Katrina's body was a bit much. She'd been a soft little thing, completely harmless, with few werewolf tells. She didn't even hunt deer with us on moon nights. Fangs and claws were simple enough to bring forth without fully shifting to wolf, which came in handy when I wanted to make a point without tearing out of my clothes. I bared a desultory eyetooth at the braggadocious hunter from the darkness of my corner before going back to my bout of heavy, ineffective drinking.

Slumped in my chair, I eyed him through a fog of cold indifference, trying to hate him but unable to muster the energy, pondering what he'd said. Maybe this clandestine war should come out in the open. Maybe *they* should see what it was like to be hunted and afraid.

Maybe the only good hunter was a dead hunter.

After finishing my drink and dumping money I didn't care enough to count on the table, I slouched out the door, catching the hunter's scent with a single sniff on my way past him. I easily located his truck in the half-empty lot. It reeked of silver, and he hadn't even parked under a light. Careless of him.

I was a predator in my own right, and used to waiting. I wondered, distantly, if killing him would make me feel anything, even the weight of my own failure for not starting sooner.

It didn't. He never saw me coming, and I slaughtered him like a particularly stupid steer.

I caught a glimpse of a stocky man with short-cropped iron-gray hair smoking a cigarette under a lamp in the lot right after the hunter fell under my claws. I shot a glare his way, and he shrugged and touched the brim of his rattlesnake-banded black felt cowboy hat before disappearing into the darkness. I had a sniff around the area, but all it revealed was ordinary human. Not one of us, not one of them.

I gazed in the direction he'd gone, and wondered.

This was war, declared or not, and I was exceptionally equipped to fight it. I'd been a soldier once, long ago and far away in a conflict no one wanted to remember or acknowledge anymore. I had retired into an obscure life as a construction foreman, but I still remembered how to fight. If I couldn't protect my pack before the hunters obliterated them, I could damn sure take bloody vengeance after the fact. Even if it was more by dreary rote than anything else.

A group of three had killed the bulk of my pack. We'd gathered in a safe house—or what we thought was a safe house—and I'd gone out to do a perimeter sweep. They hit the place hard and fast from the sides I wasn't on, firing powerful homemade bombs filled with silver shrapnel through the windows that destroyed five of my friends, along with the house, in one fell swoop.

I lived through it, burned and with several broken bones. God help me, I wished I hadn't.

But I'd gotten a sniff of the perpetrators. Hunting tended to be a family enterprise, and it didn't seem to matter to most that ninety percent of the time, we were just as human as they were, that we weren't sociopaths as a group. There are good and bad wolves just like there are good and bad people. We could police our own, and usually did, but I hadn't been given the chance.

When the hunters started coming after us, I'd been restrained. Too restrained, in retrospect. Defending ourselves in the heat of battle was one thing; no one objected to that and it was a cost of doing business for hunters. But actively hunting them back was quite another, and I couldn't bring myself to unleash my wolves on them. I was the leader, the conscience of the pack, and I needed to set an example. To be better than that, better than those who would massacre us indiscriminately.

I didn't have anyone left to set an example for.

I could cover a lot of ground as a wolf, prowling around neighborhoods until the reek of silver got me the right scent and an address. A reverse lookup gave me phone numbers and names: the Caine brothers.

It was dead easy to set an ambush for them. A breathless call about a stray wolf skulking around an abandoned junkyard brought all three running right into my jaws. Caine Number One disappeared, screaming, under a pile of flattened cars when I used my considerable werewolf strength to push them on top of him. His brothers rushed to his rescue, but couldn't get the rusted hunks of metal shoved aside in time. Screams faded to moans, then silence. One down.

They had the emotional wherewithal to be angry, the lucky bastards. They stood back to back, practically bristling like wolves themselves, radiating threat and testosterone, looking everywhere but where I was, which was on top of another stack of flat cars. No one ever looked up.

I'd grabbed a hubcap on my way, an antique one made of stainless steel, with jagged edges. Taking aim, I threw it hard, like a lethal Frisbee—

And watched with something akin to satisfaction as it imbedded itself in Caine Number Two's throat, thunking home against his spine. He fell bonelessly to sit against an amorphous pile of parts, mouth opening and closing with no sound, blood gushing from his neck and lips. He died in a matter of seconds. Two down.

Caine Number Three waved his gun around, firing wildly at shadows exactly where I wasn't. I hit him from the side like a pitiless freight train, smashing him to the ground and landing on his chest, still human except for my bared fangs and claws. The weapon skittered away, and I wrapped my hand around his throat, three-inch claws pricking but not breaking the skin. Yet. He froze.

"How's it feel to be hunted?" I asked conversationally. "Not very nice, is it." It wasn't a question. "Funny thing about pack links. I feel it when one of my wolves is hurt. Imagine how it feels to me when one of them dies." Leaning down into his face, I bared my dripping fangs, but kept my tone light. "Imagine how it feels when five of them die at the same time."

He whimpered down in his throat. "Please."

"Please," I mused. "My people didn't get a chance to say that before you bombed the house. I imagine the answer would have been the same."

With no effort at all, my claws ripped through his throat in a spray of red mist.

I sat back on my heels and watched impassively as he bled out. I thought I might feel something. Vindication, at least. But all I felt was hollow. My shoulders slumped, and my eyes were dry and aching.

I stumbled to my feet and found the same old guy standing there a few feet away, leaning against a crumbling classic Chevy with his hands in his pockets and his hat pushed back, knee bent and that foot propped against the fender. I sighed and started to scrub my hand over my face, but it still dripped blood. "What do you want?" I asked wearily.

He was quiet, not intimidated, certainly not acting as if he'd just watched me murder three people with no hesitation. "I think the question, Nate, is what do *you* want."

That brought me up short. What *did* I want? But I deflected. "How do you know my name?"

"I know a lot about you, son. Enough to know that what's been done to you ain't fair, and enough to know why you're doing what you're doing." He shrugged, keeping it casual. "And it ain't my business, so long as you keep your vengeance confined to them as deserves it and don't leak it all over innocents."

"I would never," I said, offended.

"I believe that, I do." He pushed his hat farther back with his thumb and gave me a level look. "But you know as well as I that revenge can become its own reward, and there's times you can start seein' folks as complicit because they didn't speak up when they'd oughta. Don't get caught up like that, and you and I got no quarrel."

I looked at the bodies. "I'm done. These are the ones who killed most of my pack. They needed to die for that, but—" I shook my head.

"But you don't feel any better, do you?"

"Who are you?" I demanded.

"My name is Iann MacKinnon. And let's just say I've been where you're at, a few decades gone, and I've taken an interest." His chin lifted, along with his eyebrow. "So. Again. What do you want?"

I choked. "I want to kill every hunter in this city and make it safe for my people again." Even though I was the only one left of "my people." "But I won't. It doesn't help." Nothing helped. I wondered if I'd ever feel anything again, and spun on my heel and walked away from him and his uncomfortable truths.

I still had a construction job to work and a lawn to mow, and those things didn't go away just because I had no real reason to do them anymore besides habit. Lunchtime arrived at the site of the new big-box shopping center, and I tossed my hard hat onto a handy table and walked toward the sub shop a half mile away. A low, human growl from a half-finished storefront made me stop and frown, however, especially when I smelled fear mingled with understated perfume. "Give me your purse, bitch!"

Oh. A mugging. In my territory. Well.

I stepped into the space, with its bare concrete floor and naked studs and beams, to find a homeless guy brandishing a knife at a thirty-ish blonde woman in heels and a powersuit—one of the execs checking out the site. Her dark-blue jacket was partly torn off one shoulder, and she clutched the purse to her chest. "Actually," I said to the bum, standing straight and crossing my arms, "you should think about your stupid, stupid choices, apologize to the lady, and walk away."

He spun, knife pointing at me. He'd brought steel to a wolf fight. That never went well.

"It's none of your business, man!" The guy was coming down from some drug, heroin from the stink, his voice high and desperate.

"I'm making it my business."

I dodged his clumsy, telegraphed swing of the knife with ease and caught his outstretched wrist in the same motion, slinging him face-first into a two-by-six without letting go, then twisted his hand up between his shoulder blades as he let out a pained squeak. I manfully refrained from breaking his arm. This was business, not personal, and I didn't plan to kill him unless he made me. Pressing him against the bare stud, I leaned in and spoke into his ear. "Apologize to the lady."

He made a noise down in his throat, which was echoed by the woman, as they both realized what I was. The exposed fangs might have had something to do with it. I'd made a calculated decision to let them out, to scare him and put paid to the situation as quickly as possible—and show the woman that wolves weren't all bad. Maybe that was a mistake. "Well?" I asked the bum.

"I'm sorry, lady! I won't do it again, I swear, oh God don't eat me."

I snorted with contempt. "I wouldn't do that. No telling what I'd catch." I looked at the woman, who stared back at me with wide eyes and an intensifying fear scent. Great. She was more scared of me than she was of the mugger, even though I'd just saved her. I felt suddenly tired. More tired. My teeth shrank back to human-shaped. "Both of you, just…leave. Please." Why had I even bothered?

She scuttled past me, heels clattering on the concrete. I made sure she was well away before releasing the mugger. "Get help. Idiot." He ran the other way, and I leaned against a worktable with my face in my hand.

Later that night in the Snake in My Boot's lot, I stepped out of my car and turned to lock it. A bullet whined past my ear, shattering a window concurrent with the flat crack of the gunshot. The scent of silver scorched the air, and I ducked behind a pickup truck with an instinctive growl, fur sprouting, nose questing.

Using vehicles for cover, following the reek of gunpowder, I stalked the erstwhile hunter silently through the lot. Counting shots in this day and age didn't mean much, but I did it anyway. He had no idea where I was, and he fired at shadows and errant noises, staying put instead of moving. Foolish. The cops would investigate something like that. They didn't like stray rounds flying through the city, even if they were discharged by someone hunting a wolf.

I zeroed in on his location and ghosted up behind him as he pulled the trigger the fifth time. Any notion of a fair fight I'd ever held had died with Katrina. Popping claws, I slashed sideways at his back in a move designed to cleave his spine in four places.

He wasn't wholly stupid after all. An entire small industry built around wolf hunting made specialized equipment designed to stop us in our tracks, or at least slow us down. Kevlar vests with silver threads stitched into the fabric covering were popular, and this guy wore one under his leather jacket. I'd thought the silver odor had been the bullets, but I found out I was wrong when my claws sliced through the jacket and the fabric of the vest—

And my claws retracted painfully, smoking, into my fingers.

However, I'd put significant strength behind my swing, and for a mere and squishy human, it was like getting swatted aside by a pissed-off Kodiak bear. He smashed into the door of the SUV he'd tried to hide behind, leaving a big dent and a cracked window. He lost his gun when he bounced off, dazed and winded and shaking his head.

But he kept his feet. His right hand whipped a five-inch silver-plated knife from its sheath on his belt, while I popped claws again. He wasn't slow, and he ducked under the swipe I aimed at his face.

"You wanna dance, wolf?" he gasped. His temple bled where he'd hit the SUV, and he blinked hard, coming back at me blade foremost.

"No." Cool and methodical, I jerked away from the knife and caught his outstretched wrist in the same motion, treating him the same way I'd treated the mugger, with a lamppost doing duty for the wall stud and his hand cranked higher between his shoulder blades. I was far less gentle with him, and he let out an agonized cry as the arm both broke and came out of the socket. His knife clattered to the ground, and his buckling knees tried to drop him to the asphalt, but I held him up by the broken arm. "I want to kill you. Like you just tried to kill me. Like you killed my packmates."

"Going after you was sheer self-defense, at this point! I haven't killed a wolf in *aahh*!" Something else let go in that arm, grinding unpleasantly.

"I'm sure you haven't. Doesn't mean you didn't." I snarled into his ear. It was meant to sound enraged, but all I felt was hollow. "I was done, you dumbass. The Caine brothers were going to be the last. But now? You'll *all* get to know what it's like to be afraid. Right. Before. You die. *Alone*."

He squirmed, the sharp scent of terror filling the tight space between us. "I got a family, man, don't—"

"I had a family." My voice was utterly calm. "People like you exterminated them. Like they were no better than rats." I grasped his hair in my free hand and smacked his forehead against the post. Once. Twice. Harder. A dull crack, and he went limp, but I kept mechanically pounding until his face was a ruin of blood and bone and his heart no longer beat.

He fell, and I let him, not even breathing hard. Still weighed down by blank resignation. I'd have to go after the rest of the hunters now; the cycle of retribution wouldn't stop with him. A small inner voice asked if I felt sure about what I was doing, if there maybe wasn't a better way, if I would lose myself in the pursuit of pointless, indifferent vengeance.

With a weary sigh, I turned and walked back to my car without a backward glance at the body.

Iann watched the whole thing. His jaw tightened, and he shook his head slightly with his mouth pulled down on one side. I shouldered him as I passed. "Mind your own business."

His words knifed me like a silver blade. "What do you want, Nate?"

To not feel like the failure I was, was what. I couldn't have that either. I didn't answer, and just walked away, carrying an aching black hole of loneliness that sucked up my emotions, leaving me an empty husk.

The municipality wasn't big enough to support a large contingent of hunters, and with the wolf population down to, well, me, most of them started laying low and trying to let the reek of silver fade out. By the time two more fell under my fangs, the news picked up the story, but police didn't get involved with hunter/wolf internal politics as long as I studiously kept civilians out of it.

Iann, though. He showed up again. And again. Watching with calculated non-aggression, not doing anything, pricking at the withered thing I used to call a conscience. I finally twigged to what he was.

The last hunter in town, playing some kind of sick game.

It had to be a game. No hunter was actually sympathetic to a wolf. Ever.

Unfortunately, he was ready for me when I caught him by himself, walking his dog a few blocks from his apartment. The dog, some kind of spaniel, took one whiff and bolted home through the darkness, yelping, but Iann remained unruffled as he noted my expression. He pulled a nine-mil semi-auto from under his calf-length leather duster and pointed it steadily at me. I could smell the silver ammo, but I didn't have anything left to lose.

He stood in the spotlight of a streetlamp, which left his lived-in face shadowed under the ever-present cowboy hat. "Walk away, Nate," he said gently. "Your quarrel ain't with me."

I glided forward, more wolf than human. "Isn't it? The city will finally be *safe* once you're gone."

"I been telling them numbnuts for years that indiscriminate killing is downright dumb, but they won't listen to an old man." The gun didn't waver. "I don't wanna hurt you, son, but I will defend myself."

"That's what I'm doing. Defending myself." And I launched, clothes shredding as four hundred pounds of timber wolf took the place of two hundred pounds of man.

He shouted my name, and the gun went off twice in rapid succession. One of the bullets fanned my fur, and the second sent a fiery graze along my ribs. A head or a heart shot would have been instantly fatal, and I could have bled out from an artery severed by silver, but at this point it didn't matter. He was the last. I was the last. It had a certain poetry to it.

He tried to sidestep my charge, but I anticipated that. My head snaked sideways, and I grabbed his knee in jaws that once had cracked a moose's femur. My teeth didn't shear through the leather of his duster, which he'd probably gotten from one of the hunter outlets, designed to be resistant to wolf fangs. Cartilage and bone crunched, though, and a powerful toss of my head hurled him to the sidewalk. The gun fired twice more. He couldn't miss at this distance; both rounds burned into my chest—but not my heart—as I stood over him, grunting with the impact. But they went through-and-through, and I kept the wolf form by main force and dove at his throat.

He got an arm up, and my fangs closed on that instead. "You're a better man than this, Nate," he said between clenched teeth. Radius and ulna snapped like matchsticks, though the leather held. "This is no different than what they did to you. Stop. And *think*. About what you want."

I spat his arm out....

And hesitated.

"No matter what you decide," he panted, dropping the gun. "I forgive you. I understand. And I forgive you."

What I wanted—

I wanted my pack back. I wanted to belong again. I wanted to feel more than this vacant, vengeful shell, going through the motions of life without actually living it.

Iann reached his uninjured arm up and buried his fingers in my ruff. I was a wolf who'd nearly killed him, and he petted me the way he would his dog. It felt ridiculously good. Wolves constantly touch each other, and I had no idea how much I'd missed the contact until I got some of it back. "Nate. You can stop now. You can rest, son." His soft voice caressed me as much as his hand. Maybe he was lonely too.

I huffed out a single, sobbing whine and dropped my head to his shoulder.

Slow applause made me jerk my head up. A werewolf I didn't recognize stepped out of the shadows. "Well done, my friend."

I cast a glance at Iann, who wisely let his arm fall, closed his

241

eyes, and played dead. Bristling, I ranged myself between him and the new guy, my body language radiating "my meat" under no uncertain terms. Blood dripped from my jaws. It was mine, but I was downwind from the wolf and he didn't need to know that.

Strange wolves in new territories are bad for loners. The odor of his pack covered him, along with the scent of a fresh, human kill. He had the authoritative air of an alpha.

Wounded and alone I may have been, but I was still an alpha in my own right. I lowered my head, lifted my tail, and showed him my fangs, even as my hindquarters sank under me. He squatted on his heels and smiled. It was a terrible expression. "Sending in one of my more bloodthirsty pack members worked better than I could have imagined. Both you and the hunters were laughably predictable." He dusted his hands off. "Very nice of you to take out all the hunters, Nate. Humans are sheep, and now they'll get to find out just how vulnerable they are."

His words made me feel something, finally—sick dread coiling in the pit of my stomach as I realized I'd just engineered the ruin of the city's ecology. No more hunters meant that rogues like him—and the serial killer who'd started the entire cycle— could move in and wreak as much destruction as they wanted. I shifted back to human and wiped the blood from my mouth with the back of my hand. "You can't do that."

"Sure I can. Who's going to stop me?" I straightened from my crouch and fixed him with a glare. He barked out a laugh. "You? But *why*?" He waved wildly. "It's not like they lifted a finger to help you when your pack was being annihilated. Did anyone speak a single word of caution Say 'boo'? No. They *cheered*." Contempt twisted his features. "Bunch of oblivious, bleating morons. And now they'll get theirs."

I started to say something, and stopped. Because he wasn't wrong, at least not completely. He saw me wavering and turned conciliatory. "Join us. Find a place in my pack. You're clearly good at hunting. I could use someone like you as my second."

A shudder ran through my body. We didn't do well by ourselves, as demonstrated by my little murder spree. A new pack—the idea was viscerally appealing. But... "We shouldn't. It's wrong." I knew this, down where I lived. I'd spent my life fighting a good fight, or trying to. Turning around and slaughtering humans just because I could was out of the question.

"Wrong? Is it wrong for a lion to eat a gazelle? It's nature. *We* are nature." He stood abruptly. "Come with me, or don't. It's up to you. But sheep are good for one thing, and they're about to find out what it is." He turned around and walked away, whistling through his teeth, the psycho.

Hurt, heartsick, and hopeless, I watched him go. Thinking. Was I a ravening wolf, like humans thought? Or was I better than that, a border collie saving them from their own folly, even though they'd never thank me for it?

A cough made me swivel my head around. Iann sat up, wincing. "So he's an asshole." He tilted his head at me. "I take it you ain't killing me tonight"

I stared at the ground. My voice was low and hoarse, and I shook my head, just once. "No. You're right. You're not my enemy."

"Glad you finally came to your senses." He shrugged out of his duster, wincing, and draped it over my naked shoulders. "What're we gonna do about him?"

A tiny thrill shot through me at that "we." I shivered, recognizing a kindred spirit, a fellow border collie. He hadn't murdered us indiscriminately; hell, he'd had every opportunity and plenty of reason to kill me out of hand, for weeks. I stared at the ground, still, and tilted my head, a subtle and submissive throat-baring gesture that anyone not a wolf might have missed—but Iann noted it, and nodded. I didn't want to be an alpha anymore, and he understood.

"Someone has to protect them," I said. "There's no one left but us."

"That's so. Then I guess we ought to get to it, once we patch up our hurts." He rubbed his chest with a speculative frown.

"Yessir." I shifted to wolf again and jacked myself to four feet.

Reclaiming his duster, he stood and smoothed back my ears before resting his hand on my ruff. My knee and foreleg ached, throbbing in tandem, no doubt, with Iann's. An ember of hope kindled in my heart. A pack link with an ordinary human was new... but I'd take it.

We limped after the new wolf. Hunting with renewed purpose. Together.

A Glamour in the Black

written by

Sylvia Anna Hivén

illustrated by

BRANDON KNIGHT

ABOUT THE AUTHOR

Sylvia Anna Hivén was born in Sweden and moved to the U.S. when she was twenty years old. She writes all kinds of speculative fiction, but loves dark fairy tales and weird westerns a little more than the rest. Her fiction has appeared in Daily Science Fiction, Beneath Ceaseless Skies, Escape Pod, *and others. She is passionate about her faith and holistic living, and in her free time she enjoys organic cooking, cycling, and practicing yoga.*

ABOUT THE ILLUSTRATOR

Brandon Knight was born in Shropshire, in the heart of the UK. Surrounded by small towns and green fields, Brandon spends most of his time developing ideas, which are usually inspired by a piece of narrative, either fictional or historical.

When not drawing or painting he's reading, finding inspiration for another creation.

When it comes to art he can spend hours studying works of master illustrators. The golden age of illustration is by far his favorite period, as he feels the work that was produced is unprecedented in terms of technical prowess and storytelling.

Brandon intends to graduate with a degree in Visual Communication with a keen focus on illustration.

"Being included in the Illustrators of the Future," he says, "is an achievement I've been aspiring to. I saw it as an incredible experience and stepping stone into the world of illustration. I am so honored and thankful to have been included this year."

246

A Glamour in the Black

Keani's parasite, nestled between her shoulder blades, always ached in the rain. Even the smallest of droplets slipping beneath Keani's cloak would remind her that the knotted creature was there, its shimmery form visible beneath her skin. It would shiver and burn, crackle and groan, jitter and flare. Spring drizzles annoyed it, and the rain season maddened it: when purple-smeared skies rumbled and torrents thrashed the volcano city, the parasite even split Keani's flesh open and bled crisscross marks over the embroidered hibiscus flowers on her tunics.

The rain season was almost over now, but the pain was not, and it wouldn't be for a while. As Keani slipped down the slick volcanic paths to the clam caves, the ocean roaring in through jagged crevices, there were to be many days of wet, and many days of pain, and many days of being many things but herself.

Far down the rough-hewn steps, one of the clammers appeared out of the darkness to meet her as agreed. The woman was young and barefoot, braids tangling on either side of her face like black eels. Crude knives clinked where they hung at her hips. She stopped ten feet from Keani, squinting her pale-cloudy eyes.

"They didn't lie," the woman said, her voice husky. "I've never met you, yet I want to take you into my arms. How extraordinary."

Unease crept into Keani. Not because the reaction was unfamiliar: those she visited were always conquered by the parasite's glamour. But nobody ever confessed it with such candor; never did anybody tell Keani how readily they were disarmed, and never would she expect that person to be a clam woman who dared to say it while looking into her eyes.

"I've come on the behalf of the Ialan trade company." Keani gestured toward her sack. "May I present these gifts to show our gratitude for the opportunity to know your people?"

It was a familiar speech.

The reply, however, was not. "For the opportunity to know our *pearls,* you mean," the clammer said. "We have had Volca traders visit us before with many trinkets like the ones you bring. Nothing we've been shown yet convinced us to bother with the ways of above."

A droplet wriggled beneath Keani's collar. The parasite twitched. It annoyed her, and she felt tired, and for a moment, she let courtesy go. "Yet your tribe sent you here," she said. "How curious."

The clammer shrugged. "Maybe they just want to meet the girl with the glamour. Maybe they wish to see if you turn into a great big clam in their eyes. I don't know the minds of the elders. I was just sent up here to fetch you."

The woman gestured toward the steps that plunged down into the dark. The clam caves lay below where the ocean swept into the volcano. It was an unwelcoming place, cold and salty and acrid, but the clam tribe had chosen tradition over comfort for hundreds of years to hunt the clusters of clams that clung in the watery tunnels.

"I'm Nahoa," the woman said. "I'll show you below."

"Keani." She picked up her sack.

"Can you carry that?" Nahoa said. "You're such a little thing, with those squidlet arms of yours."

The little strength Keani had left abandoned her, sucked away by the glamour's reaction to Nahoa's words—any hint of specificity, any opportunity at becoming more pleasing, and the parasite took it. Keani felt herself altering, shrinking, narrowing. Her frame thinned out. Her hands weakened and her fingers slimmed. The sack became too heavy and she dropped it onto the cave floor.

She tried to not show her frustration. "You say I don't look like I can carry a sack, and you make it happen."

Nahoa appeared startled. "I'm sorry."

"You didn't know."

"I'll carry it, then."

Nahoa picked up the sack and together they walked down into the belly of the volcano. Keani felt Nahoa's glances in the dim and the glamour feeding on the attention. By the time they reached the bottom of the steps, the glamour had completed its bond with the strange woman, and whatever reservations she'd had toward Keani were gone, leaving only admiration in its wake. The parasite settled, content, and the ache in Keani's back dissipated.

They emerged into the mouth of a cave where stalactites drooped from the ceiling like looming teeth. A cavernous opening gaped to the raging ocean outside, and a mass of people approached from a gathering of huts that were built on the slivery beach. As they approached, Keani felt herself splitting again, the glamour doubling, tripling, quadrupling its efforts: ten-fold, twenty-fold. Her soul groaned.

When she'd greeted the crowd, been bowed to and the countless versions of her caressed by admiring gazes, Nahoa took her to a small shack.

"The elders will review your offerings tonight," Nahoa said. "I apologize that you cannot be present, but the council lets in no women, even less an abover."

"I understand."

"They should know by morning if you have anything of value to trade."

"I would like to see the pearls in the meantime."

"I can show you to the shucking cave in the morning."

"Please."

Nahoa nodded and left Keani alone in the small shack. She prepared for bed. The rough-woven blankets smelled dank and were salted with tiny grains of black sand, but Keani didn't mind. The hut itself felt dry and warm, and the parasite in her back was still.

Moments like those, when that thing inside of her silenced,

Keani would close her eyes and try to remember herself. She'd imagine her own face: not the projection of someone else's comforts; not the lost husband of a widower; not the mother of a once abandoned child; but herself, Keani, a girl of fifteen. Her father claimed that she looked just like her mother: brown hair, black eyes, a heart-shaped face with a tease of freckles. Her father could still see Keani—the real her—through the glamour, as she had been before. But Keani couldn't.

Where she lay on the blankets, she lifted her hands up and opened her eyes. She had hoped to see the slim fingers of a fifteen-year old, but she just found a flash of hands, dozens of shapes and hues, too many to count and too unfamiliar to call her own, as the glamour still entertained the fantasies of the clammers outside.

As she drifted off to sleep, she wondered if she'd dream, and if she did, she questioned if the dreams would even be hers.

The council, Nahoa apologized, hadn't gotten to the matter of the trade agreement.

"They're old men, traditional men," she explained to Keani. "They care more about the tides and the color of the waters than they do about abovers. They should decide tonight if they wish to discuss it further, but I warn you—nobody ever understands our needs enough to tempt us to trade with them."

"I can wait," Keani said. "My father would not expect me to give up so easily."

Nahoa nodded. "Then I shall try my best to entertain you in the meantime."

She took Keani to the shucking cave as promised. It had an underground beach covered with shell fragments, the slivers shining in a sparse light from clay oil urns. A group of women and children hunched over piles of newly harvested clams. The water beyond the beach was black and deep, and every now and then clam divers emerged from the water, bodies shimmering wet and their nets full of blue-shimmery clams. Some were as large as a man's fist.

Nahoa picked up one of the clams, and shoved her crude stone knife into the slit between the slippery shells. She wrestled with the clam and wrenched it open. In her palm, hugged by the frothy innard of the clam, lay the largest pearl Keani had ever seen.

"That can buy someone a week's worth of food," Keani said. "It's a great treasure."

Nahoa shook her head. "It's a *curse*. The sands swept into the clams here decades ago, and now many of them come up with these defects. The giant clams are our food source, and they give less meat because of the pearls. I don't understand how these useless things help anyone."

"It matters to some. To those who already have been fed for a week. People wear them on necklaces, or to decorate their clothes."

"I don't understand such obsessions."

"You don't live above. It's very different."

"I can imagine. Must be terribly bright and windy."

"And wet." The parasite squirmed a little at the mere words, and Keani gritted her teeth at the dull pain.

Nahoa noticed. "It must be even more difficult for someone like you, with a parasite. Must be hard to never be seen as yourself. To just be what the fantasies of others make you into."

"It is."

"Was it on purpose?"

Keani shuddered at the idea. *Why would anybody willingly give up themselves to become a fractured mirror whose shards were made up of the faces of others,* she wondered. "My parents and I were in the jungle to trade animal skins from the deep-tribe, and a rope bridge snapped beneath us. We lay in the precipice for days. A shaman found us and tried to help, the best she knew how, but it went awry."

Keani had lost her memory of the incident and everything that had come before, so all she knew was from her father's feverish dreams when he cursed the shaman's spells and conjurings. He had accepted grotesquely healed bones from the poor splinters, and he had accepted leaving behind the body of his wife after she'd died from her skull cracking like a coconut. But he had not accepted his only daughter remaining infected with parasites and blood leeches to, as the shaman said, "suck her soul back from the beyond." Her father had paid dearly to have her healed by the best physicians for as long as they would extend credit. It had left her with one sole parasite and her father with countless debts.

"Physicians have told me it can be removed," Keani said. "But I won't do it until I know my father's debts are paid. We need the glamour to help us trade."

"I see the pain it causes you," Nahoa said. "I say, you sacrifice too much."

"My father is the one who sacrificed the most. He walks on twisted legs. He lost my mother."

"But he knows who he is. He knows his own face. Will you ever get to know yours, Keani?"

"Soon, I can get rid of it." Keani tried to sound hopeful. "Just one more agreement, that's all I need to afford to have it cut out."

Nahoa gazed at her with compassion. "Knives," she said, touching Keani's hand gently. "Tell your father we need knives."

When Keani returned from the volcanic caves, emerging out into the moist light of the city above, rain pounced her like a jungle cat. The parasite immediately shook and shivered, and as agony cracked along the muscles in her back, she hurried through the winding streets to her home. She knew that the pain came from the rain, but some part of her wanted to believe the parasite was angry at the prospect of being cut out. And cut out, it would be: in her pocket, she had one of the pearls, and she knew her father had agreements with a smith on the outskirts of Volca. Knives would be easy to get.

At home her father leaned on his crutches on the open balcony, gazing out over the city, the bamboo roofs slick with rain beneath the sky. He appeared frail in the waning light. When he embraced her, he shivered as much as she.

252

"I had nightmares while you were away," he whispered. "I dreamed of your mother again."

"I'm sorry."

"I shouldn't have sent you down there. The clammers are inhospitable. I should have known they'd want nothing to do with us."

"Knives," Keani said. "That's what they want."

She withdrew the pearl and handed it to her father, closing his shaking fingers over it. He stared at it with eyes as dark as the sky outside.

"They agreed?" His jaw dropped in surprise.

"They did."

"Your glamour. Curse as it is, it works miracles."

Keani wanted to say that it wasn't because of the glamour— that the success was hers: that she, Keani, had earned the respect of someone not because of the glamour but *in spite* of it. But as much as she wished it, the glamour created so much falseness she couldn't know for sure if it was true.

"Tell me about me, father," she said. "Tell me again, please."

He touched her face. "You're Keani. You're fifteen years old. Your skin is like bronze, with a spray of freckles across your cheeks. Your hair is brown and thick and lustrous. You're a beautiful girl."

"When the knives are delivered, the debt to the doctors will be paid," Keani said, taking her father's hand.

"Yes."

"You will not hold it against me if I seek a surgeon? If I go to the mainland?"

Her father's face darkened. "It's dangerous," he said. "What the shaman did, all her esoteric magic... there is no guarantee you'll come away unharmed if you try to remove it."

Keani wanted to tell him that she was already harmed—that she didn't know who she was, that she had a million faces and she didn't recognize a single one as her own, and each time someone looked at her she felt like a jungle being flooded away by torrential rain: little pieces of her were torn from her soul to be lost forever.

But she didn't tell him. She just kissed his forehead and went to bed, leaving him clutching the pearl in his hand.

The smith lived in a cramped hut on a muddy trail at the base of the volcano. He was elderly and his hands were scarred from flying embers from the fire pits, but he was skilled and his blades were as thin as banana leaves.

Keani took the knife samples back to the clammers. This time, she wasn't greeted just by Nahoa, but by a group of the clammer elders. They were pale, like the underbellies of fish, and their skin hung in tired, moist folds down hairless chests. Most of them were blind, so they examined Keani's knives with their hands, hissing in delight as the sharp blades cut their bloated fingers.

The elders agreed to her knives. In turn she was given a basket filled to the brim with black pearls. Nahoa offered to help her carry it back up the steps to Volca.

"If you walk away, the glamour will fade and I won't be the weak girl you see," Keani said. "You don't have to come along."

"I would like to. And I don't think you're weak." Nahoa took the basket gently out of her hands, and they started to walk back toward the stairs, and above.

"You'll be the last person to see the glamour," Keani said cheerfully. "Maybe one day you can tell legends of it."

"I'd rather tell stories about the girl who bore many beautiful faces and was loved by all and still fought to get her own back."

"Whatever that face may look like," Keani said. "I don't remember what came before. I don't know what people will think of me."

"I don't think you have to worry about that." Nahoa's hand brushed up against hers. "They will like you just fine."

When they emerged from the caverns and had to part, Keani's heart twinged. "I suppose I won't be able to come back," she said. "Your tribe won't let anybody in who can't fool them with a glamour."

"Don't think that," Nahoa said. "You're always welcome. You brought us blades. We will always be grateful."

254

They parted. It was the first time that a glamour bond snapped off and Keani didn't feel relief. She just felt empty.

She walked through Volca, rain fizzling in the torches that lit the wet streets. As she passed people and saw their smiles at her glamour's projections, Keani accepted the flare of pain in her back. After all, the parasite was in its death throes—and who knew how people would look at her once the parasite was gone. Perhaps these were the last looks of interest, the last glances of attraction. Maybe soon, there would be nothing left to love at all.

When she arrived home, Keani carried the basket through the darkened halls toward her father's chambers. She wasn't involved in the administrative part of the business and she told herself that's why her father didn't allow her entrance into his chamber. She suspected he was trying to protect her from the guilt of seeing him working into the early hours, bent over debt notices, worry swirling in his black eyes. But in possession of a basket that would finally end their troubles, Keani strode to the locked chamber. If her father was in there, she wanted to tell him they were free and see that weight fall from his shoulders.

She heard the clacking of her father's crutches against the floorboards, and when she reached his chamber she found the door cracked open.

"Father?"

She entered.

And gasped.

What met her was not a sad sight of her father surrounded by empty shelves or hunched over stacks of debtor's letters. Instead, she found him at a desk flanked by boxes of riches stacked on top of each other. There were silver clusters from the mountain tribes she'd visited the month before, and bolts of silks from the weavers she'd helped to convince last year. There were piles of bamboo weave mats in a corner, flanked by urns with incenses and blue-spice. At the desk, her father was not twisting his hands over bills, but instead counting shiny gold coins.

There were no bills, and there were no debts. There were only riches.

Her father's head snapped up. "Keani," he said. "Why are you in here? You shouldn't *be* here."

"You've lied," she whispered. "All this time? All this time, we were rich?"

"No," her father said, struggling to his twisted feet. "You don't understand."

Betrayal roiled up Keani's throat, and as she turned to flee, the basket slipped out of her hand. The pearls spilled all over the floor, crackling like fireworks as they dimpled the wooden boards. Or maybe that was the sound of her heart breaking, Keani didn't know.

Nahoa was alone in the shucking cave when Keani came upon her. The pale girl hunched over a heap of clams, wet ringlets of her hair plastered to her cheeks. Her face flooded with first joy, then concern when she saw Keani's tears.

"What's the matter?" Nahoa said, standing up, dropping the clams to the ground.

"He lied, Nahoa!" Keani sobbed. "My father lied to me all this time."

Nahoa took her into her arms. She smelled of salt and sand, and in the cool cave, her skin felt warm, like home. Keani burrowed deeper in her embrace.

"He has become a rich man, Nahoa," she wept. "All the while, I've suffered, and he's become rich! All that mattered was this thing inside me, and the fortune it would bring. It was never about protecting me, or keeping me healthy. It was just about keeping this cursed creature alive!"

Nahoa fell quiet for a while, holding Keani close. When Keani's sobs lessened, Nahoa let her go and picked up one of the clams. Wrestling it open was easier this time, with the thin bladed knife Keani had brought her. Another pearl lay inside, gleaming and lustrous. They both looked at it, and Keani felt angry she still marveled at its beauty.

Then, in one swift motion, Nahoa threw the pearl into the water, and the blackness swallowed it with a greedy gulp.

Keani didn't understand. "Why did you do that?"

"Some people may care about the pearls," Nahoa said. "But others know the clams are what matters: the good, nourishing parts, not those flashy jewels." She grasped Keani's shoulders gently. "Keani, I don't know whose face I am looking into when I look at you. But I know there is a soul behind that face that I want to know."

"Thank you," Keani whispered.

"If you want to know it too, all you have to do is ask." Nahoa patted the knife at her side. "I am not a physician, but that thing in your back is just beneath your skin. And while I can open things with force, I can also be delicate with my blade."

"I want to know," Keani whispered. "I want to be rid of it."

"So let me do it. I promise I would be careful."

Keani felt dizzy at the idea of that slim blade slicing into her skin, but she nodded.

"Yes," she said. "Do it. Cut it out, Nahoa."

Nahoa unsheathed her knife. "The water is cool. You'll feel less if you immerse yourself when I cut."

When Nahoa had sterilized her blade, they moved into the water. The parasite in Keani's back immediately reacted—it twitched painfully, writhing beneath her skin. It *knew*. Keani didn't care to let the agony scare her: she only leaned over, offering the parasite to Nahoa's knife.

When Nahoa cut, there was blazing pain. The world blurred, the cave around her growing concave and convex, twisting and turning. Something inside of her screamed—or was that her? Keani couldn't tell.

When the world cleared again, she was lighter, and her limbs didn't want to obey her. She saw Nahoa's face above her, huge and white like a looming moon, oddly twisted.

"Gone with you, monster," Nahoa whispered. "Gone with you, forever."

She pushed Keani away, and helpless to control herself or to speak, Keani floated off on the black surface. She tumbled in the water, saltiness stinging into her eyes—of which there were not two, but ten, maybe twenty, and she saw the world in a fracture. She wanted to scream Nahoa's name, but no words came out, for she had no tongue anymore—nor did she have legs or arms, or any other human parts.

When Keani bobbed upright enough to look around, she saw that Nahoa wasn't alone. She bent over a girl that bobbed lifelessly in the water.

Keani knew that girl. Maybe her skin had been bronze once, and maybe she once had had a spray of freckles across her face. Maybe her hair had even been dark and thick. She certainly was beautiful enough for a father to keep her alive with the conscience of a parasite. But no life was left in that girl anymore. All that was left was the shell, blood ribboning in the water.

And Keani wasn't her. It had never been her.

BRANDON KNIGHT

The Broad Sky Was Mine, And the Road

written by

Ryan Row

illustrated by

JONAS ŠPOKAS

ABOUT THE AUTHOR

Ryan Row spent most of his childhood split between the bony deserts of Nevada and the thin-aired forests of the Sierra Mountains. His father and mother both read to him as a child, and like a balloon popping, something in his head was irreversibly broken. How could he be satisfied with the absolute laws of gravity when just inside the paper-thin covers of a thousand books, men flew under the power of their own mythic wings? Wax and iron and flesh. How could he be content with the same pattern of stars every night through his narrow window when mere pages away women in silver jumpsuits sailed on solar winds through an ever-changing cipher of stars? How could he be satisfied?

He could not. Ever since, he's been hopping galaxies like a fugitive hopping train cars.

Ryan began his literary career by attempting to publish stories under the pen name Alan Wor, but now writes under his own name. He is currently studying Creative Writing at San Francisco State University, and he lives in Oakland, California with a beautiful and mysterious woman who every day makes him believe the impossible doesn't just happen inside the pages of books. The beautiful and impossible can happen right here on Earth.

ABOUT THE ILLUSTRATOR

Jonas Špokas was born in 1990 in Kaunas, Lithuania. From an early age, he felt drawn to science fiction and fantasy in video games and movies. In 11th grade, music inspired him to revive his childhood passion for art. He drew most days, copying wallpapers and characters from video games and movies.

Jonas aspired to study and draw concept art for video games, but was unable to pursue this passion as there was no such program in Lithuania. Instead, he took an undergraduate course in sculpture at Kaunas Faculty of Vilnius Academy of Fine Arts.

During these studies his interest for digital art emerged. He found that digital art wasn't as demanding as sculpting, and it was easier to generate and quicker than traditional painting.

After graduating in 2013, Jonas started working a part-time job in order to keep consistent income. In his free time, he freelances as a digital artist.

The Broad Sky Was Mine, And the Road

We're hunting a stage four in some menial wage suburb. Packed claustrophobic tight with Taco Huts and dirty white apartment buildings with no parking. Samantha drives and I hang my head out the window like an old dog, thermal goggles weighing down my neck.

The world's a blotchy mess of shifting blue and green and red and dead black. What I see when I close my eyes after staring at the sun. The colors swim across my sight like recycled dreams. The things I'm not willing to let go of when I wake up. The phosphene wonderland of no pain that's always in the middle of slipping away. All that's left of dreams upon waking are their blotchy afterimages on the insides of my eyes.

Rule: Dream whenever you can.

"Sensors'll find it before you do, David."

"That a challenge, little girl?" I say it into the wind, but I know she hears it over the com that's on at all times and burrowed in our ears with temp adhesive. I smell fire on the air.

"It's a fact."

"You got no faith in the human eye?" After two years, Samantha is still new and eager. She drinks whiskey and water, back at base, and pretends that's what she likes. She carries her own cigarettes and a personal, ice modified .45 on her hip, like me. She is afraid of not carrying her own weight. But she hasn't seen action in the hard packed, new deserts of the world. Not yet. She hasn't felt the exploding drill of an Ashland marauder's bullet through her gut. And she trusts too much in

263

the immortality of her young body. Some order in the world she still believes in. The last vestiges of childhood rooted deep in her lithe, twenty-year-old frame. I follow the pattern in the colors. The cooling centers of red and yellow.

"It's not even your eye. You're wearing goggles."

I sigh, and pull the goggles off my head with an elastic slap. The sun's high and blue. I see spots of soot on the sidewalk. A few burned corpses, covered in a film of grease and blood that shines like polish in the afternoon light.

"Will you let me feel like I'm still relevant? Please?" She maneuvers the Humvee around an overturned sedan. She keeps it steady and low, right around twenty.

"You're still relevant. You pull the trigger."

A tone sounds from the dash console. Angry and robotic.

Samantha's brown gaze darts from the road to the dash and back.

"Hit. 152.2 meters due south," she says, swinging the car tight around a corner. Kill teams used to be six guys. Then four. I like it better this way. Just a driver and a shooter. The silences are longer and deeper. The communication quick and easy.

"Running hot?" I ask, pulling one of the two German Armbrusts from its snap holster on the ceiling. It's a two foot, flat green tube. An open-backed, recoilless, anti-tank rocket launcher. Modified to shoot "Ice Packs," exploding cans of ultra compressed liquid nitrogen.

"486.6 degrees. Fluctuating up."

I grunt and load the Ice Pack. The squat, red can radiates a kind of cold I associate with empty places. I load the second Armbrust and return it to its holster. I hold one in my lap. Then I close my eyes and see, again, the recycled dream of the world. Samantha's silent. She knows I like it that way right before. I hear the air moving through the window and road crunching under us as if we are driving over bone. And an empty confusion of color is settled everywhere in my mind like a radioactive fog.

JONAS ŠPOKAS

I feel the car stop, and I open my eyes. Through the windshield, a hundred feet down the road, a black mass of carbon particles in a human shape waves in the air. Like a scribbled spot of ink on the page of reality.

Samantha's voice shakes, just slightly, in a rare show of emotion. Something we've mutually agreed to ignore.

"It can't be over four feet," she says. "It's a child?"

The way her voice rises, just slightly, makes me think she wants a certain answer. I can't give it to her.

"It looks lost." I say. I hear its low, long moan. And a column of smoke rises from its featureless, ever flowing face. I roll up the window.

"I didn't think someone so small…could…sustain stage four."

"Guess he's special," I say, stepping out. I swing the Armbrust up, resting it on a shoulder. I drop to one knee and press the first button. The heat seeker stuck to the Armbrust's barrel bleeps wild in my ear. I'm pretty close to lined up to the hottest point in the view of the sensor. Samantha speaks from the cab.

"David."

"Be quiet."

"David, what if we—"

"Whatever you're thinking, Sam, stop thinking it."

At a hundred feet, it's a gamble whether a stage four will spot you or not. And if it flares, things will get complicated. Samantha goes silent.

I listen hard to the tone. Searching for the sweet spot of crescendo that tells me to let go.

I adjust. I adjust. I adjust.

And when it comes, when I'm aimed right at its bitter-hot core, I squeeze the trigger slow. The sliding thud as the Ice Pack leaves the barrel. The hard crack of the blast out the back end.

And I think I feel the stage four looking at me. Without eyes. And moaning. Then everything's a flower of burning ice, the size of a small car, and dots of rainbow flutter and disappear in the air like dreams.

And I'm cold inside, and, for a moment, I hate Samantha, because she's not.

But then I look at her. The way she dulls her eye. Crushes the thoughts under her creasing brow. And I tell myself,

She will be.

As I stand, I see Samantha's eyes, down on the dash console, go wide and wild.

I smell it before she can speak. The bitter grit of rushing fire. Swirling in itself. Drunk on the air and its own brief life.

A storefront window explodes to my right. The sound of something giving way.

Rule: Action is life.

Twisting, I let myself fall. I let the empty Armbrust drop, reaching for the .45 strapped to my hip.

A mass of smoke pours through the newly melted hole in the front of the human world. Glowing embers flowing up its particle skin. This one's at least nine feet by three. No child. The vague shape of a man and strangled moaning from its billowing mouth. Distant and painful and aimless, as if it was crying out in its sleep.

"It's flaring!" Samantha shouts.

I ignore her. I ignore my history. Tangled in my mind. Somewhere in the accumulated grime of this edge city, church bells are ringing. I am those silver tones. Clear and empty. I draw smooth and fire without aiming in the direction of the Fall.

The .45 fits in my hand the way my heart fits in my chest. Familiar and hard. Icy. The jumping recoil of our secret language. I don't look, but I hear the Ice Cube shots bursting silver in the stage four's clouded body. Followed by the hiss of instant evaporation. If I looked, I'd see rainbow silver bursts of ice swallowed in its smoking frame, starting to glow red and yellow like a heated coal. Flaring at the sight of two beating centers of human fuel.

"Shut the goddamn door! Hit the lure!" I scream as I kick the ground with my legs and pull at the bottom edge of the Humvee with my free hand, sliding my body under the vehicle and shooting random all the mad while. The blasting is reduced to cotton popping by the com buds in my ears. They automatically mute sound over a certain decibel, and I'm thankful. Because I've got other things to listen for. I hear the door snap shut. Followed by the sound of a rapid decompression. The heat lure jettisoning off the back of the vehicle. Quiet in the wreckage of noise. Good girl.

Of course, lures only fool them half the time.

The hiss of ice converting to vapor is huge and wide and spitting. Too huge. Suddenly the air is thick and hot with moisture. Under the car, everything smells like gas. Samantha is calling to me in one ear, but I ignore her. I stop firing and drag myself backward, practically climbing the undercarriage of the Humvee, oil slick and mechanic jungle gym.

I pop out the other side into sudden sunlight. The vehicle shakes on its wheels. I know the stage four is pounding the opposite side of the Humvee, but it's not hot enough to melt the temper glass windows. Not yet. The lure hasn't gone off. Is it jammed? How long has it been? Only pieces of seconds.

I'm almost out. When I make it, I will open the back door, and Samantha will drive hard. Toward the church bells. Away from the burning moan that rises and falls in a random scale of pain. Overlapping and trampling itself as if there were two trapped, starving voices. The lure will shoot its fountain of pure white sparks, and the stage four will hesitate long enough for us to get away. And we will laugh, numb with adrenaline and another confirmation of our immortality. In the corner of my eye, I spot a white flowing. I turn. A giant cloud of steam runs over itself and spreads down the street like a pouring liquid. Liquid smoke. Like my confusion.

Samantha's voice comes to me as I start to stand. "Still live! Both flaring! Get in the damn car!"

I'm standing, reaching for the door. Ignoring the profile of her face, staring hard into the clouds of new mist.

And there is a sound like the moon cracking. Distant and sad and larger than all our little lives.

The fire child falls out of the air like the meteoric fist of a god. Ember light and atomic energy. The feather leap of a spark. A "flare jump," we call it. It lands square on the hood of the Humvee and collapses it. The blast of heat is an invisible explosion. It hits me dead in the face, and I know I'm screaming. But I can't hear it over the new atmosphere of pain radiating from the skin of my face. I stumble backward.

Don't fall. Open your eyes.

I crack them open, but they're watering, and all the edges of the world run together. I blink rapid. I hear the pounding of stage four, hellfire fists. See the Humvee rocking. The child is aglow now. A child-shaped, living ember. Flecks of soot smoke, black as unconsciousness, float off its drifting amber skin. Most of the smoke clears when they flare, and its glowing body is small, and the air around it bends and twists in the heat. It has both hands flat against the windshield. I can tell from the smell, sharp and chemical like plastic and hair, that the temper glass is melting.

I see Samantha bend over, and come back up holding the second Armbrust.

"Don't!" I shout, and my skin screams in protest at the movement. I can't get any closer to the radiating sphere of heat. It is the faceless sun in a bent, human shape. And it has melted all my wax dreams and I'm falling down into the sea of ash.

"It's okay," she says over the com.

Uselessly, the lure crackles and starts shooting its stream of sparks in the still air.

Go for it, I think. But I know it won't. The sparks make a human shape and temperature. But stage fours are hard to fool.

The child sun, in all its magma-skinned glory, falls forward into the cab beside Samantha as the last of the glass melts away like an old frost. Their moaning is high now. Closer to screaming. As if they were the ones being burned alive one bullet at a time. One wide day at a time. One trigger pull and funeral filled with strangers at a time.

"It won't always be like this," Samantha says, turning to me.

The cab is a mirage, an illusion of shifting heat. And now she seems very far away. "Remember—"

The cab explodes white with the battered thud of the Armbrust. Lightning crooked fingers of ice grow in an instant out of the hole in the windshield. Tapered to points and reaching for something beyond sight. Hidden in the fog of steam.

The com goes dead. Inside the cab, a clenched jaw of broken teeth. A solid ice-like crystal. Catching and breaking the sunlight into rainbow fragments. Scattered over everything in the bitter world. The bells are gone.

The congested silence doesn't last. On the far side of the vehicle, the adult stage four moans, and I see a new pillar of smoke diffusing in the air. It's confused by the sudden, extreme change of temperature. That's how they see the world. Hot and cold. But its confusion's not gonna last. I know.

In a second, I decide against going for the supplies in the back of the vehicle, even with the lure running ten feet back. Extra Ice Packs. Food. Temper suits. Enough to survive. But stage fours are quick as jumping light. No reason good enough to run toward one.

I'm in the middle of the street. I scan the store fronts behind me. A grocery. A bail bonds place and a pizza joint. A pawn shop. Everything is gritty brick and cracked glass and empty eyes. I give myself two vibrating seconds to decide.

Sam trusted you like a brother. Why didn't you confirm the first freeze?

I crush the thought in my head. *Not now.* I spot a sign, Vino's Butcher Shop, and I run. Away from it all. But I feel a hot wind on the back of my neck, and I smell something human burning.

Rule: Forget your history. Your purpose is in your trigger finger.

I'm running on full, beaten instinct now. Hard earned in years and burning flesh.

The butcher's shop is rotting and almost totally devoid of light. Broken tubes of florescent along the ceiling. Sprigs of crumbling herbs, rosemary and sage, hang from the ceiling by lengths of butcher's twine. They add a soft accent of the desert to the wide, wet smell of rot. And that rot is thick as cement in the air, clogging my lungs and throat. I regret my choice, but I don't stop. I scan.

Rule: Sweep your corners. Sweep the room. Know your blinds.

Blinds: The shadow behind the glass counter. The space through the open doorway at the back of the shop. To somewhere dark. Maybe more blinds mixed with the unidentifiable sludge piles of rotting, gray-green meat in the broken display case. I take my flashlight off my belt and move quick. Leading with my .45. Sweeping my blind spots as I come to them. I breathe through my mouth, but I can taste old death. The sour edge at the end of every story.

The door behind the counter leads to a small kitchen. A butcher's block stained a deep maroon. A steel sink. Knives lined up, stuck to a strip of magnet on the wall. Several missing.

I scan. The sweeping beam of my flashlight lighting everything in brief, curved seconds. Blinds: Everywhere. Small, open doorway. An office? Other side of the table. Inside the open locker. My destination. Blinds. Every shadow I turn my back on.

The locker hums soft and electric. Still running. A tattered scrap of luck.

It's dark, light creeping at my back from the front of the shop and the street. I point my torch at the locker and start moving toward it.

I hear a dry shuffle of movement. Amplified by the com buds. Skin and cloth rubbing quick. Someone choking on words through a seizing throat. I spin toward it, toward the office, shifting backward at the same time. My beam hits a shuddering human form, sudden like the appearance of a wild deer on an empty country road.

He's got a slight, teenage body and a patchy growth of facial hair. Late teens, early twenties. His skin is bright red and shines with fever sweat in the flashlight. He holds a breaking knife, a twelve inch, slightly curved grin of steel, loose at his side

271

and something dark coats it. He speaks rapid and breathy and stuttering his f's. As if trying to memorize a speech.

"It's not my f-ault. Fault. Not mine. I just, wanted to live. My f-ault?"

Late stage two.

Something in the way the kid stands, shoulders hunched and all his bones jangling under his skin, makes me think of my first girlfriend. Her strawberry lip balm. And the simple lives we've all left behind.

"It's nobody's fault," I say. Though for whose benefit, I don't know.

"It's somebody's f-ault. Mine? Mine!" He screams without moving the rest of his body, mouth so wide I expect it to pop out of its hinges. The smell of rot is everywhere, and the air is cool and has a settled feeling. I'm sweating anyway.

Rule: Don't waste. No loud noises. Usually, hiding is better than fighting.

"I've got a .45 tacked to your forehead. Ready to freeze all your thoughts and take away your dreams. If that's what you want, keep shouting."

Some stage twos can still understand. The rabid scribbles of our words. Mangled chalk drawings on the air. And the words hurt in the newly burned skin of my face.

His body twitches in place as if it's missing something. For a moment, I'm reminded so powerfully of the past, it freezes me.

And he's faster than I expect. The sudden arc of his falling butcher's knife. The sweeping sound of cut air. The blade, silver in my light. A shooting star in a void. Suddenly, I feel the urge to reach out and catch it, like the stars I watched as a child. Empty hands up to a black sky.

I jump back. Not fast enough. The blade grazes my hand. A deep graze. The flashlight clatters to the ground like mad laughter. Its jumping light bouncing off stainless steel and old meat. I lunge in and grab his knife-holding wrist with my bleeding hand. He's surprisingly strong, gnashing his teeth, wild and painfully near my face. In the semi-illumination of reflected light, I try to angle the gun in my free hand. The cut doesn't hurt yet, but I know that void of space without pain can never last.

We stumble backward. Clumsy dancers we humans are.

"Do you want to die?" I half-whisper, half-yell. But he just keeps ripping up the air with his teeth.

I feel the solid thud of a wall through my back. Enough leverage to push. I push him hard. He stumbles back. I raise my foot and kick. Feel the young spring of his solar plexus. He collapses backward and falls into the beam of the flashlight. His baby brown eyes are wide and confused. Questioning.

But I've got no answer for any of this. None but one.

The shot is loud, too loud. The Ice Cube blasts a chunk of his forehead open and backward, above his right eye. And the rapid decompression of liquid cool freezes his ruin of splintered bone and tangled, fleshy neurons. A hole gaping at the world. And the world gaping back.

I hear a moaning, and a sudden whoosh of air from the street. A sound I know. The lure must have died by now, and, as I feared, the stage four heard the shot. My rising temperature. It can see the hot core of my still beating heart through the walls. The stubborn human part of me that refuses to die.

I jerk into gear. My hand starts to sing. A bloody, familiar song. I holster the gun and scoop the flashlight off the ground. No time to worry over blinds. No time to worry about corners. I step into the meat locker and grab the door just as a crashing, flickering boom explodes in the front of the shop. And I smell things burning. Burning meat mixing with the odor of rot everywhere. I slam the door shut.

I'm surround by the jerky humming of the locker's motor, the darkness of its burned out lights, and its hanging slabs of petrified, dried out beef that, in the shadows, look like mangled bodies. Slim racks of flesh covered in a gray mold like moss or scruffy body hair. Just about Samantha's size.

Not yet.

I push thoughts of her down again.

For the smallest part of a second I can feel, I let myself breathe.

Then I'm moving again. I transfer the flashlight to my teeth, rubber grip clicking in my bite, and draw my ice lady. My .45. Fighting the smell, which is everywhere like the looming pressure of an ocean on my lungs, I gag and fight it down. Eyes watering from the effort. I try to think of other smells. I slide forward through the hanging racks and empty hooks. I move careful. My roaming eye. Blinds everywhere. A thousand crooked corners of cast shadow. And light from my teeth. Through the door at my back, I hear a muted, wet cracking. Like something breaking new bones in its teeth.

Rule: Remain calm.

The sound is probably the stage four ripping into the still warmth of the new dead I left behind. Not far enough along in the stages to be useless to the four as fuel for whatever mystic fusion keeps it burning. Jumping hydrogen, and the dance of softly splitting atoms. The hyper-slow fission of a new universe born with a dead heart from the old skin of a person.

I reach the back wall. I turn around and slide down till I'm sitting. Half my burned face pulses in dull time with my slowing heart. A blinking light. My hand sings, hard and high. I'm facing the door now. I sweep my head. Take a last scan of the room. Hanging shadows. Empty corners. Shelves half stocked with random cuts and slabs of animal. Everything sunken and spoiled by the new, inescapable heat of the world. These shadows, misshapen and only familiar through the squinting corners of my eyes, are all that's left of the childhood of the world. And the hidden places where all of us were born.

I'm alone. The world's hollow and filled with spoiled food.

I take the light out of my teeth and set it down. The cold around me is growing deeper. Blowing in from a fan on the wall.

Rule: It's best to be alone. Easier.

In the solid dark, I put down my lady and pull a tin of Vaporub out of a pocket. Dab it under my nose. Old cop trick, a Sergeant told me once. He had one dead eye and he drank flat water and vodka at room temperature. He'd been a detective, back in the dream of his real life. Before the end of the world. Then, like the rest of us, he became some form of monster hunter. Some form of insomniac. Some form of wild man who had no dreams he could remember.

The menthol fumes on my lip overwhelm the stinking dead. Sweet and eye watering. A kind of artificial mint. Cutting deep into my mind. I put the tin away and take out a knife. With some difficulty, I cut off a sleeve and wrap my hand. Tight as I can with my teeth. The pain sends bolts through my bones and into my head. But I've left it open too long as it is. Anything violent could crawl up into my blood.

There's a million ways to die.

I use the flashlight to check the dressing. It's covered, at least. I shut the light off. The dark is comforting, and it makes it easier to keep my mind from spilling out through the cracks in my skull.

I'm settling now. The sound of my breathing echoes. Maybe only in my head. Through the door, I hear small movements. Too soft to know.

It might see me. Feel me like an itch in its eye. It might not. It's cool now, in here, and the hanging meat might help obscure its vision.

Either way, I'm not letting it have my mind. Early on, on a beach along the East coast, when we were still using iron bullets with exploding copper coats, I watched a stage four melt a man. Skin like a collapsing star. And a fluid embrace like a hard sea. It looked as if the ten-foot stage four was crushing the man in a bear hug. The way a father might embrace an injured child. The four cast dirty flickers of light over the mellow flats of sand dunes. We hadn't quite worked out Ice Packs then, stage fours were something new. Rumors in a time when everyone was mad and no one could trust the sun.

We emptied our useless lead into them both. And the heat made our eyes water and turned all our skin red. The screams died quick in the impossibly wide night. The man, a private, like me, whose name I didn't know, was limp. His skin and muscles unraveling and flowing through the four's long, thin arms. And its dislocated, toothless mouth. Biting him even as the skin dissolved in the heat of its jaw.

Not me.

I hold the gun loose in my good hand.

Rule: Just in case.

And I let myself drift on my small pains. The only things in the world I know are mine alone.

I am from a city like this one. As anonymous and American as a thousand places settled at the edges of other places. Main street strip of pawn shops and liquor stores, and ten thousand tangled bus routes like knotted hair. These towns all have soft, plain names that read like the names of graveyards. Citizens' Grove. South Haven. Lock Meadow. Outer suburbs packed dirty with outer people.

Like me.

Before the end, twenty-year-old me would drive my ancient F150 down the open verse of the highway and into farm country. Pull over and walk into the huge fields of dry wheat, get high, and fall asleep. Daring the thresher and the broad warmth of the sun. Watch the tails of wheat wave as if dancing to some slow song I believed I too could hear.

At night, Mom watched me with heavy brown eyes.

"What have you been up to?" And she'd regret asking as soon as the words left her lips. I could see it. Taste it in her baked potatoes and uneven cuts of overcooked beef.

"Nothing."

Dad would make up rules on the fly and recite them like military code.

"Rule: No job, no more truck." Then he'd smile, earnest in a way I never was and never will be. "I know you can do this. Rule: It's okay to be scared."

He had a face like mine, but softer and better looking. Clear eyed and no real scars.

I'd nod vacantly at him, and later, I'd connect the battery wires and starter wires in the truck so I could go buy my kid brother and his friends beer with my fake ID.

I took for granted my eternal youth. The endless time bursting my pockets. The broad sky was mine. And the road.

When the news of the end, of a final kind of mortality, started to come, it came quick. Suddenly, a burning crowd. A field of moaning dead.

We watched the news as a family. A clumsy fear we refused to name necessitating our touch. Cities burning and spreading fever. Dangerous hospitals, centers of carnage. A heat wave emanating from our bodies.

Mom got sick. And Dad. And kid brother was bleeding from his eyes. And one night, I woke to screaming. I grabbed the brick I used as a paper weight from my desk. Flirting with the grit of a harder life.

I stumbled into blue midnight. The hallway. Kid brother—*Danial. Can't you even say his name?*—was waiting for me. Trapped in the hall's shadows like a wild animal in a net. Thrashing. An open pocket knife, two-and-a-half inch blade, in one hand.

My first scar.

He was spitting gibberish. Repeating himself. Early stage two. Later, I'd learn all the names and all the symptoms. In the hall, in the childhood of the world, I thought he was having a seizure. Back then, I still believed in the story of our fate. The world in our hands. The certainty of my inheritance as a ruler of the universe. And the screaming was my father. Fractured voice and dry throat. Somewhere beyond the standing seizure of my kid brother. In a dark that was mine to enter.

"Brother get me high. High. Hey. It's cool. Cool. Cool brother. Cool world. Oh, *cool world.*"

He laughed like the jangling mad, and I told him to relax. When I touched his forehead, he shifted and buried his little knife in my shoulder, a solid piece of the timeless night.

And instinct drove the brick into his head. And my arm, the smooth mechanism of the only true fate in the world.

Chaos.

And a road of dreamless nights to here.

In the almost dark, I could see his broken skull. Deeply dented by the corner of the brick and jagged edges sticking out wet. The body attached to it as still as the lifeless moon. My first kill.

In one, blank motion, I tore the short knife out of my arm. And dropped it. Gritting my teeth hard enough to crack.

Mom was chewing on Dad. And Dad was almost done screaming. Through their open curtains, I could see a distant fire lighting the horizon. Something terrible waking in the broken, western sky. Where the sun disappeared. And the light distorted their bent forms further, until they looked twisted and inhuman. She didn't notice me come up behind her, bare feet soft on the carpet. I broke her spine where it showed. Soft mounds at the base of her neck. With the brick. I pulled her off the bed. She was the limp heavy of the dead I didn't yet know. Dad was spitting blood bubbles. And his eyes were everywhere. Then they were on me.

"Rule: Survive no matter what you have to do."

And there was something in his voice, suddenly hard and heat wave clear, that I recognized. Something in it was like the stone promise lodged in my chest. The self-assured promise of my own importance that I could no longer believe in. That was crumbling with each new, heated breath.

A dream I was just about to wake from.

"Sure, Dad. I will."

Then his breath, jerky and short, stopped. And something was gone in the night. But I thought, delirious and cold, that he might come back, even though his neck and shoulder was a mess of open flesh. So I turned him over and broke in the back of his skull with the brick. Like a thick egg breaking. And the dull and human sound.

I buried the brick in the backyard. The sun was still deep under the horizon, but a kind of dawn was all around me. The wild light of something burning.

I buried it deep.

Later, at an evac' hospital, an Army doctor told me congratulations. I had type one resistance. Less than five percent of the population had T1R. For me, infection required intimate contact.

"Intimate?"

The doctor had hunting owl eyes, scavenger eyes of a survivor, and a sloped, protruding lip, like a beak. A night animal. Like me. He tapped his wrist with a pen.

"Blood n' blood."

Even a bite might not be enough to bring me in line with this new, atomic fate. Where all lives are short and bright as super novas in the perfect void.

The world's a blotchy mess. Always has been. Mix of dreams and broken glass pebbles of truth. I'm drifting through the useless past. The lack of light is so complete I could be dreaming one of my empty dreams. It's very cold now, and it has blunted the smell down to a stiff mold.

The pain's pretty bad. The blood in my dressing has gone stiff and the hand is numb. I wonder what my ruined face looks like, but I don't touch it. The sensation of cool air over my cheek tells me enough. It's soft and painful, like it's stroking my ruined skin. A lover or a mother.

"Oh, cool world," I mutter into the nothingness. Chuckling lightly. Which sends cracks of pain through the skin around my mouth.

The air on my face is like a woman's fingers. Small. Warm. Familiar. Exactly like fingers.

My eyes crack open. I fumble the flashlight.

"Samantha?"

My voice is dry in the air. How long was I drifting? The beam lights a section of the dark ultra white and sterile. Hanging meat, gray and green with mold. I sweep corners. The light's shaking in my hands.

Rule: Time to get up.

I stand. All my bones grind against each other like frozen gears. That, and the slow choking of the walk-in blower, are the only sounds in the world.

I take my lady in my right hand. Gently, I hold the flashlight in my left. Try to shake the past out of my head.

When I open the sealed door, a wave of warm rot hits me like sudden consciousness. The scent of burned hair and scorched human oils mixes with the now-familiar scent of spoiled neglect. I vomit, hot and cutting in my throat. Sharp and quick. I try to keep my eyes open and forward. And they water profusely. A kind of empty crying.

It passes and I spit. Try to focus on the smell of menthol wafting from my upper lip.

It's dark. Through the doorway leading into the shop, I see the brilliant, jagged reds of polluted, ashen aired sunset.

The butcher kid's a flat puddle of thick fluid, like syrup. Broken bits of bone, black and soft from heat, stick out, and the rising slope of his half-collapsed ribs and ruin of skull are lifeless islands. Empty hole of his grin.

Melted down to their lonely, elemental parts, all people smile empty and in a knowing, painful way.

I give him a wide berth. I taste something sour and acrid, lingering over everything in the room. Sweep my corners. Slow and mechanic. My gaze everywhere in the air. And the kid watches me with no eyes and only one unbroken eye socket.

Early on, when kill teams were first cut to two guys, Samantha and I pulled over along the side of a long, Midwestern highway whose old name was useless and half forgotten. Now it was called Highway 6, because it bisected zone six. A high-density zone. Recently designated. The corn and soybean crops to either side were wilted, but not yet burned down. They shivered in the wind and seemed huddled over themselves by the lack of water. In the distance, a city of a million scattered lives was burning down all at once. Flickers of light and rambling sparks. The heat made the whole thing wave and bend. As if it might not be real.

I walked around the Humvee and sat on the hood.

Samantha got out and stood near me. She held silent for a moment.

"Shouldn't we be doing something?"

I couldn't look away from the wavering mirage of our burning history on the horizon. I didn't want to look at her. I didn't know how to explain. How little power we had. How small we were, outside the cavernous galaxies of our minds. How there was nothing for us to be doing.

"It's been burning for a long time," I said. "Nothing we can do now. Let it burn."

She climbed onto the hood with me. I took out a slim, hand-rolled cigarette and let the crystal smoke soften the already blurred edges of the world. Tobacco was a luxury, an almost extinct animal paraded out only on special occasions. It made me lightheaded and easy. I passed it to Sam.

She coughed quietly and spoke into her hand, "Your parents alive, David?"

"We don't talk about the past," I said, taking the cigarette as she passed it back.

"Why not?"

My last team, three good guys, had been wiped out in the narrow halls of some dirty motel. Pincered in by a stage four with half a mind left who burned down a wall to circle us and pinch us between it and a shuttering crowd of mad men and women with bleeding mouths and eyes. Stage threes. The guys were all hard, like me, but unlucky. Like me. Samantha was a rookie and barely eighteen. We had only been on a few jobs together. But I guessed she was unlucky too.

I didn't answer her.

"My parents aren't. Alive," she said. "I watched them get torn to pieces by a couple stage threes. This was later on. After the second heat wave. At a rest stop along interstate 40. Five of them sprang out when I opened the door to the toilet. And my parents were begging me to run even as they were getting... torn apart." Her voice was as flat as the highway and as beaten down. I looked at her. She had her eyes set on the vague horizon of flame. Hard, unlucky eyes. Reflecting the living red and orange light of our future.

The wind was cool. And the weeping crops around us. Unpicked from now unto eternity.

"We don't talk about the past because all the parents, and all the kids, and all the lovers, and all the friends, and all the priests, and all grocery store clerks are dead. We don't talk about our pasts, cause everybody's got the same one. We're all from the cemetery, and we're all orphans." I said this as tonelessly as possible. Aiming it toward the fire.

The new silences of the world were always filled with the crackling of distant fire. The dry shuffle of corn and short rows of soybean. The empty road from here to there.

"Today," she said.

"Sorry?" I blew out a cloud of smoke with the word. Passed it back. The cigarette was half gone and the world seemed more alive. I wanted to tell her more. Something not so hard. How some moments can be soft. Small. Between the tired ends of our lives.

"Today, everybody's got a story. Everybody's got a whole gallery of dead behind them. But my kids are gonna grow up in a different world. Where they can meet someone, and they don't have to check their eyes for inflamed veins, and a cough doesn't mean they're gonna die painfully."

And the sure cool in her voice shocked and excited me. I didn't mean to, but I laughed.

She turned to me. Steady eyes, brown and clear as apple juice. As if she were used to being laughed at.

"You don't believe me. It's fine." She sounded as if she meant it. "Why'd you sign up, David? If not for something better. A better place."

She watched the pale smoke wafting out of her own mouth as if it might be hiding that imagined place.

I laughed again. I couldn't help it. Somewhere, God was laughing at us. And we were laughing back, insane and flickering. The breath bouncing painful in our broken chests. "Some monsters," I said to her while the world burned before us, "have to eat other monsters to survive."

And at the edge of sight, the echo of my laughter burned like everything else.

I'm on the street. The adult four is nowhere to be seen. I know they have to move often in search of fuel, and have short memories. I see the broken road, abandoned or overturned cars in either direction. Empty streets. The slight haze of smoke always in the air now. Thin in my lungs. The pollution of the burning world gives us, daily, stained glass sunsets, blood red and deep as our secrets. And dark at the edges.

I strain my ears, by which I mean I turn the dial in my ear to maximum to pick out the small sounds in the world. The paper crinkle of trash in the wind. The soft popping of burning far off. My breath, warm and wet. And something moaning, cotton dry and low, from the other side of the Humvee.

The air is sweet as caramel stuck in my teeth after the butcher's shop, and I breathe it all in as I approach the vehicle. I scan the air right above the Humvee. No heat lines. No smoke. One thing about stage fours, they're easy to spot. And this isn't one.

As I approach, I spend a second of attention on the Humvee's cab. Most of the quick ice has melted, though a few soft-edged lumps hang here and there. Everything is wet and dripping. Samantha's in there, and she's alone. The Armbrust's in her lap, and her head is back. Eyes open and glazed with a blue-white film. Her skin is wet and a sick, cold color.

"Sorry, Sam," I mutter, still moving slow and leading with my .45. "I'll pick it up from here. For somebody else's kids, I guess."

I circle wide around the Humvee, giving myself space to move. Add Sam's name to the list in my head. The list of people I've killed. As I circle, I spot it. Without its dress of smoke or suit of liquid flame, it seems infinity fragile. Black skin and the hollow bones of a bird. The kid stage four is on its stomach. It's trying to drag itself toward me, but its movements are as slow and painstaking as the movement of the earth. Whatever powered its wild, ancient fission has run out.

It's out of heat.

I holster the .45. Take the long way around the vehicle. I don't look at Samantha again.

I unhook the clasps on the back compartment of the Humvee. I sort the canvas and tempered cloth bags with my good hand until I find my pack. I pull out a small mirror. Examine my face.

It's a field of ruin. Half of it has melted and it's a raw, red color. The new plane of my face has a softness, though, and it is ruled by the same kind of feral logic as the dune beaches in my memory. My left eyebrow is gone, and that strikes me funny. I chuckle into the pain.

The first-aid kit is snapped into the sidewall. I pull it out. The dry moaning, as thin as a single sheet of skin, is constant and low. In the air like birdsong. I take out the tin of burn salve. It's a thick, clear gel with a hint of blue. I rub it into the barren field of my face. For a moment, it tingles as if it's alive, then the skin goes ice numb.

I pat down my pack till I find half a cigarette. Press it into my lip, find my lighter. I can hear the thing dragging itself toward me at the speed of time. Inevitable and slow. I peel off my ruined jacket, trade it for a heavy, temper coat. Bite and heat resistant. I'm careful of my hand. It throbs, swollen and tight. I'll re-wrap it soon.

I take a few puffs. Let it all drift and disappear into the shattered window of sky.

When I'm ready, I walk around the car to the half-live thing, dying in the street. Black strip of dried flesh. The smell that rises from it is surprising and pleasant, like the scent of charred mangoes and exotic spice. There are no features left on its face. It's naked. Cracked patches of dry skull are exposed to the human wind, in from the north. Filtered through the glass cage of the nearby city.

Every inch of its skin is blackened or gone or melted into its stringy, dry tendons, which spasm weakly, as if it's shivering. As if a cold is taking it. Its eyes are blind, but it holds them up hopefully, milk film and a dark blue fluid leaking from them like strange tears. Its useless tongue, swollen and bleeding. I know this thing. I recognize it.

And its whispered moaning is a language I almost understand.

Rising and falling. Begging. Praying. Cursing. I know all the words. I've said them all before.

I crouch down, a few feet from it, and it reaches out to me. Its voice is a burning forest. A smothered infant's cry. The mangled voice of our generation. Soft, and lost in the sound of fire. But loud in our heads.

It's so small. It must have been so young. Its life so short and painful. Yet it drags itself toward the last point of warm life on its horizon. The gun weighs as little as the heart in my chest. And I hold it as easily. Aimed right between its sightless eyes.

In the west, the sun is going. Brilliant and sad. I'll have to hotwire a car in the dark. Drive north. Into the cold. Where the last men and women huddle together for warmth in short, steel domes. I'll lead another kill team. Come back here and sweep the place with ice. That stage four and any others. I know now, for certain, there are more every day. I'll go out on my own, if I have to. I've done it before. Years ago now. A young killer with a bat, a hunting rifle. Alone on the highway.

Rule: I am relevant as long as I am alive.

Keep telling yourself that, cowboy.

My rules are cardinal truth. Doubt leads to immobility. And immobility is death. The husk of a child before me, all its chaos atoms finally stopped and dying, confirms this.

Then how come you only ever dream about the past?

I push it down. All my memories of Samantha and the rest of the singing dead. Hard and deep in my gut. Clenching it all in the fist of my mind like I'm trying to make a diamond from a fistful of ash.

I tighten my hand around the gun. Thinking of all the people still living somewhere in the world.

And here, on this American street, something, some monster with a hard shell and soft guts, is dying with a strangled moan that no one will ever hear.

The Fine Distinction
Between Cooks and Chefs

BY BRANDON SANDERSON

Brandon Sanderson was born in 1975 in Lincoln, Nebraska. By junior high he had lost interest in the novels suggested to him, and he never cracked a book if he could help it. Then an eighth-grade teacher, Mrs. Reader, gave him Dragonsbane *by Barbara Hambly.*

Brandon was finishing his thirteenth novel when Moshe Feder at Tor Books bought the sixth he had written. In 2005 Brandon held his first published novel, Elantris, *in his hands. Tor also published six books in Brandon's Mistborn series, along with* Warbreaker *and then* The Way of Kings *and* Words of Radiance, *the first two in the planned ten-volume series* The Stormlight Archive. *Four books in his middle-grade* Alcatraz Versus the Evil Librarians *series are being released by Starscape (Tor). Brandon was chosen to complete Robert Jordan's Wheel of Time series; the final book,* A Memory of Light, *was released in 2013. That year also marked the releases of YA novels* The Rithmatist *from Tor and* Steelheart *from Delacorte.*

Currently living in Utah with his wife and children, Brandon teaches creative writing at Brigham Young University. He also hosts the Hugo Award-winning writing advice podcast Writing Excuses *with Mary Robinette Kowal, Howard Tayler, and Dan Wells.*

The Fine Distinction
Between Cooks and Chefs

A lot of people want to give you writing advice. I've felt it—trust me, I've been there. During my long years trying to break in as a writer, I felt that I never lacked for someone jumping in to tell me how this writing thing had to be done.

I appreciated most of it. Writing is, in most cases, a solitary art. Every bit of advice helps, in its own way, even if all it does is express solidarity. But in most of the sincere suggestions, I also sensed a kind of worried paternalism. The authors offering advice seemed to be saying, "You poor thing. You have no idea what you're in for."

Trouble is, neither did they.

You see, every writer's path is unique. What works every time for one of us will fail brilliantly for another of us. Each bit of writing advice has to be tempered with this terrible knowledge: that for the writer listening, your advice might be the most spectacularly wrong thing that has ever been suggested to them.

For one of us, an outline is a vital tool. For another, it's a black hole that sucks the life from our story. For one of us, trimming words in revision is the only path to crisp, evocative prose. For another, cutting leads to a sense of empty, white-room syndrome in scenes. Some authors should never stop midstory to do revisions, lest they get lost in an endless cycle of tweaking, and lose all momentum. For others, this process is an essential step in discovering the voice of their characters.

As a writing instructor, this knowledge is daunting. At the same time, it's intriguing. Each new writer is at the cusp of a grand journey—a journey we have all taken before, yet one where certain tools that worked for me will be useless for you. And at the end, we all arrive at a different place. That's what makes writing so grand; each of us has something to add, and each of us has something new to discover that no one else could have found.

All of this leads to a question: If the usefulness of writing advice is so unpredictable, then why bother giving (or listening to) it in the first place? Well, unpredictable does not equate to unusable.

Your job as a writer is not to slavishly take every word uttered by a pro as gospel. Instead, you should envision yourself as an explorer. Or, if you will, as a chef.

There are two basic ways to bake a cake. The first, and the one that most of us use, is to follow a set of instructions. I can make a perfectly acceptable cake by doing this, as can most of us. However, I'm not a chef—just a cook, in this metaphor. You see, I don't know why adding eggs to a cake is important, or what the real difference between baking soda and baking powder is. (I mean, both look like powders to me.)

If you want to make your way from journeyman writer to one creating professional-quality works, you can't afford to be a cook. You can't be the person who looks at a list of story ingredients and says, "Huh. Guess I just add these in the order listed." I read far too many books (and see even more movies) that seem to have been created this way. Take everything that has been successful before, stick them in, bake at 375. Success, right?

That can't be good enough for you. I want you to think consciously about the choices you make in writing. That's how you find your way through the journey, and arrive at your unique destination. Just like a good chef knows what happens when you add a specific seasoning at a specific time, I suggest you start analyzing the fiction you love and ask yourself the hard questions.

Many "hero's journey"–type stories start with an orphan. Why? What does this do to the story? Can you get this effect in a different way?

What really makes people turn the pages in a thriller? What creates this sensation of anxiety in the reader, and why do they enjoy it? What kinds of endings satisfy this emotion, and which ones fall flat for you?

Why do some romances work, while others feel contrived? What ingredients lead to a relationship plot that readers gobble up, and which kinds of relationship plots continue to work after the two characters have gotten together?

Every bit of writing advice you get is a tool that worked for someone. It might work for you. However, chances are that even if it does, it will do something slightly different in your stories than it does in mine. You are the chef, you are the master of your own writing. Don't just follow a list someone tells you, own the process that you use to create.

At least, that's the best advice I can give. Unfortunately, it might just be the most spectacularly wrong thing that's ever been suggested to you.

Try it out and see.

The Jade Woman of the Luminous Star

written by

Sean Williams

illustrated by

DANIEL TYKA

ABOUT THE AUTHOR

Sean Williams entered the Writers of the Future Contest ten times before his story "Ghost of the Fall" won third prize in the first quarter of 1992.

He has since become a #1 New York Times *bestselling author, with over forty novels and one hundred short stories to his credit, not to mention the odd* odd *poem.*

*He has been called many things, including 'the premier Australian speculative fiction writer of the age' (*Aurealis*) and the 'king of chameleons' (*Australian Book Review*) for the diversity of his writing. As well as his original fiction for adults, young adults and children, he has worked in universes created by other people, such as* Star Wars *and* Doctor Who. *He also enjoys collaborating, for instance with Garth Nix on their Troubletwisters books. He has a PhD in the literature of matter transmitters, which trope he has used many times, most recently in his acclaimed Twinmaker series.*

Now an international judge of the Writers of the Future Contest, he still lives in the dry, flat lands of South Australia, just up the road from a chocolate factory, with his wife and family and pet plastic fish.

ABOUT THE ILLUSTRATOR

Born in 1983 in Warsaw, Poland, Daniel Tyka was raised with the smell of oil paints, as his father was a painter. It was a difficult time, when Poland was ruled by communists; Tyka didn't have fancy toys or computers. To fill his time, he could either go outside to play with other kids or draw.

In high school, Daniel loved art, but instead of art school, followed a path into the financial industry where he lost nine years trying to fit into the financial corporate life.

Then, eight years ago, inspired by a website called "CGSociety," he began watching free tutorials on the net and studying by himself.

With a little push from his friends, Daniel decided to quit his job and spend all his time drawing. He began spending 16 hours per day working on his laptop. After a year he began getting his first jobs, which enabled him to slowly make a living. From then on, art has been a wild ride until now.

The decision to take art seriously was the best decision in Daniel's life. With all of the resources on the net, he didn't think that art school was necessary anymore.

Today, he is living his dream. Daniel won the Illustrators of the Future contest in 2014 and he was featured in Volume 31.

The Jade Woman of the Luminous Star

You must get me out of here, Michaels. I have important work to do."

Those were the first words uttered by Hugh Gordon in my presence. I remember them clearly. On the one hand, I was relieved that he was willing to acknowledge me as a fellow professional, for a man of his standing, even in his dire circumstances, might have been tempted to dismiss me as a physician of no great renown, as in fact I am (and would very much like to return to being, Inspector Berkeley, once you have read this deposition). On the other hand, he seemed genuinely convinced that I could effect his release.

When I declared that this was quite impossible, he became irritable and aggressive. He accused me of gloating, of malpractice, even of spying. The last is outlandish, of course, but might have seemed plausible before his arrest. You are no doubt aware of his reputation—as a scientist, I mean. His advances in aeronautical engineering have been considerable; many have even been adopted by the Ministry of Calculation for employment throughout the empire. Now that his laboratory has been razed, is it too ghoulish to imagine that someone might want to pick his brains for knowledge the gallows might otherwise claim?

Eventually, he took me at my word. He had no alternative, and I remember thinking that there was no predicament too alien for a keen intellect to confront. I admired the power of his mind, you see, even under such duress. I had not yet glimpsed the depths of his delusion—or of his cunning, depending on your interpretation of subsequent events.

He warned me: "You will think me certifiable, Michaels, if I tell you the truth. I despaired too, at first, and with good reason: this vile place, with its loathsome inmates and equally loathsome porters, and all that preceded it. . . . But then I wondered. Could it possibly be that she sent me here deliberately? You see, I felt something intangible when the door you just came through slammed shut behind me, something profound beyond words. Was this the 'precipice of light' Pattinattar wrote of nine hundred years ago? Had I chanced upon the secret of the ancients, which I must find anew or never see her again?"

His eyes had taken on a remote and urgent look, staring beyond the walls of Exeter Vale Asylum toward vistas unknown. I endeavored to bring him back to more immediate mysteries.

"Margaret, do you mean?"

He sank back onto his cot and put his head in his hands. "No, not Margaret. And no, this was not the right place. I tried, but could not follow in the great poet's footsteps. So here I am, Michaels, at your mercy."

I had been apprised of the statements he had made upon his arrest. I was aware that another woman might be implicated in the affair, although she had neither come forward nor been named. For your part, Inspector, you know that my purpose that day was to ascertain if this woman existed and, if so, whether she was complicit in the murder of Margaret Gordon. I resolved to be resolute in my pursuit of the truth, lest a great man of science be ruined over something of which he might be completely innocent.

I thought, then, that he might be shielding a jealous mistress. I would come to wonder if injured pride and his fall from grace drove him to perpetrate violent acts on all the women around him.

I do not know what I think now.

"You must tell me what happened," I said to him.

"Yes, yes—and if I must tell someone, it might as well be a scholar like me." He raised his head, regarding me with bloodshot but startlingly blue eyes. "I think it was Pattinattar, again, who said: 'I do not mix with idle, useless men. I do not listen to their speech.'"

He was trying to distract me with flattery.

"Tell me who she is, Doctor Gordon. Where did you meet? Where was it she wanted you to go?"

"Such difficult questions! You have no idea what you ask."

I said nothing.

"Very well." He shifted so his shoulders rested against the wall. "Her name is Abiha, and Margaret—poor Margaret—thought she was a ghost."

It started on the twenty-fifth (he began, speaking with the clipped precision of one used to addressing the Royal Institution) and I say this, Michaels, with certainty, because it was the night of the lunar eclipse and I had been studying craters by telescope. My thoughts were as full as the face of that distant world. I imagined myself standing upon those jagged, airless mountains, staring up at the darkened globe of the Earth. For all the advances we have made in recent decades, our trains, steamers, and airships are no closer to taking us there. We need infinitely more powerful forms of transportation to make these dreams reality, and I, unlike most dreamers, have the means to do just that. I had been working on them that very evening.

It was well past midnight when Margaret came down for me, complaining about the noise. "What noise?" I asked. The household was asleep and the laboratory closed. All of Exeter was hushed. The eclipse had put the town in a somber, premonitory mood.

"Someone has been knocking," she said. "If not you, then who?"

I could tell that she would not be pacified until the matter had received the attention she believed it deserved. Abandoning the telescope, I went inside to prove to her that there had been no knocking, by me or anyone else. With no one to upbraid,

I hoped she would let the matter go, return to her bedroom, and leave me to conclude my observations in peace.

We found no one in the house, no windows open, and no note at the front door. The house was empty and silent.

Yet, as I was leading Margaret back to her rest, there came a sound from below—hard and sharp, a sudden clap as of a book falling face-first onto the floor.

Margaret jumped, and I confess I started too. Barely had the echoes faded than I was on my way back down the stairs, convinced that the sound had originated in the laboratory.

Have you seen my laboratory, Michaels? No? Well, it is as big as a barn, and needs to be, for I have tested engines in there and reconstructed whole sections of airship frames at one-to-one scales. These days, it is full of glass bells much larger than a man, dozens of them, connected by copper wires and containing delicate Faraday cages of my own design. If someone were in there, they would find little they understood, but much that they could damage. It is—

Ah, yes, I forget myself. It's all gone—and why not? My research will benefit no one now.

Poor Margaret. The irony that she was the one to draw this phenomenon to my attention is not lost on me.

She waited in the doorway as I searched the vast space, leaving no cupboard or nook untouched. I found nothing, and the sound was not repeated. Yet I had heard it: the evidence of my senses was not to be denied.

All I found was a slight crack in my newest bell, a crack that I was certain had not been there before. The bell was spoiled, but I dismissed it as a simple case of thermal compression in the cooling house, coupled with stored stress in the curved glass, suddenly releasing itself. I ascended with Margaret in tow, confident that I had found enough evidence to put her mind at rest. If it occurred to her to ask how a single crack could have made all the other noises she reported, she said nothing.

I slept soundly. I may have dreamed, but I do not recall. I do have a sense of being plagued by my nightmare all that month, and I suppose this will interest you, Michaels: it is what drives me, day and night, in my quest for the perfect transportation device. It is a dream that has haunted me since childhood, a dream of a world poisoned by the fumes of its industry, where inefficient coal boilers spew smoke and char, interminable lines of vehicles choke the streets, and overloaded airships rain ash upon the sickened races below. For all my successes, all my novel advances, my greatest fear is that I have not done enough to prevent this calamity from coming to pass. I am far less afraid of being forgotten than of leaving no one behind to remember my efforts.

(He chuckled at that, without humor, and I reminded him to adhere to the subject.)

Margaret was the first to talk of haunting. I, of course, wouldn't credit the idea, but it was indisputable that in subsequent days noises were heard in the house that could not be explained away as the servants at work or the walls settling. Strange thumps, scrapes, and sighs came at random intervals, utterly without warning, sometimes seeming near, other times as far away as Selene herself. I told Margaret she was imagining things, but I knew she was not. I could not explain it, and would not accept her explanation, and so the phenomenon had to be ignored.

I am embarrassed to admit to the willful disregard of data—data that might have led me much sooner to the understanding I now possess, and might even have prevented the calamity that befell dear Margaret—but there you have it. My mind was fixed on other matters. One week after that first night I was expected to address my peers at the Institution on my latest experiments, and my speech was not yet prepared. Instead of pursuing the matter of our spectral interloper, I worked long hours distilling my thoughts and combing the library for references I might have overlooked. There was no time for Margaret's uneasy superstitions.

On the day of my departure, I descended early to the

laboratory, intending to add the final touches to my speech before anyone else awoke—only to find that my notes had been rifled through and scattered across the desk. Several pages had fallen to the floor, there to be trodden on like so much refuse. You can imagine my alarm. I woke the house with Herculean wrath and demanded that every maidservant be questioned. They swore that no one had entered the laboratory during the night. It had in fact been securely locked, by me, before retiring, and the lock had not been tampered with. I had the only key, but I did not believe them. Someone must have entered the laboratory and examined my work. Someone!

My interrogation of the staff might have continued all day had not the urgent need to prepare for my departure intervened. I gathered up the notes in a fury, secured my valise, and rushed out to where my carriage was waiting to whip me to the station. Margaret farewelled me at the steps, in something of a state herself. Unnatural noises in conjunction with physical disturbance added up to a poltergeist in her mind, and she was reluctant to remain in the house without me to protect her.

It would be easy to say that she had been reading too much fabulous fiction—but that would ignore a facet of her character that I had always admired, and which is essential for any wife of mine: an open mind. Some would say that I have said much stranger things, and indeed I proposed a few of them that very day.

I said "peers" earlier, when I referred to my audience at the Royal Institution, but what I mean is my critics. You may not be familiar with my most recent theories—of life on this earth as a river, and an individual, such as you or me, as an eddy in that river, a self-sustaining whirlpool of vital dynamism that endures even though the particles of water comprising it constantly change. This philosophical principle has received a warm welcome in some quarters—but the same cannot be said of the theories of transportation that naturally arise from it. Doesn't it strike you as odd, Michaels, that we lug this ponderous sack of tissues around with us every time we go hither and yon? Wouldn't it be easier to abandon it and adopt an identical one when we arrive—to move the eddy alone and leave the river behind?

Well, you are not alone, and some of my critics dislike my methodology as much as my philosophy. If I am so interested in transportation, they say, why base myself in Exeter, so far from the great steel machines of the north? There, I say, is the answer. Those machines are not in my vision. They crush the landscape and foul the sky. They are the nightmare, not the dream.

Yes, yes, the ghost. I am getting there, have no fear, if by my own slow and torturous path.

It was well after nightfall by the time I returned home. I was exhausted. My ears rang with the bleating of pedants, and I was in no mood for what greeted me. Who would have been? The house was in an uproar, due to a rash of "manifestations," as Margaret called them, from eerie whispers to strange explosions; even a minor earthquake, I was told, that had upset a row of plates in the kitchen, shattering every one. I was inclined to regard at least the last of these incidents as carelessness, perhaps even willful trickery, but in the face of Margaret's distress I could not dismiss them all. Something was afoot. The question was, what?

Two of the servants had resigned, citing good, Christian horror at such devilish pranks, though not above accepting generous severances if they kept silent in the parish. My presence reassured those who remained, and when they had gone home, leaving me and Margaret alone in the unsettled house, I was able to put my mind to the problem, for that was how I now regarded it—something to be solved and put behind me, rather than dangerously ignored.

Already I knew that the phenomena came at all hours, not just during the night; and that apart from the dishes and the cracked glass bell—both of which might have been coincidence—they consisted solely of sensory impressions. Nothing concrete had been detected. What other data we had were as elusive as the atoms of my imaginary river.

299

I told Margaret that I was going to make camp in the laboratory that night, in order to study the phenomenon more closely. She told me I was addled even to consider it, but I was adamant. The manifestations were confined to the ground floor, so it made sense to conduct the experiment in situ. I gathered a decanter of sherry and several books from the library to pass the time. Exhausted though I was, I planned to stay awake the entire night and record what I experienced.

Ah, Michaels, if only my notes survived! One sheet would provide you with all the evidence you need, although perhaps you would interpret it as the product of a deranged psyche. You would see in those notes my keenest observations, with each incident dutifully timed and described, accompanied by speculations as to cause, where such was not immediately obvious.

Of the sounds, many were mechanical, such as tiny clicks and whirrs that came at irregular intervals, as though a vast and invisible calculating machine surrounded me. Others were natural: once, for instance, I swear I heard a bird call, and there were the faintest hints of voices, coming and going at the very fringe of perception.

I monitored several thermometers and recorded numerous wide swings in temperature. Different parts of the room often disagreed by several degrees, and I was forever loosening and tightening my cravat.

At least twice, I swear, something poked me gently, once between the shoulder blades and once in my chest. Nothing at all was to be seen.

I accumulated several pages of notes over the course of the night, but came to no conclusions. My attention wandered back to my work, and to the books I had brought with me for the long vigil. They were translations, mostly, of texts dismissed in these enlightened days, but in which I hoped to find a gleam of inspiration. For thousands of years, you see, alchemists have written of moving in ways that would seem magical to us. Lu Yen's Chu T'ang shu described traversing the tapestry of stars to the edge of day—that is in third-century China, when the most famous Chinese alchemist of all, Ko Hung, believed that he could fly to heaven by mounting the air and treading on light, echoing the Daoist Dance of Yu, where adepts physically trace out the constellations in order to travel to the stars. Such apparently preposterous claims are not confined to China, by any means. Egyptians believed that certain words provided people with the power to travel safely through different worlds after death, while The Coffin Texts claim that one can learn how to cross over the sky and explore the entire universe. Thoth boasted of descending to the Earth with secrets belonging to the horizon, and that claim was later taken up by the Greeks: in Corpus Hermeticum, Hermes Trismegistus instructs students to fly into the heavens without wings. Scholars have often suspected that there was something these venerable philosophers understood that we have forgotten, but my intention was not to recover that supposedly lost knowledge, instead to make it a reality and put it to the salvation of our civilization. If people dreamed thus, once upon an age, then I could make them dream again.

When dawn arrived, the carafe was empty and I was utterly exhausted. The maidservant found me asleep at my drafting table with my head on my arms when she knocked gently at the locked door to see if I required breakfast.

I roused myself and told her that, yes, I would require something even heartier than normal to get the day properly underway. I did not reveal to her that my quest had come to nothing. I was, if anything, more mystified than ever. After a nearly sleepless night, I now faced a long day of research, and questions from Margaret that I was no nearer to answering.

When I returned to the desk, what I saw sent all thoughts of food to the four winds.

Daubed in thick ink across my careful notes was a symbol I had seen before, but which I had not drawn. It was a sign used by alchemists of the fourteenth century to capture the union of the sexes.

Don't scowl at me, Michaels. I'm not being unnecessarily prurient. One must describe what one sees: that is the most important rule of science, particularly if one has broken it already that week!

This crude drawing, this arcane symbol, was the first confirmed, physical manifestation of the creature that was to change my life forever.

You must imagine my wary excitement upon this discovery. I was not frightened by the phenomenon itself, but I very much feared being taken for a fool, and so I conducted a thorough search of the desk and its surroundings, the door and its lock, even the windows, tightly sealed against the night's chill, lest someone had waited until I slept to deliver this cryptic sigil. I found nothing to suggest that it was anything other than an anomaly; and, perhaps, a message from beyond.

Breakfast arrived, with Margaret hard on its heels. I hid the defaced sheet under the rest of my notes and told no one about it. Why? Well, instinct played a part. Margaret was unsettled enough; I didn't want her crying the house down, demanding exorcisms or séances or whatever is the latest fad in London these days. And we had lost enough staff already. Better, I told myself, to keep this development to myself for the time being, until I was absolutely certain of its import.

I know what you must be thinking: I was tired and had been reading alchemical texts all night. The sherry, too, might have played a part. It is only natural for you to assume that I had doodled the symbol myself in some deep hypnagogic state and woken unaware that I was its author. That is in fact the complete reverse of the reality. The symbol appeared because I was reading the texts. The hand that so crudely crafted it was drawn to me for this very reason.

Margaret was not persuaded by my assurances that nothing untoward had occurred that night, but the events of the day went some way toward reinforcing the white lie. As though the production of the drawing had calmed our so-called haunting, all further incidents were greatly reduced in magnitude. Nothing happened that could not be attributed to natural causes, and I was careful to ensure that calm prevailed.

That night, to be certain I was not interrupted, I slipped a dose of chloral into Margaret's evening cocoa. When at last she was breathing peacefully, I returned to the laboratory, intending to open communication with our provocative ghost.

You see, several things had occurred to me. The ghost knew I was there: why else would it have placed that symbol directly in front of me, where I was certain to see it? That it had waited until I was asleep suggested that it had divined my purpose. Furthermore, it understood what I was reading, or at least recognized like symbols on the pages before me. All this spoke strongly of intelligence, so making contact with it was not only possible, but desirable. If replicable, the exchange might dwarf all my other achievements to date.

I had acquired numerous blank sheets of paper, upon which I reproduced other alchemical symbols and wrote messages in several different languages, including Archaic Chinese. I placed them all about the laboratory, and waited. For several hours, nothing happened. I reread The Writings of the Hidden Chamber recovered from the tomb of Tuthmosis III in Luxor, which talks of the gates and ways of the gods, and I revisited the teachings of the Indian saint Bogar, who boasted that he could travel freely throughout the three worlds by means of astral projection. I began to grow sleepy, but drank cup after cup of coffee to ensure I did not succumb. If my alchemically inclined phantasm was to put in an appearance, I would be awake to welcome it.

At shortly after four in the morning, I heard footsteps approaching me across the floor of the laboratory. I sat up, but saw no one. My skin tingled. The hair on the back of my hands and neck stood to attention. I smelled something—the faintest hint of another person near me—and felt a puff of air against my cheek.

"You are close," whispered a voice into my ear, "so very close."

I leaped to my feet, filled with excitement and atavistic dread. I was alone in the laboratory, yet someone was speaking to me. An invisible being, a spirit—a ghost, why not? We don't have words for such an experience. It is something that calculating machines could not calculate, that analytical engines could not analyze—yet I was experiencing it. I alone!

I flailed about, vainly seeking substance in the empty air. The ghost laughed, as though at the clumsy efforts of a child. One of my hasty pictograms fluttered into the air, and I caught it, crushing it in my fist. I felt taunted, belittled. Angrily, I demanded that the ghost reveal itself to me at once.

"I cannot," said that faint whisper in my ear. "You must wait, Doctor Gordon."

"How long?"

"One more night, and then the congress of our worlds will be complete. Will you be here to greet me?"

"Yes," I said, without hesitation. Who would not? "I will be here."

"Bring no one else," the teasing spirit said, and fell silent. She said nothing more that night, and I felt no further sign of her presence.

Yes, I said "she." The creature haunting my laboratory was plainly a woman, a woman of some intelligence and spirit by the sound of her, although her accent was unfamiliar. There was none of the breathless, echoing death rattles the writers of popular fiction would have us imagine. She clearly was not that kind of ghost.

Naturally, after the encounter, I could not sleep, and I spent the rest of that night and the following day in a fever of anticipation. Margaret was worried. She could sense that something had inflamed my intellectual passion, yet she saw my regular work go ignored. I paced about the laboratory, unwilling to leave, responding only vaguely to her entreaties, barely eating or drinking. I must have seemed like a man possessed; it is a wonder she didn't accuse me of this very thing. A more credulous mind might have wondered if I had somehow fallen under the ghost's spell. Not Margaret. She understood my moods as well as I understood hers. She knew when I had been seized by the power of an idea.

But what, really, did I have? Little that would have impressed the overly critical gentlemen of the Royal Institution, those who had jeered and catcalled at my latest presentation. I needed far more if I was to declare a breakthrough of such magnitude—a breaking through, indeed, between different planes of existence. I didn't for a moment contemplate secreting an observer to witness what might follow that night. If nothing occurred, I would be an instant laughingstock. I needed more evidence before even considering public engagement.

I suppose I am a laughingstock now, Michaels. I expect people whisper terrible things about me and my behavior— that my mind gave way before the derision of my peers and I killed my wife in a moment of mania. If I had braved the possibility of further humiliation, this story might have had a very different conclusion, though I suspect that my visitor would easily have detected an observer and disappeared for good. The truth would have been denied me, and I would forever have wondered what I might have lost.

Again, I dosed poor Margaret so she would not be disturbed. Again, I sealed myself into the laboratory, armed with nothing but my books and my wits. Again, I endured hours of uncertainty before the stillness of the night was broken. Again, I started, but this time not at any mere wisp of air or whispering voice.

I jumped because right in front of me, from absolutely nowhere, appeared the most beautiful woman I have ever seen. Not as a ghost or phantasm. There was nothing ectoplasmic about this visitation. She was as real as you or me.

Describe her? I cannot do her justice. She was Oriental, I thought at first, with full lips and dark eyes, and hair so brown it was almost black. The cut of her tresses was short but finely styled, not like a man's, and her ears were pierced with gold. She was dressed in a way you would find most immodest, I am sure, in some kind of silken uniform, with trousers instead of a dress, a high collar, and gloves; all deep purples and greens, very harsh to my eye. Her smell was rich and tropical, like Amazonian flowers. She looked curiously about her, nodding as though finding her surroundings familiar, before she turned to me.

When she spoke, I knew that she was the being who had visited the night before. I will hear that voice the rest of my days.

"Hello, Doctor Gordon," she said. "My name is Abiha, and I have been looking for you."

At this point in his tale, Doctor Gordon became too distraught to speak. He begged my indulgence, and I allowed him a moment or two to gather himself. When it became clear that his distress was mounting, not receding, I offered him a calmative draft, which he accepted.

"Don't knock me out, though, will you?" he asked me. "I must finish what I have begun."

I left the cell and returned some minutes later with a sedative of my own concoction. He drained the vial readily enough. Before long, he grew calm again and his limbs lost some of the restless energy that had made listening to him an exhausting experience. I felt that he was nearing the crisis at the heart of his story, and that he knew, at some level of his being, that to continue would be to confront the true depths of his illness.

I was not disappointed.

"Abiha stayed for one hour," Gordon told me. "She assured me that she was not a spirit from beyond the grave, and that she was no more or less human than I. She said that she had journeyed to our world from another, one called Surobia, although that was not the place of her birth. That was yet another world, Arora, which she had left more than a year ago—to explore, she said, like some female Livingstone. These other worlds she spoke of are not transcendental dimensions or heaven's empty halls, apparently. They orbit the sun as the Earth does, home to animals and plants and civilizations like ours. Sometimes they approach one another, and for periods lasting around a fortnight, which Abiha described as 'congress,' those few individuals who have the trick of it can make the crossing.

"Yes, Michaels, raise your eyebrows. I won't deny I did the same, at first. Where are these worlds, exactly? If they were as real as she claimed, would we not see them through our telescopes and feel their effects in our world's stately progression about the sun? But as she talked, I remembered the alchemists of old and their insistence that this world was not the only one of human experience. I thought of the ice ages and the various other cataclysms that have befallen our changeable Earth. What if there truly are such worlds in a reality alongside ours, orbiting a sun that exists in all realities? What if the ancients were right and we moderns so very, very wrong?

"Take Philolaus. He imagined a Central Fire that bright Sol orbited, and about which another Earth, the Antichthon, also circled, forever hidden from us. Then there are the levels and spheres of Cabalism, all reaching out from a central, fiery point. What about the Heart of the Sun in Uthman ibn Suwaid's Turba Philosophorum? Or Hermes Trismegistus' Utmost Body, that alchemists could fly to with the Philosopher's Stone?"

I cut across his lecture—almost a sermon, such was the intensity with which he spoke—to convey my surprise that a man of science could place any faith at all in the ravings of lunatics and mystics. Hadn't their theories been proven wrong centuries ago, or exposed as the carefully encoded ceremonies of a depraved cult of sensualists?

"Sir Isaac Newton was an alchemist," Gordon responded. "Did you know that? The man who gave us calculus and the laws of gravitation, perhaps the greatest scientist who ever lived—he would scoff at your skepticism, sir, and with good reason, I think.

"And as for the allegation of copulation, well—all the alchemists I've spoken of believed in the union of the sexes and the power it unleashes, so perhaps there is something to that too. Take *Asclepius,* or *Kulacudamani Tantra* and the Realized Ones of the tantric arts, or *The Yellow Emperor's Canon of the Nine-Vessel Spiritual Elixir*—look them up yourself if you don't believe me!"

Needless to say, Inspector Berkeley, I have not done so. I am no prude, but I have no use for the ravings of charlatans. I was, however, keenly aware of the word *congress* in the context of Doctor Gordon's narration, and the close relation between its appearance and that of the mysterious other woman. His description of her spoke volumes, as did his confusion of intellect with passion, and his willingness to drug his wife in order to conduct an illicit nocturnal rendezvous in his laboratory. It seemed clear to me, then, what dark truth his own mind could not yet bear to look at directly.

I gave him a moment to compose himself, then asked that he tell me all that had transpired between him and the nocturnal, exotic Abiha.

As best I can remember (he said) this is it.

"We all of us, Doctor Gordon, have places of significance," she said. "Mine are the workshops of men like you, great thinkers who propel our species out of the darkness of ignorance and into the light of the intellect. I am drawn to such places and to the work performed there. That is why I have come to you. I felt the power of your experiments rippling out across the Helioverse, calling me to you.

"No, do not speak. Listen first. You have evidently mastered the art to some degree, or I would never have found you, congress or no congress, and I see by the books you have assembled that you are treading in the footsteps of great men— and great women, too. Sex is no impediment to inspiration, as your research will have revealed to you, I hope.

"Soon our worlds will diverge once more, and I have, therefore, only a brief opportunity to examine your progress.

I desire to know how far along the path you have come. Will you tell me? Will you hold nothing back? Knowledge shared is knowledge doubled, as we say on my world. Together we will travel much farther than apart."

Thus she set me off into the very same presentation I gave to the Royal Institution, three days earlier. I prefaced it by describing my nightmare of a polluted world and my dream of the perfect means of transportation, at which she nodded most vigorously, her eyes alight with interest. I thought I had found the perfect audience—from whom I expected to learn much more in turn—and I roamed about the laboratory, gesticulating, and demonstrating each piece of equipment as I came to it. She followed me closely and did not interrupt, not even to ask questions about the more esoteric details of my theory.

I mistook her attention for understanding, even approval.

I did not notice her furrowed brow until my demonstration of the prototype flux duplicator, the core component of my dream transport system, concluded.

"What is it?" I asked her. "Where have I erred? The theory is new, I know—I am, perhaps, the only person in this world who could understand it—but I am sure it is as familiar to you as a child's multiplication tables."

"Familiar?" she said. "Hardly, Doctor Gordon. Machines mean nothing to me. I came here to see you, to hear about your work, not theirs. What set you off along this path? What strange occurrence? There must have been some kind of spatial bilocation to prove to you the possibility of this method."

"Bilocation?" I echoed her in turn, and it felt suddenly as though we were speaking different languages.

"Yes, a transference from locus to locus, possibly achieved by accident rather than design. You clearly know nothing of the Helioverse, but that doesn't rule out travel in this world alone. What is your significant location?"

"I don't understand," I said, with utter frankness.

"You don't? So what made you think you could ever enslave this talent to a mere device? Where is the practical principle that guided your research?"

"In all honesty," I said, reminded of my ordeal at the Institute, "I possess nothing other than thought experiments, but I am close to demonstrating a functional circuit—"

"A working execution-machine, you mean. It is guaranteed not to work."

"But my theories—"

"Your eddies in a river are marvelously metaphoric, Doctor Gordon, but you have failed to pursue them to their logical conclusion. What would happen if you froze an eddy long enough to re-create it? On being released from the icebox the eddy would dissolve into ordinary water, and you would be left with nothing. Put yourself through this contraption of yours, and you too would dissolve. Die, if you prefer. Better that these devices remain harmless trinkets, as I originally thought them to be, or you dismantle them and direct your efforts to more accomplishable aims." Abiha flicked the edge of one of my precious glass bells, making it chime a resonant, deep G. "I'm sorry, Doctor Gordon, but I beg you not to eradicate yourself in pursuit of a fundamentally flawed notion."

I stared at her in shock and dawning horror. Could what she said really be true?

"How do you travel, then," I asked her, "if not by machine?"

"By will," she said, "and by art. That is all you need to swim the river of life."

"Will you teach me?"

She didn't answer immediately. On my desk lay a rare edition of the Picatrix, and she flicked through it as though seeking guidance. I sensed disappointment in her, along with disapproval, and waited anxiously for her response. I am a proud man, but I am not afraid to admit when I am wrong. A rigid mind is not a scientific mind. I would abandon all my research if it meant attaining the reality she had demonstrated to me that evening.

My mind flew with the possibilities. World upon world

upon world, all full of human life! She must not be the only traveler of her kind. How many times had voyagers made the crossing during our planets' intimate conjunctions? Magical texts are full of magical visitors who instructed the alchemists of old: you might already know about the giants of Genesis, but what about the companions of Horus who founded the original Egyptian dynasties, or the *Fankuang Tzu* of the Taoists, the Sons of Reflected Light who came from far across the sea, bringing wisdom and insight with them? Could Abiha's people and these beneficent visitors be one and the same?

In some ancient Chinese traditions you will find reference to the Highest Clarity, a place beyond the sky, where live the Jade Women of the Luminous Star. Was I looking at such a woman right now, in my very own laboratory?

"I am sorry, Doctor Gordon," she said again. "You are not ready."

She closed the book and stepped back from the desk, and in her eyes I saw the certainty of her decision, the futility of all forms of protest I might offer, and a determination to leave.

That was when I made the greatest mistake of my life.

The prospect of losing her was intolerable. She possessed the secret I had pursued for so long; I would not let it slip through my grasp! I lunged for her and took her arm, but she had already begun the charm or spell she used to travel between worlds.

The moment my skin touched hers, I felt a foglike ether envelop me, and all the light and heat was sucked out of the world. She gasped and tried to pull away, but I resisted, gripping so tightly I fear I hurt her—but not out of anger, I swear, or fear of losing her. A terrible sense of emptiness in the ether, of dissociation, had me mortally afraid for my life. If I let her go, I thought, I would be lost between worlds and surely die.

We struggled back and forth, she beating at me with her fists, and me imploring her to return with me, or take me with her. Whether she heard my cries or not, I do not know. The laboratory faded from sight, and the features of a new world appeared, one with metallic columns and bright lights. The air was dry and smelled of spark-gaps. Shapes rose up around us, and I felt their hands gripping me, pulling us apart. They snarled and spat at me in a foreign tongue. I strained to hang on to her, but could not resist them.

Finally, a stout blow to my forehead tore me loose. I was hurled back into the ether, where I tumbled for an instant, insensate, before landing with a bone-jarring impact on the floor of my laboratory.

I lay there for perhaps a minute, stunned. My skin was cold. I felt frost on my eyelashes. The chill seemed to penetrate right to my bones. But for the hammering of my heart, I might have been frozen solid.

Then the sound of smashing glass stirred me from my delirium.

I sat up, feeling her eyes upon me: Abiha's dark eyes, devoid of pity, demonically invisible. I staggered to my feet and stared wildly about the laboratory.

One of my glass bells chose that moment to shatter. It exploded into a thousand crystalline pieces, struck powerfully by an invisible hand, and I gasped in alarm. What cruel sabotage was this? Denying me her secrets was punishment enough, surely. Why destroy my greatest work as well? If I died in error, wasn't that my own business?

A third bell disintegrated. I picked up a spirit level and went on a rampage of my own, striking at the empty air in an attempt to catch one of my spectral tormentors off-guard—to no avail, of course, although I raged and swore. I begged. My cries went unheard beneath the shattering of the bells. The ground was soon covered in tiny shards, as though an artificial snow had fallen from the roof. My feet crunched at every step.

Soon just one glass bell remained, and I lunged for it, determined to save it at least from the slaughter. When I was barely a hand span away, it shattered in my face, and I thought I heard someone laughing.

I threw the spirit level at the empty air and roared my

frustration. And still I could feel her, in the laboratory, all around me, mocking my impotence in silence.

A hand touched my shoulder.

I spun around with fists upraised, ready to do battle with the Devil himself.

Margaret fell back, white-faced. "Darling! I heard the noise and came down to see. What in God's name are you doing?"

I dropped my hands and fell back, imagining how this must look to her. To her senses, the laboratory was empty apart from me, and she must surely have witnessed me lunging at that last bell with spirit level in hand. She would of course imagine me the architect of this disaster.

But what would she think had occurred in my mind to make such actions possible? What possession, what madness?

In that moment of self-realization, I understood everything.

"My darling," I said to Margaret, striving my utmost to keep my tone level and my expression one of sincerest sanity, "do not be alarmed. I know how this must seem to you. Be assured that the reality is not as it seems. Our visitor—well, as you can see the haunting has got entirely out of hand, and we must leave immediately. It is not too late."

She looked at me without understanding, but with recognition. She knew me and trusted me. She would have left with me—I know it. She was my wife, and I had never before done anything to harm our happiness.

It was then, Michaels, that the most terrible thing of all occurred. Margaret made a soft cry, like a child, and staggered forward. I supported her before she could fall to the ground and cradled her in my arms. Her head lolled backward, and I felt a vile rush of blood over my hands. Struck a fatal blow from behind, she was dead before I caught her.

Only when I smelled smoke did I begin to fear for my own life.

A second time, Doctor Gordon broke down, but this time he forswore all forms of chemical relief. He declared that he would finish or be damned—for damned he already seemed to be.

DANIEL TYKA

The demons from the other world, he said, had set about demolishing his reputation as well as his work, and in that he acknowledged they had totally succeeded.

The rest of the story differs little from eyewitness testimony. Firemen attending the scene found him lying in the lane at the back of his library, spared by mere inches from flaming debris. He was liberally splashed with blood and in a state of maniacal frenzy. Several witnesses heard him cry out, "Come back to me! Come back!" When asked if he was referring to his wife, he clearly declared that he was not. "The other woman," he said—"And if she can't have me, she means to destroy me!" Upon which, he collapsed unconscious and was borne away for treatment.

Only when investigators found Margaret's charred skeleton in the remains of the house, the back of her head apparently staved in by a hammer, and he was formally accused of murder—only then did Doctor Gordon emerge from the catatonia that had gripped him since his discovery. But he remained stubbornly mute. Even when he was charged, he said nothing. He was transferred from the hospital to Exeter Vale and has remained here ever since, sleepless and to all appearances unrepentant, pending a proper psychological examination.

On the fourth day, he seemed at last ready to talk.

"And here we are," he said when he had finished his sorry tale. "What do you think? Am I deluded? Depraved? Both?"

I refrained from commenting on his condition. It seemed clear to me that the man had suffered a major breakdown. Perhaps he truly believed that someone else had killed Margaret, but the facts of the case are plain. He was alone in the laboratory when Margaret entered. He admits that himself, invisible spirits notwithstanding. She came upon him unexpectedly while he was in the midst of demolishing his recent work. Who knows what he imagined, in the grip of such ungovernable emotions? She intruded; he was discovered. So Margaret Gordon died a violent death in the house she had shared with her husband for twenty years, and only her husband could have killed her.

I believe he understood my conclusions without requiring me to declare them. He was merely deluded, not deprived of his faculties. I knew that, Inspector Berkeley, but I nevertheless allowed him to get the upper hand.

"If you will not release me," he said, "then I would like to see Margaret. Where she lies, anyway. She must have been buried by now. We have adjacent vaults reserved in the Catacombs of the Lower Cemetery, and I hope to lie next to her when this grisly business is over. Do you think that might be arranged? If so, I will go quietly—plead guilty and of sound mind, confess whatever you like. You have heard my story, and if I cannot convince you of the truth of it, then I have no wish to cause further inconvenience to you or anyone else."

The request was not altogether surprising, nor the granting of it wholly unjustified. I will defend that conclusion to the grave. For a dangerous madman, there would have been no question of release. But he, who seemed sane enough, lacking only the honesty and good character to reveal the whole truth about what happened that ghastly night—him I could not deny. It seemed certain to me that, in a deranged state brought on by insomnia, and by romantic circumstances he was naturally wary of revealing, he had murdered the one person he had ever been a danger to, and that I or anyone else was therefore safe in his presence. Granting his request could ease the conclusion of his trial and leave the resources of both judiciary and asylum free for those in greater need.

"Tell me just one thing," I said, before taking my leave to obtain permission from Superintendent Gilfoyle.

"Anything, Michaels."

"You said you felt something when you came here—an intangibility, a profundity, or words to that effect. What do you think that might have been?"

He studied his hands as though looking for bloodstains.

"Perhaps no more than my imagination," he said. "I shouldn't have mentioned it. You will think it the nearness of the Creator, perhaps, or fate's cold hand upon me, some such nonsense."

316

"Hardly," I rebuffed him. "I am, as you say, a scholar, and I read extensively in the new theories of mind. My speculations on such matters lead me in very different directions—inward, not outward. The feeling came from part of you, I would say, from some unnoticed or suppressed corner of your mind. You felt it when the woman Abiha abandoned you, leaving you trapped in your marriage with Margaret, and you felt it again when locked in this cell. Could your dissociative impulse be nothing more than a method of achieving freedom by the only means available to you—via a fantasy? Could that be why a disturbed mental state accompanied each occurrence of that feeling, and why you seem compelled to expound this unlikely tale to the bitter end?"

He regarded me with a critical eye for a good minute. I felt that he was surprised, and perhaps even slightly amused, by my claims.

"You may be right," he said, finally. "I was wrong to belittle you, Michaels. I'm sorry."

I dismissed his apology as unnecessary, but was secretly pleased to have earned it.

On that encouraging note, I left him to see about the visit to Margaret's resting place, in the hope that this would put the dreadful affair behind him for good, little knowing how complicit I was about to become in the conclusion of these events.

I wish you to understand and accept, Inspector Berkeley, that I acted unknowingly, and in full faith of Doctor Gordon's good intentions. I will swear before any judge you name, in this world or the next, that I thought him resigned to his fate, that this last concession would see him walk to the dock and ultimately to the gallows. He spoke no more of his work, or of the woman he felt had betrayed him. When I returned to his cell with the escorts assigned to him, he was already on his feet, his head bowed and his attire as neat as he could manage, given his circumstances. He seemed a gentleman fallen on hard times, not a villain.

317

Constables Teale and Collison secured his wrists with handcuffs and led him from the cell. A small steam carriage awaited us at the exit from the administration wing, where the patient's temporary release forms were properly signed and witnessed. I rode with the driver, while my unfortunate companion sat between the two constables in the locked cab. We made our way down the long drive and through the main entrance under a sky as gray and leaden as granite, its featureless expanse broken only by the oval silhouette of an airship rising in stately fashion from the station with propellers deeply droning— one of Gordon's own designs, if I am not mistaken.

The journey to Longbrook Valley and the catacombs of Exeter proceeded uneventfully. We were met, at the steps leading up through the Lower Cemetery to the entrance in the grim hillside, by the priest and, rather disconcertingly, the catacombs' bricklayer, who was of the impression that we required his services. On the discovery that all of our party were living and no vaults needed to be sealed that day, he left muttering under his breath while Doctor Gordon and I ascended.

The arrangement was that the two constables would wait without while I accompanied the patient to the vault. The priest unchained the gate and allowed us through, then secured the entrance behind us. The air was cool and close within the catacombs themselves, and I longed for more light than my meager lantern provided. The walls were made of heavy, dark stone and fashioned to convey a sense of Egyptian antiquity. I was reminded of Gordon's alchemical fantasies and wondered what he made of them now.

"I feel it again," he told me, on that sepulchral threshold. "And I know now that it is fate, after all, brought me here."

He seemed feverish to my quick inspection. "Do you wish to proceed? There would be no dishonor in turning back."

"No," he said. "I must see her. And I know now that I shall."

We walked into the catacombs and followed the priest's directions to the Dissenters' section. There we scoured the sealed vaults, looking for fresh brickwork and a new brass plaque. I found Margaret before he did and stood in silence before telling him, reading the graven message that marked out the record of her days.

"Margaret Josephine Gordon, beloved wife, 1842–18—."

It seemed very little to me then, and still seems so now.

"This is it," said Gordon. He had come up behind me without making a sound. "Do you carry a journal with you, and a pen?"

"Of course," I said—and that is the last thing I remember. Constable Teale found me unconscious on the floor of the catacombs with a large bump protruding from the back of my skull, struck from behind just as Margaret had been—by her husband, Doctor Gordon.

You might say that, if what I tell you is true, I am lucky to be alive. I assure you that I curse the error of my judgment with every breath, and I wish I could explain what happened that day with any more clarity than this.

Certain facts are indisputable. The catacombs were sealed; the only entrance was attended by the two constables and the priest. No one entered or left until sufficient time had passed for them to come in search of us. When they found me unconscious and alone, reinforcements were summoned and the catacombs meticulously searched. Even Margaret's vault, the most recently sealed, was opened, but her body was the only occupant.

Of Doctor Gordon there was no sign. He vanished that day as thoroughly as any ghost, my notepad and pen with him, and I believe you when you assure me, Inspector Berkeley, that no trace of him has been found.

I maintain that I had nothing to do with his disappearance, although I do not blame you for reaching the opposite conclusion. The only material way for the accused murderer to escape from the catacombs was with the assistance of an accomplice, and the constables' solemn oath that they let no one enter or exit is supported by the priest's eyewitness account. If these three are excluded from the list of possible collaborators, that leaves only me. Furthermore, I had the obvious opportunity to concoct this scheme, while supposedly interviewing him in Exeter Vale.

I am, however, sanguine about my confinement, for it has provided me with the opportunity to write this full and frank testimony—and to make one small but possibly critical discovery that escaped my attention in the catacombs.

In the inside pocket of my coat, folded carefully in four, I came upon a note written on one of my own note papers, but in a hand very unlike my own. I enclose it with this account as evidence of the fugitive's state of mind, and its bearing on the matter of my innocence.

Your conclusions must be your own, Inspector Berkeley. I have nothing left to reveal, and no further speculations to offer. (I presume, however, that you have interviewed the bricklayer, along with the porters of the asylum, and are doing everything in your power to find the woman Abiha, about whom Doctor Gordon speaks so vehemently.)

Yours most sincerely, et cetera,

John Wesley Michaels, M.D.

Michaels—

I am sorry to have used you in this despicable way. On entering the catacombs, I find that hope has returned; for the attainment of another possibility, the one that has thus far eluded me, is now within my grasp.

How much you believe of my story, I may never know. Perhaps none at all—in which case this short missive will provide yet more evidence to support a diagnosis of madness. If, however, you have detected the faintest ring of truth in my account, then you should attend carefully. The import of what I have to tell you has repercussions for not just this great empire, but all humanity on this world.

Abiha told me that my experiments were flawed, and perhaps they were in application, but not in essence, for what else could possibly have drawn her to me? My machines sent ripples through the ether between worlds, alerting her and her allies to the existence of my work. They came to investigate; they misunderstood what they saw; they approached me, thinking me like them, free to wander the wondrous Helioverse she spoke of. Perhaps they hoped to recruit me. That I do not know—but now I know their cause, I can safely swear that I would never ally myself with such beings.

You see, Michaels, it occurred to me that night to wonder: if so many alchemists in our world had made the same discoveries— how they could possibly have been forgotten. Why, when their conclusions are so openly discussed in their texts, isn't this means of travel available to us all? The answer lies in how you yourself described them: "lunatics and misfits," I believe, were your very words. Someone must have calculatedly driven them into disrepute—but, again, why?

It is clear to me now that the one thing Abiha and her people do not desire, under any circumstances, is for someone to build a machine that replicates what they alone can do. Giving such a machine to the masses would open up whole worlds to exploration and exploitation, robbing them of the advantage that they are careful to maintain.

I said that I had made a mistake that night, by resisting her. Had I meekly abandoned my theories, Margaret would not have died, and I would not be as I am now, the center of scandal, my work in disrepute, all that is dear to me in this world dead and demolished—entirely by her hand.

So much for the "light of the intellect"!

What has also become clear to me is the possibility that Abiha too made a mistake. When I grasped her and was pulled into the ether, I did not return unscathed. The ether altered me, as it must alter everyone who touches it. I recognize it now. I feel it when it is near, and I have concluded that I could enter it again, under my own volition, if only given the opportunity.

But how to navigate such formless spaces? How to avoid being lost forever in the void between worlds?

321

"We all of us have places of significance," Abiha told me. Hers are laboratories like mine, where great men dream of traveling the universe. What if some places resemble the poles of a magnet, except that like attracts like, tuned to an individual's vital experiences? This explains why she came alone to me, not with an army of fiends at her back. Such a navigational mnemonic would enable her to cross the gulf between worlds as easily as stepping from room to room, unfettered by mere matter!

And I could do likewise, if I could manage the trick of it.

Far from egoless acceptance of guilt, dear Doctor Michaels, the dissociation I felt in my cell offers me both the means to escape and an opportunity to gain revenge upon the woman who killed my Margaret. I feel it even more strongly now, here in this place of mourning and loss. The ether presses hard upon the reality of this world—this world I now suspect to be paper-thin and as easy to puncture as water. For the ether is none other than my river of life, the universal fluid we ride like swans, not realizing we can take flight at any time.

In a moment, I will make the attempt. If I succeed, I will follow this fateful catacomb to one in another world—hers, perhaps, if the congress has not ended, or another nearby—leaving you a mystery, this apology, and a further exhortation to read the authors I named during our brief discourse. Don't let the silence subsume their voices, for each is a victim of those who would condemn our world to isolation and ignorance. Take up their dream of the ultimate transportation, and follow, if you can.

And when you think of me, remember their words, not mine:

"I touched the state when only truth remains.
"I swept away pleasures and pains.
"The Highest which is beyond the reach
"Of the four ancient Vedas
"came
   "here
     "to me!"

[Author's note: Every reasonable effort has been made to trace the copyright holders of "I left the world" and "The Eightfold Yoga" by Pattinattar, English translation by Kamil V. Zvelebi, and to obtain their permission for the use of this copyright material. The author apologizes for any errors or omissions and would be grateful if notified of any corrections that should be incorporated in future reprints of this story.]

Freebot

written by

R.M. Graves

illustrated by

DINO HADŽIAVDIĆ

ABOUT THE AUTHOR

R.M. Graves is a born-and-bred Londoner. Due to his mother reading only Asimov during her pregnancy, something she had not done before nor since, he is genetically preconfigured for speculative fiction. He started by reading Andre Norton, followed by his mother's Asimov, and moved on to Orwell and Huxley because they were banned by his Catholic school.

He finished writing his first book before he'd finished reading his first book and secretly wrote all through his schooling. Later he secretly wrote all through his architectural studies and still secretly writes despite having a family and his own illustration company.

In 2012 he joined the Online Writing Workshop to learn how to write stories that people would want to read. Now his fiction appears in Interzone *and* Escape Pod, *among other places. His art book* Postcards from the Future *is available on Amazon UK.*

He lives in pre-apocalyptic Camden Town with his wife and two children.

ABOUT THE ILLUSTRATOR

Dino Hadžiavdić was born in 1986 in Bosnia and Herzegovina. His artistic tendencies became apparent quite early. Art was a personal refuge during the time of war, when no other distraction was available. With his father being a history teacher, historic books became his main source of inspiration.

Later his focus changed to costume and character design, being heavily influenced by sci-fi and historic genres, mostly by works from Ian McCaig and Colleen Atwood. Determined to pursue a career in that field, he continued to study fashion design and illustration with a local art teacher, Gordana Mehmedović.

After graduating from high school, despite his wishes to attend the Academy of Fine Arts, he went on to study architecture, obtaining a Masters Degree. Skills obtained during those years continue to change his style, and expand the artistic medium toward CGI, digital art and animation.

He is currently attending the Academy of Fine Arts at the University of Sarajevo, studying Industrial design. His goal is to become a costume designer in the sci-fi genre.

Freebot

Danny charged down the high street toward the hospital, dodging freebots all hell-bent on being useful. He could still make this, he could still get to Sally in time.

"Danny Clark, a dad? Congratulations!" A chromed, headless horse skittered toward him and dropped to its knees. Danny stumbled to a halt, thumping his thighs in frustration, his chest fit to burst.

The horse waggled its saddle. "You need a ride! Sorry you lost your benefits, big guy. Hard times. Can my sponsor help you out over the next few months? Hop on, they'll sort out the details on the way."

It was only then his hoodie buzzed. The hospital. He propped his wheezing body against a lamppost.

"Mr. Clark?" The nurse's voice was tiny against the blare of the street. He wedged the hood hard to his ears. "If you are interested," she said, "you're wife just had a baby girl."

Danny doubled up and spat on the pavement. His hands were blackened and raw from the dawn shift, his arms still trembling. He screwed his eyes shut. He should not have taken that job. He should have stayed with Sally.

"Right," he said, his voice coming out in a strangled falsetto. He cleared his throat. "Sally? Is she—"

The nurse gasped. "Frankly, sir, whatever you're doing that is so important right now? I'd keep doing that for a while."

More freebots peeled off the throng and barreled toward

him. Danny had stood still too long. He creaked upright, blurting apologies into his hood but the nurse had already gone.

"Down to your last ten quid, eh?" A job-cart trundled toward him, feathered in leaflets for jobs that needed brains, not brawn. He balled his fists, and pictured smashing freebot casing, reaching through the Internet and crushing the parasite sponsors in their holes.

Instead, he forced himself to walk away, striking off in a random direction. He didn't stop until he hit a pub, then he didn't think until he was inside.

The "King's Shilling" was dark, wooden and rammed. The only space at the bar was beside a loitering freebot. Either that or next to the Wipe-Clean Lady; plain scary from her broken, droopy eye down to her dusty stilettos.

"I kept a seat for you, fella," said a white plastic flea the size of a football. "Just 20p a month. Free pint, too!" White fleas occupied all the pub's chairs, untouched pints in front of them. Danny shook his head and headed to the bar.

A real bar girl met him with a taut smile. "I can offer you the ad-free experience, sir, if you'd like to join the member's club?"

"Pint of Black," Danny said, before the guilt could step in. That's when the loitering freebot piped up.

"Ah, death," it said, spinning binoculars at him, its voice crackling and old.

"Mate, check the credit," Danny said. "Can't afford your life insurance."

"Ha, ha, ha." It clattered on its wheels. Danny frowned at the ugly machine, just a tripod bolted into the arms and back of a motorized wheelchair. "Daft bugger, no," it said. "Guinness. Your drink. Death is like Guinness. Thick, black. Warm as blood." It spun at the bar girl and boomed, "Not. *Cold!*" She frowned and plonked Danny's pint down, leaving finger prints in its bloom of frost.

Danny swigged and closed his eyes at the deep, bitter rush.

DINO HADŽIAVDIĆ

That was it. All gone. No more money. He heaved a sigh from his boots and pulled his hood over. He should have done the right thing, should have saved the wages. No job. No benefits. That meant no flat. What would he tell Sally?

He kicked at a tangle of shoe-worms, before they could re-tie his laces in patented knots and bill him for undoing them. There would be more crap from the freebots now that he couldn't afford protection. Streetlight subscription would lapse, too, probably have to walk home in the dark. While they had a home. It didn't bear thinking about, moving his family out to the slums, or face living on the street. Poor Sally, and poor little baby girl. They deserved better. He was no husband, no father. No man. Just a dumb lump, dragging them under.

He stared into the sinking cream of his pint and tried not to recall the terrible morning, but did. Hefting junk out of an old house and competing with yabbering freebots for the pleasure. Worse, under the foremanship of another freebot, sponsored—as it turned out—by social services. Danny was done, on the spot, for benefit fraud; signing-on while "employed." As if a morning's casual labor counted as employment. That sarcastic freebot laugh, as it printed out ten quid's worth of voucher codes. "Ha, ha, ha."

Danny drank the way he'd learned as a kid, small sip, big swallow. Trick your body. Make it last. Then the ugly machine burst into song next to him, "Oh Danny boy...the pipes, the pipes are ca-alling...." Suddenly that empty seat next to the freebot hooker didn't look so unappealing.

Something prodded his shoulder, a black mannequin in a yellow suit. "Danny," it said, "let me get your next drink, pay me when you can."

"Can't," Danny said.

"No problem. We can lend you something, you know, against your daughter's future earnings."

Danny blinked. "Seriously? She's less than an hour old."

The mannequin shuffled on its feet. "You haven't signed her

up yet? With a model agency?" It spun, right round at the waist. "Yo Stella! This one needs an agent!"

A candelabrum shuddered over, squeaking.

"Clothes! Clothes!" another shrieked.

"This one is with *me*." The ugly freebot reared up over their heads, its distorted roar rattling glasses. The freebots scarpered, and Danny considered necking the pint and going too, but the contraption bellowed over at the bar girl, "Sweetheart, put this sad bugger on my member's tab will you?" Then it sang again, to the tune of "The Red Flag": "The working class can kiss my arse! I've got the foreman's job at last!"

"Keep it down, John"—the bar girl frowned at Danny's bloodless knuckles—"or you're out."

Danny glared into the machine's cold, binocular lenses. He was sick of the world knowing his business. "You taking the piss, freebot?" he said, quietly.

The lenses didn't move. "Name's John. Loser," it said.

Danny could hear Sally, his better half. She would say: *Dan, there's no sense letting the machines get to you.* But his face prickled, and his lips twitched.

"What's this?" The freebot, *John,* whirred its lenses closer to Danny's face. "Think you can break me, big fella? That's the answer is it? That's going to put a roof over your family's heads?"

Danny wrenched his gaze away, downed the rage with his pint and went to the toilet, John shouting, "Ha, ha, ha," behind him.

Danny lodged his forehead on the cool tile above the urinal. He hadn't eaten since the night before and the gulped pint had his skin tingling numbly. He even felt a little dizzy already.

At least being on John's membership tab meant the piss was free, and the hawking freebots all ignored him, even now, at his most vulnerable. He eked out the primal bliss of unhassled privacy, savoring the old-school moment. It was as if the Internet had never escaped.

When he came back out, another pint waited. The bar girl nodded at the freebot and shrugged. Danny went to walk by, but the machine rolled into his path.

"It's a warm one. The way it should be," it said. "I'm sorry, son."

Danny stared at the pint, at John. There was a horrible ghostliness to that empty wheelchair, moving about on its own. But at least its binoculars seemed apologetic. Danny should go. He needed to look for work. Beg the council. He needed to see Sally and his baby.

He took the offered drink. There was time. After this one.

"Wife in hospital with the baby?" John said, its goggles tracing the arc of the pint back and forth from bar to mouth. Danny wiped his hand across his top lip and nodded.

"So they're safe and warm," it continued. "God bless the National Health, eh? What's left of it. I remember my first. Like a bomb going off, it was." It rolled a nudge at Danny's foot. "You need to get your head together, Danny Boy. Plan your next move."

Danny slumped. He hoped the machine didn't see the tear he thumbed from his eye.

"Oh Christ," it said. "That's bloody disgusting. Don't make me change my mind, Mate, getting you that pint."

"Mate?" Danny snarled through clenched teeth. "You don't know me."

"You make a lot of assumptions, son." The freebot swiveled on its wheels to face Danny square on. "Would you talk that way if you knew I was flesh and blood? A man?" It rolled so hard at Danny's shin it nearly knocked him over. "A blind, deaf, mute and paralyzed man? That these machines are my only way to connect with the world? That I also have a family and it still depends on me?"

Danny's ears grew hot, "You're *disabled*?"

"Ah, now son, we don't say that." It nodded at his pint. "But spare your blushes, go on, steady your nerves."

Danny glugged and the freebot—or whatever it was—filled him in. "Tower-crane operator, I was. Went to grease the hook-gear one day—pissing with rain—didn't fasten the safety properly. Dropped."

Danny gawped. "And you survived? Lucky sod— No. I mean—"

"Ha, ha, ha," John said, "your face. The rain, you see? Muddy. 'A soft day' my Da' would have called it. Helped break the fall, that and I twisted, you know, so I could land on my feet."

Danny imagined the bones of his legs crunching their way up through his body. He winced.

"Didn't feel a thing." John shook his lenses. "Doc said I hit the ground fast as a bloody skydiver. So fast, there wasn't time for the pain to hit my brain before I was killed. Ten minutes dead, they say. You'll have another in there?" John flicked his lenses at the empty glass, and before Danny could react, the bar girl had swapped it.

Danny waved at John's ugly rig and haunted seat. "How'd you get that?"

John hummed, "Oh, this old thing. Kids made it for me. Not bad, eh?" It buzzed a pirouette. "Got me on a program. Research, like. All these probes in my head."

"Like mind control?"

"Ha. Yep, suppose so. Sounds fancier than it is, though. Moving this fly-shit tiny dot around. You know by concentrating: 'up-up-up, left-left-left.' Bastard slow. At first, anyway."

An ambulance, rolling up outside the pub, distracted them. Its lights pulsed the bar blue.

"Now, I got all kinds of gizmos. Sound, pictures. And different rigs, for different jobs. Speech, too, obviously. Got my singing voice today." John drifted, staring at the vehicle outside. "Don't need the keyboard now. God that was shite. Like trying to text on a phone at the end of a long tunnel, by lobbing a football at it."

Danny's chest heaved.

"Ah, a smile," John said, "That's more like it."

"So where are you?" Danny said, "I mean, really?"

John's binoculars fixed him, "Now that's a question ain't it, sunshine? Where am I really? In my body? Or here with your sorry ass?" the lenses minutely tracked Danny's eyes.

Danny averted his gaze, feeling foolish.

"Oh Danny boy..." John started singing again. Danny watched a real paramedic—not a freebot—climb out of the ambulance and hang about. He wondered if the bloke might just saunter in for a pint, he looked so relaxed. Why the lights, then? The medic clocked Danny, and looked at his watch.

"Switzerland," John said, "My body is in a comfy drawer in Switzerland, somewhere. To answer your question. Oh." He twitched at a clock above the bar. "I gotta go. Afternoon shift. So Danny Boy, what are you going to do, eh?"

Danny's stomach lurched at the thought of John going. He shrugged.

John looked around, as if checking for earwiggers. "I'll let you into a little secret. No. Two. You know, it was me. Earlier. Your foreman who turned telltale?"

Danny went rigid.

"No wait. Listen. Another secret." John rolled closer. "We're hiring. The company I work for."

Danny stammered, questions tumbling over each other. His brain crunched and stalled. John's goggles locked to him, nodding slowly.

"You'll die, of course. While they disconnect your nerves. But then. Son. Wings!"

Danny's head bobbed on his shoulders like a balloon. He gripped the bar. How many had he drunk again? John didn't help, rolling back and forth, talking bollocks: "Travel anywhere in a blink. A digger in Beijing. A sub in the Atlantic. A trash-collecting electromagnetic-net in sodding orbit. Real jobs. It's the new frontier!"

"'s a joke, right?" Danny's voice came out his ears. That was wrong. He should go. Sally. His daughter. When was the overwhelming love supposed to start? Where was the door?

"You got poison in you, son." John rolled behind him. "Couldn't have you bolt. Waste all that money we spent on the 'sad buggers' list, you know, those most likely to give up, do themselves in. Not to mention my work, prepping your ass. Course, you're free to ask this fella's help." Danny blinked at the pursed lips of the bored paramedic, materializing at his side, fiddling with a needle. "Just say the word. He'll give you the antidote. You're back out on the street. With your family."

John nuzzled the chair at the back of Danny's knees. He swayed, and locked his legs, trembling from the bones out. "Sally," he said into his hood, to call her, but it didn't recognize his thick mumbling.

"Pipes are calling, Danny boy. Do your duty! As a man. For your family. Take the king's shilling. Fight. For them. Or live knowing you're a coward. That when it came down to it, you weren't prepared to do what it takes."

The bar girl caught Danny's eye and shook her head emphatically, in warning or in judgment, he couldn't tell. She pressed her lips and turned away. He swallowed at a rise of bile, forced leaden eyelids to stay open. The room boggled.

John shoved him again and he teetered. "Got to be your choice, sunshine. Cry for help? Or hold your tongue and man-up?"

Danny gripped John's tripod, warm metal vibrating in his palm. He bared his teeth, shuddering uncontrollably. He could snap its neck, rip the thing apart. Then what? The world had a list. Of people who were too crap to live, and he was on it. Danny's life, Sally, the baby, spilled with the tears off his chin. He never had a grip on them at all, and everyone knew it.

He shut his mouth, and shut his eyes.

"Good lad!" A crackling, old voice filled the black, strong hands guiding him into a seat. "Hop on, fella. We'll sort out the details on the way, eh? Ha, ha, ha."

Last Sunset for the World Weary

written by

H. L. Fullerton

illustrated by

CAMBER ARNHART

ABOUT THE AUTHOR

H. L. Fullerton was born in New York and still lives there; has never watched the world end from the deck of a star cruiser; writes mostly speculative fiction; tends toward the apocalyptic; likes semicolons and the occasional interrobang; prefers penguins over pandas, fiction over non, and Monopoly over Jenga; verbs nouns; wonders if this should be a bulleted list; thinks thirty-two is a lucky number; occasionally indulges in run-on sentences; once came in third for a Parsec Short Story Contest; sometimes tweets as @ByHLFullerton; might be in trouble with prepositions; uses words instead of emoticons; believes commas are apostrophes gone wild; can't remember what goes here; finds sunsets more accommodating than sunrises; saves dangling participles; binge reads while watching television; has had (or will have, depending on the time-space continuum one is using) stories published in places like AE, Daily Science Fiction, Freeze Frame Fiction, *Parsec's* Triangulation anthologies, Urban Fantasy Magazine, *and hopes to sell enough stories to support a growing tsundoku habit.*

ABOUT THE ILLUSTRATOR

Camber Arnhart was born in 1996 in Albuquerque, New Mexico and raised by her two artistic parents. She spent many days creating arts and crafts with her mother and watching her father play fantastic video games, all of which inspired her.

Her life changed when her dad brought home a Wacom tablet and she became addicted to digital art. She started with basic paint programs but moved on to her favorite digital tool: Photoshop. Along with creating digital paintings, she fell in love with the gaming genre and aspired to create videogames for a living.

During her time at Volcano Vista High School, her art skills improved dramatically, thanks to the rigorous AP art program. She received a number of art awards, including a national gold medal in the 2015 Scholastic Art & Writing Awards.

Now she attends the University of New Mexico, where she intends to obtain a degree in computer science and a minor in art. Equipped with both technical and artistic skills, she aims to create her own games that inspire audiences with engaging stories and environments.

Last Sunset for the World Weary

We watched the world end from the observation deck of the star cruiser. Pickets sat on my right. "To new beginnings," he said, raising his champagne flute.

"To those left behind." I kissed his glass with mine. My cheeks blushed at the clink. With all the crying going on, it seemed... *sacrilegious*? (Could one even use that word anymore or was it outré like "skyward" and Latin nomenclature?) I half expected someone to spit on us, but if anyone would know the proper etiquette for witnessing a planet's death-gasms, it'd be Pickets.

And Earth had put on a show. If one overlooked the deaths-of-millions thing. Which I was a tad uncomfortable doing. But then, I'd always been moved to donate when confronted with pixels of starving children or pandas. I thought of the tiny bamboo stalks on my cabin's nightstand and how no vegetarian ursine would ever taste them. I teared up and turned to Jawry on my left.

"To the last sunset," he said—always the poet—and we all sipped. Earth's spacely remains did resemble a sunset. Something to do with the gases released from the vaporization—Pickets had explained it to me when he invited us to his little on-deck soiree for Earth's send off, but I didn't understand much of his scientific ramblings. Pickets is much more entertaining when he isn't being pedantic. (Secret? I stopped listening after faux-tropo-*something*. I've never had much patience for knock-offs.) Seeing my expression, Pickets had rolled his eyes and said, "Think of it like a rainbow segregation party for your eyes."

I told him he wasn't allowed to use that word.

"What, 'segregation'?"

"No, 'rainbow.'" He'd laughed and I accepted his invite as long as he promised not to be boring—I so hated boring. So far he'd been very bon vivant. It almost made up for the captain's impromptu evacuation drill this morning. Completely in bad taste. Reminding us of our mortality while others were dying. As if there were any point. Who planned for disasters? It simply begged for trouble. And those bulky life-preserver suits might sustain a person until another star cruiser sailed by; but, frankly, I'd rather go down with the ship than be caught dead in one. Plus, there was no guarantee I'd get the same caliber of cabin on another ship.

"Pickets," Jawry said, leaning forward to make eye contact— eye contact was very important to Jawry. (My dear poet claimed it let you touch a person's soul. Making connections was something of a must for him. Without them, he'd be cast off into zero gravity or reduced to server status—and the poor man can't mix a margarita to save his life.) "You always hit just the right note for the occasion. Thanks for sharing your seats with us. Fida wanted to commemorate this occasion sitting in a pitch-black cabin spouting eulogies for marsupials."

Pickets patted my hand. "The colors. Aren't they beautiful?" Jawry and I both agreed they were. "Better than the aurora borealis," Pickets murmured.

"Person, place or thing?" I asked.

"Thing," Pickets said, a moue of disappointment twisting his lips, "but not animal, vegetable, or gem."

"Then, no, darling. You know I have no use for *things*." I found it unkind for both Pickets and Jawry to laugh and was gladdened to see the other passengers glare at them. A small giggle might be overlooked at a funeral, but guffaws never. "Hush," I said. "Pandas are dying."

"Fida, dear. *We're* the endangered species now. Remember to put me on your list to be saved. P-I-C-K-E-T-S."

Maybe the morning would've gone different if I hadn't opened my eyes and seen my pot of bamboo first thing. Normally the sight of it gave me the serene greens, which was why I kept it on my nightstand, but this morning it reminded me of a home lost and I plunged into the blue glummlies. Jawry's lips grazed my shoulder. I sighed, rolled over and pushed him out of bed. He climbed back in and tried to tease me into a happier mood.

"Really, Jawry. A planet went poof last night. Our home is gone. How can you smile?"

"We are our home, Fida. Earth was a place we once lived. I'm here; you're here. What isn't there to be happy about?"

For a sensitive soul, Jawry doesn't wallow in grief the way he should. Probably too grateful he wasn't on Earth when it ended. If not for me, he would've been. I pushed him away again; he went easily. "Today is not for happiness," I said, feeling a frown gather at my back teeth.

"I will write you an elegy for yesterday." He padded toward the shower; he did his best composing in there.

"No poem," I called. Jawry's laments are particularly moving. His ode about a lost earring—how I loved that earring!—critics hailed as a lyrical allegory about souls parted, never to be paired again. One nasty critic (I heard he was Earth-stuck and thought it served him right) blogged: "It's overblown drivel about a goddamn earring left at the opera. Buy another pair, for christsakes, and get some effing perspective." This morning I agreed with that ass: the loss of Earth was no different to Jawry than the loss of my earring. I supposed the mourning must be left to me. I dressed in gray—because black washed me out and white reminded me of dead Chinese pandas—and went looking for Pickets.

I checked the breakfast room, the observation deck, the pool, then the bar, and finally had a steward track Pickets down for me. He'd switched to the blackside deck and was still staring into space at the place Earth used to be. "Pickets," I said. "Mourning

341

is one thing; maudlin's another." I had my chaise turned so I faced him rather than the black and bright of space ruined by purple and pink smudges.

"This," he waved a hand at the view, "is a once-in-a-lifetime thing. Another few hours and we'll be out of range. It's the last piece of Earth we'll ever get. Enjoy it." He patted his chaise for me to join him.

I signaled to a nearby steward and had my lounge repositioned. Pickets offered me his hand and I took it. We sat, side by side, and watched the smeary rainbow sunset disappear from view. "That's it then," he said. "We're *star-stuck*."

Pickets persuaded the staff to serve scones and coffee despite us being blackside. With no one else about, we raised the lights to dim so we could break our fast. Pickets looked wistful, as if he were suffering the blue glummlies himself. "It was beautiful, wasn't it?"

I shrugged. There'd been something ominous in the colored ash against a black backdrop, not a true sunset but a disturbing reproduction. Maybe I was reacting to how the display had been created—the end of the Earth—rather than the art itself. "Did you watch all night?" Night was a relative term, but Pickets understood I meant the hours our half of the cruiser faced away from the sun.

"I wouldn't have missed a second of it. We're one of the few cruisers with sight line. Best view in space. You can tell your great-grandkids about it one day—if you have any." He sipped and switched expressions, watchful now. "Where's Fida's shadow?"

"Commemorating the event in quatrains. And do stop calling him that. Play nice." I swatted him.

"You wouldn't like me half so much if I did." He closed his eyes and clasped his hands across his rumpled suit. He was right. Part of Pickets' charm was his bite. I wondered which of us would tire of the other first. When he drifted off, I left him to his dreams and wandered about blackside. A day of all night seemed just the thing. (Plus, my desertion would worry Jawry. He pretended not to mind Pickets nor envy the time I spent with him, but what artist wanted to see their patron's gaze caught elsewhere? Not one that liked eating.)

I explored deserted corridors, tiptoeing so as not to disturb this half's inhabitants. Without Jawry or Pickets at my side, the cruiser was a strange beast. I wondered if—like Pickets—the longer I was aboard, the more claustrophobic this life would seem.

Probably not, I wasn't the adventurer Pickets was. Long before new orbit life became necessary, he was one of the first permanent star cruiser residents—back when the end of the world seemed a doomsayer's mantra rather than a realism.

Besides, I liked my creature comforts (even if Jawry had grated my nerves this morning) and entertainment was always easier to find than adventure. I'd be just fine.

That night Jawry and I joined Pickets at the captain's table for dinner and Pickets began his catalog of sunsets. "Not," Pickets said about a Saharan sunset, "that it could hold a candle to what we viewed yesterday."

The captain said, "I trust you found the view to your liking?" and Pickets assured him he had.

"No trouble with the ship?" Pickets said. "I know you were concerned about our proximity."

"Everything worked out fine," the captain said. "We broadcast the demise, and sales from that video will more than compensate for the extra fuel expenditure our delay required. We'll resume our orbital path by tomorrow. If you'll excuse me, I have some matters to take care of on the bridge."

And I thought, *We changed orbit for Pickets?*

Life went on as usual; the way it does. I hardly even noticed Earth was missing. Pickets stopped moping and returned to his buoyant self; Jawry fawned and scribbled; and the blue glummlies left me alone as soon as I moved my bamboo plant to a less conspicuous spot in my cabin. I considered getting rid of it altogether; maybe making Pickets a gift of it. He'd appreciate the symbolism of the gesture if not the gesture itself—"What,

Fida? Am I to be next on your list of unsaved things?" But Jawry seemed to derive inspiration from it, so I let it be. I didn't even object when my darling poet made something of a shrine out of it, though I thought that rather tasteless myself. Pagan, even. (Unless that word, too, has been decommissioned; then I mean something else.)

Then Jawry had to bring the whole dead planet thing back up. Those lines he'd been scribbling? A poem about the end. Even though I adamantly asked him not to.

"If I succumb to the glummlies again, it'll be your fault, Jawry, and I'll never forgive you."

"Ignore her," Pickets said, making fly-shooing motions at me with his hand. (One of the best things about star cruisers? No flies, no gnats, no nasty mosquitoes. Well, maybe second best. The service was out of this world. I've never been so well taken care of.) "Fida has no idea how to act as an audience. That's the trouble with stars. Too blinded by their own importance to care what we mortals suffer. Give us a listen, poet Jaw-reate."

"It's called: *From Blackness We Go*."

"Does that even make sense?" I asked. Pickets assured me it did. I wasn't totally convinced, but deferred to his cultural expertise.

Jawry read his poem; he didn't mention extinct ursines once. Pickets clapped when my poet finished. I managed a wan smile.

"You didn't like it?" Jawry was crushed.

"It's very nice," I said. "Very... astronomical. I'll have to listen to it again. But not now."

"Fida," Pickets chided. "You owe the boy more than that. He made you the Earth in his poem—the center of his moony universe."

"He killed me!?"

"No, no." Jawry rushed to hold my hand. "My Earth never ends. She is with us always. *'And tho we see her not again, her kiss resides deep in our hearts, her dust settles upon our heads. Forever she does carry on, we spin orbit* dance! *in her stead.'"*

I couldn't decide if being compared to a vaporized planet was flattering or not. "You can recite it again for me tonight."

CAMBER ARNHART

Pickets snorted. "You *are* solipsistic—the perfect Earth."

"And I suppose you'd make the perfect sun? Everything begins and ends with you?"

"Some of us have more gravitas than others. I'd make a grand sun," Pickets said. "But let's not fight. I, too, have a surprise for you. A gift."

"A gift? For me?"

"And Jawry—if you'll share."

"What is it?"

"You'll have to come see." Pickets led us into the bowels of the cruiser. Everything clanked and hummed and vibrated. Not to mention the dirt and grease. It was very factory-ish. I have to say, I didn't think much of Pickets' presentation. It made me appreciate Jawry's poem all the more. Until Pickets threw open a door marked CULTIVATION BAY 111-G and stepped aside to let me enter.

"Your gift—my sun, my earth, my moon." Pickets bowed, a smirk upon his face.

I stepped inside and there it was. A bamboo forest. Complete with one giant panda. Just for me. *"Oh, Pickets!"*

If Pickets hadn't bought me that panda... Ordinarily, gifts don't make me suspicious—and I adored pandas. Then Jawry had to go wondering *how* Pickets procured the panda, *when* Pickets got it, *where* he'd found it. On and on, he went. I paid no attention to Jawry's jealous ramblings—a little rivalry does the heart good, or so my mother claimed—until Pickets told that story about a mountain in China that ruined his view.

Pickets sighed. "Such a majestic mountain; too bad it grew in the wrong place."

"I don't think you understand how mountains *work*, Pickets."

"No, Fida, it's you who doesn't understand. A man with ambition can climb mountains. A man with enough yuan can move them. I climbed it twice; it was an improvement from every angle. I should've taken photos—though you know I don't hold with capturing moments; an event is meant to be *experienced*—then you could see my vision realized. You'll just have to take my word."

"Wouldn't it have been easier to change apartments?" Jawry said. "Found one with a view of the setting sun more to your liking?" Ever since the gift of the panda, Jawry had been trying to provoke Pickets. He insisted Pickets was trying to entice me into bed, and my dear poet was probably right. Not that it would happen. I understood Pickets perfectly and wasn't about to let him make a memory out of me. (That mountain he moved was the only thing he'd climbed twice.) But I'd let him try. I loved my little amusements, and Jawry could only provide so many.

Pickets gave him a disdainful look. His expression did what Jawry's words couldn't. It made me wonder about my black-market panda: the foresight needed to procure one; the people who might've been saved in my pet's place; the menu changes necessitated by the amount of food Chyna needed each day (a small sacrifice for preserving a species if you asked me); and, of course, about Pickets.

Pickets," I said when he joined me in CULTIVATION BAY 111-G one afternoon, "I don't hold with moving mountains."

"Of course you don't, Fida. You much prefer other people to rearrange things for you."

"Well, I value comfort, yes; nothing wrong with that," I said and Pickets nodded his agreement. "But you do things on whim—that result in destruction."

"I am a man of vision. I seek out beauty. That is hardly whimsical."

"You don't argue about your destructive nature?" I'd thought quite a bit about Pickets and his sunset obsession. A man who moved a mountain might be inclined to hurry a dying planet along.

Granted, it would've happened anyways, but I couldn't help feel a tiny bit that Pickets was something of a mass murderer. I worried whether it was my responsibility to do something about him. Certainly, no one else would rebuke him.

"A man can neither create nor destroy."

"Where do you get such ideas? I swear, Pickets, the things you make up. I thought I could at least trust you to be *honest.*"

"Honesty?" He laughed. "Between us? Fida, it cannot be. You'd never stand for it."

"Oh, hush. My panda's eating and you'll give her indigestion." I could spend hours watching Chyna peel her bamboo, chomp and suck—if not for the smell. Pandas have an odor—they don't mention that in the brochures. One you couldn't wash away with strawberry-scented shampoo no matter how many gallons of reclaimed water you squandered.

I asked Pickets to see about putting up a glass wall to separate the natural habitat and its nasty scents from my viewing pleasure. He said, "I should've guessed you'd prefer zoo over safari. But, yes, let us indulge your little wish."

"*Why* does the captain indulge you?" I asked.

"Because I own this cruiseline. Or a fraction of it. Do you require the exact percentage?"

I didn't. "Pickets? If you wanted to *make* another sunset, could you?" For this was my concern. That he would grow bored. A restless Pickets might prove hazardous and we were, after all, on the same boat. I wouldn't care for him to rock it—or worse.

"I hardly care to do a thing twice when once will suffice. Repetition is for the unimaginative. See you at dinner?"

It was Jawry's poem that made me do it. Not that horrible astronomical one with the sun and Earth and moon all spinning about in love. No, he wrote another one: *Those We Leave.* There's something about intentions gone wrong and *vows we take to the grave because we kept them not.* The last line—*and all the goodbyes I wished I said*—made me weep, especially following that list. *Goodbye, sparrow; goodbye, goose. Goodbye, Mother, Child. Goodbye, rabbit; goodbye, moose. Goodbye, creatures wild.*

Jawry's courtly recitation of all the things that died along with the Earth woke the judge in me. Saving one smelly panda couldn't make up for extinctioning everything else. (Plus Pickets rather nastily categorized my Jawry's lovely poem as Seussical, but without the imagination or catchy rhymes.) Would Pickets' cruelty never end?

First a mountain, then a planet. What next?

I wasn't willing to find out. I hated to get my hands dirty, but poor Jawry was no match for Pickets. His heart was too big to stop someone else's; his hands too soft.

I lured Pickets below decks with promise of an adventure.

"Fida, what mischief have you planned?"

"Oh, the mischief's already done," I told him, thinking bribery and extortion barely counted as crimes if done in redress of a greater wrong. No one has ever accused Justice of being pretty. After all, the poor woman has scales and wears a bag over her head. "I merely borrowed a key or two—and arranged for us not to be disturbed. I threw your name around some. I hope you don't mind?"

Of course he didn't. Although he was confused when we reached our destination. "I have an exquisite stateroom," he said. "Why are we cramped in here? It smells like dry rot."

"You and your sunset. That's why. You can't go moving mountains and vanishing planets for your own amusement."

"It was a *moment,* not an amusement. Your panda is an amusement. To compare my last sunset with your latest pet..."

"Pickets, you did a bad thing." I shook my finger at him. Vulgar, but it made my point. Then I locked him in with the life preservers. He banged on the door, furious. I knew once he calmed down he'd laugh at the irony. Although maybe not. You never could tell with Pickets. It's what I found most charming about him. Dear Pickets.

The Sun Falls Apart

written by

J. W. Alden

illustrated by

CHRISTINA ALBERICI

ABOUT THE AUTHOR

J. W. Alden has always had a fascination with the fantastic. As such, he's made science fiction and fantasy his literary domain—though some other weird things sneak in from time to time.

Growing up along the coasts of Florida, James learned to hate the sun and love the shade. While most kids his age spent their weekends at the beach or on the basketball court, he buried himself in books. He now lives just outside West Palm Beach with his wife Allison, who doesn't mind the odd assortment of musical instruments and medieval weaponry that decorate his office (as long as he tries to brandish the former more often than the latter).

J. W. Alden is a graduate of the 2013 class of Odyssey Writing Workshop. His fiction has appeared in Nature, Daily Science Fiction, *the* Unidentified Funny Objects *anthology series, and various other publications.*

ABOUT THE ILLUSTRATOR

Christina Alberici is a freelance illustrator and BFA graduate of the University of the Arts in Philadelphia, Pennsylvania, where she studied illustration and animation.

Her style features a combination of surreal and fantastical characters, each painted in deeply imaginative settings. Her work is created completely in digital form, and her portfolio includes book covers and editorial articles, as well as sci-fi and fantasy artwork.

The Sun Falls Apart

A crack between the boards revealed a meager smattering of light, but Caleb took any glimpse of the sun he could get. Thick wood and rusty nails denied it everywhere else in this house. Here in the old guest room, it struggled through. The razor-thin sunbeam cut a swath through the darkness and landed on his chest. Stepping into the light felt like stepping out the front door.

"Wait until Dad hears," Josh said.

"What?" Caleb put a hand over the crack. Too late this time.

His brother's silhouette loomed in the doorway. At fifteen, Josh was only a few minutes older, but half a foot taller. "You're trying to look out that window."

"So?"

"So that's cheating. I'm getting outside first, so you're trying to cheat. If you'd earn something for a change, maybe you wouldn't be such a shit-stain."

Josh took off, yelling for Dad before he'd even reached the stairwell. The one thing he loved more than getting Caleb in trouble was letting him know first. Caleb slunk out of the room and ran his fingers along the bronze picture frames lining the upstairs hall. Portraits of people he'd never met and would never know the names of glared like a jury with sentence in hand. Dad was already pounding up the stairs.

"Show me," he said when he reached the top.

Caleb led him to the musty guest room and gestured at the window. Dad broke the stream of light, sending an array of dust motes into a wild dance. He approached the crack much the same way Caleb had—slow, deliberate, as though facing a holy relic. He traced it with his thumb, shaking his head.

"I'll seal it after the next supply run." His eyes left the boards and took a quick survey of the room, stopping on the attic hatch above the bed. "We'll have to cover it until then. Don't run off. I'm not done with you."

Dad climbed onto the mattress and yanked the dangling cord. The hatch popped open, and a metal ladder descended with a high-pitched wail, its feet pressing dimples into the mattress. He stepped up into the dark, returning a moment later with a framed canvas tucked beneath one arm. When he held it up to the window, he revealed the blurry golds and greens of a glistening meadow, the type Caleb pictured when daydreaming about the outside. Dad hung the old oil painting from one of the crooked nails, stifling the only sunshine in the house with a two-dimensional imitation. He didn't even hang it straight.

"Okay," Dad said. "Talk."

"I wanted to see the daylight," Caleb said. "Why can't—"

Dad seized Caleb's chin between thumb and forefinger, squeezing hard. Caleb didn't resist. "You *know* why. That privilege is earned. Have you tested today?"

It always came back to this. Work harder. Practice more. "Yes, sir."

"And?"

It all felt so useless. "Failed again."

"Then don't talk to me about daylight." He released Caleb with a jostle, then cocked a thumb toward the covered window. "That's cheating. If you want to see the sun, follow your brother's lead. He's almost ready. In the meantime, you don't set foot in this room until that crack is sealed. In fact, consider upstairs off limits until further notice."

"The *whole* upstairs? What about the library?"

"Closed for business until you finish the maze."

"But Dad—"

CHRISTINA ALBERICI

His father silenced him with a look. Not *the* look, but one that made it clear what pressing his luck would get him. "You're not ready for what's out there, Caleb. Hunting for shortcuts takes you further from the finish line. Until you've proven you have what it takes, your world ends where these walls begin."

Caleb ground his knuckles into the dining room table, jaw tensing and relaxing in a steady rhythm. The chandelier above seemed like the closest thing in the house to daylight, which made this his favorite room to test in. He frowned at the wooden maze in front of him, trying to will the steel ball inside to move. Josh had beaten this test at thirteen.

"You're trying too hard." Mom leaned against the arched entryway. "You're quivering like a leaf."

"I wouldn't know what that looks like." Her looming presence made this harder.

"Don't get smart, Caleb. I'm trying to help."

"Why? I'm not like you and Dad. I'm not like Josh."

"Nonsense. You have the same genes, kiddo. You just need to get out of your own way. You beat the last test in half the time you've spent on this one."

"That was just knocking a domino over."

"And this is just rolling a ball around." She walked up to the table and rapped her knuckles against it. "Your perception of this table, this room—it's a distraction. It's all made of the same stuff. It's all intertwined. The space between is an illusion. One little stir in the right place will get things moving. Don't think about the maze. Don't even think about the ball. Think about the goal."

Caleb squinted, trying to puzzle out what she meant. The maze *was* the goal. Still, he pretended it didn't exist. He let his focus blur and imagined the walls of the dining room dissolving away. He pictured the vivid beam of light upstairs. How wondrous its source must be, if such a small part of its brilliance could dispel the gloom that swallowed this house. A light like that would envelop him—free him. It would cover him in warmth and burn away cold moments like this, when he thought he might never leave the house.

The sun entered his mind now, suspended somewhere above, far from reach. The hairs on his arms stood on end, and he swore the temperature rose. But when he took in this phantom sun, its rays began to fade. A giant, spherical mass rolled in front, eclipsing its beauty and ushering the dark back into Caleb's world. With an audible grunt, he reached for the enormous obstacle—not with his arms, but with his mind. When he did, he felt its cold, hard surface, as though he'd pressed naked flesh against it. He threw himself at it, yearning to push it aside and reclaim the light. The object yielded, tumbling away under sheer force of will. Daylight poured in, warm elation gripped him, and—

The ball moved.

The imaginary sun vanished and the wooden maze returned. The ball rolled along its corridor, heading straight for the first obstacle hole. But Caleb's mind was back in the dining room now, and he couldn't steer it. The ball refused to turn or slow. It just kept gliding toward another failure. Without thinking, he reached for the maze and gave it a jerk, sending the ball back toward the starting point.

Caleb sighed, expecting a reprimand for using his hands. But Mom didn't yell or scold. She hadn't even seen what happened. She stared above Caleb's head, brow line frozen and distorted. He followed her gaze to the chandelier. It swayed to and fro in a violent arc, like a giant crystal pendulum.

"How long were you upstairs this morning?" Mom said.

"What?"

"You'd better head to your room for a while." She bent forward to collect the maze from the table. It almost slipped from her trembling hands.

Mom and Dad beamed as Josh took his first step past the yellow line and into the front entry hall. Caleb glared down at it. He'd imagined himself claiming this privilege a thousand times. He'd even crept up to it when no one was looking, sliding a toe or two across the yellow paint to see if the floor felt different on the other side.

"Watch and learn," Josh said under his breath as he passed. "Until you take things serious, this is as close as you're getting."

Mom squeezed Josh when he joined them in front of the door. Dad gave him a firm handshake, then reached into his back pocket. He pulled out a white, plastic keycard. Black marker spelled Josh's name on one side. Josh grasped for it, but Dad yanked it out of the way.

"Nah-ah," he said. "Don't treat this frivolously. It's part of your outdoor trials. Keep it on you at all times. The card lives in your hand. Your hand lives in your pocket. Lose your key, I lose my temper."

"Yes, sir. I'm ready."

"Then the world is yours." Dad handed the card over. "Show me you've grown and you'll get to keep it."

Josh smirked at Caleb from across the hall, displaying the side with his name like a first-place trophy. He slid the card into the receiver next to the door. The indicator light changed from red to green.

"Caleb, congratulate your brother," Mom said. "He worked hard for this."

"Congratulations," Caleb said, then left them.

Most days, he loved hearing the thud of the maglock retracting, watching the door swing open. Sun would spill into the entry hall, glorious and warm. But he couldn't love those things today. He couldn't bear to watch Josh step into the light.

Caleb rifled through the open drawer of the dining room hutch, running a hand from corner to corner. He slammed it shut and traced a slow path back to the table, scrutinizing the floor. Mom walked in as he turned the maze upside down again, shaking it.

"Thought I'd find you here," she said.

"I can't find the ball. It fell out somewhere."

She pulled up a chair and sat. "Your father took it."

"You're kidding." Caleb let the maze clatter on the table. "He's the one telling me I'm not testing enough. He just lectured me the other day."

"I'm sorry, kiddo. We had a long talk after your last attempt. He thought you should take a break. Just for a little while." Her gaze flickered away, bouncing from the chandelier to the overturned maze.

"You don't agree. You know he's wrong."

Mom smiled. "We both want what's best for you, Caleb. Sometimes it's tough to figure out what that is. Your dad gets tunnel vision. He finds a way that works and sticks to it. Me, I think it's possible there's more than one path to the finish line."

"I don't know what you mean."

"Neither did he." She drummed her fingers on the table, silent for a moment. "He'll be out with Josh for another couple hours. How bad do you want to test?"

"Bad. I'm tired of these walls. I'll probably fail, but I want to try."

"There's a catch. The ball's in your dad's pocket, so the maze is still a no-go. You'll have to skip to the next test."

A wisp of heat crept up Caleb's neck. He didn't even know what the next test was. How could he tackle something new when the maze still gave him problems?

"If you don't want to, say so," Mom said. "We'll pretend this talk never happened, and you can go back to the maze in a day or two."

"Is it even worth trying?"

"It's always worth trying, Caleb. If watching Josh walk out that door lit a fire in you, I say let it burn." She stood and slid the maze away from the center of the table. "Wait here."

Caleb eyed the unbeaten maze after she left. He knew what Dad would say about this. He knew what Josh would say. Another shortcut. Another *cheat*. When she returned, Mom held a petri dish with a black dot at its center. She slid it onto the table, and Caleb squinted. The dot twitched. It had legs, wings, and a pair of prismatic eyes.

"A fly?"

"This test is a little different," Mom said. "You're not knocking anything over or pushing anything around. This one's about precise manipulation. You need to separate the fly's wings from its body."

"You mean spread them? Hold them out?"

"Pluck them. Pull them off. I know it sounds tough with only two hour's practice, but give it your best shot."

"Won't that hurt it?" Caleb prodded the dish with a finger. The fly beat its wings in futility. "How long will it live without wings?"

"It's a fly, Caleb."

"If I had wings, I wouldn't want them torn off."

"What it may or may not want is irrelevant. It's had a short, futile life, serving nothing but its own impulses. It's vermin. Its wings are the only important thing about it. They're between you and the goal. Remove them."

He leaned into the table with a slow breath—in through the nose, out through the mouth, like they'd taught him. His mind cleared of all but a few lingering thoughts about the maze. Once he'd set his mind in the proper place, moving that ball had felt effortless. He'd failed in the end, but it had gone farther and faster than ever before. So Caleb tried to do now as he did then. He tried to melt the room away, to fill his mind with daylight. But it didn't come easy this time. Every time he drew near, the fly twitched, shattering his concentration. Caleb spread his mind apart again and again for the better part of an hour. Each time, the fly wrenched him back into reality with a single beat of the wings he meant to deprive it of.

Just as he wanted to grab the petri dish and fling it across the room, Mom slid it away. Failure. Again.

"You said two hours."

"I could let you stare at this thing all day, Caleb. You're not going to pass. Not like this." She tapped a thumb against the dish in her palm. "Why don't we try something different?"

"Like what?"

Mom left the dining room, motioning for him to follow. She

360

led him across the house to the foot of the stairwell. Caleb froze at the bottom.

"Dad says I'm not allowed upstairs," he said.

Mom turned around, already halfway up, and gave him a crooked smile. "Well, *Mom says* time's wasting."

Caleb complied, but couldn't help glancing over his shoulder toward the entry hall, as though his father might emerge at any moment and catch him in the act. When he realized where Mom headed, a bevy of unplucked wings fluttered about his belly. Reluctance waned, and he followed her into the guest room, where she placed the petri dish on the floor. Above it hung the meadow painting Dad had used to cover the boarded window. She picked it up and tossed it onto the bed, letting Caleb's stifled sunbeam burst into the room.

"All right, kiddo," she said. "Take your shirt off."

"What?"

"This might be your last chance to have the sun on your skin before your Dad seals this. Do you want clothes in the way, or do you want to feel it?"

Caleb slid his t-shirt off, then stepped into the beam. He'd known the sun's kiss on more than one occasion, but having it snatched away days before made the sensations all the more vivid. Warmth radiated outward from the bright spot on his chest where he and the sun joined. It spread across his flesh, one electric inch at a time. For a few blissful seconds, he forgot about this musty prison and the impossible tasks keeping him within. He forgot about Mom, about Dad, about Josh. The light was all there was.

Mom put a hand on his shoulder, reminding him she existed. "I know how that feels, Caleb. I know it's intense. Put it to use."

He examined the petri dish. The fly twitched at his feet, as though sensing the weight of his gaze. Caleb let the world crumble again, but this time the fly entered the void with him. He *felt* its presence now, like the steel ball. When it moved inside its glass prison, he sensed the tickle of its trembling legs somewhere in his mind.

The sun manifested again, a mass of brilliant flame suspended above. Caleb reached for it...and touched hairy, insectile flesh. A silhouette grew against the light, pulsing and swelling, almost as large as the sun itself. Either the fly had grown or the sun had withered. The revolting creature threatened to eclipse its warmth. The fly spread its wings, dimming what light remained into a sickly gray haze. Every bit of pity Caleb possessed for the thing left him. Mom was right. It was vermin. He had to overcome it. He had to conquer it, to cast it aside in pursuit of the sun. He had to—

A shower of glass exploded outward from the petri dish. Caleb covered his eyes, back in the real world again. Mom raised her arms as well. When they lowered, she gaped at the floor. A perfect circle of shards surrounded a spot of untouched carpet where the dish had been. A tiny, yellow smudge lay at its center—all that remained of the fly.

"Oh," Caleb said.

Mom said nothing. He reached for her, and she jerked her arm away as if touched with a hot iron. The unease written across her face didn't stay long. She washed it away, eyes apologetic.

"I messed up," Caleb said.

"It's okay." Her eyes darted now, as though searching for anything to look at but Caleb. The sunbeam caught a piece of glass in her hair, one of many. She began to pluck them out. "I'll clean up. Just head downstairs."

"Uh-huh."

He slipped his shirt back on and made his way toward the door. The brief expression on her face when he'd tried to touch her still burned. He'd grown accustomed to tests ending with disappointment in his mother's eyes, but this was different. This was something else. In that moment, however fleeting, she'd been *afraid* of him.

"Caleb," she said.

He stopped in the doorway and faced her. Some of that fear slipped through again, whether she knew it or not.

"Don't tell your father about this."

Caleb's stomach tightened. He nodded, then left his mother amid the ruins of his failure.

The next night, Caleb dreamed of a meadow. He'd never seen one except in the painting upstairs, but it felt as real as any room in the house. A halo of trees circled the clearing. Morning dew glistened over swaying blades of grass. Birdsong lilted in every direction, and flowers bloomed before his eyes—reds, yellows, everywhere. A white sun shot into the sky, hours passing like seconds. When he woke, he half expected to be lying in a mound of leaves.

He wasn't.

Caleb rolled out of bed for a glass of water, mouth stale and parched. The clock on the nightstand said it was four in the morning, and the stillness of the house agreed. On the way back from the kitchen, he passed the winding stairwell his father forbade him to ascend. He stepped onto the bottom step and ran a hand along the cool, wrought-iron banister. Had Dad sealed the crack yet?

He took another creaking step, thinking about the painting, the room. There was something wrong with him. He'd seen it in Mom's eyes as they followed the sway of the chandelier, again when they drifted up from those scattered shards of glass. Not only had he failed his tests, but he'd failed them *wrong* somehow. Now the testing had stopped, and his parents wouldn't tell him why. Maybe they'd given up on him. Maybe these walls would hold him for the rest of his life. With his sunbeam shut away, he might never know daylight again. Caleb shivered.

Blackness enveloped him a step at a time, and a nervous tingle swelled within. Scaling the stairs felt like proving Josh right, yet again. What was this, if not cheating? But he had to look. He had to know. If the crack remained uncovered, he could wait out the night and savor the rising dawn while the others slept. If Dad found him in the morning, he'd be furious. But one last glimpse of the sun would be worth his wrath.

The grooves in the hallway picture frames guided him to the

guest room. When the door closed behind him, he hit the switch for the corner lamp, and the uneven meadow came into view. When he'd first seen the painting, he thought little more of it than a cheap facsimile. Now that he'd walked those hills in his dreams, he breathed heavily when he took it in. He gripped the dusty canvas, inhaling. With an exhale, he yanked the painting from the boards like a stubborn Band-Aid. A white band of caulking stretched across the middle of the window where the boards had once parted. Caleb ran a fingertip across it.

Dry and hard.

His fingers threatened to pierce the meadow in his hands, but he forced them to unclench. He rehung the painting, doing his best to reproduce its crooked angle. Then he stared. He regarded the tiny trees, the grass, the flowers. He contemplated the imitation sun, no wider than the tip of his thumb. He reached out and covered it whole. The meadow refused to darken.

When his gaze left the painting, it found the attic hatch above the bed. Dad had climbed into that black hole and emerged with a meadow beneath his arm. What else waited up there? More paintings? If they'd condemned him to dreams alone, maybe there were more to be had. Caleb climbed onto the mattress and grasped the pull cord. He fumbled for the ladder as it slid from the hatch, but it still screeched on the way down, piercing the calm in the house. He scrambled for the lamp switch, then sprinted back to the stairs to see if anyone stirred. No one came to investigate the noise.

With persistent silence at his back, Caleb returned and made the climb.

Odorous dust and mildew confronted Caleb as he groped his way into the gloom. His arm brushed a hanging chain, and he gave it a yank. Yellow light poured from an exposed bulb, casting angular shadows about the hardwood floor. Boxes and bins lay scattered around the room, many ripped and taped, barely holding together. Against the pitched wall to his left, a row of metal filing cabinets gathered what looked like years of dust. Decaying newspaper clippings and magazine covers hung from exposed rafters. WAR, they said. MENACE PREVAILS, they said. DESPERATE ACCORD STRUCK. Caleb didn't know what the headlines meant, but the images captured him at once: city skylines, towering skyscrapers, bustling crowds. None of the people looked happy. But even in the worst pictures, the sun was shining.

Caleb made his way to the file cabinets. Streaks and fingerprints broke the layers of dust surrounding one of the drawer handles. He opened it with a low rumble. A row of manila folders stared up at him. He drew one at random and flipped through the papers inside. Most of it was unreadable—unfamiliar terms, equations, strings of numbers. None of it meant anything. Then he found a page with words that screamed at him.

Assessment Log: Subject 19
See referenced video files under observ.index
Age 11
Dominoes: PASS (19070817.avi)
Maze: PASS (19072017.avi)
Age 13
Housefly: PASS (19080317.avi)
Mouse: INCONCLUSIVE, subject refusal (19081217.avi)
Mouse: PASS (19081417.avi)
Age 14
Dog: INCONCLUSIVE, subject refusal (19093017.avi)
Dog: INCONCLUSIVE, subject refusal (19093117.avi)
Age 15
Dog: INCONCLUSIVE, subject refusal (19100117.avi)
Controlled exposure (19100217.avi)
Dog: FAIL, anomaly (19100217.avi)
Procedures halted pending analysis
Age 17
Handler injured, see incident report (19112417.avi)
SUBJECT TERMINATED (19112517.avi)

Caleb flipped the page. More unfamiliar words and characters. Another flip, and there she was, staring at him. She had Dad's gray eyes, Mom's auburn hair. She could have been a sister. He glanced at the open drawer, stuffed with identical folders, each with a number on the tab. Did he have a folder in there? Did he have a *number,* like the girl?

He scanned the room again, eyes bouncing from newspaper to newspaper, box to box. They stopped on a chest-high, wooden crate set flush against the far wall. Nothing special amid a sea of browns and grays, but something about the wall behind it seemed odd. A raised section of wood peeked out on both sides, lighter than the rest. Caleb dropped the folder and raced across the room, dust stirring in his wake.

A window frame.

He curled his fingers around the crate's edge and pulled. It didn't move. He drove his shoulder into it, shoes sliding on the dusty floor. Finally, they found purchase, and the crate inched forward, revealing a vertical strip of window—no boards.

Caleb pressed his face against the glass, grinning. Dirt and grime caked its surface, but moonlight shone through. He dug into the crate again, hoping to uncover the rest. He grunted and strained, unveiling the world one blurry inch at a time. Then he backed away and gaped at the first bare window he'd ever seen, hair on his arms standing at attention. The ugly yellow bulb overpowered the moonlight pouring in. Caleb longed to see the silver rays he'd read about in the library, pure and undiminished. He spun back toward the hatch to shut the light off.

Josh stood in his way.

"What are you doing up here?" he said.

Caleb didn't speak.

Josh peered over his shoulder at the window. "Wow. You don't learn. I guess we'll need to lock you in your room."

"Leave me alone. This is none of your business."

"Mom and Dad told me to keep an eye on you. That means *everything* you do is my business. I'm in charge of you. You do what I say when I say it." Josh took a step forward. "Now get downstairs."

Caleb planted his feet. "I'm not going anywhere until the sun rises."

"You'll never see the sun. Trust me. I'm a man now. I've been outside. I know how the world works. You don't have what it takes."

Josh shot forward and shoved Caleb to the floor. Caleb scrambled to his feet, but Josh wrestled him back down. Their limbs tangled together—tan skin against pale flesh—pushing, grasping, yanking at hair and shirt. Josh managed to get his hands around Caleb's wrists and straddled his hips. He pinned Caleb's arms to his chest, squeezing the wind out of him. Caleb tried to buck him off, but he was too strong.

Josh glanced up at the window with a smirk. "Too bad you couldn't keep from snooping, shit-stain. When I'm done with you, I'm going to board that up."

When Josh said it, Caleb saw it. He pictured his last door to daylight shuttered away, draping this dingy place in darkness again. It made him want to cry, to scream, though he couldn't inhale deeply enough. Josh had stolen the sun. Again.

Josh pressed harder, forcing more air from Caleb's lungs. The attic faded, and his mind came alive. A demonic parody of Josh with black eyes and fanged teeth loomed above, its hideous body as big as the sky. It pinned Caleb to the ground with a cloven hoof and wrapped its clawed fingers around the sun. The light disappeared into the palm of its hand, held out of reach forever.

"No."

With a single word, Caleb thrust the might of his mind at the Josh-shaped phantom. It yelped and shrank away from his will, relieving a tremendous weight. When light swelled and he could breathe again, he realized the beast's cries had not been imaginary.

Caleb's eyelids snapped open. Josh groaned several feet above, pressed against the sloped roof by an unseen force. Droplets of blood leaked from his nostrils. Instead of dripping onto the floor, they rolled upward across his cheeks and splattered onto the ceiling. The shattered remains of the light bulb covered Josh in a silver luster.

Caleb screamed. Josh fell.

Caleb rose with a stagger and reached for his brother, whispering his name. Josh lay in a heap on his stomach, silent now. Caleb rolled him over, then yanked his hand away when slivers of glass speared his fingertips. He stuck two fingers in his mouth and watched his brother's chest as he spit the shards out. Dim light made it hard to discern the rise and fall, but it was there, keeping time with the steady drip of blood from the ceiling. Josh was hurt, but breathing.

Cold relief washed over Caleb, but didn't remain. His brother's prophecy would come true now. His parents had to be stirring, and soon they'd find him. They'd condemn him to a life between these walls. Or worse. Two words echoed in the recesses of Caleb's mind, in the whispered voice of a girl he'd never met.

SUBJECT TERMINATED.

Caleb looked down. A white rectangle lay at his feet, plastic sheen gleaming in the moonlight. The keycard with Josh's name on it said hello.

The moon was not the sun, but it was still glorious. Its light danced upon Caleb's flesh, and the shimmering expanse that carried it made his throat tighten. The night greeted him like a new friend; warm, humid air caressed every exposed inch. Countless competing scents beckoned on the breeze. His parents had carried a few of them into the house before, but most were as alien as the night sky. After taking in the heavens, his gaze drifted earthward. He dropped to his hands and knees to smell soil and grass for the first time in his life. When he found his feet again, he carried handfuls of it up with him, tossing it into the air like green confetti. If not for fear of being followed, he would have sprawled in the dirt and rolled in it.

Caleb strode across the lawn, tears welling, but stopped short of the street. Several black shapes surrounded the house, rectangular and massive. He'd seen pictures of these things before—cars, trucks, jeeps—but they were even bigger than he'd imagined. They had strange words emblazoned on their sides. POLICE, they said. NATIONAL GUARD, they said. U.S. ARMY. As he drew near, his shoe crunched on something hard and brittle. He stepped back to look, and almost lost his footing.

Bones.

Reeling away from the tawny remains, Caleb collided with the nearest vehicle. He peered inside. Tattered blue clothing lay in the driver's seat, barely concealing more lumps of bone. A human skull smiled from the passenger's side.

Caleb moved on, pace quickening. What had happened here? How long had corpses rotted outside his bedroom walls? He ducked and weaved between the derelict vehicles, stepping over more piles of human remains. Some of them still clutched the rusted weapons that had failed to save them. By the time it was all behind him, Caleb ran at full clip. The road bore him into the unknown, but he couldn't turn back. Not after what he'd seen. Not after what he'd *done*.

Dilapidated houses on either side of the street gave way to woods and telephone wires, a sweet scent rising with them. Caleb slowed to a jog, then a walk, lungs heaving. He'd never run so far, so long. The trees whispered as a burst of cool air caressed him; the world seemed to breathe Caleb in as he did likewise. When the wind receded, an altogether different sound emerged. A low, mechanical rumble swelled somewhere on the road ahead, growing louder with each passing heartbeat. Caleb considered standing his ground. Part of him yearned to learn what this world was bringing him. But the remnants of death outside the house burned in his mind. He ducked between the trees, dropping down to wait for the thing to pass, whatever it was.

The rumbling grew louder, and a shape emerged beneath the starlight. Blinding light erupted from twin spots on its fore.

Caleb covered his eyes, and the thing made a wild screech. Two loud thumps followed, then boots against blacktop. *People*.

When Caleb could see again, two men stood in the road, bathed in the headlights of a truck. They wore black jumpsuits with white emblems on the left breast. Each held a rifle. Each pointed it at Caleb.

"Out of the woods, vagrant," one of them said. "Now."

Caleb thought about running, slipping deeper into the trees. But something told him their weapons would outrun him. He complied.

"A kid?" the man said when Caleb emerged. "This far in? Are you shitting me, Tucker?"

"Don't look at me," the other said. He wore some kind of visor over one eye. "None of the infrareds further back caught him."

The first man gestured with his weapon. "You're in a lot of trouble. Who are you? What are you doing on this road?"

"My name is Caleb. I'm exploring."

Tucker let out a snicker, and the men exchanged puzzled looks.

"Well, sorry to interrupt your expedition," the first man said. "But I'd rather not have to answer for an idiot kid being reduced to a thin, red paste in my quadrant. How did you get past the checkpoints?"

"I don't know what you mean. I walked."

"From where?"

"From my house. Up the road."

The man lowered his rifle with a cockeyed look.

"Sarge," Tucker whispered. His rifle pointed somewhere behind Caleb. "There's more out there. Reds missed it somehow, but I'm staring right at it."

The first man, Sarge, gave Caleb a hard, combative look, as though he'd committed some great wrong. "Christ. One of them."

"No way," Tucker said. "We made tribute. They shouldn't—"

"In the truck. Now."

Without another word, they lowered their weapons and piled into the vehicle. The truck spun around, cutting across the road and bathing Caleb in fumes that made him cough. The tires screamed against the asphalt, kicking acrid smoke into the air.

But the truck refused to move, as though held in place. Caleb knew why.

He faced the darkness behind him. His father gave it a voice. "Everything that happens now is your fault."

"Don't hurt them, Dad. Please."

"You've condemned them, not me." Caleb had never seen such a grim expression on his father's face. "Now watch."

Groaning metal punctuated his last sentence. The truck's doors flew from their hinges, and the men inside spilled out. Tucker clung to the doorframe, but an invisible hand wrenched him away. They tried to right themselves, to raise their rifles and fire, but the guns ripped away from their hands, slings tearing like paper. They rose from the ground, tumbling and spinning in the air, grunting and moaning. Caleb looked away. He knew what he'd see if he didn't.

"Nah-ah." Dad seized his chin, steering it back in their direction. "You wanted the outside. You hurt your brother to get it. Well, here you are, son. Watch how we deal with vermin. Watch how this world works."

Sarge drifted forward, hanging upside down. Their eyes met. For a second, Caleb thought Sarge might say something. His head drove into the concrete before he had the chance. Caleb slammed his eyes shut.

"No, no, no."

Dad gripped his shoulder. "Open your eyes."

"I can't. I can't watch this."

"Tell you what. I won't kill the other one. I just want you to look at him. Look at the life you've ruined."

Caleb did as his father asked. Tucker no longer floated in the air. He knelt a few feet from them, shivering, staring at his unmoving partner.

"I'm sorry," Caleb said, tears blurring his vision. He didn't know if he meant the apology for Tucker, Sarge, or his father. "I've learned my lesson."

"Not yet, you haven't," Dad said.

"You said you wouldn't kill him."

"I won't." Dad gave Caleb a shove toward Tucker. "You will."

"What?" Caleb's stomach lurched.

"This is what you wanted. You wanted to cross the yellow line, whether you'd earned it or not. You wanted a shortcut. Here it is. Forget dominoes. Forget mazes. We'll skip you right to the final test. Your brother hasn't even made it this far."

"No." Caleb tried to back away, but his father shoved again.

"This man is nothing, Caleb. He's an insect—vermin. They all are. Remove him and the world is yours. The *sun* is yours."

"I can't."

Tucker rose into the air again. He let out a frantic gasp, which became a pitched howl.

"What are you doing to him?" Caleb said.

"Just breaking a bone or two."

"Please don't!"

"Then put him out of his misery. I know you can. You showed Josh what you can do. Now show me. Otherwise, it's going to take him a long time to die."

Caleb tried to block the world out, to build the sun, as he'd done before. He doubled over, scrunching his eyes and covering his ears. He tried to ignore Tucker's pain, to fade into a reality of his own making. But this time, he failed. His imaginary sun never came. All he saw was black. All he heard were screams.

He opened his eyes and aimed them at the night sky. They drifted straight to the brilliant orb that had so entranced him when he took his first steps outside. He'd spent his life chasing the sun, but he knew about the moon from books in the library. He knew why it beamed so bright amid this dark sky. The energy crawling across his exposed skin didn't belong to the moon—it was sunlight. The moon was merely its vessel.

Caleb stood up straight and met his father's eyes. He removed his shirt, letting the sun embrace him from somewhere over the horizon.

Dad smiled. "And I thought Josh was the quick learner. Do it, son."

Caleb didn't need to shut his eyes for what came next, though part of him wanted to. He didn't need to block the world out. He didn't need to visualize his obstacle. It stood right in front of him. Caleb knew what he needed to do, and for the first time in his life, he knew he had the power to do it. This time when he called on it, his mind leaped forward as easily as a hand swatting a fly. A loud popping noise halted Tucker's screams. Save for a final, rasping cry, the night fell silent.

Tucker collapsed onto the ground. Caleb's gaze drifted from him to the twisted mass that used to be his father. His back had inverted like a question mark. His head faced the wrong direction. Dad's eyes—eyes that once held immense power over Caleb—had gone white and empty.

Caleb fell to his knees and sobbed.

"You helped me," Tucker said, clutching one arm. "Your kind never helps. You just hurt. And take. *But you helped me.*"

Caleb stood and wiped his face with his shirt. "I couldn't help your friend."

Tucker shuffled to his feet and leaned against the truck. He limped toward the driver's side, then turned back to Caleb. "Is there anything I can do for you?"

The sound of shoes pounding pavement echoed toward them. Caleb looked up. Against the night sky, which now faded to purple at its edge, a featureless silhouette bobbed along the road. Caleb heard his name, a long howl against the wind—Mom calling after him.

"Take me some place high," Caleb said. "I want to watch the sun rise."

Flawless Imperfection

BY SERGEY POYARKOV

*This year, Sergey Poyarkov celebrates his 25th anniversary as
a winner of the L. Ron Hubbard Illustrators of the Future Gold
Award. He arrived in Los Angeles in 1991 to receive his award,
directly from his home in the Ukraine, as Communism was falling
in his homeland.*

*Sergey has since gone on to a successful artistic career as an
illustrator and made a transition to fine artist, with his works
displayed in exhibitions across Europe, the UK and the United
States. He has published five books of his art, in which he conveys
not only his art but his own philosophy of art, expressing pride in
his roots and appreciation of his new friends in other countries.*

*Sergey's whimsical art graces the cover of this anthology. The
piece is entitled "Do Not Stop," which he described with these
words: "I do not remember when I made the discovery that the
world is a system of obligations. Here a man is flying and playing
the piano. As soon as he ceases to play he will fall. Each of us lives
in his own definite rhythm, sits at his keyboard. This rhythm is
set to us by society or by ourselves. And when one tries to stop, to
change this rhythm, all the complex mechanism of his life starts its
descent. One may beat the keys more often and then the device will
mount higher, the horizon will widen. If you beat them less often,
the machine will fly closer to the ground. So don't stop: fly farther."*

Flawless Imperfection

A long, long time ago, art split into two opposite directions. One of them is described by the word *art-ful,* the other by the word *art-ifical.*

There exists the art of bizarre fantasy so masterfully performed and polished over years that you can't take your eyes off it. There also exists an art of marketing, in which one can't determine whether all this has been brought from the rubbish heap or a museum.

When this split occurred is hard to determine, but one has to admit that with the appearance of "experts" in art, the practice of painting has become, shamefully, a pastime one is likely to be embarrassed by.

Back when people lived in caves, they desired with all their might to draw beautifully, as can be seen by the painting in Lascaux, Spain. Painters in antiquity also attained perfection in their arts. It's from them that the Renaissance masters took the baton.

In fact, over the past nineteen centuries, artists tried to paint beautifully. Artistic skill achieved its highest point as a rather pleasant and delightful thing until a marvelous stream of hooligans and—at first even nice—rebels appeared at the end of the nineteenth century.

At the beginning of the twentith century, there appeared a number of "experts" who said it was inappropriate for a viewer himself to decide what he liked.

I dislike many aspects of Modernism—namely those works

376

where one can't see any skills of drawing. I don't like them for the same reason any doctor or scientist doesn't like palm readers, astrologists, or other swindlers.

There is a boundary that separates these two different businesses: the art of painting and the art of marketing.

Palm reading and astrology are cheating on a commercial level. If Mark Twain were alive today, he would jeer at the tribe of conceptualist artists and their followers. Modernism began as a piquant cheese with a rind of mold, where the bits of mold emphasized the taste of the cheese. But the cheese disappeared quite soon and only the moldy rind remained.

You must have seen the film *The Thomas Crown Affair*. A teacher takes her pupils to the Metropolitan Museum and points out an early impressionist painting. The children don't appreciate the piece until the teacher tells them it costs 100 million dollars. At which point, they open their eyes in admiration, saying in chorus: "WOW!" But it was the sum of money, not beauty, which created the impression.

Just because millions of people believe in something, it does not make it true or good. If these millions adopt cannibalism, fascism, fall into religious trances, or believe in the rightness of Marxism or beauty of conceptualism, I don't have to agree with them.

Only those who are unsure of themselves must listen to "experts." Do you seek the opinions of "experts" while choosing your favorite dish, convictions, hobbies, friends, or your wife?

The art of Rauschenberg, Chagall, Warhol and Picasso is the art of positioning in the market using PR technologies, conveyor goods, and masterful marketing. Their professional position is, "It's my view."

It's truly ingenious to adopt that stance, and I take off my hat to them.

The art of Breughel, Andrew White, Bosch and Norman Rockwell is the art of imagination, fantasy and masterful professional skills. Their professional position is "This is how I can do it." Their position and philosophy belong to them, and it was not invented by their art dealers for them. To be honest, we have to say that they successfully combined both positions, and one must give them their due.

There are two reasons why I respect Picasso. First, I respect success. Second, in his last interviews he jeered at his admirers and laughed publicly at those who considered him a great painter.

From my observation, the worse one can paint, the louder and more hysterically he tends to shout: "This is how I see it!" and the more furiously he calls those who have all grounds to declare with dignity, "This is how I can do it," "craftsmen" and "cheap shopkeepers."

I believe it's better to be a jolly, capable, and joyful craftsman than a dull, incapable conceptualist.

The principle goal of the artist is to gradually make his work simpler and simpler or more and more complicated. My New York friend Sasha Zakharov sometimes checks whether his work of literature is a success by the reaction of his girlfriend Yana. If while looking at the plot she starts weeping, it means that the work is a success. This is more objective than any expert's evaluation.

I hate questions like, "What do you call your style?" or "In what direction do you work?" It's easy to invent a pseudo-scientific term ala "narrative descriptivism" or "anti-conceptual out-modernism," but for whom or what is it needed? Viewers are taught to ask questions: "What stream (trend, or direction) is it?"

Really, what difference does it make? There is no stream. There is only one person in the world who determines what you like and what you don't like, what is good and pleasant and what is unacceptable and ugly, and *that person is you!*

I think that for mentally healthy viewers, the most important thing is *their* perception—not mine, not an art specialist's, or a curator's, a journalist's nor a neighbor's.

You, yourself, are capable of having your own opinion, and it is the only true and correct one for you. If, in order to learn what he truly likes, a man needs advice from an "expert," then he is sick.

When I became an art student, I stopped painting my "childish" pictures where maps of fairy islands and my own fictitious heroes mingled with heroes of the books I read. I proudly began to learn how to paint academically correctly. Then one day, my childhood friend Igor Sudak came to see me. Naturally, he asked me what I was engaged in at the moment.

I joyfully unloaded a heap of portraits, landscapes, still lifes, and staging routines—feeling justifiably proud of my evident progress.

"It's understood," said Igor. "And what do you paint for yourself?" I realized then that this school of drawing plaster heads, paraffin apples and naked bodies on the background of conventional drapery is simply a method to gain professional painting skills. And it's my personal choice to paint exactly what I wanted after I obtained the skills. I want to paint my own personal realities, and not the things only accepted, or things that are considered to be "proper."

A painter learns to paint staging and all the rest in order to return on a high aesthetic, a higher level of technical expertise to the things he wanted to paint before he got engaged in academic studies. It's very important not to lose track of the childish feeling of awe in front of a white sheet of paper. However, while studying, many forget what they began studying for, like adults who forget that they once were children. When one gets bored with everything, including diversity, those who are truly original remain true to themselves.

I recall a story about a rabbi named Dzussi. He said: "When I die, God won't ask me why I wasn't Aristotle, he'll ask me why I wasn't Dzussi." I want to be myself, and I think that this should be the goal for everyone.

Directing the Art

BY BOB EGGLETON

*Bob Eggleton is a successful science fiction, fantasy, horror, and
landscape artist, encompassing twenty years of putting brush
to canvas or board. Winner of nine Hugo Awards—he has been
nominated an amazing twenty-eight times over twenty-four years—
plus twelve Chesley Awards, as well as various magazine awards,
his art can be seen on the covers of magazines, books, posters
and prints—and of late, trading cards, stationery, drink coasters,
journals, and jigsaw puzzles. He is considered one of the most
"commercially successful" artists in the fields of science fiction and
fantasy.*

*He has also worked as a conceptual illustrator for movies and
thrill rides, including Star Trek: The Experience in Las Vegas. He
did concept work for the feature film Sphere and for the Academy
Award–nominated film Jimmy Neutron: Boy Genius.*

*Between demanding deadlines for book covers and movies, Bob
has illustrated two books of experimental artwork about dragons:*
Dragonhenge *and* The Stardragons.

Other books of Bob's artwork include: Alien Horizons: The
Fantastic Art of Bob Eggleton, Greetings from Earth: The Art
of Bob Eggleton, The Book of Sea Monsters, Primal Darkness:
The Gothic and Horror Art of Bob Eggleton, Dragon's Domain:
The Ultimate Dragon Painting Workshop, *and* Tortured Souls,
*a collaboration with Clive Barker. For Easton Press he has done the
Centennial Edition of* Tarzan of the Apes *by Edgar Rice Burroughs.*

Also, he and his wife, Marianne Plumridge, have a children's book:
If Dinosaurs Lived in My Town, *available from Sky Pony Press.*

*Bob is a Fellow of the New England Science Fiction Association
(NESFA). His work has appeared in professional publications and
books in the world of science fiction, fantasy and horror around the
world. Spacewatch/NASA named asteroid 13562 Bobeggleton in
his honor. Most importantly, he was a running extra in the 2002
film* Godzilla Against MechaGodzilla.

Directing the Art

This is the second year that I have been asked to serve as Art Director for the Illustrators of the Future Contest winners. In the second phase of the competition, each artist is assigned one of the winning Writers of the Future stories in this volume and they are commissioned to create an illustration for it. Each art piece competes for the best of the year, which merits the Golden Brush Award and a check for $5,000.

It's hardly a chore.

I practice what I preach in these regards. I just believe, in essence, in letting the artists do their very best work. I can guide and I can suggest, using my own years of experience based on what I think makes a great illustration.

What you have in your hands is some of the very best, upcoming illustrator's work (oh, and the writer's work, too, but that isn't what I am here for). Illustrating what goes on in a writer's head, becomes text and is supposed to trigger a visual response, is a juggling act.

The truth is, I see little difference between "Art" and "Illustration." Perhaps it has one difference: Art can invite you to make up a story, Illustration tells you one. Either way, it's a visual delight.

This year we have some amazing work. I'm not going to single anyone out because that, for me, is impossible, as every artist has a wonderful style that is solely their own. There are works that take us in subtle directions, with limited color palettes to tell the story. Two in particular were total stand-outs. There are dinosaurs, pandas, road warriors and surreal imagery. What awesome talent.

As I always attest, the best illustrations are the ones that juxtapose prosaic imagery with something completely unearthly and weird. What this creates is a sense of recognition of something "normal," and yet something completely otherworldly is happening! It is in the flux between those points that a great illustration is formed.

As far as techniques, it's fair to say that whether a person works digitally or traditionally (with brushes, paint, etc.), as far as communication goes, it's the final image that counts.

Believe me, illustrating a story is no walk in the park! Some authors, while having written a terrific story, have no visual "hooks" in their narrative. Sometimes it's just a mood. As the great illustrator Norman Rockwell once said, "Some come easy, some come hard." One idea may just jump at you from page one. With others, several re-reads of the story are required. That is how it goes.

For me as an art director, I tend to like simple, "to the point" images. It need not be cluttered or have too much going on, but an area of focus that is spot on and makes all the areas around it sort of subordinate to it—that's how I do my own work.

The point is, it's not only hard work, but it's fun. If a sense of fun is present in the art, then this will translate to the viewer that the illustrator had some joy doing it.

My opinions, I am sure, differ from other people's, but I find that in the long run, it's a popular appeal which judges how well an illustration worked.

Art directing is a learning experience for me as well, as I see how others work. I love seeing the "thumbnails" and concepts for the art. Often the best one, the one the illustrator themselves liked...is the one I like. I enjoyed the feedback from the artists. One person even gave me more information, which helped me see where they were going and why they felt strongly on their concept. I like that interplay.

Anyway, behold. Before you is a feast for the eyes and the mind. Go to it!

LIST OF ILLUSTRATIONS BY ARTIST

CHRISTINA ALBERICI
The Sun Falls Apart
387

CAMBER ARNHART
Last Sunset for the World Weary

DINO HADŽIAVDIĆ
Freebot

ROB HASSAN
Hellfire on the High Frontier

BRANDON KNIGHT
A Glamour in the Black

ADRIAN MASSARO
Squalor and Sympathy

KILLIAN McKEOWN
The Star Tree

393

VLADA MONAKHOVA
Cry Havoc

PAUL OTTENI
Images Across a Shattered Sea

395

IRVIN RODRIGUEZ
The Last Admiral

TALIA SPENCER
Möbius   397

JONAS ŠPOKAS
The Broad Sky Was Mine, And the Road

PRESTON STONE
Dinosaur Dreams in Infinite Measure

DANIEL TYKA
The Jade Woman of the Luminous Star

MARICELA UGARTE PEÑA
The Jack of Souls

401

ELDAR ZAKIROV
Swords Like Lightning, Hooves Like Thunder

The Year in the Contests

The L. Ron Hubbard Writers and Illustrators of the Future Contests are undoubtedly two of the largest and longest-running contests of their kind in the world—and still growing by leaps and bounds. In 2015 we celebrated the highest number of entrants ever for both the Writers of the Future and the Illustrators of the Future Contests.

Publishers Weekly, the publishing industry's highly influential news publication, said of the 2015 anthology, "Genre insiders will find this an excellent place to spot fresh talent," as the title reached the #7 position on the *Publishers Weekly* science fiction bestseller list.

Contest entries have originated in 176 different countries, with our first submissions this year from Swaziland, Samoa, Syria, and Saint Vincent.

This year, our writer winners, which include our finalists, semi-finalists, and honorable mentions came from 14 countries, while our illustrator finalists and honorable mentions hailed from 31 countries.

PUBLICATIONS BY PAST WINNERS

Each year, we go to great lengths to try to discover what our past Writers and Illustrators of the Future winners have been up to. It has become a major task. Given the proliferation of online books and magazines around the world, any numbers that we throw out will probably not reflect *everything* that has been released, though we counted nearly 370 books and stories by our writer winners this past year alone.

So rather than try to list so many titles, we're going to pass. Listing just the "major" novels somehow doesn't seem fair.

The same is true for our illustrators. We found dozens of book covers, illustrated books, graphic novels, comics, and so on, and of course much of the artwork done by our illustrators goes into products like video games, movie and television designs, and so on, when the art is only seen once the work hits the big screen. So rather than attempt to summarize all of it, let's just go straight to our awards.

AWARDS NEWS FOR PAST WINNERS

Tony Pi won Australia's Aurora Award in the category of Best Poem with "A Hex, with Bees."

For the Endeavor Award, for Best Novel written by a Northwest American Author, the winner was Jay Lake, for *Last Plane to Heaven.*

The Hugo Award, granted by Worldcon for Best Novel of the Year, went to the novel *Three-Body Problem,* written by Cixin Liu and translated by Ken Liu.

Ken Liu also won the Sidewise Award for Alternate History for his short story "The Long Haul from the ANNALS OF TRANSPORTATION, The Pacific Monthly, May 2009."

Jay Lake won the Locus Magazine Award for Best Collection with *Last Plane to Heaven.*

Past winner and current contest judge Sean Williams won Australia's Ditmar Award for his story "The Legend Trap."

The Legend Award for Best Fantasy Novel of the Year was won by Brandon Sanderson, our contest judge, for *Words of Radiance.*

Contest judge Nancy Kress won a Science Fiction and Fantasy Writers of America Nebula Award for her novel *Yesterday's Kin.*

The Jovian Award was presented to our contest judge, Mike Resnick, for Best Editor, Short Form for his work on *Galaxy's Edge.*

Our long-standing judge Larry Niven received the Science Fiction and Fantasy Writers of America Grand Master Award.

NEW ILLUSTRATOR OF THE FUTURE JUDGES

This year we added two new art judges to our distinguished panel:

Artist Rob Prior is unusual in that he often paints with both hands at once—and even does it live, onstage. As a graduate of both the Art Institute of Pittsburgh and Carnegie Mellon University, Rob went on to earn his MFA from the University of Toledo and began his career as a storyteller through his artistic skills at a young age. Using his numerous skills as an illustrator, screenwriter, storyboard artist and more, Rob's career spans over thirty years of gaming, comics, film, and television experience. He has also been recognized as one of the top intellectual property creators, by his peers, for creating incredibly detailed worlds, characters and stories.

In comics he has worked with *Spawn, Terminator, Deep Space 9, Evil Ernie, Melting Pot, Lady Death,* and *Heavy Metal.* As a leading storyboard artist, Rob has provided storyboards for video games, television, and movies such as *Terminator 3, Buffy the Vampire Slayer,* and *Ghost Rider,* just to name a few.

Our second new judge, Echo Chernik has over twenty years of experience as a professional commercial artist in the advertising field, and five years as an instructor of graphics and digital illustration. She specializes in art nouveau–influenced poster design, advertisements, package design, and book covers.

She currently works out of a studio in Sammamish, Washington, and when not illustrating, she also enjoys kick-boxing, target shooting, volunteering in the community, baking and outings with her daughters. She has won numerous awards for her work.

That's it for 2015. Now on to another stellar year!

THE YEAR IN THE CONTESTS

For Contest year 32, the L. Ron Hubbard Writers of the Future Contest winners are:

FIRST QUARTER

1. *J. W. Alden*
   THE SUN FALLS APART

2. *Rachael K. Jones*
   DINOSAUR DREAMS IN INFINITE MEASURE

3. *Sylvia Anna Hivén*
   A GLAMOUR IN THE BLACK

SECOND QUARTER

1. *Stewart C Baker*
   IMAGES ACROSS A SHATTERED SEA

2. *Ryan Row*
   THE BROAD SKY WAS MINE, AND THE ROAD

3. *R. M. Graves*
   FREEBOT

THIRD QUARTER

1. *Matt Dovey*
   SQUALOR AND SYMPATHY

2. *H. L. Fullerton*
   LAST SUNSET FOR THE WORLD WEARY

3. *Christoph Weber*
   MÖBIUS

FOURTH QUARTER

1. *Jon Lasser*
   THE STAR TREE

2. *Stephen Merlino*
   THE JACK OF SOULS

3. *Julie Frost*
   CRY HAVOC

PUBLISHED FINALIST

K. D. Julicher
SWORDS LIKE LIGHTNING, HOOVES LIKE THUNDER

For the year 2015, the L. Ron Hubbard Illustrators of the Future Contest winners are:

FIRST QUARTER
Camber Arnhart
Talia Spencer
Maricela Ugarte Peña

SECOND QUARTER
Christina Alberici
Vlada Monakhova
Dino Hadžiavdić

THIRD QUARTER
Killian McKeown
Paul Otteni
Jonas Špokas

FOURTH QUARTER
Brandon Knight
Adrian Massaro
Preston Stone

Our heartiest congratulations to all the winners! May we see much more of their work in the future.

NEW WRITERS!
L. Ron Hubbard's
Writers of the Future Contest

Opportunity for new and amateur writers of new short stories or novelettes of science fiction or fantasy.

No entry fee is required.

Entrants retain all publication rights.

ALL AWARDS ARE ADJUDICATED BY PROFESSIONAL WRITERS ONLY

Prizes every three months: $1,000, $750, $500
Annual Grand Prize: $5,000 additional!

Don't delay! Send your entry now!

To submit your entry electronically go to:
www.writersofthefuture.com/enter-writer-contest

E-mail: contests@authorservicesinc.com

To submit your entry via mail send to:
L. Ron Hubbard's Writers of the Future Contest
7051 Hollywood Blvd.
Los Angeles, California 90028

WRITERS' CONTEST RULES

1. No entry fee is required, and all rights in the story remain the property of the author. All types of science fiction, fantasy and dark fantasy are welcome.

2. By submitting to the Contest, the entrant agrees to abide by all Contest rules.

3. All entries must be original works, in English. Plagiarism, which includes the use of third-party poetry, song lyrics, characters or another person's universe, without written permission, will result in disqualification. Excessive violence or sex, determined by the judges, will result in disqualification. Entries may not have been previously published in professional media.

4. To be eligible, entries must be works of prose, up to 17,000 words in length. We regret we cannot consider poetry, or works intended for children.

5. The Contest is open only to those who have not professionally published a novel or short novel, or more than one novelette, or more than three short stories, in any medium. Professional publication is deemed to be payment of at least six cents per word, and at least 5,000 copies, or 5,000 hits.

6. Entries submitted in hard copy must be typewritten or a computer printout in black ink on white paper, printed only on the front of the paper, double-spaced, with numbered pages. All other formats will be disqualified. Each entry must have a cover page with the title of the work, the author's legal name, a pen name if applicable, address, telephone number, e-mail address and an approximate word count. Every subsequent page must carry the title and a page number, but the author's name must be deleted to facilitate fair, anonymous judging.

   Entries submitted electronically must be double-spaced and must include the title and page number on each page, but not the author's name. Electronic submissions will separately include the author's legal name, pen name if applicable, address, telephone number, e-mail address and approximate word count.

7. Manuscripts will be returned after judging only if the author has provided return postage on a self-addressed envelope.

8. We accept only entries that do not require a delivery signature for us to receive them.

9. There shall be three cash prizes in each quarter: a First Prize of $1,000, a Second Prize of $750, and a Third Prize of $500, in US dollars. In addition, at the end of the year the winners will have their entries rejudged, and a Grand Prize winner shall be determined and receive an additional $5,000. All winners will also receive trophies.

10. The Contest has four quarters, beginning on October 1, January 1, April 1 and July 1. The year will end on September 30. To be eligible for judging in its quarter, an entry must be postmarked or received electronically no later than midnight on the last day of the quarter. Late entries will be included in the following quarter and the Contest Administration will so notify the entrant.

11. Each entrant may submit only one manuscript per quarter. Winners are ineligible to make further entries in the Contest.

12. All entries for each quarter are final. No revisions are accepted.

13. Entries will be judged by professional authors. The decisions of the judges are entirely their own, and are final.

14. Winners in each quarter will be individually notified of the results by phone, mail or e-mail.

15. This Contest is void where prohibited by law.

16. To send your entry electronically, go to:
www.writersofthefuture.com/enter-writer-contest
and follow the instructions.
To send your entry in hard copy, mail it to:
L. Ron Hubbard's Writers of the Future Contest
7051 Hollywood Blvd., Los Angeles, California 90028

17. Visit the website for any Contest rules updates at:
www.writersofthefuture.com

NEW ILLUSTRATORS!

L. Ron Hubbard's
Illustrators of the Future Contest

Opportunity for new science fiction and fantasy artists worldwide.

No entry fee is required.

Entrants retain all publication rights.

ALL JUDGING BY PROFESSIONAL ARTISTS ONLY

$1,500 in prizes each quarter. Quarterly winners compete for $5,000 additional annual prize!

Don't delay! Send your entry now!

To submit your entry electronically go to:
www.writersofthefuture.com/enter-the-illustrator-contest

E-mail: contests@authorservicesinc.com

To submit your entry via mail send to:
L. Ron Hubbard's Illustrators of the Future Contest
7051 Hollywood Blvd.
Los Angeles, California 90028

ILLUSTRATORS' CONTEST RULES

1. The Contest is open to entrants from all nations. (However, entrants should provide themselves with some means for written communication in English.) All themes of science fiction and fantasy illustrations are welcome: every entry is judged on its own merits only. No entry fee is required and all rights to the entry remain the property of the artist.

2. By submitting to the Contest, the entrant agrees to abide by all Contest rules.

3. The Contest is open to new and amateur artists who have not been professionally published and paid for more than three black-and-white story illustrations, or more than one process-color painting, in media distributed broadly to the general public. The ultimate eligibility criterion, however, is defined by the word "amateur"—in other words, the artist has not been paid for his artwork. If you are not sure of your eligibility, please write a letter to the Contest Administration with details regarding your publication history. Include a self-addressed and stamped envelope for the reply. You may also send your questions to the Contest Administration via e-mail.

4. Each entrant may submit only one set of illustrations in each Contest quarter. The entry must be original to the entrant and previously unpublished. Plagiarism, infringement of the rights of others, or other violations of the Contest rules will result in disqualification. Winners in previous quarters are not eligible to make further entries.

5. The entry shall consist of three illustrations done by the entrant in a color or black-and-white medium created from the artist's imagination. Use of gray scale in illustrations and mixed media, computer generated art, and the use of photography in the illustrations are accepted. Each illustration must represent a subject different from the other two.

6. ENTRIES SHOULD NOT BE THE ORIGINAL DRAWINGS, but should be color or black-and-white reproductions of the originals

414

of a quality satisfactory to the entrant. Entries must be submitted unfolded and flat, in an envelope no larger than 9 inches by 12 inches.

7. All hard copy entries must be accompanied by a self-addressed return envelope of the appropriate size, with the correct US postage affixed. (Non-US entrants should enclose international postage reply coupons.) If the entrant does not want the reproductions returned, the entry should be clearly marked DISPOSABLE COPIES: DO NOT RETURN. A business-size self-addressed envelope with correct postage (or valid e-mail address) should be included so that the judging results may be returned to the entrant. We only accept entries that do not require a delivery signature for us to receive them.

8. To facilitate anonymous judging, each of the three photocopies must be accompanied by a removable cover sheet bearing the artist's name, address, telephone number, e-mail address and an identifying title for that work. The reproduction of the work should carry the same identifying title on the front of the illustration and the artist's signature should be deleted. The Contest Administration will remove and file the cover sheets, and forward only the anonymous entry to the judges.

9. There will be three co-winners in each quarter. Each winner will receive an outright cash grant of US $500 and a trophy. Winners will also receive eligibility to compete for the annual Grand Prize of an additional cash grant of $5,000 together with the annual Grand Prize trophy.

10. For the annual Grand Prize Contest, the quarterly winners will be furnished with a specification sheet and a winning story from the Writers of the Future Contest to illustrate. In order to retain eligibility for the Grand Prize, each winner shall send to the Contest address his/her illustration of the assigned story within thirty (30) days of receipt of the story assignment.

The yearly Grand Prize winner shall be determined by the judges on the following basis only: Each Grand Prize judge's personal opinion on the extent to which it makes the judge want to read the story it illustrates.

The Grand Prize winner shall be announced at the L. Ron Hubbard Awards Event held in the following year.

11. The Contest has four quarters, beginning on October 1, January 1, April 1 and July 1. The year will end on September 30. To be eligible for judging in its quarter, an entry must be postmarked no later than midnight on the last day of the quarter. Late entries will be included in the following quarter and the Contest Administration will so notify the entrant.

12. Entries will be judged by professional artists only. Each quarterly judging and the Grand Prize judging may have different panels of judges. The decisions of the judges are entirely their own and are final.

13. Winners in each quarter will be individually notified of the results by mail or e-mail.

14. This Contest is void where prohibited by law.

15. To send your entry electronically, go to: www.writersofthefuture.com/enter-the-illustrator-contest and follow the instructions.
    To send your entry via mail send it to:
    L. Ron Hubbard's Illustrators of the Future Contest
    7051 Hollywood Blvd., Los Angeles, California 90028

16. Visit the website for any Contest rules updates at www.writersofthefuture.com.